SOME WERE HUNTERS, SOME WERE PREY . . .

John Reilly—A naive American expatriate . . . behind his innocent blue eyes lurks a deadly secret . . .

Ben Ames—A brilliant history professor . . . a harmless favor turns his Greek vacation into an odyssey of terror . . .

Caroline Hooper—An innocent tourist . . . she sought a new life among the ruins of ancient Crete, but found herself a target in a deadly game of international intrigue . . .

Stavros Papandakis—A mysterious Greek landowner . . . he was willing to risk all his wealth and power to save the one person he loved . . .

Yevgeny Vlatchkov—The shadowy Russian . . . he devised deceptions no one could fathom . . .

BUT ALL WOULD BE VICTIMS IF THEY DIDN'T FIND . . .

THE BREZHNEV MEMO

THE BREZHNEV MEMO

Morton Marcus

A DELL BOOK

Published by
Dell Publishing Co., Inc.
1 Dag Hammarskjold Plaza
New York, New York 10017

Copyright © 1980 by Morton Marcus

All rights reserved. No part of this book may be
reproduced or transmitted in any form or by any
means, electronic or mechanical, including photocopying,
recording or by any information storage and retrieval
system, without the written permission of the Publisher,
except where permitted by law.

Dell ® TM 681510, Dell Publishing Co., Inc.

ISBN: 0-440-11034-3

Printed in the United States of America

Map by Clarice Borio

First printing—May 1980

For Eric Ambler, with homage

Prologue

The announcement in several American newspapers of the death of a young American named Henry Reese, who was killed in a hiking accident while vacationing with in-laws on the Greek island of Crete, attracted almost no national attention. The New York Times gave it a box on page 31. The Chicago Tribune mentioned it as a filler item on page 65, opposite its daily comic and crossword puzzle page.

The San Francisco Chronicle did run the story on the front page, primarily because Reese's family had lived in San Francisco for more than eighty years, his father was a prominent physician, and Reese himself was still a resident of the city at the time of the accident. The local television news teams even interviewed the tearful parents in their living room, where Reese's father said that he and his wife had just received the information from the State Department and were still in "a state of shock."

In Athens the incident was given similar front-page coverage by the daily English-language newspaper, the Athens News. Several hundred tourists read the article, shook their heads and sighed that an Aegean vacation should end so tragically for one so young.

Benjamin Ames, a vacationing professor of history

at Claremont College, Claremont, California, who had arrived in Athens that day, read the article during the taxi ride from the airport, shook his head, and promptly forgot the incident in the ensuing argument with the driver, who attempted to overcharge him for the fare to the Hotel Athena.

Two days after the accident an unacknowledged radio message originating in the town of Rethymnon on the north coast of Crete was monitored by a United States National Security Agency (NSA) radio surveillance ship on routine patrol in the eastern Mediterranean. The message was repeated three times between 1500 and 1505 hours and simply read "Transcendentalism defective." It was transmitted on the U.S. Navy FleetComm frequency in a code used by a U.S. intelligence unit whose area headquarters was in Athens but none of whose operatives were on Crete at that time.

Chapter One

Something was bothering him about the package.

He leaned against the railing, hugging the package to him and using it as a cushion against the cool metal. The ship thrummed beneath him, and to all appearances the moon was keeping its distance beyond the silvery track it had laid on the water.

The package was an inconvenience that irritated him, an extra responsibility he didn't need. Since he knew the value of its contents, he had resolved not to leave the package in the cabin. For that matter he had decided to keep it with him at all times until he delivered it, and in the last several hours he had begun to look at everyone around him as if they were planning to steal it.

And then there was his apprehension about its contents; the way the package had come into his possession just didn't sit right.

He knew he was being his "old paranoid self" again, as Julia used to say with a smirk. He smiled to himself; in this case she was probably right. No one gave a damn about the package or what was inside it, even if he were to lug it, cumbersome as a wrapped ham in its brown paper, into the captain's dining area and drop it with a resounding thud on the table. As for his doubts—Reilly was a former student of his and he was doing a simple favor for him, and that was all there was to it.

Julia. He wondered if he'd be able to think of anything without relating it to her. The smile vanished and his lips tightened. He stared at the moon-flecked water.

"Excuse me. Are you all right?"

He turned to see a tall, slim woman with straight, shoulder-length hair. Her face was in shadow. "What?"

"My friend and I—we thought you might be ill."

"Oh. No, it's cooler on deck, that's all."

"It is stuffy inside," she said, brushing her hair out of her eyes. "Well, sorry to bother you."

"No bother. It was a nice thing to do."

"Not really. I've been seasick myself, so I know what it's like."

She turned to go.

"Been over here long?" he asked, wanting the conversation to continue.

"Three days. Two in Athens and one in Delphi," she said, turning toward him. "You?"

"Five days. You enjoying it?"

"Yes, enormously. Gail and I are going to have a hard time adjusting to Chicago again. You on vacation, too?"

He nodded.

"What do you do?"

"I teach history at Claremont College in California."

"Oh, really," she said, her voice rising slightly.

He shrugged and didn't reply.

"I'm Caroline Hooper, Professor. Why don't you join us. If I'm not mistaken, you're headed to Crete for the same reason we are."

"Oh? What makes you think that?"

"Crete's the only place this ship is going, for one. And I'll bet half the tourists on it are going there for the same reason—the Minoan ruins. Am I right?"

He smiled and nodded.

She led him into the lounge, sliding gracefully through the crowd as she made her way over to a skinny blond woman sitting alone at a table near the window, just inside the door. Cigarette smoke swirled through the room, and voices reverberated around them. Greek families were chatting in groups waving their arms as they laughed or argued. Children chased each other through the thickets of adults, and old women in shapeless black dresses sat apart, moaning and pressing lemons to their nostrils, attended by young men and women with concerned, slightly exasperated expressions.

"Guess what?" said Caroline to the blond woman. "We've found ourselves a professor."

The blond woman raised her eyebrows and grinned. "Hi, I'm Gail Hutchinson," she said, holding out her hand and looking up at him.

"Ben Ames," he replied, taking her hand and smiling, aware of how awkward the package felt in his other hand but happy to be talking with fellow Americans after five days alone in a strange country.

"You going to see the ruins, Professor?" asked the blond woman.

He nodded.

"We're fanatics on Minoan art," she continued.

"I'm known as something of a nut on the Minoans myself," he said, remembering the conversation with Reilly at the museum earlier that day.

"Really?" asked Gail. She seemed to be the more animated of the two.

He smiled and sat down, holding the package on his lap.

Gail grinned and hunched her shoulders in reply to his smile. She was thinner than Caroline, almost bony, and had a childlike way of twitching her body and tugging at the edge of the red plastic tablecloth that Ben found annoying. In contrast Caroline's relaxed manner had drawn his attention as she had moved through the crowd, and now he kept glancing at her every few moments. She was sitting across from him, a willowy brunette with warm, hazel-colored eyes, watching the scene in the lounge and apparently only half-listening to the conversation.

"Where are you going to be staying on Crete?" Gail asked him.

"Heraklion first: I've got some business there. But after that I don't know." He looked at Caroline. She looked at him. He felt as if they were Gail's parents. He smiled at her. She smiled back.

"We've got reservations at a town on the south coast called Ayia Galini. Ever hear of it?" Gail asked.

Ben shook his head.

"Neither have we, but it's the cheapest place we could find. Probably another mistake. Ever been to Crete before?"

"No," Ben said, "not in this life anyway."

"That's great," Gail replied, grinning again. "Why don't the three of us meet somewhere and explore the island together?"

Ben looked at Caroline. She smiled and nodded. "Why not," he said.

"It *would* be nice to see you on Crete," said Caroline. "You can probably show us a lot of things off the beaten path that we'd never find on our own. I hate taking tours; the guides rush you through everything."

"Yeah, or some old couple wants to show you snapshots of their grandchildren in Oregon—like yesterday. What a drag!" added Gail.

"So it would be good to see you on Crete, Ben," said Caroline. "We've got reservations for tomorrow at the Hotel Minos in Ayia Galini."

He bought a round of drinks, and the three of them talked for a while longer. Both women were in their mid-thirties and divorced. They worked as architectural secretaries in the same office and had come to Greece to see the ruins and to relax in the sun on their annual two-week vacation. They had planned to go to Mykonos first, but the island was filled with tourists, not a bed to be had, so they were taking the ferry to Crete a week early.

"Did you take the trip to Delphi while you were in Athens?" asked Gail.

He shook his head, and they talked some more, finally agreeing that if Ben happened to come south in a day or two, he would get in touch with them at Ayia Galini, and together they would work their way through the Minoan sites at Phaestos and Ayia Triadha and maybe go on to Knossos.

He offered to buy another round of drinks, but Gail said she was exhausted, and both women got up to go. He shook hands with them, they repeated that they hoped to see him in a day or two, and then they left.

He watched them walk through the lounge. They turned and waved at him from the far door, and he waved back. The lounge was almost empty now, and several young men were stretched out in booths or asleep on sofas at the far end of the room. He ordered a beer and drank it. Then he went out on deck again, carrying the package under his arm, and resumed his place at the rail, feeling lonelier than he had before he met the women.

And for good reason. Here he was, standing on a ship grinding its way to some godforsaken island while his past receded behind him like a burning town.

Well, things weren't that bad, really. At forty-one, he was still healthy, his six-foot-two-inch frame had all its limbs and organs, and his athletic build was still apparent in whatever he wore. In fact his gray eyes continued to retain their quickness and clarity, without the need for glasses; there was not even the hint of a jowl beneath his well-defined jaw; and now that his black hair was silvering at the sides, his looks would have been considered distinguished if he didn't have that mountainous broken nose in the center of his face, which Julia insisted gave him the appearance of a grazing buffalo.

Actually, he'd accomplished quite a bit in his life. He was a full professor of history at Claremont, and proud of the title, although at times he thought it misrepresented him. He was no Harvard-bred scholar but the son of an Oklahoma dust-bowl farmer who in the mid-Thirties had migrated to Manteca, a small town in central California, and had ended his days there as an electrician.

Ben shook his head and leaned forward, pressing the package against the rail. He hadn't thought about Manteca in years. It was a faraway world where he had left his boyhood, his high-school football career, and several girls whose names he no longer remembered. He had even enlisted in the Air Force there, two months after graduating from Manteca High. That was during the last days of the Korean War, and he had been trained as a squad leader on one of the Air Force's newly formed air-base defense teams before being sent to Korea, where he took part in several of the bitter firefights and hand-to-hand struggles at Kimpo Air Force Base.

The War came flooding back: the mud, the gunfire from the trees beyond the perimeter, the yelling figures charging at him, the young Korean wrestling for the carbine, his neck tendons quivering, his face all mouth as his shout became a gagging gurgle and the saliva flew past his lips. . . . And then there were the bar girls and the week-long drunks in Japan. In fact it was during one of those R and R leaves in Tokyo that Ben had become interested in history.

The strangeness of Japanese life and manners aroused his curiosity, and he soon found himself forsaking the girls and ginmills on the Ginza in favor of an armchair in the USO club and books on Japanese history. This stimulated his interest in history in general, and after his discharge he enrolled in the University of California at Berkeley on the GI Bill, where he majored in history.

By the time he received his B.A. degree, he had decided to become a historian, not only because he was intrigued by the differences among peoples, but because he hoped to find "some underlying sense of order in the seemingly random rise and fall of nations," as he wrote in his senior thesis. Ah, innocent youth! All he got for his troubles was four more years of scholastic drudgery, another degree, a wife named Julia Sloan, who had been a nursing student when he

met her, and two daughters. And somehow at the end
of those years he had become Benjamin the historian.

No, he was no genteel, Harvard-bred scholar, as his
colleagues liked to remind him. He was a storyteller
who could transform the words in books into landscapes that whitened in winter and greened in summer, a lecturer who could make his students see the
shadows shifting over the pearls on Marie Antoinette's
bodice and hear the silk hissing as she steered her
hooped peacock-blue skirt through the halls of Versailles, a professor whose vocabulary was still partly a
trucker's and whose voice continued to be edged with
the rough intonations of his early life. Old Henderson,
the medievalist, said Ben was a poet who had chosen
the wrong profession and the wrong life, and once,
while drinking with him and several other colleagues
after a departmental meeting, Henderson had drawled
that Ben was "a seer, a half ar-tic-u-late seer whose
words could summon to life the ghostly shapes of the
past." The trouble was that Ben never knew if Henderson was being flattering or sarcastic. But one thing
was certain: Ben was obsessed with history, his obsession infected his students, and it was this obsession,
he knew, that made him a good teacher.

He stood at the railing, only half-aware of the moonlight trailing the ship. He was alone on deck except
for a man smoking a pipe who stood farther down
the rail. Instinctively Ben's fingers tightened on the
package. Then he relaxed, reminding himself that
there was no reason to worry about it. He was letting
his imagination get the better of him again. The
pleasure of talking with the two women should have
told him how alone he had been the past five days,
and he knew how easy it was to imagine the craziest

things when a person was lonely and in a strange environment.

His thoughts strayed back to the package. There certainly was something about it that was nagging at him, and now he realized that it was the phone call the day before his meeting with Reilly that made the meeting seem, in retrospect—well, yes, why not say it?—suspicious.

The phone call had come yesterday. He had just returned to the hotel from the Benaki Museum, damp and wilting in the mid-June Athens heat, and the hotel manager was standing behind the registration desk as she usually did—her lips compressed, her smoke-gray eyes an arctic mist, and her face a mask of make-up beneath her bluish bouffant hairdo. "Monsieur Ames," she had said, "there was a phone call for you while you were out."

"For me? But I don't know anyone in Athens," he replied, and then, for an instant, he thought it might have been Julia. But, no, the manager would have specified that the call was long distance from America. Anyway, his life with Julia was over, had been over months before the divorce became final. Julia had another man now—Elegant Elliott of the English Department, suave and slim in his Ivy League tweeds and his phony Harvard accent—a guy the kids liked, too. And that was that: ten years of a continually disintegrating marriage that had finally collapsed. After all these years, after all the planning with Julia, Ben had come to Athens alone, and found that the crumbling city reflected his own mental condition.

The caller had not left his name and did not phone back, and Ben had assumed that the whole thing was a mistake on the hotel manager's part and thought no more about it. Then, today, as he was wandering through the National Historical Museum, nodding and smiling at each portrait and artifact as if recognizing forgotten objects from his childhood, he was startled out of his daydreams.

"Professor Ames? Professor Ames, is that you? Well, I'll be damned."

Ben was in the Naval Heroes Room, and when he turned toward the voice he found that he was looking at the portrait of a stocky grandmother with stern eyes, standing at the railing of a nineteenth-century frigate, her head and shoulders swaddled in a fringed beige shawl. *Good old Bobolina, the matriarch as admiral!* Below the portrait stood a slim young man in his mid-twenties with tousled, butter-colored hair and a chicory-brown tanned face which made his even white teeth and doll-blue eyes look almost luminous. He was grinning broadly at Ben. "Well, I'll be! Of all places. But, hell, where else? Don't tell me you don't remember me?"

As a matter of fact Ben didn't remember him. There was something familiar about the face and the slim build, but Ben was still half-immersed in fantasies of Greek heroes and intrigues and blood feuds.

"Reilly," the young man said, still smiling. "John Reilly. Western Civ. And then the seminar in Nineteenth Century Revolutions."

Ben nodded. Reilly, yes—John Reilly, an average but likeable student who hadn't contributed much to any of the classes and in the seminar had presented a less than inspired paper on the student uprising in Vienna, was it? Or was it on the Magyar revolt under Kossuth in Pest? He hadn't seen the boy in what—five, six years?

"If there was one place I would find you in all Greece, sir, I guess it would have to be here, or at Knossos."

Ben smiled at him. "What are you doing in this out-of-the-way mausoleum?" he asked.

"Same as you. Looking at the portraits. Matter of fact, you're the reason I'm here. Your lectures on the 1821 Revolt really got me into it and inspired my little visits here. This has become my favorite museum in Athens. I find the atmosphere—how can I put it—almost transcendental."

Ben smiled again. "Transcendental?"

The boy hesitated, flashed a smile in return, then glanced at the portraits on the walls. He was wearing a low-necked blue-and-white-striped pullover shirt, a pair of loose-fitting white trousers, and sandals. His tanned forearms, neck, and ankles seemed to be jutting out of his clothes, and with his khaki army-surplus knapsack resting on the floor at his feet he looked very much at home.

Although he didn't want to admit it, Ben was flattered that the boy had been inspired by his lectures to visit the museum.

"Have you seen Admiral Kanaris' heart yet?" asked Reilly. "It's over here," he said, and led Ben past dozens of portraits of legendary sea fighters and their ships, all hung frame to gilded frame on the crowded walls. At the end of the room, in a purple niche surrounded by faded brown-and-gold battle flags as large and dusty as old quilts, a small gold urn sat on a white pedestal. Reilly pointed to it. "I didn't believe it when you told us, but there it is all right."

Ben smiled at the boy's enthusiasm. "You seem to be well acquainted with the museum," he said.

"Yep. I've been here three or four times, and this is my good-bye visit, so to speak. It's back to the good old US of A now. . . . How long have you been in Athens, sir?"

"Just five days."

Reilly shook his head and smiled. "Then you haven't seen anything yet. I'd love to show you around, but I'm on my way out. How long are you going to be here?"

"I'm leaving for Crete tonight."

"Crete! Well, well, well. So you're finally going."

"Yes, *fi*nally," Ben said, suddenly thinking of Julia and hearing the bitterness in his voice.

"You won't be disappointed, sir."

Ben nodded, still thinking of Julia and imagining the ruins at Knossos as they appeared in the glossy color photographs in his books at home. He and Julia had planned the trip for years, plotting their route from Athens to the Peloponnesus and on to Crete.

"I'm headed there myself," Reilly was saying, "though I don't want to go. I was visiting my father-in-law—"

"Your father-in-law?"

"Yeah. I married a Cretan girl I met in Berkeley, a student there."

"Oh," said Ben. "And you're not looking forward to going to Crete. Well, I don't want to sound pedantic, Reilly, but—"

"Wait a minute. Hold on. I'm not putting Crete down. And I know your Minoan civilization lecture by heart. It's just that we've already been there. Visited her father and toured the important sites for two whole weeks. And when we left, my father-in-law gave Stella this old family icon to take with her. Now

Customs won't let us leave the country with it. They say it's a national treasure, it's so old. So we have to get it back to the old man, and I don't trust the mails."

"So you're going back to Crete."

"So we're going back to Crete and losing a ride all the way to France for nothing but gas money."

"Too bad," said Ben.

"Yeah, it's a lucky ride this time of year," said Reilly. He paused, then suddenly looked at Ben with a smile. "Say, I've got an idea. Why don't *you* take the icon back for us?"

"Well . . ."

"Come on. You're going there anyway. Besides, you can meet my father-in-law. He'll probably give you a meal and a place to stay and introductions to people all around the island."

The request was simple enough, and it had been pleasant seeing someone he knew after five days alone in a foreign country; Ben even meant to ask Reilly to lunch.

"I've got it right here in my knapsack," said Reilly. "Wrapped and all. Come on, what do you say? You'll like my father-in-law. He's a sweet old guy with plenty of stories about the Big War."

Why not? Ben had met no Greeks, had experienced none of the famous Greek hospitality. This would be a perfect opportunity. Besides, the previous day he had had the uncomfortable thought that he might be even more lonely and alienated on the island of Crete than in cosmopolitan Athens. In fact he had begun to think of the Cretan trip with trepidation. He also did not want to offend Reilly and lose his companionship for the afternoon. "Okay," he said, "on one condition—that you have lunch with me."

"That's great," said Reilly, bending down to untie his knapsack. He withdrew a rectangular package about a foot wide and a foot and a half long wrapped in heavy brown paper, wrote a name, address, and phone number on it, and handed it to Ben. "Thanks again for this, and for the invite to lunch, but if I'm going to make my ride, I've got to hustle back to the wife and get our things together. The car leaves this afternoon."

Reilly showed him some other things of interest. They talked about California for a while, about Reilly's M.A. in political science, and even touched on Ben's divorce and lonely pilgrimage to Greece. Then Reilly took his leave with a grin and a vigorous handshake in the foyer of the museum.

When the massive door closed behind Reilly, Ben felt more alone than before, and he stared at the door for several minutes. It was only when he realized that he had been clutching Reilly's package to his chest like a hymnbook that he noticed it at all.

And that was all there had been to it. It had been so innocent, so matter of fact. No overtones. No innuendoes. Nothing suspicious. Yet something about the meeting was still nagging at him.

He pushed away from the railing and looked down at the package. It was crisscrossed with white twine and trussed with brown tape from end to end, and he couldn't get a look at whatever was inside without leaving some evidence that he'd tampered with the wrapping. What did he think was in it, for God's sake? Drugs? Stolen jewels? Those things happened only in newspapers. He was letting his imagination gallop away with him again, making trivial incidents into historic events, as Julia was always ready to tell him.

He shook his head, turned away from the rail, and went in to bed, but not without noticing that the man standing farther down the rail followed him in.

Chapter Two

The steamship docked in Heraklion, Crete's most populous city, at six the next morning, and Ben, not seeing Caroline or Gail among the disembarking passengers, wandered away from the harbor looking for an inexpensive hotel.

Everything about Heraklion depressed him. If Athens had been crumbling, Heraklion was plain dirty. Heaps of old brick and mortar and ripped-up wood lay in many of the streets, along with grimy fruit rinds and soiled paper; and white two-story Turkish houses with overhanging balconies and red tile roofs crouched together in pockets beneath square concrete and glass hotels similar to the new buildings in Athens. Some of the Turkish houses still had tiny shaded gardens behind their whitewashed walls, but most of them seemed to have been abandoned.

Within an hour after his arrival Ben checked into a small pension, unpacked, showered, and, feeling desperate and alone, went to the front desk and asked the manager to place a call to the telephone number Reilly had written on the package. The manager, a bald, rotund old man in undershirt and trousers, was still as unshaven and sleepy as he had been when Ben arrived. He dialed the number and waited a few moments, snorted and spat on the floor behind him, and suddenly shouted into the mouthpiece in a rising frenzy, "*Yassoo! YASSOO! Stavros Papandakis? STAVROS PAPANDAKIS, PARAKALO!*" handed the receiver to Ben with a toothy grin, leaned both elbows on the desk, and propped his head on his hands so that his ear rested on the opposite side of the telephone from Ben's. Throughout the conversation that followed he nodded his approval or grunted his disapproval, and bowed, smiling toothily, whenever Ben glared at him or attempted to pull the short phone cord farther down the counter.

"Stavros Papandakis?" Ben said into the mouthpiece.

"*Nai,*" said a husky voice at the other end of the line.

"Do you speak English?"

"Yes. Who is this, please?"

Ben told him about his meeting with Reilly and the occasion of his phone call. There was a long silence on the other end of the line. The man seemed hesitant, but finally, as Reilly had predicted, he insisted that Ben come to his house for the night. Ben declined, saying he had just checked into the hotel and wanted to visit the sights around Heraklion. They agreed to meet the next afternoon at four. Papandakis gave him directions to the meeting place, and as they were about to hang up said, "Please, Professor Ames, which hotel are you staying at?"

"The Pension Circe."

"Ah, yes. That is a pleasant one. Until tomorrow then, Professor. Are my directions clear?"

"Yes. Thank you. Good-bye, sir."

"Good-bye."

Ben stood at the registration desk, ignoring the grinning old man. The call to Papandakis had left him more depressed. He had refused an offer to send a car because of Papandakis' initial hesitancy. It had seemed that Reilly's father-in-law had invited him for courtesy's sake alone—and Ben hated the thought that he had forced himself on the man. But there was nothing he could do about it now, and he did have to return the icon. He shrugged and left the hotel, taking Reilly's package with him.

He purchased a guidebook of the island, read the sketchy historical introduction with an indulgent smile, and visited several points of interest it recommended.

Heraklion still depressed him. But as he strolled by the Minoan art treasures in the galleries of the Archaeological Museum, he became convinced that his disappointment with both Athens and Heraklion was due to his readings of their histories, readings which had not prepared him for the poverty, the stench, or the dirt, but which had erected in his imagination two cities that existed outside of time, as if they survived in separate bell jars where dust did not gather, the temperature did not change, and human beings did not suffer. Somehow he had fallen into the Great Error he had warned his students about many times: he had forgotten that history books were only "fragments of chapters from the Book of Existence," as old Henderson liked to put it. Consequently, Ben had romanticized both cities and lost the sense of the living world in them.

Lost. He and Julia had *lost* something. That was her word for it. The implication was that he had lost something that was vital to the relationship, and she had gone elsewhere, to Elliott, to find it. And, yes, Ben had to admit that he had lost touch with the children, with her. *The books:* he had retreated more and more into his books, thinking he was confronting the world through history when in reality he was escaping from it, losing contact with race riots, starving children in Biafra, senseless murders in Northern Ireland, oil shortages, hijackings, assassinations, and all those daily events he was unable to control. He imagined what he must have looked like to Julia and his daughters, stooped over his texts late into the night, solitary, uncommunicative, just as his father had looked to him when he was ten years old, after his mother died. He would watch the old man night after night, staring at the light from the lamp to the left of the blaring radio until he fell asleep in his chair.

And as he stood in the glaring sunlight outside the museum it seemed to Ben that he had come to Greece on a pilgrimage, a quest for everything he had lost—his wife, his daughters, and his father.

He returned to the pension in a dismal mood, and decided to postpone his first sight of Knossos until after he returned from visiting Reilly's father-in-law.

"S'cuse, sir," said the old man, still unshaven, from behind the front desk as he handed Ben the room key.

Ben looked up.

"Man here. Ask for you."

Not again, Ben thought, remembering the unexplained phone call at the Hotel Athena two days before. "What did he want?" he asked in a neutral voice.

The old man shrugged, pursing his lips and raising his eyebrows. "Just want to know you here."

"What?"

"He ask your name, say 'is here?' I say, 'Is here.'

'What room?' he say. 'Three-ten,' I say. 'Which one?' he ask. 'Three-ten, one with balcony in front,' I say. And he go."

"That's all?"

The old man nodded and lazily rubbed the bristles on his jowls with the back of his hand.

"Well, what did he look like?"

"Dressed like old time *Kriti*. Country people, they still dress in such way—boots, black kerchiefs around head, daggers in sash."

"Nothing else?"

The old man thought for a moment. "Yes. Black cloth here," he said, gesturing to his left arm. "For someone die in family—you know."

"Did he say he'd be back?"

The old man shook his head. "He just go."

Ben went to his room, wondering who the visitor had been and what he wanted, and he was still wondering when he returned to the pension after supper that night. Without turning the light on in his room, which was stuffy and uninviting even in daylight, he tossed the package on the bed, strolled onto the balcony, and looked down at the street.

The pension was located on a corner in one of the older neighborhoods. That was why he had chosen it— a neighborhood of small Turkish houses with white garden walls and recessed doorways that were now transformed into gaping caverns by the exaggerated shadows thrown against them by the dim streetlamp on the corner.

The neighborhood was quiet, far from the noisy traffic of the boulevards and the promenading crowds in the plazas, and it was several minutes before Ben realized that someone was standing in the shadows of the alley directly across the street, smoking a cigarette. Ben tensed for a moment, straining to see more clearly, imagining nothing in particular, just puzzled to see someone standing motionless in a dark alley. Then he looked away, wondering in passing if he had discovered a peeping tom or merely someone waiting for a friend. But when he turned back to the alley several moments later, he realized that he was looking for the person and that his tension hadn't eased.

Several minutes passed. The person in the alley didn't move. All Ben could distinguish was the firefly light of a cigarette brightening and dimming.

Finally a car approached the corner from the left, opposite the alley, and its headlights swept into the narrow passageway, sliding over the figure of a young man with a cigarette in his right hand, dressed in black boots and tan jodhpurs. He looked like an eighteenth-century pirate with the black bandanna tied around his head and the thick black mustache. A black armband circled the upper left sleeve of his silky white shirt. But that wasn't what surprised Ben. What did was that the man did not move when the headlights shone on him, but stood there, continuing to smoke, his face tilted upward, his lips suspended in what seemed a lazy smile, as though he had been watching Ben all along.

Ben stood on the balcony a few moments longer, nerves jangling. He peered into the alley, but could see nothing, not even the cigarette. Then he went into the stuffy room, shaking his head and smiling. *Come on now, man!* he said to himself. *Here we go again! The phone call in Athens, and now this strange-looking character in the alley, who looks just like the guy who asked for me downstairs today. Coincidence,*

that's all. Even the black armband was coincidence.
Once more his imagination was beginning to get the
better of him.

He looked down at the package. *Why not open it
and put an end to these fantasies once and for all?
Just listen to me, for God's sake!* Besides, as he'd already realized, the package was trussed up so elaborately that any tampering he did would be only too
apparent, and it wouldn't be worth that much embarrassment just to indulge his paranoia.

He shook his head and went to bed, attempting to
put the whole day out of his mind.

But he slept fitfully, and toward dawn dreamed the
nightmare for the first time since coming to Greece,
and this time the nightmare took place in Knossos.

Knossos was the reason he had come to Crete. It
was one of the wonders of the ancient world, a vast
palace-city which may have had as many as 80,000
inhabitants by 1800 B.C., and from those pillared passageways and stone throneroom the Minoan Empire
had ruled not only the other cities on the island but
settlements throughout the Mediterranean. Knossos'
indoor plumbing and scores of other technological conveniences, as well as its inhabitants' carefree yet sophisticated art, were not to be matched in Europe until our
own century. And it was one of the few Minoan population centers to withstand the huge volcanic eruption
that occurred somewhere around 1500 B.C. on the
nearby island of Thera, an eruption which sent tidal
waves hundreds of feet high crashing against Crete's
north coast and showered the island's farmlands with
toxic ash. Neither Knossos nor the Empire could survive the effects of this catastrophe for long, though,
and finally the palace, its pillars and passageways top-

pled and overgrown with weeds, became a fabled ruin hidden from the world until its rediscovery in 1900, almost 3500 years after it had been abandoned. Until then Knossos was remembered as the legendary site of the Labyrinth, whose hundreds of interconnecting passageways, according to mythology, were prowled by the Minotaur, a monster with the body of a man and the head of a bull. At prescribed times, the myth went, the Minotaur was offered sacrifices of maidens and youths who were set loose in the Labyrinth and roamed aimlessly through its stone corridors until they encountered the Minotaur and he devoured them.

Ben's fascination with the palace had begun in his boyhood when his father had read him the story of the Minotaur from a child's mythology book. The story had been the only bond he remembered with his father, and had ended, as had all communication with the old man, when Ben's mother died. After that their only close contact occurred when the old man would beat him with his thick, callused hands, filling the room with his whiskey-sweet breath, or in Ben's dreams, when he would walk into a room or around a street corner to find the Minotaur lunging toward him with his father's bloodshot eyes and tobacco-seared breath. These nightmares had persisted into his adult life, and even though he had written an undergraduate psychology paper in which he identified the monster as the embodiment of the bestial aspects of man's nature which "inhabited the shadowy, convoluted lair of the mind," he still woke from these nightmares trembling and sweating.

Now, in his nightmare, Knossos was surrounded by a blurred gray light, and he was wandering through partly reconstructed courtyards with wide staircases and blood-red columns, seemingly endless passageways lit by airshafts, and stone chambers whose walls were covered with brightly-colored murals of birds and flowers and dallying youths. Suddenly he smelled it. He sniffed and looked up. He had wandered into a section of passageways he did not recognize, and a tepid breeze had tunneled toward him through the gray underground light, surrounding him with the overpowering stench of warm hides sour with urine and sweat. He almost gagged, and instantly knew that he had wandered into the area of the palace inhabited by the Minotaur, and that the monster, clothed in the heavy odor of his childhood nightmares, was there, waiting for him around the next corner or standing behind him, watching his every move with bloodshot eyes. He whirled around, but just as he tensed, expecting to see the bull face rushing at him, he woke up.

Slick with sweat, he flung back the sheet, threw his legs over the side of the bed, sprang to a sitting position and remained there, frozen, his muscles locked, staring straight ahead. It was first light, and as soon as he was fully conscious he went to the balcony window and looked into the alley. No one was there. In fact he didn't see anyone resembling the man in the alley as he strolled the streets that morning, and he had almost forgotten the incident and the nightmare by that afternoon when he left the city to meet Reilly's father-in-law.

Chapter Three

The meeting place was twenty-five miles west of Heraklion, at the turn-off for the town of Garazon. This was a few miles inland on a two-lane road that paralleled the main highway along the northern coastline. After an hour's jolting bus ride over a precipitous, treeless landscape, with panoramic views of the sea on one side and valleys green with olive groves and grape arbors on the other, Ben was let off at the Garazon junction.

The sun was dumping vats of late afternoon heat on the highway. The heat billowed around him and he was sticky with sweat. Just as he was beginning to have misgivings about whether he had been left in the right place, the bus drove off in a gale of exhaust fumes and dust and blatting engine noise, leaving him on the empty roadway.

A black Citroën was parked across the highway on the edge of the side road, facing inland, and a short, stocky man in his early sixties with closely-cropped white hair and a square clean-shaven face was trudging toward him. He was wearing black, knee-high boots, tan jodhpurs, and a white shirt with a brown-striped tie beneath a white linen jacket. Even in the dusty heat of the road his grooming was immaculate.

He was, in fact, the picture of an English country squire, except for the black armband sewn to his left sleeve. Ben observed the armband, his heart jumping, but forced his expression to remain impassive. He'd soon know what was going on.

"Benjamin Ames?" the old man said.

"Yes," said Ben, smiling.

"I am Stavros Papandakis," the man announced somberly, ignoring Ben's smile as he shook his hand. "Please." He made a slight bow, led Ben to the Citroën, and directed a small wiry man with a black mustache to take Ben's valise and load it into the trunk. The wiry man, who was also wearing a black armband, performed the old man's instructions with nods and bows—opening doors, loading the trunk, and scurrying back and forth around the car. Then, with Ben and Papandakis comfortably installed in the back seat, he drove the Citroën inland past miles of olive groves toward a huge mountain range that loomed thirty or forty miles ahead.

"You said you were my son-in-law's teacher in America. What do you teach?" asked Papandakis.

"History. European history."

"And are you acquainted with *our* history?"

"Yes, I am."

The old man nodded, his expression still grim. "Our life has been a tragic one. Turks, Venetians, Germans. But we have survived." He had been looking out the window as he spoke, but when he completed the last sentence, he turned to Ben with expressionless black eyes whose very blankness made Ben uncomfortable, not merely because their gaze was so direct and powerful, but because they implied more than the old man's statement had said, things about Ben which were highly unpleasant, for they seemed to be peering deep inside him as into a messy closet.

Ben was startled. Was this the person Reilly had described as "a sweet old guy?"

Papandakis continued to stare at him. "We are not Greek, you know. We are a nation of martyrs. That is our heritage. You do not mind that I speak to you in this fashion, I trust? You are a teacher, and I am sure such statements do not seem presumptuous to you," he said, still staring into Ben's eyes.

"No," said Ben, once more sensing that Papandakis was trying to tell him more than his words expressed. Was the old man mad? What the hell was going on?

"You speak excellent English," Ben said, smiling at the old man once again.

The old man nodded once more at this comment and turned abruptly toward the window, as if the compliment was of no consequence to him and the smile possibly distasteful. "My father sent me to England for my education," he said finally, still looking out the window. Then he turned toward Ben and smiled for the first time, although his smile was thin and his eyes were still insinuating. "I have retained the language and happily misplaced the accent."

Ben really *was* impressed by Papandakis' English, although he noticed that the old man tended to thicken consonants and round vowels, and his sentences were too formally constructed. There was something definitely foreign about his English, as though a pungent herb were being used to lend an exotic flavor to boiled mutton.

"What did my son-in-law tell you about me, Professor?" Papandakis asked in a more relaxed tone.

"Nothing. Just that he was your daughter's husband

and he couldn't take the icon you had given him out of the country."

"Ah, yes, the icon." The old man nodded and lapsed into a somber silence once again.

These sudden shifts of mood were unnerving, and Ben felt his discomfort turning to apprehension as he remembered the old man's long silence on the phone the day before when he had told him about the icon. There sure as hell was something fishy about that package! No two ways about it.

They rode in silence for several minutes, then the old man tapped Ben on the shoulder, pointed out the rear window, and began to speak, never taking his eyes from Ben's.

"Several kilometers farther down that highway, Professor, is the cave of Melidhoni where the Turks smoked to death more than three hundred and fifty of us in 1824. Women, children, everyone. It is a Cretan shrine, a place where we renew our courage. Do you understand what I am saying to you?"

Ben's apprehension was now turning to alarm. What *was* the old man saying?

Papandakis fell silent once more, and did not speak again until they reached a large village cluttered with two-story whitewashed houses with red-tiled roofs, similar to the Turkish houses in Heraklion.

"This is my village," the old man said, and the way he said it made Ben think that he owned the entire town.

A mile beyond the village they turned onto a driveway in the middle of an olive grove. The driveway led to a squat but spacious two-story concrete house, freshly whitewashed, with a veranda circling the lower story and a balcony above it. The doors and the window shutters were made of well-kept wood, newly shellacked, and the proverbial red-tile roof had been replaced by a flat concrete one painted white.

"My house," said Papandakis more by way of explanation than welcome.

The car followed the driveway to the back of the house, where there was a graveled yard surrounded by outbuildings and beyond them on all sides the olive grove.

They stepped out of the car, and the old man pointed to the mountain range ahead which towered over the valley. Patches of snow were visible in the shaded crevices near the tallest peak. "Psiloritis," the old man said, "your Mount Ida, Professor. It is said that Zeus was born there. You will be able to see it from your room." He turned to Ben with his expressionless eyes. "Nikos will take your valise," he murmured, and they both followed the driver through the back door, into a large kitchen with an open hearth, then through a dining room, a wide hall, and up a curving stairway to a room on the second floor, where the wiry man placed the valise on a bed.

The three men stood by the bed looking at each other. Ben felt the other two wanted something, but he couldn't figure out what. He looked at the white walls on which hung cloth rectangles embroidered with maroon and yellow flowers. The room had a fireplace at one end and a double bed at the other. The varnished floor was covered with three white throw-rugs, also decorated with embroidered flowers. A bureau, a chair with a leather seat, and a desk, all made of the same heavy dark wood, were the only other furnishings. But if the furnishings were sparse, they were also tasteful, almost aristocratic. The windows on either side of the curtained glass double door looked onto the balcony and beyond it to the olive groves which seemed to spread all the way to the rock-bare mountains at the end of the valley.

Papandakis cleared his throat.

"It's lovely," said Ben in response.

Papandakis nodded, then glanced toward the valise.

"Oh, yes," said Ben, realizing what Papandakis wanted. He went to the bed, unlatched the suitcase, took from it the bundle Reilly had given him, and handed it to the old man.

"Thank you, Professor," said Papandakis with a slight bow. "Now wash, rest, amuse yourself in whatever way you desire. Supper is at nine. Nikos will call you for aperitifs and *mezedakia* at eight thirty." And with that he strode from the room with Nikos following him, leaving Ben to wonder at both his behavior and his connection with the man who had watched the hotel room the night before.

Ben walked onto the balcony. It was cooler outside. The sun was low in the west, casting a rusty patina over the tops of the olive groves and the outcroppings of the mountains. *Psiloritis. The mountain on which Zeus, father of the gods, was born.*

Ben took a deep breath. Papandakis was certainly strange, but maybe there was a simple reason for his odd reception. Even for this coincidence of the armbands. One thing was certain: Ben's imagination could no longer be blamed for playing tricks on him. Something was going on all right, and that something had to do with the package. He'd think twice before questioning his paranoia again. Strangely, he wasn't frightened. He figured that now that they had the package, he wasn't in any danger. And any way he looked at it, whatever this was all about had nothing to do with him. He shrugged and looked at the mountains again.

Psiloritis. Melidhoni. Papandakis had spoken of "our heritage," of the cave where "more than three hundred and fifty of us had been smoked to death by the Turks," as though past and present were one here. And Ben knew that he was now in a Crete closer to its past, both historical and mythical, than was Heraklion, a Crete that had given birth to Greek civilization. Why, Zeus had been born on the very mountain he was looking at. . . .

He'd give Papandakis another chance. If he didn't get along with the old man tonight, he'd leave in the morning. This evening he was going to be a cheerful, inquisitive guest and find out as much about Cretan life and manners as he could—packages, armbands, and moody patricians be damned!

Chapter Four

Supper consisted of grilled lamb rissoles, fried potatoes, a tomato and vinegar salad served with slabs of white cheese and a sharp white wine—a plain but welcome meal after seven days of Greek restaurant cooking.

The dinner was served in the dining room, a long, narrow whitewashed chamber decorated with embroidered-flower wall hangings. The room had three entrances: one, opposite a large study, was through the main hall; another, at one end of the table, was through two glass doors that led onto the veranda; and the third, at the opposite end of the table, was through the kitchen.

It was dark by then, and in the thick heat of the room the overhead bulbs spread a grainy sulfurous light over everyone seated at the table, which made their faces all seem yellow and haggard.

There were five man at supper besides Papandakis, who was sitting at the head of the table in front of the glass doors, and Ben, who was sitting opposite him. The others ranged in age from the early twenties to the late sixties, and the energy they had expended in eating in the stifling room had left their faces slick with sweat. All were dressed in Cretan knee-high boots and jodhpurs; all wore wide purple sashes around their waists, from which protruded the ivory handles of daggers with pommels shaped like the heads of human thigh-bones. And although the colors and textures of their shirts were different, all had black armbands pinned to their sleeves.

The two older men were seated on one side of the table. They were both bareheaded and wore coarse, long-sleeved charcoal-gray shirts. Like Stavros Papandakis, they were short and thickset. One was in his late fifties and had been introduced as Stavros' brother, Pandelis. He had furious black eyes and a huge sweeping mustache shaped like a whale's upturned flukes. The other, the oldest man at the table, sat between Pandelis and one of the younger men and had been presented as Uncle Kosta; he had a drooping white mustache and smoky black eyes that moved in a slow, stately manner from one person to another.

The other three men were tall, lean, and young. They wore silky black shirts that rippled across their chests; they had wrapped their skulls in the black net bandannas, fringed with tassels, that gave Cretan men the appearance of pirates; and each of them sported a thick black mustache.

Of the two sitting opposite Pandelis and Uncle Kosta, one, named Manoli, had a lazy left eye that bulged slightly and kept glancing off somewhere behind Ben's right shoulder while the right eye locked the American in its gaze—a phenomenon that gave Ben the uneasy sensation that someone was coming up behind him whenever Manoli glanced his way. Pavlo, sitting on Manoli's right, had perpetually indrawn eyebrows and a pained, almost bewildered expression, as if he didn't quite understand what was going on around him. His watery eyes were continually turning toward the glass doors with a dreamy, faraway stare which made him look as if he were on the verge of tears.

The third young man was seated on the other side of the table, between Ben and Uncle Kosta. His name was Yorgo, and his straight back and calm bearing suggested an almost arrogant self-confidence, an impression that was increased by the half-smile that was always on his lips and which Ben soon realized was caused by the size of his teeth, which were like thick white slabs aligned without a gap. His protruding teeth and small squinting eyes gave him the appearance of a dangerous but contented whale dozing in the sun.

When Ben had been introduced to the other members of the Papandakis household in the study before dinner, he had immediately recognized Yorgo as the man who had been watching from the alley the night before. But once again, he had hidden his anxiety, reminding himself that he was in no danger. He'd soon know what they wanted from him—if they wanted anything. After all, they had the package, and that was that. Obviously Yorgo had been sent to Heraklion to insure Ben's welfare, or, rather, the package's. That was all. And the ominous atmosphere in the dining room was merely a combination of the heat, the raffish Cretan costumes, and a prescribed code of social behavior of which he was ignorant. But he *was* uneasy. There was no doubt about that.

Since their grunted acknowledgments of Papandakis' introductions in the study, the others had not addressed a single word to Ben. They spoke among themselves in low voices, occasionally darted a furious glance in his direction, then settled into long silences which made Papandakis' efforts at small talk seem all the more forced and inappropriate.

The old man's spirits had lifted since the afternoon. Dressed in white dinner jacket and black tie, he didn't seem to mind the heat, which had left his face damp and shiny and had soaked Ben from head to toe. Except for several stretches of tight-lipped silence, he seemed almost chatty, describing the ingredients of the dishes they ate and the tradition of the wall hangings, commenting on this aspect of Cretan garb or that detail of Cretan history, and generally being an effusive host.

The only women who were in evidence in the Papandakis household were two hunched old crones in black shawls and black skirts who carried in the platters of food. At one point, Ben remembered Caroline Hooper, the woman he had met on the boat two nights before, and wondered how she would like to find herself this far off the beaten path. He was not surprised when he immediately decided she wouldn't.

The dishes had been cleared away and everyone was sipping small cups of Greek coffee when Papandakis whispered something in Greek to Manoli, the tall young man with the bulging eye. Manoli slid from the table and left the room, returning a few moments later with the package. It was still wrapped.

Papandakis put the package on the table in front of him, rose, placed his right hand on it as if he were about to take an oath on the Bible, and smiled at Ben.

"Now to our business, Professor Ames," he said, still smiling. "Your phone call interested us greatly. Yes, greatly." He paused and drummed his fingers on the package, the smile hanging on his lips. "And my friends here, not talkative on most occasions anyway, are most eager to see what you have brought us, so eager that they have said nearly nothing all evening. That is Cretan patience. Mark it well."

The five men were completely still now, all looking at Ben. Nikos, the chauffeur, had appeared from the hallway when Manoli had reentered the room, and now stood leaning against the dining room entrance with his arms folded and a sleepy expression on his face. There was another man, dressed like the others, whom Ben had not seen before, standing behind his chair in the entrance to the kitchen.

Ben's nerves were ringing like tiny burglar alarms. The situation would have seemed even more ominous had not Papandakis continued to smile at him.

"You call me up, Professor, and tell me that you have seen my son-in-law in Athens. That alone would have kindled our interest. You see, Professor," he said, tapping his forefinger on the black armband sewn to his jacket sleeve, "eight days ago my son-in-law was killed in an accidental fall while hiking through the Gorge of Samaria. Pandelis there, my brother, and our cousin Grigori were with him but had dropped behind to allow a group of German tourists to pass them on a high, narrow part of the trail, and the next moment my son-in-law was tumbling down the ravine. When they got to him, they found that his neck was broken. That is why I sent Yorgo"—he nodded in Yorgo's direction—"to watch your hotel yesterday, for you told me on the phone that you had met my son-in-law in Athens two days ago, which would be six days after his death."

Papandakis was no longer smiling, but he continued to speak evenly, almost calmly. Pandelis, the thickset one in his late fifties, was glaring at Ben with small black eyes, his lips tight beneath his fish-tail mustache.

Ben could hear his heart thumping. Sweat was pouring down his face. Papandakis' words had been clear enough, but they made no sense. *Son-in-law dead? A fall? Gorge of what? Where? Reilly's tan, smiling face, the blond curls, the doll-blue eyes—yes, it was two days ago in Athens. What was the old man talking about?*

"It is a joke in very poor taste, Professor Ames. We Cretans are known for our violent tempers, but you also say that this *ghost* you met in Athens gave you a package for me. An icon I supposedly had given him. And, Professor, that is why you are here digesting a good meal now, and not leaking your life's blood away in a ditch somewhere on the road to Rethymnon."

Papandakis' voice was still calm, but the threat in his words was too clear for Ben to deny. The five men at the table seemed about to spring at him.

Papandakis continued, relaxed and unhurried, as if explaining the solution to a chess problem. "'What,' I asked myself, 'can this man be bringing me in that package? My son-in-law is dead, yes. I have seen his body myself and given the police his belongings. And I had given him nothing while he was here.' No gifts, nothing, Professor. So what have you brought us in this package, which is obviously the reason for your masquerade? Why do you look so shocked, Professor? The situation is indeed a strange one, stranger than I have told you—but you already know that, do you not?"

And with these words he suddenly flipped the package over, at the same time grabbing one of the strands of twine that bound it. The wrapping sprang open like a flower, coming undone so easily that Ben immediately knew that the package had been opened before and that all these words had been a show for his benefit. Still he leaned forward to see what was inside, sure it would be an icon, but fearing it would be anything from drugs to—what? The creaking of his chair sounded like a pistol shot. Everyone was looking at him.

"Now, Professor," said Papandakis, his tone no longer calm and his teeth cutting each word into a precise, snarling shape, "where is she?"

Chapter Five

Ben was unable to tell how much time passed before Papandakis spoke again. He was aware that his mouth was open, that his throat was dry, and that the room was as still as a yellowing snapshot. A drop of sweat slid in a slow track from his forehead to his chin.

"I asked you where she was, Professor. I would appreciate your answering me and telling me what these things are all about." Papandakis gestured at the contents of the package. From the wrapping he lifted a photograph of a pretty dark-haired young woman in her twenties who was staring moodily out at the men at the table. "Where, Professor?"

Ben knew he was in extraordinary danger, but he couldn't make any sense out of the situation. "I've never seen her before," he heard himself say.

"Really? Then why do you bring me a photograph of her? And why this?" Papandakis lifted from the wrapping what looked like a folded map.

"Come, why the silence, Professor? You are the courier, are you not? What did they instruct you to tell us?"

"Courier?" A smile fluttered on Ben's lips and vanished as Papandakis continued to stare at him without changing his expression.

"I am talking about my daughter, Professor. And make no mistake, I *will* have her back. I should have known something was wrong when Henry arrived without her."

"Henry?" asked Ben.

Papandakis slapped the folded map on the table with his open hand and leaned forward, his fingers spread. His eyes were black fire. "I do not appreciate your humor, Professor. Deliver your message, and let us get on with this."

"Mr. Papandakis, I don't understand a word of what you've been saying. I met your son-in-law at the Historical Museum in Athens three days ago, and he asked me to deliver that icon to you, since I was coming to Crete anyway. That's all I know."

"Your icon, Professor." Papandakis reached into the wrapping and tossed a blank slab of wood trussed with torn masking tape onto the table. He pointed at it. "The documents were taped to that," he said in a voice suddenly hoarse with weariness.

Ben felt his lips part, but no words came. He wondered why the revelation of the blank piece of wood should have surprised him after he had been shown the other unexpected objects in the package. But even before he had finished asking himself the question, he knew the answer. All through Papandakis' revelations and insinuating remarks he had believed that the icon was lying heavy and immobile underneath the wrapping and in the end would vindicate him. Now that this last connection with any kind of sense had been denied him, he was virtually in a state of shock.

"Well, Professor?" said Papandakis after a few moments. Everyone was waiting, but Ben didn't know what to say. Papandakis frowned and gave him a curious glance, and Pandelis leaned toward the old man and whispered something to him. Papandakis nodded, still looking at Ben. "My brother wants to speed up this business, and he suggests a few cuts of the dagger will do it. He is not as patient as the rest of us. If you know something about our Cretan sense of honor, you will understand why. Henry was in his charge at Samaria, and the young man's death has weighed heavily upon him. Besides, Stella is his favorite niece, Professor. I would not keep him waiting much longer."

Ben glanced at Pandelis' square face with its wiry iron-gray hair. It was turned toward him, and he saw the hatred in the man's black eyes. He was relieved that he was sitting at the other end of the table. He looked back at Papandakis.

"Professor Ames, we are well aware that ransom will have to be paid, and we will comply with the request. But you must give us the figure."

"Ransom? Now wait a minute—"

"You are not asking for ransom, Professor?" Now Papandakis was showing surprise.

"Mr. Papandakis, I don't even know what you're talking about. This whole situation is as startling to me as it is to you."

"You still maintain that you met my son-in-law three days ago at the museum in Athens and that he gave you this package for me?"

"Yes."

"And you knew nothing of its contents?"

"That's right."

"Even of this letter?"

Ben didn't reply as Papandakis, without taking his eyes from his, removed a folded sheet of typewriter paper from the wrapping. "Let me read it to you in order to refresh your memory," he said as he unfolded the paper.

> To: Stavros Papandakis
> Garazon, Crete
> Sir:
>
> Your daughter, along with four other American citizens, is being held in the town jail at Söke in Turkey, on drug-smuggling charges. I do not need to tell you what this means. She and the others will be transferred to a state prison within the week.
>
> Please make plans for her release and the release of the other Americans in any way you see fit. I am aware of your unique abilities in this area. Mark down all monies and materials you will need.
>
> The release must be effected within three days of your receipt of this letter. A courier will be in touch with you within twenty-four hours.
>
> Sincerely,
> Another Concerned Father

"It is written in an efficient Greek. Now tell me, Professor, are you that 'concerned father'?"

"No," said Ben, suddenly angry at the way Papandakis was attempting to manipulate him with these theatrical tactics.

"Then you must be the courier."

"No."

"Do you know the meaning of the sentence about my unique abilities to release my daughter from a Turkish jail?"

"No."

"I see. Let us pursue another way of looking at this.

Would you say that the letter could be the first communication of a kidnaper?"

"That's what I thought as you read it, yes."

"Then why the elaborate disguise of the concerned father, Professor?"

"I don't know."

Papandakis looked down at the letter and bit his upper lip. When he spoke again, his voice was calm. "Let us say that you are telling the truth. Unless you or the writer has a morbid sense of humor, you would have presented his demands by now. If that is the case, what do you have to do with all this, Professor?"

"As I've already told you, nothing," said Ben, his anger rising.

"If for some reason this letter should prove genuine, then I must assume that my daughter is actually in a Turkish jail and that the concerned father is the parent of one of the other prisoners and that is why he wants them all released. Would you not say so?"

"Yes, that's what I understood the letter to say," said Ben, his jaws tightening.

"And I must also assume that this concerned father is powerful enough to have access to a dossier on me and to be able to deliver whatever money and materials I might request."

"It seems that way."

"And you still maintain you do not know what we are talking about?"

"That's what I said."

"Professor Ames, when I opened the package this afternoon and read the letter, I was proceeding on the assumption that this situation could be solved by my finding out the names of any Americans who were being detained in the town jail at Söke. Several phone calls confirmed that five Americans are being held in the Söke jail on drug-smuggling charges." He paused, took out a slip of paper from the right side pocket of his jacket, studied it, then raised his head and continued. "Their names are Stella Reese, my daughter; Douglas and Stephanie Hodges; Stephen Robinson; and Jeffrey Stone. Do these names mean anything to you?"

"No."

"I see," he said, setting the paper on the table near the wrapping. "Well, Professor, I have made my plans on the basis of those phone calls. I will need one hundred thousand American dollars. You may use the phone in my study to relay this information."

"To whom?"

"You still say you know nothing about this letter?"

"That's right."

"Then, Professor, I ask you once again, what is your concern in this affair?"

"As I've been telling you, nothing. Absolutely nothing. And I'm getting goddamn sick and tired of your not listening to me!"

"Would you listen to me if I were in your place?"

Ben said nothing.

"Exactly. You are not a stupid man, Professor, and I am sure you are aware of your position. I shall give you the remainder of the night to consider your role in this affair. If you do not tell me in the morning, I shall allow Pandelis to have his way with you, I am afraid."

He turned to Nikos, who was still slouched in the doorway, and said several words to him in a clipped, precise Greek. Nikos pushed himself out of the doorway and started toward Ben.

At that moment there was a sudden movement on

Ben's right, and he turned to see Pandelis lunging toward him across the table. The thickset man's right arm was sweeping downward toward him in an arc. His hand clenched the handle of a dagger, its blade gleaming like the blade of a guillotine as it sank into the table a foot from Ben's chest.

"*Pandeli, oshee! Oshee!*" Papandakis shouted, but the men seated on either side of Pandelis had already wrestled his arms behind him and pushed his head and upper body down on the table. His body tense and straining, he turned his face toward Ben and glared, then spat and muttered something in Greek that didn't need to be translated.

Ben hadn't moved. He had watched the attack like a paralyzed man witnessing his own death. His body had refused to function, and now his nerve ends were jangling. Everyone was looking at him with mixed expressions of concern and loathing, except for Papandakis, who was simply staring at him with his empty black eyes.

Nikos put a hand on Ben's shoulder. Ben rose and allowed the man to guide him toward the hall.

"One thing more, Professor," said Papandakis, still standing erect and calm at the head of the table as if nothing had happened. "Does the name Henry Reese mean anything to you?"

"N-no," said Ben, his jaw trembling. All the anger was drained out of him.

The men in the dining room continued to stare at him, even the two who were still holding Pandelis pinned to the table.

"He was my son-in-law, the one you tell me you met in Athens, Professor."

"N-no, I-I met John Reilly in Athens."

"Ah, so finally you volunteer an answer. John—what did you say his name was?"

"Reilly."

"But my daughter Stella was married to a Henry Reese, Professor. Four months ago in San Francisco, where she has been going to college for the last three years. Do you understand? My daughter and this Henry Reese belong to what is called a meditating society, whose leader is in India. I do not quite understand all that, but I do know that they were going to spend several months in India and return to America by way of Europe so she could introduce me to her husband, since I had been unable to attend the wedding. As was natural, they meant to come through Turkey. I objected to this route, of course, considering the strained relations between that country and mine, but Stella wrote that she had an American passport and that there was nothing to worry about. I had several postcards from her in India. Then Henry arrived alone nine days ago, introduced himself, and said that Stella had remained in Athens with a sick traveling companion but had insisted he come to Crete ahead of her because he was suffering from dizzy spells. That was odd, but since the young man seemed unconcerned about it, I assumed that it was a strange thing for my daughter to do and nothing more. She has always been a willful girl, anyway. Then Henry was killed in the accident the day after his arrival, and we have heard nothing from Stella until your phone call, Professor. I hope this explanation will allow you to appreciate our position, and will even excuse Pandelis' assault."

"I see," said Ben, but he said it just to fill the silence. In reality he saw nothing. Things made less sense than before.

"She is my only daughter, Professor. And by tomorrow morning you had best be ready to begin negotiations. I do not know why you have insisted on playing the fool tonight and can only assume that you are waiting for someone to contact you with further instructions."

"Believe me, Mr. Pap—" Ben began, but Papandakis stopped him by raising his hand.

"We have had enough conversation for one evening, especially if it is going to be more of the same. Good night, Professor." He shifted his gaze to the wiry man at Ben's side. "*Niko!*" he said curtly. Nikos took Ben's arm and led him toward the stairway.

Chapter Six

Ben stood just inside the bedroom door without switching on the light. He wanted the anonymity of darkness. He wanted to be lulled by it, soothed by it; and shutting his eyes, he began to sway in the room's stuffy heat.

Then he heard Nikos locking the door from the outside and the clatter of the turning key exploded through him like buckshot: he was actually a prisoner, a prisoner in a house where some insane bastard had just tried to kill him!

What was this all about? He had done a simple favor for a rather dull ex-student, and now he found himself mixed up in fraud, kidnaping, and possibly drug smuggling.

Ben shook his head and walked to the center of the room. Moonlight was glazing the windows on either side of the gauze-curtained glass door.

The situation seemed inexplicable, the questions endless and unanswerable. Could the package have been switched? *Impossible.* It had been with him day and night since Reilly had given it to him. And what was Reilly's role in all this? He had set Ben up and fed him to the wolves. *Why?* When he got his hands on the little bastard, he'd beat the answer out of him.

But Ben knew he wasn't going to get his hands on him: Reilly was probably halfway across Europe by now. And if he, Benjamin Ames, was going to get himself out of this situation, he had best control his anger and think clearly.

He took another deep breath and turned to the window again.

Why should Reilly impersonate a dead man and thus announce himself as a fraud to Papandakis from the outset? And what was Reilly's relation to the concerned father who had written the letter? And why did the concerned father work in such a devious manner? Why not show himself? Call or write Papandakis directly? And what did the phrase in the letter mean that had referred to Papandakis' "unique abilities," a phrase the old man had pointedly asked Ben about? For that matter, why use the package to begin with? And biggest question of all, what did he, Benjamin Ames, professor of history at Claremont College, Claremont, California, have to do with all this?

The dark room, which at first had seemed so comforting, had become more stifling with each question. Ben walked to the glass door that opened onto the balcony and stepped outside.

A cool rush of air enveloped him. He was surrounded by the sky's moon-bright dome. A few stars were sprinkled on it, but the light of the lopsided moon, low in the southeast, dominated the heavens. The hulking mountains at the end of the valley were chalky with it, and the olive groves below them washed toward him like a cobweb-covered sea.

Then the scratching of gravel and the crunch of footsteps brought Ben's attention to the moonlit yard below. A man, half in shadow, was wandering around, kicking stones and swatting at branches with a stick. He continued to move around the yard, stopping every once in a while in the shadow of an outbuilding to stretch, yawn, or stand quietly in the darkness. Once he stepped into a rhombus of yellow light cast by a first-floor window, dropped the stick and lit a cigarette, and Ben saw that he was one of the young Cretans, the one called Pavlo, whose dreamy eyes and mournful expression had caught his attention at supper. Now he was standing guard, although quite casually, for he had no weapon and was nonchalantly smoking as he continued his tour about the yard.

He didn't seem to notice Ben standing on the balcony, but his presence reminded Ben that he was a prisoner, and once more he began to brood. By morning he had to have answers for Papandakis that were totally beyond his powers to provide. And if Papandakis turned him over to Pandelis—well, he didn't want to think about that.

A prisoner and his guards, Ben thought. *Nikos beyond the locked door and Pavlo in the yard below and a houseful of Cretans besides, one of whom had already tried to kill him.*

A prisoner. Think of that. Absurd! He was a history professor on vacation, not some swashbuckling adventurer. But the fact remained that he was a prisoner, a prisoner among his guards. True, he didn't feel like one: he was taking the night air on a wide balcony overlooking a peaceful landscape. But he *was* a prisoner. Why did he refuse to feel like one? He realized the answer almost immediately: Papandakis, Nikos, or whoever was responsible, had forgotten to lock the glass door that opened onto the balcony. That was why Pavlo had not looked up. They had probably not been planning on holding him prisoner. They had thought he was a courier, and when he failed to provide them with the information they had expected, they had to improvise.

An excitement seethed through him. Already he was calculating the distance from the balcony to the ground. Ten, fifteen feet, at most. He could jump that easily. And with the least bit of luck he wouldn't twist an ankle or break a leg and could sprint into the olive grove before anyone could stop him. What then? *Think of that when the time comes. Here there would only be morning and Pandelis' snarling face; out there, there was a chance.*

He smiled in the darkness, a bitter smile, and began to plan his escape.

He tiptoed back into the darkened room, leaving the light off, got a sweater and the guidebook from his valise, and made sure his passport, wallet, and matches were in his pants pocket. He tied the sweater around his waist, tightened his shoelaces, and placed all the coins from his pocket on the bed. The luminous face of his wristwatch read eleven ten by the time he stood ready in the center of the room, wondering what he had forgotten, and noticed that he was sweating and breathing rapidly. He decided to wait another twenty minutes for the household to settle down to sleep, and sat stiff-backed and tense at the desk, watching the sharp-angled patterns of moonlight on the floor.

It was then the doubts began. Maybe this was the wrong move. If he was caught, it would definitely be the worse for him. Papandakis, certainly Pandelis, would be infuriated. And whether or not the escape was successful, it would prove that he was guilty. *Of what?* Ben shook his head, remembering Pandelis' furious face and his rendezvous with the dagger the next morning. What would happen if Pandelis caught him trying to escape? What if he broke his legs—hell, his neck was more like it—when he jumped from the balcony? He wasn't a kid anymore, and he was out of shape besides. How long could he run? How fast? Was he really up to this? He might make the jump successfully only to be brought down by a coronary two steps into his dash to the olive groves. He saw himself writhing on the moonlit gravel while the Cretans laughed uproariously in a circle around him.

But with each objection he came back to the image of Pandelis lunging at him, the knife glinting as it began its descent toward him, and the expression on the thickset man's face as he lay pinned across the table by his comrades. "I've got no choice," Ben breathed into the darkness, as though saying this aloud would somehow validate his plan. But he knew he did have a choice, and was taking it, and knowing that made him feel better, stronger. *But what if* . . .

He sneered at the timid voice inside him, and as if to silence it once and for all, he rose, picked up the guidebook, and stepped onto the moonlit balcony once more.

The cool night air strengthened his determination. He tiptoed to the railing and calculated the length of his drop again. He stepped back, looked at his watch: it was eleven thirty-one. Then he tightened his grip on the guidebook and stood as still as he could, waiting for the guard to show himself.

He heard footsteps scraping on the gravel. Pavlo's shape came into view; it bent down in the center of the yard, then straightened. Within seconds tearing sounds began to punctuate the darkness. Ben held his breath. *Stones,* he thought, *he's throwing stones into the trees.* Pavlo's right arm swung like a lazy pendulum. He was standing in the middle of the yard, his back to Ben, facing the groves below the mountain range. In a few minutes he clapped his hands together several times—*Slapping dust from them, I guess*—and resumed his patrol.

Ben didn't move. He listened to the man make four lackadaisical circuits of the yard, trying to determine his routine, but could find none. Pavlo's haphazard roamings told him that he was not taking his guard duty seriously, and Ben knew that he would have to make his move on impulse and hope for the best.

His body ached from standing stiffly in one place, and he couldn't control his breathing. He stepped forward, gripped the railing, and began to balance himself on the balls of his feet. After Pavlo had passed below him on his next circuit, Ben swung himself silently over the railing without the least hesitation, an operation made difficult by his trembling arms and by the guidebook he still clutched in his right hand. He gripped the railing with his fingers as best he could and let his body hang down as far as possible, and let go.

The jolt came sooner than he had expected. His shins seemed to splinter, his kneecaps went numb, and he landed on the seat of his trousers. The sound of his landing echoed like a handful of thrown pebbles against the house, and a grunt popped from his lips as he expelled air from the impact.

Then he was up and running for the trees, both legs, thank God, working well, everything in operational order and propelling him forward.

The shade of the olive grove closed around him.

"*A! A! Amerikani, stomata!*" shouted a voice behind him.

Other voices joined the first, calling, inquiring, finally shouting. A dog barked.

By that time Ben was deep in the grove, sprinting down a dim corridor between two rows of trees, listening to the air shriek past his ears, and watching the moonlight spear through the jagged openings in the leafy roof above him.

He stumbled on large, dry clods, almost fell several times, but kept on, never slowing down, repeating to himself again and again that the first part of his escape was a success. *I've done it! Done it! Damn!*

In a few minutes he slowed to a trot, listening for sounds behind him. He was drenched with sweat, his breath wheezed through a rusty crevice of pain in his chest, and an ache as big as a football was knotting in his right side.

He began to sprint again, although now he ran in an awkward gallop, and idly realized that the trees around him had been planted in rows and that he was four rows deep in the grove, running parallel to a road.

He didn't know how long he went on in this way, but when he dropped exhausted and gasping for breath beneath a tree, there were still no footsteps behind him. His heart was racing. His muscles trembled. The ache in his side had grown so intense that it was difficult for him to draw breath, and he placed an open hand on his side until his body began to quiet.

Between shudders and gasps he listened for sounds in the grove behind him. Soon he could hear small voices in the distance. He looked at his watch. It was eleven forty-five.

A truck rattled by on the road, sliding the white beams of its headlights into the grove for a moment as it changed gears before going around a turn. Then there was silence again.

As his other agonies subsided Ben became aware of a cramp in his right hand, and he realized that he was still clutching the guidebook. He smiled down at it, a shadowy oblong on his lap, and pictured himself sitting there under the olive trees in the middle of the night, somewhere on this island at the end of Europe, his body aching and sweaty, knowing that angry men were making their way toward him through the grove, men who wanted to maim and possibly kill him.

He lifted the book to his face and his smile widened. Then he began to chuckle, and the chuckling turned to chortling, and soon he was snorting huge uncontrollable gusts of laughter.

Chapter Seven

The laughter continued only for a minute. When it had subsided, Ben was once more aware of his predicament. The shouting and calling, although still in the distance, was getting closer. He was alert, tense.

He rose, yet remained in a half-crouch, ready to move in any direction at a moment's warning. His legs trembled, his calves ached, and the muscles in the back of his thighs had tightened.

He quickly reassessed his situation. Outside the grove the moonlight had transformed the night into a chalky brightness. He would be an open target on the road. If he stayed in the grove, he might be safe until dawn, but then what? If they were searching the grove with any kind of precision, they could conceivably find him tonight. They might even employ villagers, a sort of Cretan posse, to hunt him down; he remembered the way Papandakis had spread his arm that afternoon and exclaimed, "This is my village," as the Citroën had passed through the crumbling town. Which brought up another thought: If Papandakis was as powerful as he seemed, he would know and probably command the allegiance of a great number of people in the area. Ben nodded, memorizing an axiom he knew he should not forget: *Ask no Cretans for help*. Almost simultaneously he reasoned that he had to get as far away from this part of Crete as quickly as he could.

He stood in the darkness under the trees, looking out at the road, not knowing what to do next. He was thirsty and a little nauseous from his unaccustomed exertions.

Several moments went by. Then he heard the wheezing sound of a truck in low gear, and a moment later a sheet of light shot into the grove as the truck came around a turn and passed on. This one had come in the opposite direction from the truck that had gone by before, and it had seemed to be descending, from the way its engine noise had screamed against the meshing of the gears. The other truck had changed to a lower gear before it went around the turn—that meant it had probably been going uphill.

Ben realized almost immediately that he had found the answer. When a truck slowed to change gears for the uphill turn, he would run out of the grove, jump into the back, and let the truck take him where it would; *provided, of course, that the truck had an open back, and provided there was a truck at all.*

He smirked at his own stupidity. It was eleven fifty, ten minutes before midnight, and only two vehicles had passed in the last five minutes. Why did he think that more would pass at this hour on what was clearly a secondary road, and, further, what made him think that one of them would be an open truck?

The voices behind him were louder now. They were cursing and hollering to each other and seemed only moments away.

Should he wait or head on through the grove? The question was academic. He knew he would wait, at least for another few moments, for on foot he would be an easy quarry and would be caught, at the latest, a few hours after daylight. But in a truck he could be transported anywhere and would in a matter of minutes put miles between himself and his pursuers.

He heard another vehicle on the road, but its engine noise was too light to be a truck's and it was coming from the wrong direction anyway. He didn't want to go back to the coast, since he would have to pass Papandakis' house and the old man could very well have set up a roadblock.

A moment later headlights shot into the grove and swept on.

Ben jogged on tiptoe to the row of trees that bordered the road and stood behind a gnarled, thick trunk and waited. He thought he could hear footfalls behind him, but he knew that his senses could be playing tricks on him, especially since the footfalls sounded as if there were an entire regiment beating its way toward him through the trees, and his heart was thumping so loudly.

Beyond the trees the road was a grainy silver. He waited. Several moments passed. Then he saw two circles of light inching toward him on the road, nodding and dipping. They seemed to be nudged forward over the irregular surface of the macadam by a heavy weight. A vehicle. It was coming from the right direction, but even in the moonlight Ben couldn't tell whether it was a car or a truck.

He dashed from tree to tree, maintaining his cover, until he reached the bend in the road. His heart was hammering faster now, and he was breathing shallowly. Was it a truck? Did it have an open back? Would it be going slow enough? He leaned against a tree trunk, his body bathed in sweat again, and looked out at the road, guidebook still in hand and his fingers ready to push off the rough wood.

The vehicle continued to slide toward him, its headlights nodding and dipping, nodding and dipping, so hypnotically slow that Ben almost forgot to pull his head behind the tree when the wash of lights from the twin beams shot into the grove and swept through it.

Then Ben was pivoting around the tree, running behind the vehicle, and, yes, it was a truck, a truck with a canvas cover and an open back. He sprinted toward it, almost stunned by the brightness of the moonlight beyond the grove and the feeling of total exposure it gave him.

The truck shuddered as it slowed, and the driver shifted gears.

Ben ran by the side of the road, caught up with the truck, dashed onto the road behind it, threw the guidebook into the back, raised his hands above his head, grabbed the end of one of the wooden frame panels to which the canvas was lashed and half-jumped, half-threw his body upward toward the opening, at the same time swinging his left leg up like a high jumper. But instead of throwing his leg onto the floor of the truck, he braced his left foot against the edge of the side panels, hung in space for a moment with his right leg dangling over the road, then, with a final tug, heaved himself up and forward, and rolled into the darkness beneath the canvas roofing.

He lay there, arms aching, listening to the stuttering of his heart and the truck's wheezing engine as it strained up the steep turn. He waited for several moments, his body tense and still, until he was sure that the driver had neither heard nor seen him jump into the truck.

With a deep sigh he let his body go slack.

The back of the truck was bare, except for a lot of empty gunny sacks that were strewn over the floorboards. A heavy animal smell surrounded him, reminding him of his nightmare encounter with the Minotaur, but he was unable to tell if it was rising from the sacks or from the bed of the truck.

The truck jolted and shook as it continued on. He found the guidebook as he pulled several of the sacks into a heap and lay on top of them; then he dragged several more sacks over him for a blanket and let his mind and body relax.

The sky, which filled most of the opening, was still pale with moonlight. The road continued to twist and turn, mounting from one switchback to another, then climbing through ghostly white outcrops of rock and bare, steep ravines. The olive groves came into view far below in a toy-enamelled countryside complete with hills, the curving silver track of a river, and, here and there, minute specks of yellow window lights and winking car beams. He could even make out the shoreline in the distance, and beyond it, stretching to the horizon, the smoked glass of the sea.

Despite his predicament Ben felt light-headed, almost giddy. He smiled to himself. It was ridiculous, sure, and he should have been thinking about what he was going to do next, but he hadn't felt this way since the homecoming game in '51, since bootcamp, since he and his buddies had cruised the Ginza so long ago. He sucked in an enormous breath and let it go and couldn't suppress the grin that tugged his lips apart despite his clenched teeth.

* * *

The truck continued to haul itself up through a barren landscape drenched in moonlight. At first it passed through several small villages, but soon there were no villages, no trees, only steep uplands that dropped away into deep ravines or rose into sharp inclines, and, at turns, beyond the edge of the road the countryside he had just been riding through would suddenly appear far below in the distance.

Ben didn't know how much farther up the truck could go. He felt he had already reached the top of the world, and he was getting thirstier by the minute. He looked at his watch. It was twelve forty-five. He had been jostled and tossed about in the truck for close to an hour and had grown accustomed to the almost sweet animal odor that surrounded him. But the air had turned cool, and he could feel the change in the temperature through his sack blankets.

Just as he was beginning to shiver, the truck slowed down and suddenly entered a large village, rumbling down a long street with paved sidewalks and square two-and three-story buildings on either side. The buildings were an eerie blue-white in the moonlight as they slid past on either side of the opening. The street was deserted, the lights were out in the buildings, and even though there were evenly-spaced streetlamps every fifty yards or so, Ben realized that what made the scene so forbidding was not only that there were no people, but that the buildings were fairly new, and the absence of life in such a place, high up in an empty moon-swept landscape, gave him the impression of being in the ruins of a dead civilization on a dead planet. He remembered Knossos. The gigantic volcanic eruption on the island of Thera. The tidal wave and the showers of toxic ash that had destroyed the Minoans. Thirty-five hundred years ago.

The street continued, stretching on for the length of several football fields before the buildings on one side gave way to a small concrete square with some sort of public building beyond it. Then the close-packed square buildings began again. But within moments the truck turned into a side street and stopped.

Ben tensed. There was nothing the driver could want from the back except the empty sacks, but Ben was annoyed with himself for not having prepared for the possibility that he might come back to inspect something or pick up a tool and find him there.

As quietly as possible, Ben covered himself with several sacks, and lying on his back as still as he could, the guidebook clasped to his chest, he held his breath and waited.

Chapter Eight

The cab door opened and slammed. Footsteps slapped on the pavement. A dog barked.

"*Scazmos!*" said a gruff voice.

Keys rattled, a door opened and shut, and once more there was silence.

Ben released his breath. He waited for several minutes, then slipped from the truck, guidebook in hand. Staying in the shadows, he made his way back to the main street, where he looked at his watch. It was one o'clock.

He was stiff and sore, and after the long ride his thirst was enormous. He felt like a giant cramp, and although he walked some of the stiffness out in several moments, his muscles were still sore.

He came to the square he had seen from the truck. A streetlamp stood at the entrance and shone down on it, just managing to disclose a rectangular white plaque conspicuously displayed in front of the shadowy municipal building behind the square.

Ben limped up to the plaque. It was made of white marble and designed to look like the pages of an open book. Both pages were crowded with neatly chiseled Greek words edged in black. The only word Ben could distinguish in the dim light was on the right-hand page, four lines below an intaglio of black laurel leaves arranged in a circle around a black medal shaped like a cross suspended from a ribbon.

ΑΝΩΓΣΙΩΝ

Haltingly, he sounded out the letters. AN-OY-ION. Then he converted the Greek ION to its English equivalent IA. ANOYIA! So that's where he was. The day before he had read something about the town in the guidebook, but he couldn't remember what.

Keeping his back to the streetlamp so he could not be easily seen from the main street, he lit a match and opened the guidebook to the index. He found the name of the village and the page number. The match went out. He lit another, turned to the page, and read:

> At 20 1/2 miles from Heraklion the village of *Anoyia* sits on a saddle between the mountains, 2,200 ft. high. It is the northern approach to Mt. Ida (*Psiloritis*), and from it one can reach the Idaian Cave (4-6 hrs.) where the ancient Greeks believed Zeus, ruler of the gods, was nurtured (see p. 53), and the 8,058 ft. summit (another 5 hrs.). Known for its weaving. A center of rebellion in WWII, the village was completely destroyed by the Germans in reprisal, but has been rebuilt. A plaque in front of the town hall commemorates the event. Villagers can still be seen crossing themselves on passing it and greeting each other with the words *Kali Eleftheria,* a phrase literally meaning "Good freedom" and usually addressed to pregnant women, wishing them an easy birth,

but used here during the war both as a slogan
and a password.

The match went out.

So that explained it: the modern buildings, the eerie feeling. The memory of death was almost palpable here. Ben had sensed it before he even knew where he was. *Kali Eleftheria.* Yes, freedom was good. Ben could attest to that. Although he was thirsty and bone-weary, he also felt triumphant. He had taken the initiative, escaped, eluded his pursuers, and was now on his own.

At the same time he was uneasy, and not only because of his predicament. The guidebook had written of the destruction of Anoyia in the same terse style in which it had described the fall of the Minoan Empire, yet Ben felt more for the people of this little town than he did for the remote earthshakers who had originally inhabited the island. He knew that both events were part of history, but Anoyia was closer to him in time and experience, and its loss struck him as human instead of—dare he say it?—historical. *What did he mean by that?* When he was in high school, he had thought history was only in books and was not related to daily life. Now he realized he had never lost that idea, despite his professorship, and the realization almost made him curse aloud at his stupidity. But he had other, more important things to worry about.

Still standing in the shadows near the plaque, he calmly reorganized his thoughts. There was no one on the sidewalk, and the street remained empty.

He lit another match and found Anoyia on the guidebook map. One road ran through it, the one on which he'd come; it ran south from the coast and at

Anoyia turned north and east toward Heraklion, twenty-odd miles away.

Going back was out of the question. He wanted to stay as far away from Papandakis' territory as possible. The road to Heraklion seemed the likely answer. But as he stood in the silence of the sleeping village he quickly realized that the possibility of finding a ride at this time of night was almost non-existent. And if he attempted to walk part of the way on the road, he might well be exposed on this desolate landscape for ten miles or more with no trees or buildings to hide behind should Papandakis send a car to search the road, and since this was the only road, that was a likely possibility.

The match went out, he lit another, and looked at the map again. Besides the red line of the road there was a dotted black line leading south from Anoyia to a small blue circle under which was printed *Idaian Cave*. From there, more black dots led south in a snaking path to another blue dot marked *Kamares Cave* and continued to the southeast until they reached a black circle which identified the village of Kamares. Another dotted black line led directly south from the Idaian Cave to the same village.

South! What was it? "We've made reservations at a hotel on the south coast in a town called Ayia Galini. Ever hear of it?" *Caroline!*

The match went out. Feverishly, Ben lit another one and scanned the south coast on the map. There it was: *Ayia Galini*, marked with a blue beach umbrella signifying that it was a first-rate tourist town with excellent beaches. He traced the roads from it in several directions before the match burnt out. He lit another; finally he was able to link Ayia Galini with Kamares by two connecting roads, and he estimated that the distance between them was no more than sixteen miles.

"Thank God," he whispered.

The match went out. He took a deep breath and relaxed. It wasn't the perfect answer, but it was the only one. Papandakis would never expect him to go over the mountains, certainly not at night, and would probably continue looking for him along the north coast. The darkness would protect him. And finding Caroline and Gail in Ayia Galini, where he could disappear into the crowds of tourists, solved the two questions he had not allowed himself to think about until now: who was he going to turn to for help, and how was he going to get off the island?

For all he knew the police and the other Cretan officials were in Papandakis' pocket and would turn him over to the old man if he came to them for help. If they were honest, they might open a prolonged inquiry which would provide Papandakis with the opportunity either to kidnap him, or kill him.

He shuddered again.

With Caroline and Gail it was different. He could work with them. They could even hide him, give him time to figure out what this was all about. At least they could go to the American Consul in Heraklion, or wherever he was, without attracting the attention of any black-booted Cretan with a black bandanna tied around his skull who might be watching the consulate.

Things were finally going his way. All he had to do was get to Ayia Galini. All he had to do was find Caroline and Gail.

Doubts began to shake him almost immediately.

Would Caroline help him? She hardly knew him. And what if she and Gail were part of the plot? The meeting on the ship looked pretty damn suspicious in light of what had happened since. And if Caroline were innocent, did he have the right to bring her into it? But even as he asked himself these questions he knew Caroline and Gail were his only way out, and he had to take whatever risks were involved. If they refused to help—well, he'd face that when the time came.

He lit another match and found a small sketch map of the Mount Ida hike on page 53 of the guidebook. The map used the Anoyia War Monument as a final landmark in sketching a path from Kamares to Anoyia by way of the Idaian Cave. He reversed the line of march, figured out where he was and where he was going, and pointed himself in the right direction.

He looked above the buildings at the mountain peaks that shone dense as packed talcum in the moonlight and sensed that it all had been child's play up to now. What worried him was not just his doubts about making it to the other side, nor the fear of confronting that moon-drunk landscape alone, but the realization that just as these mountains were a physical barrier between one side of the island and the other, for him they were a psychological barrier between two kinds of life.

He smirked and shook his head. The high mountain air must be making him giddy. Crossing the mountains was the most practical plan, that's all.

At night? Without even a flashlight?

His muscles were stiff and sore, but with a grunt and clenched teeth he suddenly set off toward the mountains, as if getting off to a brisk start were enough to conceal all the misgivings he felt about the journey ahead. *Conceal his misgivings? From whom? The gods?* Jesus, the night was really beginning to get to him.

Within ten minutes he was out of breath and his heart was batting against his ribs like a heavy blind bird in a cage. Once more he was depressed, although he recognized that the depression was more physical than mental.

After finding a public fountain and drinking in long swallows, he had left Anoyia by a side street, as several dogs barked at him from back yards. Beyond the last house the street had become a track wide enough for a car but strewn with pebbles and loose stones, and he had immediately begun to ascend a high craggy landscape of ledges and rounded ridges over a series of gravelly switchbacks.

The bare slopes above and the shadowy clumps of bushes that dotted them were powdery white in the moonlight. The moon was setting on his right, to the west, as he continued to struggle up the switchbacks, his breath burning like a brush fire in his chest before it rasped from his throat.

It was quite cold by now, and his exertions, which at first had warmed him, spreading a slick map of sweat over his body, soon left him shivering and chilled. He put on his sweater, but it didn't help much.

His thirst returned, but he could find no water—still he kept on, grimly checking his watch again and again as if he could determine his progress by it.

After two hours he was totally exhausted and reeling from one side of the path to the other. Once he slipped and fell, cutting the knee of his trousers and scraping his palms and knees on the stones. He sat there panting, his mouth open, staring at the ledges and outcrops around him, listening to the silence, and cursed himself for the stupidity of his plan. But he rose and went on.

An hour later he was hallucinating. First he was startled by both a patter of stones falling from the slope above him and a sharp, familiar animal odor. And when something rustled in a bush several moments later, he imagined that the Minotaur was there, waiting in the shadows among the rocks, watching him with its burning red eyes, and he was terrified and stumbled on.

It was five o'clock and the moon had just set, leaving a pale blue light over the landscape, when he reached the Idaian Cave, crawling more than walking and numb with cold. At least he assumed it was Zeus' cave from the description in the guidebook, which put it in some godforsaken place ten or twenty yards from a small white chapel, like the one he now saw ahead of him on the trail.

The light had dispelled whatever fears he may have had, but he was so tired by now that he had no desire to look into the elongated slit in the hill just off the trail, and he didn't give a damn whether Zeus had spent his infancy there or in a jet airliner. He even ignored the small round chapel when he passed it. All he wanted to do was get this damn walk over with and drink several gallons of water. But at the same time he was pleased that he had made it this far, and although he didn't want to admit it, he knew that getting to the cave was a triumph of sorts, as well as a point of no return. And he was glad that he had not entertained thoughts of turning back once he had left the plaque in Anoyia's tiny square. He also recognized that his anger of the past few hours was directed against himself, for he knew that the hike was not difficult, that tourists did it every day (even if they did accomplish it on muleback), and that only his poor physical condition had made the climb so arduous.

From the cave the trail led through a flat upland plain that was carpeted with a dense soft grass and surrounded by rounded slopes. After climbing for so long, he almost enjoyed the level walk, although the cold was still making his teeth chatter. The trail led through the center of the plain, and he followed it, smelling oregano and thyme. Before he had walked halfway through the fragrant highland, he heard the warbling of wrens and the crying of large black birds that flapped overhead. With each step he kicked up swirls of pungent dust that stung his nostrils.

The plain seemed to be oblong in the predawn light. After he had walked a mile into it, it was covered with masses of stone and scrubby brush, but where it finally disappeared into long, rounded boulders and large flat broken stones beneath wide slopes, he found a row of drinking troughs fed by an underground spring and drank greedily.

By dawn he was stumbling downhill, the path leading in easy curves through stunted hollylike trees with prickly evergreen leaves. At first he welcomed the descent, feeling the worst was over, but the trail proved steep and clattery with stones, and he kept slipping and jolting his body. Soon his back and kneecaps ached and his legs were trembling.

Half an hour later the sun rose full in his eyes from behind a distant mountain range, casting a dim ruby light into a vast depression of smoky land where there were many villages separated by groves and roadways. The sight of civilization jogged his sprints.

By eight he had tied his sweater around his waist again, and he was pouring sweat. But even though he seemed to be wandering aimlessly down the trail, his spirits were vaulting with each step. He felt light as the blue butterflies fluttering around him, almost giddy, as though he had shed ten years of mental and physical flab in the last ten hours.

An hour later he passed several tourists rocking through the sunlight on muleback, led by an old Cretan with white stubble on his face who was wearing a black handkerchief knotted around his head and jodhpurs and black boots. He stared inquiringly as Ben lurched by. Ben paid no attention, even ignored the man's calls of "*A Keria-istay kala? Istanistay kala?*" He imagined how curious he must look to them, stumbling down the mountain wild-eyed and covered with sweaty dust.

He smiled. He liked the picture, suddenly felt like turning to the old man and yelling "*Kali eleftheria!*" and found he was doing just that—wildly, joyously shouting it up the mountainside, "*Kali eleftheria!*"

The old man halted, turned toward him. "*Té ipate?*" he called.

"*Kali eleftheria!*" Ben shouted again, a big grin on his face.

The old man stood there a moment, one leg in front of the other. Then he shrugged, turned, and went on his way, followed by the mules and their passengers.

Ben didn't care. He continued to grin. *Kali eleftheria!* Damn, he'd made it!

* * *

He was in Kamares by ten forty-five. He found a small café, drank four bottles of icy lemonade, ate a sticky pastry filled with nuts and honey, and then washed his face and slapped the dust from his clothes in the filthy bathroom of the café. He looked at himself in the broken mirror. The washing hadn't improved his appearance much. He was rumpled and grimy, and when he returned to the dining room, the owner stared at him with inquisitive frog-like eyes from his stool behind the bar, his face propped up on several chins.

Ben didn't care what the man thought. He was impatient to get to Ayia Galini.

He paid his bill and left. He was brimming with energy, but five minutes after he had gotten into the taxicab at the fountain in the village square and was bouncing along the dusty road in the heat, he was already fast asleep.

Chapter Nine

He woke to find the taxi driver leaning over the front seat, shaking him, and repeating, "*Se kotheti! Se kotheti, Americani! Se kotheti!*"

Ben's lips and throat were parched, his eyelids stuck together, and he felt gritty under his clothes. But he sprang to a sitting position immediately, mind whirring, and looked around the street before getting out of the taxi.

There was only an old woman in black who waddled down the shaded sidewalk with a covered basket on her arm and disappeared around the corner.

Come on. Ease up. No one is going to look this far away.

He paid the driver and got out, every muscle groaningly sore. The taxi had stopped on a narrow street in front of a white three-story building with bright blue enamel window shutters and matching entranceway. The white wooden sign above the door read Hotel Minos and was lettered in the same blue as the window trimmings. There was a small outdoor café nextdoor.

Although there was no sunlight in the street, the heat was oppressive, and after a moment Ben entered the shadowy lobby and rang the bell on the registration desk. A square middle-aged man came trotting down the hall in slippers and undershirt and slid behind the counter. He looked Ben up and down with some concern, and when Ben asked for Caroline he opened his hands as if he were playing an accordion, tilted his head to one side, and said with relief, "Two woman gone now. Back this afternoon."

The mid-afternoon heat rolled against Ben from all sides as he lumbered to the outdoor café, sank into a chair beneath a dark blue awning, and ordered a beer. He had chosen a table back from the others, where he could see the street but not immediately be seen from it.

The town was a jumble of whitewashed houses and narrow streets tumbling down to a small harbor. New, taller buildings, obviously hotels—the Hotel Minos was one—lifted their sun-glazed windows and enamel-trimmed balconies above the older ones. But the new buildings had been erected with no eye to order and merely added to the sense of crowding, so that the whole town looked like an unruly crowd of white-jacketed men all desperately trying to reach the sea at once by the same route.

Ben drank his beer and waited, every so often scanning the street for signs of Papandakis' men, but only as a precaution. He didn't really expect to see them. His fear of them was still real, but he knew he had come too far, was too much "off the beaten path."

Caroline and Gail returned an hour later. Ben watched them pay the taxi driver, carefully placing bills and coins in the driver's upturned palm and asking, "Enough? Enough?" with each offering. The driver kept nodding and staring at his palm and finally looked up, selected several coins from their hands, smiled, said *"Efcharisto,"* lifted his cap, and drove off.

Both women were flushed and perspiring; their faces still looking pinched and bewildered after the transactions with the taxi driver. Caroline, dressed in white slacks and a pink T-shirt, carried a wide-brimmed straw sunhat at her side. Gail was wearing powder-blue slacks and a matching blouse. They started to walk toward the entrance of the hotel.

"Hello there," Ben called.

Caroline turned and squinted in his direction. "Well, hello," she replied, the tightness in her features relaxing.

"You look as though you can use something cold," he continued and smiled.

Caroline nodded, brushing the hair out of her eyes. "Can we ever!" Both women walked to the table, fell heavily into the canvas chairs, and sighed simultaneously.

Gail was the first to look at him. "My God, what happened to you? You're a mess!"

Ben looked down at his crumpled, dust-covered clothes. Grime was smeared on his shirt cuffs and, he knew, on his collar and the neck of his T-shirt. Even his hands, one of which encircled the beer glass and the other of which lay flat on the table and was sliding back and forth over a hump in the white plastic tablecloth, were crusted with dirt. He remembered what he had looked like in the cracked bathroom mirror at Kamares, and he was still weary from his all-night hike and groggy from the heat and his fourth beer.

"Well, I didn't mean to make you feel gloomy—" Gail continued and suddenly stopped.

Ben looked up. Caroline's hand was on Gail's wrist and she was looking at him with concern. "Are you all right?" she asked.

"Not really," he said, not meaning to say it, but moved by the urgency in her voice.

Caroline lifted her hand from Gail's wrist and reaching across the table, covered his fidgeting hand with her own. He took her hand and held it. "What is it?" Caroline asked. "Bad news from home?"

"I look that broken up, huh?"

"You look pretty bad."

He tried to smile, but the smile didn't work right, and he realized that he was gripping her hand tightly.

Caroline turned to Gail and nodded.

"Well, folks, that's my cue," said Gail. "I think I'll go up to the room and freshen up, as they say. See you."

And the next moment she was gone.

Caroline and Ben didn't say anything for several minutes.

The waiter came over and Ben ordered two beers. He was still holding on to Caroline's hand.

"If there's anything I can do—" she began.

"Look, I don't know whether I should get you involved in this."

"Try me," she replied, squeezing his hand.

He hesitated, stared at the table, remembered his suspicions about her, and looked up. Her face was still full of concern and made him realize how alone he was. "Okay," he said. "I have no one else to turn to anyway." And he told her everything that had happened to him since their meeting on the ship three days before.

When he had finished, they both sat in silence, looking at the table. With each succeeding event the meaning of the story had seemed more elusive than before. Did she believe him? Could she believe him? He looked at her face. She was still staring at the table, her eyebrows drawn together in a frown. "I'm not crazy, Caroline. Every word I've said is true, as impossible as it all sounds."

She waved his words away as though they were flies buzzing around her head, then brushed her hair from her eyes again. Ben noticed that her hair fell straight as a curtain as she tilted her head, a curtain that not only framed her face but also seemed to provide a backdrop for her features. "Are you positive that fellow at the museum was your former student?" she said.

"Yes. Why?"

"Because the answer to this has to do with him. Papan—whatever his name is—was obviously surprised by your phone call and as you said was not prepared to hold you prisoner. And it was Reilly who gave you the package with the photograph and letter already sealed inside it and told you to get in touch with Papandakis. Reilly's the key, all right, unless someone switched packages on the boat or in Heraklion."

"No, I kept the package with me at all times, and Reilly's handwriting was on it, remember?"

"Anyway, Reilly's probably the one who called you at the Athena."

"Yeah, I guessed that."

"And the meeting at the museum was all an act," she said.

Ben nodded.

"You're still positive he was your former student?"

"Absolutely."

"Did he have a grudge against you or anything like that? You know—bad grades, discipline?"

"No, no. He wasn't the brightest student I ever had, but he was pleasant, and we got along. To tell you the truth, I didn't even know he was in class most of the first term, and I only really noticed him when he took other classes of mine."

"Would the classes have anything to do with this?"

"How?"

"The subjects."

"No, not that I can think of."

"Well, something about your past relationship with him must be the key to all this. Or maybe with the concerned father's kid. Maybe they were friends, even classmates."

"But I didn't recognize any of the names on the list that Papandakis read. Besides, I wasn't close to Reilly. He just happened to take three of my classes, and we'd nod to one another around campus. That's all."

"There has to be more," she said, "or this doesn't make any sense."

Ben nodded.

She looked at him and bit her lip.

He squeezed her hand and smiled, relieved at having told someone about his predicament and grateful that she had listened. He had no suspicions about her any longer. He hadn't talked to a woman this seriously since his break-up with Julia. But now Caroline was involved in all this craziness, and he felt guilty about having transferred his confusion to her. He covered their joined hands with his other hand. "Let's take a walk," he said, rising to his feet.

* * *

He had been sitting for so long that his sore and aching muscles had locked, and he winced as he stood up.

They strolled down to the plaza lined with outdoor cafés and pastry shops that fronted the tiny harbor. Small white fishing boats trimmed with swaths of blue, yellow, or lime-green paint bobbed at anchor in the sunlight.

Ben and Caroline walked through the port and out to a rocky beach, making their way around a cliff that jutted into the water and hid the town from view when they had passed it.

They hadn't spoken much. Caroline was still preoccupied, and Ben was still exhausted from his trek over the mountains—almost too tired, in fact, to worry about Reilly or Papandakis or the house in the olive groves. At the same time he was strangely, almost drunkenly content to be ambling along the beach with this tall, brown-haired woman, and when she tripped on a stone embedded in the sand, Ben put his arm around her and kept it there, as if he had been doing this for years.

The sun was glaring off the sea, but a cool offshore breeze was blowing, and the water nudged the beach with a soft flopping sound. They stopped and looked at the surf. It swayed, an iridescent blue.

Ben looked at her. She turned to him, brushing the hair out of her eyes once more. "I don't understand any of it," she finally said, and he could see the confusion in her face.

He smiled. "Come on now. It's nothing for you to get upset about. I'll go to the embassy, and that will be that. And I'm perfectly safe here. Papandakis will never suspect that I've come all this way."

She turned her head and looked down the beach, as if to verify what he had said.

"Hey, come on," he said, "I appreciate your concern, but you're more worried than I am."

She turned back, smiling.

"That's better. Now let's talk about something else. You, for instance. How come you and Gail are so interested in the Minoans?"

"I know what you're trying to do," she said, her smile widening and her face relaxing, "but okay. It was our boss, Eric Heinhardt. Ever hear of Heinhardt and Magnuson, architects? Mr. Heinhardt kept regaling us with the wonders of Minoan architecture, which he insists is the beginning of Art Deco, one of my favorite styles of decorative art. He has several Piet de Young sketches hanging in the office. You know anything about De Young?"

"Nope," Ben lied, wanting to keep her talking and her mind off his troubles, and delighted at having discovered another aspect of her personality. His arm was still around her.

"De Young was the man Evans got to draw reconstructions of the way Knossos must have looked when it was inhabited," she continued. "They're beautifully done. Mr. Heinhardt would lend us books on the Minoans, and soon we were as excited about them as he was. I was especially interested in the frescoes, since I majored in art history in college."

"Oh?"

"Surprised?"

He shook his head.

"I'll bet," she smiled. "Anyway, that's how I got the job at Heinhardt and Magnuson after my divorce. I could type, and I knew the way buildings had been constructed down through history—that impressed Magnuson. But the Minoans were new to me. We only touched on them briefly at school. . . . " She stopped. "Why are you looking at me that way, Professor?"

"I was just thinking that you are a handsome woman, Caroline Hooper," Ben said, not meaning that, but not unhappy that he had said it.

"Does that mean that I just chatter on and on?"

"No. It means, thank you."

Her smile widened at that and she looked up at him. They stared at each other. He slid his other arm around her and kissed her. She drew away for a moment and then moved into his embrace and was kissing him back. He pushed his tongue against her teeth and she opened her mouth for him. She was smaller than he had thought—height, bones, build—and he was surprised by her softness.

Finally she pulled away, and they continued down the beach, hand in hand, saying nothing. She was looking down at the sand and occasionally kicking at stones or pivoting on the balls of her feet, so that she seemed to be curveting like a pony, whirling inward with each step. Since the kiss her body had taken on a spirited, almost expectant quality, that was arousing him more with each footfall.

"You know—" she said, clearing her throat.

"Yes."

"Oh, I don't know. I forgot what I was going to say." And she turned to him suddenly and began to laugh, her face bright and merry. Then she threw her arms around his neck, kissed him quickly on the lips, and ran down the beach.

Ben was still physically weary from his previous night's climb, but he was filled with an overall sense of well-being, a confused mixture of gratitude, tenderness, and lust that he hadn't felt in years.

She turned toward him fifty yards down the beach, beckoned him on, pointed to a low rock ledge twenty-five yards or so farther down the sand. She yelled, "Last one there gets a dunking," and started to run toward it.

He felt his body lurch forward. Despite his sore muscles, his legs began to churn, and with a shout deep in his throat, he sprinted after her.

She turned and screamed when she saw him coming, then kept racing toward the ledge.

She reached it before he did. It was a low shelf of gray limestone, smooth as a whale's back but scored with numerous potholes. Ben was right behind her, and when she turned around again, he was on top of her, scooping her up in his arms and carrying her to the other side of the ledge. She screamed again. He plunged into the water in a humping gallop, until all at once they landed in a tangle of arms and legs and flying foam and sat there laughing, coughing, both out of breath, as the surf sloshed around them.

She lifted a dripping arm and plastered his hair back over his forehead. He buried his face in her neck and gave her several loud growling kisses. She put both arms around him. The water dripped from her arms and slid cool and slow over his shoulders and down his back.

"You're a handsome man, Ben Ames," she said.

"And as I've already told you, you're a handsome woman," he replied, pushing himself away and looking at her.

"Thank you, sir," she said with a nod.

"Feel better?" he asked.

"What do you think?"

He smiled.

Her eyes narrowed. "Has that smile always got you what you've wanted?" she asked.

He must have winced at that, because she slid a wet finger against his lips and traced a smile with it. "Yes, I'm sure it has," she said, more to herself than to him. She was no longer smiling.

"Wait—" he started to say, confused by the sudden change in the conversation.

She pressed her fingers to his lips. "My husband was a charmer, too. There were always women around him. I could stand that. But it was the indifference, the cruelty, when we were alone, that I couldn't take— the way he was driven to seek acceptance from others, and beneath it all there was no real feeling for anyone."

"I'm not like that, Caroline."

She smiled. "I know. I knew it by the way you changed the subject back there when you saw I was upset." She smiled again. "No, of course you're not like that."

"He seems to have left a few scars," Ben said.

She had taken her fingers from his lips when he began to speak, and now, her head bent to one side, she was skimming them back and forth over the surface of the water and staring at them. "Yes. He was older, a big official in the Teamster's Union. I met him just as I was about to start graduate school. And there went my career. I spent the next eight years caressing his ego, telling myself that his outside interests meant nothing. Then I couldn't stand the cruelty and the neglect any longer, and I left."

"How long ago was that?"

"Two years. And I question myself with every man I meet."

Ben nodded. "I'm not going to hurt you, Caroline. I didn't plan this and I don't know what it means—if it means anything. You were good enough to listen to me, and I appreciated that. And, well, what happened, happened."

They sat there, waist-deep in the water, staring at each other. Then she smiled, darted her head forward, and kissed him quickly on the lips. "I'm being silly," she said and began to get up. "Forget what I said." She was standing now, and held out a hand to him. "I think we better get back before Gail begins to wonder what's happened to us, don't you?"

Ben stood up, and she put her arms around him. "I do like you, Ben Ames. I really do," she said, and kissed him on the mouth before he could reply.

Then they walked back to Ayia Galini with their arms around each other.

Everyone seemed to be watching them when they got back to the plaza on the harbor—taxi drivers, waiters, other tourists sipping from small glasses at the outdoor tables. Ben felt the stares immediately. Within moments Caroline tugged his sleeve, and the alarm in her face told him that she had noticed it, too. Her face didn't express fear exactly, but rather the paranoia of the hunted that he'd been feeling since the previous night, and he knew that she was thinking about Papandakis.

"It's nothing," Ben said to her. "It's our clothes. We look like we've been washed ashore, all the way from Egypt." He smiled at her. "And who knows?" he added. "We may be glowing."

She squeezed his waist, her arm still around him, and smiled back. "Where are you going to stay?" she said. He thought for a moment, but before he could reply, she added, "Wherever it is, I want to stay with you tonight." He smiled at her. She was quiet for a moment, then said, "There are vacancies at the Minos."

"I can't risk that," he answered. "I'd have to show the manager my passport when I registered. I don't see how Papandakis can know where I am, but to give my name would be asking for trouble."

"Why not stay with us, then? I'm sure we can sneak you past the manager."

"Good. But look, I don't want you to tell Gail anything about this. You may be doing her a favor."

She nodded.

At her room, he showered and shaved with the tiny razor she used for her legs, while she and Gail went out to buy him some new clothes. Although the shower refreshed him, he was so exhausted from the previous night's exertions that afterward he lay back naked on one of the room's two beds, draped his towel over his groin, and waited for the women to return.

He awoke in the dark, needing to go to the bathroom. At first he didn't know where he was, and he tensed. The room was stuffy, and only dim slats of light showed through the closed shutters.

He was still on the bed, still with the towel draped over his groin, his throat parched. But when he stumbled toward the bathroom, his muscles felt so stiff that he winced, gasped audibly, and inadvertently dropped the towel.

"Hello. How you feeling?" breathed a voice from

the other side of the room when he returned. It was Caroline's voice, but husky, heavy with sleep.

"I'm okay," he whispered, and made his way toward the voice.

She was on the other bed, her body dim curves and hollows under a sheet.

"Gail and I decided to let you sleep. You were dead to the world," she said, her voice still husky.

"Where is she?" he asked, squinting into the corners of the darkened room as he sat down on the bed and caught the faint fragrance of jasmine and sleep, like pressed flowers, rising from Caroline's body. He was suddenly aware of her warmth and his nearness to her.

She shifted, propping herself up on one elbow. A stronger scent of jasmine wafted up at him, and he tensed again, realizing he was aroused.

"She had a date, a fellow she met yesterday. I guess she won't be back tonight."

"Oh," he said, unable to think of anything else to say.

They sat there. He knew she was looking at him, but he couldn't see her face.

He put a hand out and touched her raised shoulder. It was bare. He hadn't expected that. All his nerve ends quivered, and at the same time he remembered he was naked.

Then he was kissing her, or she was kissing him—he didn't know which. Her arms were around him, and he was swooping down into jasmine. He remembered them both snatching at the sheet that had settled between them like a slackened sail and his muscles shrieking at him. But these were forgotten as soon as their bodies made contact and she opened herself to him, her hands and arms fluttering white shapes, and he entered her. Almost immediately she began to come, throwing her legs up to draw him deeper, and he came, too, with massive, jarring strokes that left her gasping long after her body had tensed and subsided for the second time.

They lay there, breathing heavily. Finally, he eased himself off her and lay down beside her. Her hand strayed over the hard ridges of his stomach.

She released a long, final sigh. "That was beautiful," she whispered. "I can't remember when . . ." Her voice trailed off.

"I know," he replied. "Same with me."

Her fingers slid lower, at first touching his penis lightly, then grasping it as if trying to determine its shape and weight. It began to rise.

"Oh," she said.

This time they made love slowly, exploring each other's responses and effortlessly slipping from one position into another, sometimes with her on top, sometimes him. They were both tender and savage, so that once as he battered her from behind she cried out, but not in pain, and several times she whimpered and uttered words he didn't need to understand.

When he awoke, sunlight was pouring through the shutters. She was staring at him, alternately sliding her fingers over his face and body and looking at the places her fingers touched. An overwhelming wave of tenderness rose up in him, catching in the back of his throat.

They made love again, learning with their eyes what they had learned in the dark with their fingers, and now sipping, now tasting one another, like wine connoisseurs—a slow, elaborate unfolding of uninterrupted movement that continued even when the room became a warm bath around them and their bodies were slippery with sweat.

Around noon Gail returned to change clothes and then left once more, saying she'd be back by seven. Shortly afterward they went for coffee and rolls at the café nextdoor to the hotel, where they made small talk and exchanged significant looks and smiled. Then they returned to the room and made love for the rest of the day, unable to keep from touching one another.

Gail came back just before dark. Ben, dressed in the black trousers and white shirt the women had bought for him the day before, had showered again and was refreshed, but the all-day lovemaking had left him as exhausted as he had been on the previous evening.

Gail continually glanced from her friend to Ben. She was obviously curious about what was going on. And when Caroline went in to shower, Gail's impatient finger-tappings, sudden risings and sittings and impulsive postcard jottings confirmed that Caroline had told her nothing about why Ben had arrived in Ayia Galini in such a disheveled state the day before.

"Well, it looks like we're a trio," she said when Caroline came out of the bathroom rubbing her head with a towel. "And this third is hungry."

Caroline looked at Ben.

He nodded. "It will be okay."

"What do you mean, okay?" asked Gail.

All along he had known that he would have to tell her something, and now was the time. He fluttered a winning smile at her, then suppressed it after looking self-consciously at Caroline. But Caroline smiled warmly back at him. "I'm in a little trouble, Gail. Nothing with the law or anything like that. But some people want to see me, and I don't want to see them."

Gail's eyes narrowed.

"It's nothing to worry about," he said. "I'm sure we're all safe here. I'm just going to spend one more night in your room, if it's okay with you. I'll be gone in the morning."

"What?" said Caroline.

He turned toward her, but didn't meet her eyes. He had come to the decision just then, as he was speaking, but he knew it was the right one. "For a couple of days, anyway," he said. "Until I get this all straightened out. I'm going to head for the American Consulate. In fact, you can find out for me from the manager where it is. I'm sure this is all some kind of a mistake that I can clear up in a day. We'll arrange to meet back here or in Heraklion."

Caroline shook her head and looked down at her hands.

"It's best," he said, moving to her and touching her hair. "And I'm not going to disappear, believe me. And I'm only leaving because I don't want to get you involved in this thing."

The three of them stood there, Gail looking from Ben to Caroline again. No one said anything for a few moments.

"Well," Ben finally said in a jovial voice, fighting against fatigue, "you two ladies are going to be my guests for a real Greek meal."

"Are you sure it will be all right?" asked Caroline, attempting a smile.

"Sure. I'm safe here for another twenty-four hours. Maybe more. And there'll be so many tourists down at the harbor, no one will notice me, especially since I'll be with such ravishing, eye-catching females."

He was right.

It was dark and balmy by the time they reached the port, and the crowds at the tavernas and pastry shops were pressed together and constantly moving. The fishing boats, which had displayed such gaily painted hulls that afternoon, bobbed anonymously in the shadows beyond the bare bulbs strung from lampposts and poles around the perimeter of the cobblestoned plaza. Thirty or forty tables and chairs had been set up in the open at the edge of the pier, and two hundred or more had been placed on the other side of the plaza, in front of the restaurants and pastry shops, under heavy blue and gold canvas awnings.

Even before they had finished eating, an electrified bouzouki orchestra had struck up in the taverna nextdoor, filling the plaza with exuberant metallic music. Soon crowds of tourists, led by a tall mustached man in almost theatrical Cretan garb, were doing chain dances in the center of the plaza.

Gail's friend of the past few days, a young Danish tourist, had returned to Heraklion late that afternoon, so the three of them joined the festivities. Ben attempted to ignore his new and more pleasant exhaustion brought on by the day's activities with Caroline. They danced and drank, consuming bottle after bottle of a sharp-tasting retsina, switched to the sweet licorice-flavored ouzo, cold and milky over ice, then switched back to retsina again.

They were joined by two paunchy Germans, flushed and boisterous, who kept slapping the table and laughing and throwing their arms around the girls, but by that time everyone was so dizzy with drink that no one cared.

Ben was so tired that two retsinas had made him surprisingly drunk. He had decided just to go with it, shrugging off all caution in a devil-may-care silent toast to himself with his third glass of retsina, which he downed in one gulp after intoning with great solemnity *"Kali Eleftheria!"*

And so the evening continued: the music of the steel-stringed instruments shrill and blaring, backs and shoulders, people bumping into each other, sweat, laughter, licorice breath, mouths shouting and calling, Caroline hugging him, holding on to his arm, laughing, Ben kissing her, Ben and Caroline holding each other.

Somewhere around eleven Gail disappeared into the crowd and Caroline scanned the plaza for her, standing on tiptoe and turning her head from side to side. It was their pact, she explained: one mustn't lose sight of the other in a crowd.

Ben nodded, his head as heavy as an over-cooked cabbage.

"Ben!" Caroline said suddenly, catching his arm and calling his name with such urgency that he looked up, his heart jumping. "I think there's someone watching us. Over there, to the right. In the taverna beyond those people, standing at the edge of the crowd."

"You sure?"

"Yes."

"I can't see anything."

"Wait till the dancers go by. Right below the blue awning. There. Now do you see him?"

"Jesus Christ!" said Ben, jumping to his feet, his head instantly clear. "It's Reilly."

Chapter Ten

Ben lurched from the table, furious with himself for entering into his confrontation with Reilly when he was drunk and exhausted. He pushed his way roughly through the crowd. Several people called angrily after him, but he paid no attention. He was intent on the blond man with the doll-blue eyes who was still wearing the white trousers and the blue and white striped pullover shirt.

Reilly saw him coming and smiled, remained slouched in his chair behind a white metal table with a hole in the middle where a beach umbrella should have been. A middle-aged man in a white suit, standing behind his right shoulder, bent down to say something to him, but Reilly waved him away, keeping his eyes on Ben and continuing to smile.

Ben kept losing sight of Reilly in the crowd, but each time he knocked away arms and shoulders and the path cleared in front of him, there was Reilly sprawled behind the table, grinning at him.

Finally, Ben was leaning over the table, and Reilly was looking up into his eyes. "You bastard!" Ben said, swaying, feeling ponderous and old standing over his youthful adversary, and realizing he was even drunker than he had thought.

The man in the white suit had slipped around the table and grabbed Ben's arm. Ben shook him off.

"Please, Professor, let me explain," Reilly said and gave him a boyish smile.

"Explain! Damn you, you almost got me killed!"

"I don't really think so. Look, I've been sitting here for over an hour advertising myself like a red flag in front of a bull, waiting for you to see me so you'd come over and we could talk about this sensibly, so calm down."

"Calm down! Listen, you son of a bitch, you've got a lot of explaining to do, and then you're going to get me out of—"

"That's why I'm here, Professor. Now sit down or let's go somewhere where we can talk, privately."

The man in the white suit clamped his hand on Ben's shoulder and pushed down, and Ben practically fell into a chair. The man's hand remained on his shoulder.

"You tell this guy to get his hands off me, or I'll break his fingers one by one," Ben said.

"Andoni!" snapped Reilly. Andoni removed his hand and took a step back. "Satisfied, Professor?"

Ben nodded. The confrontation with Reilly hadn't gone as he'd imagined it. He was dizzy with drink, and the exertion of fighting his way through the crowd had left him spent and limp, draining the anger from him. He knew Reilly was right, too, and if he wasn't willing to talk sensibly, at least he wanted to hear Reilly's explanation of what was going on.

Caroline had come up behind them and was standing in back of his chair. He could feel the tension quivering from her, but didn't look up.

"What's going on here?" she began, a slight quaver in her words.

"It's all right, ma'am. Everything's going to be all right now," said Reilly with a friendly grin.

"But—"

"He's going to come along with us for a while—"

"No!" Her voice was high and unnatural.

Ben reached up, touching her elbow. "It's okay, Caroline. I've got to find out what this is all about. It's the only way."

"I don't think you should go, especially alone."

"It's best—"

"No, it's okay, Professor. She can come along if she wants." Reilly was so calm, so much in control, so boyish, and seemingly so concerned with Ben's welfare. Still the student.

"Yes," she said. "I want to."

"Professor Ames and I will have to talk in private, but you can wait in the lobby, and afterward you can both be on your way."

Reilly rose to his feet, came around the table, and helped Ben up, aided by the man in the white suit. Ben did not resist. His physical activities over the past forty-eight hours had finally caught up with him. He was exhausted and very drunk, and his legs wouldn't work right.

A waiter came up to them with a curious expression on his face and gestured to Ben. The man in the white suit spoke several words in Greek to him and he shrugged, pursed his lips, and turned away.

The crowd had apparently noticed nothing unusual, and the dancing and loud music continued.

The four of them made their way through the roiling mass in the plaza and up several narrow streets with tall streetlamps at the corners. The tinny music from the harbor echoed through the streets, and by the time they entered a hotel high on the hill, Ben's head had cleared somewhat and he was regaining control of his legs.

"A drink, Professor?" Reilly asked. They were in his third-floor room, and he had switched on a small table lamp near the bed. Caroline had remained in the lobby with the man in the white suit.

Ben shook his head.

"Well, I'll have one," said Reilly. He took a green bottle from the dresser and poured an inch of amber liquid into a glass.

The hotel was one of the new buildings. The furniture in Reilly's room was matching dark wood, arranged tastefully, and a sliding glass door led onto a private balcony facing the sea. A full moon sat low over the water, and the sea looked like a giant silver coin beneath it.

Reilly motioned Ben to one of two brown upholstered chairs that faced a glass-topped coffee table with a white note pad on it and sat down in the other. He put his drink on the table, stirred it with his forefinger, withdrew the finger and sucked it slowly, all the while staring at the pad on the table. With only the light of the small lamp the room behind them was a vague presence of comfortable shadows.

"Okay, Professor, I'm going to tell you what this is all about. We don't have time to beat around the bush and play games anymore."

"Why should I trust anything you say?" said Ben, surprised at how weary his voice sounded.

"Because you have no choice. And because we need you."

"Why the hell did you give me that package, Reilly?"

Reilly looked up. There was no smile on his face now. His eyes were steady and somber. Ben could not remember having seen him in such a serious mood, and Reilly's expression made him stop speaking.

"Let me start at the beginning, sir. If you have any questions when I'm done, I'll be happy to answer them."

Ben nodded and leaned forward.

Reilly took a gold ballpoint pen from his pants pocket, clicked the point down, and every so often jabbed the exposed point on the pad to emphasize key words as he spoke.

"My name is John Reilly, and several years ago I was your student. That much you know. In fact, it was your classes that inspired me to study political science at UCLA. While I was there, I was approached by a U.S. intelligence agency—it doesn't matter which one—and when I graduated I went to work for them full-time on Balkan and Greek affairs. That was three years ago. I wasn't kidding when I said you had whetted my appetite for Greek history, and the Historical Museum *is* one of my favorite spots in Athens. I go there all the time.

"As I'm sure you know, things have been pretty turbulent in Greece the last few years, and we've been accused of engineering this or that faction's rise to power. But what you may not know is that we're really over here as a sifting channel for information coming out of Russia via Turkey. We've got agents and cutouts—that is, contacts—all over Turkey, monitoring, buying, and otherwise procuring information about, or from, Russia that they pass on to us. That's right, we've got units inside Russia, organized and manned by Russians, several with no prompting from us. Fact is, most came to us, and they now feed information to our agents in Turkey, and our agents bring it out.

"Sixteen days ago we received word from headquarters in Langley that one of our most highly placed operatives in the Kremlin had gotten hold of a document which was vital to world peace. It contained information so important that the chances of averting World War Three may depend on our getting it through. World War Three—do you understand what I'm saying, Professor?"

"Jesus Christ, Reilly, what the hell are you into?"

Reilly dropped the pen on the pad, got up, and held one of his hands up in a gesture that asked for patience, then continued to speak, pacing around the shadowy room.

"The operative in question was unable to bring the document out of Moscow, but since the document itself was the important thing, Headquarters decided to bring it out by assigning our Moscow network to pick it up and bring it to a drop in Ryazan. Then we put several units in southern Russia in touch with each other so the document could swiftly pass in a chain to one of our agents in Turkey, the area where Soviet border security is the most lax. That put the operation in our sector, and we quickly arranged our part of the show. The agency, of course, was taking an enormous risk. There were five of our Russian networks involved, and if you know anything about intelligence, you know that none of them knew anything about the existence of the others. This is for security reasons. By linking the networks, we were breaking completely with precedent. We did this for two reasons. First, the information was contained in a document. Usually it comes by word of mouth, or radio transmission. Now it was a piece of paper, and the paper was so important that we didn't want to fail to get it out, and out in time. Second, this document described events that would be set in motion after a specific date in the near future, the result of which could be so catastrophic that we had to get the document out of Russia before these events occurred, in order to avert them. In other words we were working against a deadline.

"Then just what we had feared began to happen. We got word that as the document traveled from link to link, the unit which had just passed it on collapsed behind it. The KGB was pulling in one network after another, and this continued all the way to the Turkish border, where our man picked up the document. There was a leak or something, of course, but we had arranged this operation so that it couldn't be stopped. The document is that important. Anyway, we got it out of Russia within three days of its being, shall we say, 'appropriated.'

"That takes us to thirteen days ago, eighteen days before the date on which the first of these events is slated to occur. Now everything depended on our agent in Turkey. He had a long trip to make, all the way across Turkey from the Georgian border, but he could make it in two or three days by pre-arranged routes and a whole network of cutouts, residents, and agents to use as resources. He's also one of our best men.

"Well, we lost him right after the transfer was made. Maybe he thought he'd been spotted and went to ground. I don't know. We gave him four days, then instituted a search. Nothing. Anyway, six days ago, one of our Turkish contacts reported seeing a police report with our man's name on it. Seems he had been arrested in a hotel in the town of Söke, along with four other Americans, on drug-smuggling charges.

"The Turks don't take kindly to Americans transporting drugs out of their country. They won't even negotiate with our embassy people about it, and they usually sentence the accused to life imprisonment. Including innocent bystanders. And that's the situation we think our man's in. The police arrested every American in the hotel, with or without evidence, and the Turkish government hasn't officially announced the bust yet. We couldn't go in; we can't even show our faces. We're not even supposed to know about it. And the agency's public image is so bad in Greece and Turkey right now, to say nothing of everywhere else—well, you know about that. But there's the added problem of not wanting to tip our hand before we get hold of the document and can use it. We don't want to let on to the Russians where it is, either.

"Anyway, we had to get our man out, and quick, but our hands were tied. We did have our contact get us the names of everyone who had been arrested, hoping one of them would be the kid of some prominent American who had enough punch to raise hell—you know, heart-throb stuff in newspapers that might whip up world opinion and pressure the Turkish government into releasing the Americans or at least publicly announcing that the bust had been made. Then we could

get to our man with someone from the consulate and
find out where the document was.

"We were working on other plans, too—still are—but
it would take time to implement them. We knew the
concerned father thing was a long shot and would
probably take too much time to bring off, but it's routine to run a background check on everyone involved
in an operation. Anyway, we could feed the story to
the media back home, and if for some reason it
worked, it would be the cleanest operation for us—no
one would be able to spot us turning the dials in the
other room.

"Anyway, one father was a cattle rancher in Texas,
another a prominent preacher in Kansas City, but
they didn't have political connections and weren't big
enough to pull the headlines on such short notice. The
other two were small fry. The fifth was odd, though—
the father of the girl identified as Stella Reese. He
turned out to be a Cretan named Papandakis who had
sent his daughter to school in America three years
ago, and while she was there she had married an
American named Henry Reese. When we checked on
this Papandakis with our Greek informants, we found
out some interesting things.

"Papandakis' father was a wealthy Cretan landowner and a well-known political figure, a member
of the Revolutionary Assembly in the abortive revolt
of 1905, and one of the men responsible for Crete's
union with Greece in 1913. The old man was a friend
and political crony of Venizelos, Crete's and later
Greece's great political leader. He sent his son to be
educated in England in the 1930's. Young Papandakis
returned to administer the family's holdings on his fa-

ther's death, and he became a hero of the Cretan Resistance in World War Two.

"His father had been a friend and business associate of a Cretan Turkish family named Kursad. The Kursads were repatriated to Turkey in the exchange of populations in 1923 after the disastrous Greek invasion of Turkey the year before. Papandakis and the eldest son of this family were fast friends and even went to school together in England. Eventually the Kursad boy, whose name was Nazmi, became a powerful cabinet minister in the Turkish government, a position he maintained until his death seven years ago.

"The families have never lost contact, but after the end of World War Two Papandakis was content to administer his estates instead of going into politics like his father and his friend. He seems to have disliked the brutality of both sides during the Civil War in the late 40's, and this presumably affected his decision. But that hasn't kept him from engaging in a bit of smuggling from time to time. Turkish art objects—rugs, jewels, antiquities—things like that, nothing big. He wormed it through his old school chum, Nazmi, exclusively at first, but his Turkish contacts have grown with the years. He's kept his Resistance organization together and employs them in his smuggling operations, of course. And since he's a hero of the Resistance, and wealthy besides, the Greek government and the Cretan officials look the other way. There's no reason why they shouldn't—he pays them off royally.

"Anyway, it was my station chief who got the idea to use him. His daughter was involved, he obviously had the contacts inside Turkey who could bribe the appropriate officials, and, finally, he was close to the target and could go into action immediately. What made the plan attractive was that we were limited by two time factors—one, we had to get the document out within nine days, as I've already said; and, two, we knew that any attempts at bribery would have to be made before the Turks officially announced that the drug bust had taken place. We were well aware that once the announcement was made, bureaucratic wheels would start turning that would be difficult to stop. We also knew from past experience that when the official announcement of a bust involving foreign nationals was made, the prisoners would be immediately transferred to a maximum-security army jail, in this case in Izmir, where our bribery attempt would have to be elaborate and much less likely to succeed. At present the prisoners are still being held in the town jail in Söke, which is only guarded by local police.

"The chief also reasoned that if the bribe didn't work, or if the plan should in some way be exposed, only Papandakis' participation would be revealed, and it would be thought that he had gone into the project from personal motives. We would in no way appear to be involved. The only other person who might, in fact, would be the man who financed the operation, our fictitious concerned father, whose motive would be considered as personal as Papandakis'—and in everyone's mind the Texas cattle baron would be a good candidate for the job.

"Anyway, all we needed was a courier to pass the information on to Papandakis, someone who was in no way connected to our organization, someone we could trust to set up the concerned-father ploy convincingly, because he wouldn't know what was really going on. And that's where you came in." He stopped and looked down at Ben. "Any questions?"

Chapter Eleven

Ben sat in the chair, staring at the table, only partly drunk now. But he was completely worn out, and in this state trying to make sense of Reilly's words was difficult. So much didn't seem to connect.

"And if Papandakis fails, World War Three is upon us. Is that what you're trying to tell me?"

"Not exactly," said Reilly, sitting down opposite Ben and picking up his glass. "We're working on two other plans. But they'll take time. Hopefully, with some well-placed bribes Papandakis can bring everyone out in two or three days. According to our schedule we've got only five days left until the strike date mentioned in the document and no more than four days before the Pentagon steps in with something more drastic."

"What do you mean by that?"

"Use your imagination, Professor."

"Like Lebanon and Santo Domingo?"

Reilly looked into his glass and didn't reply.

"Sending in the Marines to bust your man out of jail?"

Reilly kept staring into his glass.

"But you gave me that package four days ago. How was I to know?"

Reilly looked up.

"I know. We've lost a lot of time. That was the weakest part of the plan—when you took the package to Papandakis. I decided not to urge you to bring it to him immediately because I thought I might scare you off or make you suspicious. I was counting on your going there immediately to get rid of the responsibility. That's why I told you the icon was considered to be a national treasure."

"Are Papandakis' contacts so extensive that he can buy five Americans out of a Turkish jail?"

"We don't know. He's never done anything like this before. But he's smart, he *does* have contacts, and the girl *is* his daughter after all. We checked that out, too. They're very close, especially since his wife died. And Stella is his only daughter."

Ben nodded, still confused, unable to remember the questions he'd been asking himself for the past forty-eight hours.

"Why did—Jesus, listen to me! I'm sitting here asking you questions as if all this were real. This is crazy, Reilly! I don't believe a word of it."

"But it's true, Professor, no matter what else you want to believe. Let me get you a drink; it might clear your head." He was smiling again, but the smile was thin and ironic. *No longer boyish,* Ben reflected. *And maybe it never had been.*

Reilly brought him his drink, an inch of whiskey in a glass half full of tapwater from the bathroom. It tasted like dishwater.

Reilly was still standing. He looked down at his drink. When he spoke again, his tone was gloomy. "I told you that we had no time to play games anymore. For my part, I've blown my cover: told you who I was and what I'm doing here. Do you know what that means, sir? It means that I'm finished: I'll never work in the field again after this. From now on it's a desk or retirement." He smiled bitterly. "Retirement at twenty-six. Now do you see how important that document is? You're not the only one hurting, and there'll be others hurt before this is over—maybe millions of them. But for what it's worth, I'm sorry I got you mixed up in this."

"Your concern is touching," said Ben. "Look, I don't want to be sarcastic, and everything you've said makes a crazy kind of sense, but I can't help feeling that you should have thought about making your apologies before you gave me the package in the first place."

Reilly nodded.

"And now that we're on the subject—why did you choose me to begin with?"

Reilly seated himself on the upholstered arm of his chair and looked down at Ben, his eyes serious and troubled. Absently he picked up the gold pen and began stabbing the pad with it once more. "I told you we needed a courier to make contact with Papandakis, someone not connected with the agency. At first we were going to hire someone off the street, someone to represent the concerned father in the letter—a delivery boy, so to speak. That was chancy, though. What if the guy dumped the package and ran off with the money? It might be days before we found out. And if he wasn't with the agency, it would take time to check him out before we even gave him the package, and we didn't have the time. As far as our residents were concerned—"

"Residents?"

"Sorry. Jargon for 'local operatives and contacts'—in

this case Greeks. Anyway, as far as they were concerned, we wouldn't even consider using them. To ask them to approach anyone about this, especially after the bad press we've been getting for our activities over here, would be just setting them up for a bad fall. So as a last alternative we began to look at friends or acquaintances of American operatives who might be visiting Greece—tourists, businessmen, or . . . teachers on vacation. If we hadn't come up with anyone in two days, we were going to approach an American working at the Athens branch of an American bank. But I found your name and your hotel after just twenty minutes of looking through the Customs register."

"That was pretty easy. Should I be flattered that you remembered me after all these years and that you considered me a likely on-the-spot spy—I mean, 'delivery boy'?"

Reilly smiled grimly before replying, then began doodling on the pad as he spoke, writing something in heavy strokes that he went over again and again, apparently unaware of the furious energy his hands were releasing. Ben looked at the pad but couldn't make out the drawing.

"It could have been anyone, sir. But if it helps your ego, you were the perfect choice. We started with that day's arrivals and moved backward. That way we had a better chance of finding the man we wanted at the address he'd given when he entered the country. I found you five pages back and knew immediately that you were the one we were looking for. My only reservation was whether I wanted to involve you."

"Pray tell, student Reilly, why was your tired old professor the perfect choice for this delicate mission?"

"Be sarcastic, if you want, Professor, but you were. First, I knew you could be trusted to deliver the package. I knew you were scrupulous and, well, let's face it, there was no reason why you wouldn't get in touch with Papandakis within a day of your arrival here."

Ben nodded.

Reilly continued to color in whatever he was doodling, pushing the pen on the pad with greater and greater pressure. Ben's interest in the doodling increased.

"Second, our relationship was so casual that no one could trace you back to me. Third, I knew you would be going to Crete because I remembered your lectures on Minoan civilization. You always ended them by saying that one of your dreams was to visit Knossos. I'd even made up several ploys to lure you into coming here within two days of our conversation. Then I just called the hotel to verify that you were there—"

"So you *were* the caller. Very clever."

"Not really. Remember, you weren't suspecting anything. You didn't see any of our people tailing you in Athens after that or on the boat to Crete, because you had no reason to imagine that anyone was following you. You haven't been out of our sight since we verified that you were at the hotel."

"And you found me by looking at the Greek Customs register?"

"Yes. Don't underestimate us. We've got contacts everywhere."

"I'll *bet* you do. But I wasn't thinking of that. I was wondering—why me?"

"Chance, Professor. You happened to be there. That's the element that either makes or breaks all plans. Wasn't that one of the eight basic ways you taught us to view history, the one you said Henry Ford preferred—history seen as an unrelated jumble of names, dates, and events?"

"You've learned your lessons well, Reilly. But if you remember, I dismissed that theory immediately."

"That's because we were in a classroom where you could categorize and compartmentalize the lifeless events of the past, since you weren't part of them. Theories, Professor. They were only meaningless theories."

"So now you're attacking the whole discipline of history."

"No, I'm just getting sick and tired of your damned sarcasm. Such bullheadedness doesn't become a man of your intellectual attainments."

Ben tried to haul himself out of the chair and attack Reilly, or protest, or he didn't know what. But he was too tired to rise. He wanted to throw his glass in Reilly's face, but that seemed like a feeble gesture. And so he downed the rest of his drink instead, remembering with another spasm of fury that Reilly was the one who had gotten him into this situation. But immediately the fight went out of him, and the weary tone of his voice almost made his words seem an apology when he said, "I'm going to whip your ass, Reilly. So help me God, I'm going to whip your ass."

"I can't seem to make you understand what was at stake—what *is* at stake!" said Reilly. He exhaled wearily, took the glass out of Ben's hand, went to the bureau, and then into the bathroom to refill it.

When he had gone, Ben hauled himself out of the chair and floundered over to the pad. Staring up at him in heavy block letters was the word

TRANSCENDENTAL

He blinked and swayed, then turned back to his chair. Reilly was standing in the doorway of the bathroom, watching him.

Ben tensed, but Reilly merely nodded and came toward him, gesturing at the pad with the refilled glass as he handed it to Ben. "What do you know about Transcendentalism, Professor?"

"The nineteenth-century New England literary movement?" Ben asked incredulously.

Reilly nodded.

Ben shook his head. "Not much. Not my field," he mumbled. His legs suddenly felt waterlogged and he stumbled back to his chair and fell into it.

"You know as much about it as I do, then," said Reilly standing over him.

"Transcendentalism," said Ben, looking up at the ceiling, his head heavy as a fishbowl. "Let me see . . . Emerson, Emerson. A mixture of Brahmanism and Kant. Kant. It was his idea. He claimed that anything we know about the world, we know through intuition *a priori* rather than through experience. Emerson agreed with the intuition part but thought we knew everything from experience."

"That's it. Then Emerson applies that to the Brahmanic idea of the Oversoul, the godhead in which all souls merge."

Ben smirked. "Pardon me, Reilly, but isn't this a little off the subject? I realize you're obsessed by it, but—"

"Obsessed by it? Why do you say that?"

"Because of that," said Ben, pointing to the pad. "And because you mentioned it at the museum."

"Did I?" said Reilly, looking into his glass. "I'm not surprised. But it's not as far off the subject as you think."

Ben looked up. "Oh?"

"In time, Professor. Everything in time. Don't worry, we'll get to it. But I'm sure you've got more pressing questions to ask first."

Ben thought for a moment. "Yes," he said. "The obvious one. What's in the document?"

Reilly took a deep breath, released it, and looked Ben directly in the eye. "What I'm about to tell you may sound melodramatic and long-winded, but I've got to impress upon you the importance of what's on that piece of paper. It goes beyond capitalist or Communist, democracy or dictatorship, Cold War or—"

"Well, that's pretty melodramatic all right," said Ben.

Reilly shook his head, turned away, went to the balcony door, stared at the sea for a moment, then turned back. "Are you going to listen to me or not, sir?" he said quietly.

Ben nodded.

Reilly walked back and sat down. "You know what's been happening with the weather lately." It was more of a statement than a question.

Ben nodded.

"Drought in California alternating with deluge, and record snowfalls and low temperatures in the Midwest and East. Temperatures in the Mediterranean recorded at over one hundred and thirty degrees. Earthquakes in Eastern Europe and China. Agriculture affected everywhere. Some people think climate is changing—"

"Yes, yes, I know all that."

Reilly nodded and began again. "Do you remember the earthquake in China a little over a year ago? The epicenter was in a city of one million people called Tangshan? We now know that the city was levelled and that more than 750,000 people were killed. Did you know that Tangshan was a center for heavy water production and uranium conversion—in short, an urban industrial complex whose most important industry was the manufacturing of fissionable materials?"

"What are you getting at?"

Reilly held up his hand for silence and continued. "Do you remember the quakes in Italy that killed thousands of people last year?"

Ben nodded again.

"Did you know that the agricultural devastation and the economic ruin that followed them were the final blows that brought down the moderate government and caused a large Communist minority to be voted into Parliament, the first Communist minority to figure strongly in any Western European coalition government since World War Two?"

"I don't see—"

"What if I told you, sir, that the changes in weather, as well as the recent Italian, Chinese, Greek, and Turkish quakes, and the quakes in Yugoslavia, which just *happened* to occur when the government was starting to move decisively against Croatian separatists whose activities threaten the unstable unity of that anti-Soviet country—what if I told you, sir, that all those meteorological catastrophes were manmade?"

Ben blinked. He hadn't expected that. Then a slow smile crept across his face. "I'd say you were talking science fiction, Reilly."

"I figured you would. So would a lot of other people, sir, but they'd be wrong. The manipulation of weather conditions has been one of mankind's dreams since long before the Cold War or Détente. You as a historian know that. It can mean the avoidance of famine and flood; it can mean optimum growing conditions for crops, and thus assure the world supply of food. Unfortunately, it can also mean the discovery of a weapon more terrifying than any that has ever been invented—one whose use cannot be detected and whose power is almost unimaginable."

"Come on, Reilly, what are you handing me?"

"Professor, we *know* the Soviets have been engaged in weather-control experiments for years. Ostensibly they want to melt the permafrost of the tundra and use that vast expanse of land in Siberia for agricultural purposes. We even know how they're doing it. It has to do with the transmission of electricity without wires, designed by a man named Tesla in the 1930's. He was a scientist who worked for a time with Edison, and was a pioneer in high-tension electricity. He was especially interested in the transmission of high-frequency electrical charges without the use of wires, which he called 'terrestrial stationary waves.' With the technological advances since Tesla's death in 1943 his discoveries could easily be adapted to upper-atmospheric testing: great electrical forces could be released high in the atmosphere, changing the normal paths of the jet streams that flow above the earth's surface, which are, as I'm sure you know, responsible for weather patterns.

"So, when a Soviet scientist visited Quebec several years ago and interviewed a man named Arthur H. Matthews several times, we looked up. Why, right?

Well, this Matthews just happened to be Tesla's last assistant, and was living in total obscurity in Canada. That the Soviets knew of his whereabouts was suspicious enough. But that they wanted to interview him was more than that, especially when several months later—in mid-1976—we heard that high-frequency radio transmissions in Russia had disrupted radio communications in several nearby countries. The Russians even admit that they're testing something, but they won't say what.

"I could go on like this for hours. But let me cut this short by saying that all of this is no surprise to us, because for years we've been experimenting with the weather, too. Not using Tesla's ideas, it's true—following a different direction. But that may change now. Anyway, Honduras and El Salvador have been complaining in the United Nations since 1973 that our weather-modification project off the Florida coast has robbed them of vital rainfall, and Haiti, whose government we're not exactly enamored of, has been hit by such severe droughts since 1967 that its climate has changed from tropical to semi-arid. . . ."

"Are you implying—"

"I'm not *implying* anything, sir. These are facts. Why else do you think President Carter and Brezhnev instructed Vance and Gromyko to sign a pledge that neither the U.S. or Russia would tamper with the weather for military purposes? And isn't it interesting that that's just about the only thing both men have been able to agree on?

"Russia's violated that agreement a number of times, but so have we. Both sides had been conducting their experiments long before the agreement was signed, and they just continued them afterwards. All the experiments have been on a small scale, of course, and any damage to climate patterns has been accidental—we thought.

"But for a year or so we've been hearing rumors, and we've been able to filter out enough oblique references from communiqués and Soviet publications to convince us that the Russians have applied Tesla's theories to the earth's interior. Tesla claimed that by employing terrestrial stationary waves he could use the earth as a conductor and make it respond like a tuning fork to electrical vibrations of a certain pitch. What does that sound like to you, Professor?"

"Earthquakes?" asked Ben thickly.

"Exactly. We think the Russians have perfected their experiments to the point that they can direct electrical energy into the earth and induce seismic movement either by exciting the convection currents just beneath the earth's crust or by disturbing—maybe *influencing* is a better word—the earth's plate tectonics. Put simply, sir, and as you've just said, they've learned how to make earthquakes. . . .

"We don't know how, can't even conceive of what they're doing to achieve this. Our weather experiments have been atmospheric, except for underground atomic testing and a few piddling attempts at earthquake prediction. That's how far behind we are.

"We don't even know if the Russians have to bounce a beam off a satellite to activate some mechanism from there, if they have to put the satellites into orbit pre-armed so to speak, or if they can send tremor-inducing electrical impulses from the earth's surface that travel through the interior in such a way that they will cause seismic disturbances only at a given point—or, to call a spade a spade, only at a given target.

"It's so hush-hush that we've only been able to get snatches of it here and there through those rumors and references in communiqués and articles I just mentioned. We've put enough together to make the world quake picture I described before. From these and from certain photographed Soviet dispatches we have been able to identify three installations inside the Soviet Union that appear to be the focal points for their seismic operations. One is in the northwest, in the Urals; another is in the southwest, in the Caucasus; and the last is in the Yablonoi Mountains near Irkutsk. But two more are under construction, it seems—one in the north on the Taimyr Peninsula in Siberia, and the other in the east, on the Kamchatka Peninsula, on the Pacific coast, which would put it right across from us—on our doorstep, so to speak. It seems evident from the locations of these sites that this seismic weapon—and there seems little doubt that that's what it is—works on a directional principle. That's all we know about these installations, except that we've figured out that the seismic attacks against Italy, Yugoslavia, Greece, and Turkey must have been launched from the Caucasus, and the massive one against Tangshan from Irkutsk, which sits right above the Chinese border near the curved southern tip of Lake Baikal. Anyway, we figured all this out afterwards—just sixteen days ago, in fact. Before that, how the Russians planned to use these installations, was a mystery to us. Then, sixteen days ago, the document came into the picture."

Reilly paused. Ben was groggy and said nothing: he was also frightened. The dimness in the room seemed to have deepened, and beyond the glass door the moon-polished sky was brighter.

Reilly poured them both drinks, repeating his circuit to the bureau and the bathroom. He handed Ben his glass and took a sip from his own, staring down into it afterwards. He began to speak again.

"That little slip of paper was the break we were waiting for. One of the most highly placed members of our Moscow network copped it and was executed within hours. He recognized how important it was the minute he saw it, the poor bastard, and knew that he had to get it out to us no matter what.

"The paper is nothing more than a memo in Brezhnev's handwriting, with his signature, that directs the Irkutsk installation to begin 'seismic transmissions'—those are the words—five days from now against ten specifically named Chinese cities—but for what purpose we don't know. It seems that the cities are to be destroyed as a sort of softening-up operation, maybe a prelude to an all-out invasion, although we doubt this. It could be that the Russians just want to take out China's atomic plants and research centers; or it could be that instead of invading, they will walk in after the quakes as China's good neighbor from the north, with food, medicine, medical advisors, and other technicians to begin reconstructions. In reality those regiments of technicians would contain demolition and assassination squads who will eliminate all the remaining atomic centers and anti-Soviet Chinese political leaders. Choose any one of the scenarios you want.

"Clashes along the Russo-Chinese border have been common knowledge for years, of course. We're aware not only of how both countries are vying for leadership of the Communist nations, but the almost paranoic fear the Soviets have of China's location beneath their soft underbelly. And it's no secret that in 1969 the Russians asked us to join them in a 'surgical nuclear strike' against the Chinese. They had even massed several divisions armed with tactical nuclear weapons on the Ussuri River two miles from the Chinese border, before we could talk them out of it. Now, with the added threat of Chinese nuclear development, we've been expecting the Russians to do something drastic for the past five years. One thing's certain: the Tangshan quake was a test run. If the Russians could kill 750,000 people and arouse no suspicion, they were home free.

"Anyway, our position in this seemed clear enough. All we wanted to do was head off the whole thing. If China got wind of the Soviet plan, they'd most likely open up on the Russians with everything they have. We wanted to avoid that as much as we wanted to stop the quakes.

"So we had the information, but not the memo. As you can see, the physical fact of the memo's existence is what's vital. We had to have it, and within twenty-one days. Without it, we were hamstrung; neither side would deal with us. The Russians would laugh in our face, and so would the Chinese. And if we got the memo after the dates the quakes were scheduled to occur, the Chinese would say we were making it all up to foment trouble between them and the Russians.

"All of us in the office figured that if we got the memo in time, the U.S. would blackmail the Soviets. Tell them to abandon their plans or we release the memo to the world. Next, with our date of receipt clearly postmarked on the envelope, so to speak, we would give it to the UN Secretary General for safekeeping, just in case the Soviets thought of going ahead with the quakes after promising not to. We didn't think they'd risk that. It would be World War Three for sure if they did, and they want to gain the world, not destroy it. The memo was our only proof—the order to Irkutsk, Brezhnev's signature—that's what makes it so important.

"Well, we prepared a hurried report at Headquarters' request, and by the time they processed it and got it to the President, who was in Miami addressing a Democratic fund-raising dinner that night, it was early the next day. When he read the report, he bounced off the walls. He was so angry, he picked up the hot line and told Brezhnev that he was going to turn the memo over to the Chinese the minute he got his hands on it. And he let the Russians know that we'd started secret talks with the Chinese in order to establish full diplomatic relations with them. Letting the Chinese know about the memo would demonstrate our good will, he said. Brezhnev replied that he didn't know what the President was talking about, but gave his word that he would take care of it, and asked the President not to do anything rash before he did.

"We hadn't anticipated the President's reaction, and I guess the Russians hadn't either, because after the call there was a flurry of activity between the Premier's office and KGB headquarters. Trouble is, we didn't know what was going on because, as I've said, we'd just lost our main operatives in Moscow, especially the ones in key positions, and because the Russians were using their version of our DES system to communicate with each other."

"Our what?"

"Our Data Encryption Standard system. It's one of the new coding systems that's virtually impossible to break. A message is fed into a computer-like electronic device that mixes the message up, divides it in half, adds the coding key to one half, mixes the two halves back together, and runs the entire mess through a series of anti-code-breaker circuits that prevent any code analysts from working the code back to its plain text. Even if we had a computer that could trace the message, it would take years to work through all the possible permutations."

"That one lost me."

Reilly shrugged. "Makes no difference. It's more important to know what NSA could monitor than what it couldn't—and what it could was the volume of telephone and radio traffic, which it usually does anyway. Not only were messages flashing hot and heavy between the Kremlin and Two Dzerzhinsky Square— KGB headquarters—but also between Two Dzerzhinsky Square and regional KGB headquarters all over the western and southern USSR. This went on for a solid day, the calls moving in an orderly outward blanket pattern from Moscow, west all the way to Riga, Kaliningrad, Brest-Litovsk, Lvov, and Kishinev, and south all one way to Yerevan and Tbilisi. Know where Tbilisi is, Professor?"

Ben licked his lips, but before he could reply Reilly had continued. "Georgia. It's the capital of the Georgian Soviet Socialist Republic, and just happens to be the biggest Russian city near Turkey's northeast border.

"Routinely NSA also monitors air-traffic signals in the USSR, on the lookout for unexpected troop movements. And guess what—thirty-six hours after the President's phone call, and within an hour after the call to Tbilisi, one of Yuri Andropov's personal adjutants—Andropov's head of the KGB—is being flown in the boss's plane to Tbilisi.

"Something was up all right, but we didn't know what. It sure as hell was a flap—all that movement is not routine. Point is, the Russians were acting as if they'd got caught with their pants down. But they knew our top man in the Kremlin had got hold of the memo and radioed its contents ahead to us, because they had eliminated him within hours after the theft. So why the turmoil? Did they think the memo would evaporate or we wouldn't try to get it? Made no sense, unless, as it seemed to me and everyone else in the office, the President's announcement of our Chinese negotiations had caught them by surprise and either made their plans for the memo more necessary than ever or rendered the very existence of the memo undesirable, to say the least.

"Going on either of those assumptions, it seems obvious that the Russians want the memo back at all costs. But why? To hide from the world an ugly cancelled plan or to insure that the plan can be carried out without interference from us, since we wouldn't be able to prove any allegations we might make? It also seemed obvious that we had to get the memo before the Russians did and get it before the strike date.

"All this, of course, happened more than two weeks ago. Since then, both sides have played a wait-and-see game." Reilly paused to sip his drink before continuing. "It's interesting that neither of us is making any direct moves against the other—no alerts, no mobilizations. Both of us are keeping everything on the diplomatic chessboard level and forcing the other to act accordingly, while both intelligence communities continue their scrambling around behind the scenes. But I can't help remembering that if we don't get the memo, not only will the Russians be able to do what they want with China, but with everyone else, and in the subtlest ways. Undetected, mind you, they could cause a quake in southwest Iran along the Zagros thrust line that would destroy most of Iran's oil production, the world's second largest, which supplies five percent of our oil, ninety percent of Japan's, seventy percent of Israel's and almost thirty percent of Europe's. That quake alone could cripple the free world's industry and cause economic disaster. And don't forget, their Kamchatka installation is less than six months from completion, and then the bastards could zap the San Andreas fault in California, which is blocked and therefore prone to disastrous earthquakes at points just northeast of LA and immediately south of San Francisco. A major quake, timed to occur during rush hour, could kill ten million people in a matter of minutes."

Ben's lips parted, pursed, but no words came. Cities toppled in his head. Under their debris somewhere were Julia, his daughters, old Henderson—his life. Minoan civilization gone in a day. He shuddered, then shook his head slowly. "I can't believe the Russians would try anything like that, Reilly," he said in a thick voice. "They'd never take the chance—"

"No? What about the Berlin Wall? The Cuban Missile Crisis in '62, or the planned surgical nuclear strike against China in '69? I could go on all night. Let me assure you they could and did take the chance, and the proof is in the memo. That's why they want it back so badly. Come on out of the classroom, Professor, and enter the real world."

Ben didn't reply.

Reilly stopped his prowling and gestured at the pad on the coffee table. "And then there's Transcendentalism." He stared into his glass and twirled the almost melted ice cube again. "This is the screwiest part of the whole thing, as far as I'm concerned. It goes back three years—at any rate, I think it does—to when my cover was still clerk typist in our embassy in Athens. The entire embassy, along with the rest of the Athens diplomatic community, was invited to the Russian Embassy for a reception in honor of the Georgian National Dance Troupe when it came through on tour that summer. Diplomatic parties are ideal places for making contact with potential operatives so everyone in the intelligence community looks forward to them. But diplomatic functions with the opposition present also afford both sides opportunities to see each other face to face. You don't really try to recruit one another, despite what the manual says, but you do get to observe.

"Well, during the party I was approached by a member of the Soviet Ministry of Culture who was traveling with the Georgian dancers, a tall, blond-haired young guy with a small, bubble-gum-pink birthmark on his right cheek, named Yevgeny Andreievich Vlatchkov. I knew who he was—captain, KGB, a slick twenty-eight-year-old on the way up. Not one of the old timers, served his own ambitions more than he did the state. With this trip he was getting his chance to turn the corner of his career. Traveling around with the dance troupe, he was, in reality, recruiting anyone he thought ripe and making contact with perhaps dozens of KGB residents, from whom he was gathering information and to whom he was handing out assignments on an itinerary that would take him through the satellite countries, the Far East, and the West—a total of twenty thousand miles. Ukrainian by birth, Vlatchkov grew up in Georgia when his father, a doctor, moved the family to Kutaisi. He graduated third in his class from Tbilisi University, a specialist in cybernetics and mathematical logic, although he's well-up on literature and the arts and an expert in languages, especially English, French, and German. Dossier says he's arrogant, aggressive, overbearing, but mentions only two faults that might affect his work—he's a little too proud of himself, and he likes to show off his knowledge. Both of these traits make it difficult for him to keep from announcing his successes with women, chess, or anything else.

"The dossier was right on all counts, for within a few minutes of introducing himself, he lets me know in so many words that he is aware of my real identity. Very uncool. But even more uncool was the way he was downing water glasses of embassy vodka, and getting louder and more belligerent by the minute. In this state he engaged me in a conversation on American literature and its European antecedents, obviously delighted that he knew more about the subject than I did. I tried to excuse myself, but he grabbed me by the arm and began lecturing me, after somehow steering the conversation around to Transcendentalism. I guess the fine points of his English were pretty good, because when I muttered that he was acting like an asshole and had better get his hands off me, he got even more riled up and began haranguing about how 'Emerson was bourgeois' and that the notion of Transcendentalism was 'nothing more than a capitalist fraud to promulgate a pseudo-mysticism among the masses in order to stupefy their sense of dissatisfaction with their lot.' He was talking so vehemently that people were turning to look at us. I didn't know what to answer. It was so damned outlandish, and he was in this enormous rage, his eyes burning. At one point he even balled a fist while he was talking. As crazy or drunk a bastard as I've ever seen. Then people nearby separated us and the boys from the Russian Embassy led him off to bed. They apologized, of course, and except for a frown from my station chief and an assignment to make a report on the incident in triplicate, I never saw Vlatchkov again. I heard he got a good bawling out, and it went against him on his promotional report, but his behavior that night was not typical, and he's supposedly so sharp they've kept him on as an active case officer.

"Then seven days ago, nine days after the memo was stolen and eight days after the President's call, an NSA radio ship picks up a message from Crete transmitted in a code we haven't used in more than a year. It says simply 'Transcendentalism defective.' Everyone's walking around the office scratching their heads. No one knows what the message means, and we have no one running a project on the island. But I know who it is, and I quickly put two and two together about Andropov's plane flying to Tbilisi within an hour of Moscow's phoning there. All I have to do is check Vlatchkov's whereabouts on our computer back home. Sure enough, he's stationed in Tbilisi, still in Georgia and still a captain. When I tell my station chief, he assigns me to handle the matter as I see fit, peripheral to my main project—and everyone's at the station—to find our missing agent and the memo. That, of course, was the day before we knew about our man being in jail at Söke.

"Anyway, there was no doubt that Vlatchkov was on Crete. Why, I don't know. And the message was so strange, I still can't figure out what he's trying to say. Why had Andropov's personal adjutant flown to see him? Why is he on Crete? Does the word *defective* mean he wants to defect? I'm sure of one thing though—that message was for me and me alone. And I'm almost sure about another—he's issuing me some sort of invitation or challenge—probably to come and get him. But it's so screwy."

Ben shifted in his chair. "Has he contacted you again?" he asked, his tongue heavy in his mouth and his jaw hardly moving.

"No. And that makes it screwier," said Reilly, resuming his pacing. He strode across the room to the balcony and looked out at the sea for a few moments. Then he strolled back and stood looking down at Ben. "And now you know as much about the memo as I do," he said in a low voice.

Chapter Twelve

Ben sat in his chair holding his drink at an oblique angle on his thigh; it was about to slop over. He couldn't speak. He was weary beyond belief and stunned by what he had just heard. *My God!* he kept thinking. *My God!*

He had to have time to sort out the information, to make sense of it—yes, to categorize and compartmentalize it.

He lifted his glass and downed the drink in three swallows, his arm as heavy as a shovel. He was a lot more tired than he had thought.

Reilly took the glass from Ben's hand and refilled it. "Any more questions?" he asked from the bureau, his back to Ben.

"I have to have time to sort all this out," Ben heard himself say. There was no sarcasm in his voice now, and he pronounced his words thickly. His tongue wouldn't work right.

When he reached up to accept the fresh drink, he was almost alarmed at how slowly his arm moved. He felt as if he was dragging it through mud.

Reilly gave him another friendly smile, but Ben couldn't see anything boyish in that smile any longer. It was difficult for Ben to focus his thoughts. The whiskey was really hitting him, and the already shadowy room was fading in and out of his sight in a pulsating haze. Still, he understood the twinge of irritation he felt when he realized that Reilly was not the dull, grinning student he had known five years ago. He was a keen-witted young man who had been four steps ahead of his teacher at every turn. Ben was annoyed that he had underestimated Reilly—and worse, that he had allowed himself to view him as the stereotyped naïve student, which was the way Reilly wanted others to see him. At the same time, somewhere far back in the sluggish vapors inside his head, Ben admired Reilly and was flattered that the young man had thought him important enough to employ him in this situation and entrust him with such vital information.

"Now, let's get to you, sir, so we can wind this thing up," said Reilly, leaning toward him. "Have you told anyone about the contents of the package?"

Ben considered the question. He had heard it clearly enough, but it took him an excessively long time to remember the answer to it. The whiskey was certainly slowing down his responses.

"How about the girl?" asked Reilly.

Ben nodded. "Yes," he said.

"And her friend?"

Ben shook his head. "Kept her out of it." He could hear himself speaking from a great distance away, as though his mouth was somewhere down a mountainside. His words were slurred.

Reilly stood up. "Then since we're just about finished, why don't we get the lady out of the lobby and have a nightcap?"

Ben nodded again. "Sounds . . . fine," he said, but

it didn't sound fine, the shift in the conversation had been too abrupt. Suddenly he was on his guard, but the whiskey was lulling him, and by the time his thoughts had sharpened into objections Reilly had left the room.

He returned a few moments later with Caroline and the man in the white suit. Ben hadn't moved. He was so exhausted that the whiskey had acted as a depressant, and he was practically in a stupor. Caroline looked at him and he nodded to her, heavily, slowly, as if he were tilting a bowling ball. She turned to Reilly, who smiled at her as he handed drinks to her and the man in the white suit and refreshed his own. *The boyish smile again*, thought Ben, and through his blurriness he felt twinges of apprehension.

Reilly looked at his glass, then lifted it above his head. "A toast to a better world, sir. That's what this is all about. *To a better world!*"

He downed his drink in three gulps, and Caroline and white suit followed his example. Ben didn't touch his; it remained balanced on his thigh, circled by a hand that felt as big as a catcher's mitt.

"Reilly," he heard himself say. "Why tell me . . . all this? You . . . could have . . . sent me off . . . with some story . . . or other." He seemed to have little control over his faraway mouth now, and was forming his words with great difficulty.

"True," said Reilly.

"That's . . . all?"

"No, but let me be a good host first," he said, and motioned for Ben to finish his drink, but Ben couldn't lift his arm, even if he had wanted to.

Reilly collected the other glasses and refilled them, saying to Ben over his shoulder, "The only thing I haven't done is congratulate you on your hike the night before last, sir. That whole episode was unexpected and caught us off guard—me, at least."

The room was still lit by the one lamp near the bed, but it seemed to be fading further into a deepening haze each moment. The walls had already vanished and had been replaced by a grainy, oscillating dimness.

Reilly returned with the drinks and handed them around, raising his as a signal for the others to drink. They did, except for Ben. "That hike wasn't like you, sir."

"Maybe . . . more to me . . . than meets the eye. . . . Shouldn't underestimate . . . old teachers . . . any more than they . . . their students," said Ben, breathing heavily with each phrase. His mouth was in another province now.

Reilly lifted his glass in a mock salute, as if acknowledging the barb, and said nothing. But his comments had stirred a question that emerged as big as a ship from the fog in Ben's mind. "How did . . . you find me?" Ben asked.

Reilly smiled again, still standing in front of Ben, backed by the palpitating dimness. When he spoke, his words were clear, but seemed to be coming from a great distance away. "That was easy. There were only three ways you could go. The road to the coast, which would have taken you by Papandakis' place—I didn't think you'd do that—the road over to Anoyia and down to Heraklion—in which case you'd have to depend on standing out in the open by the side of the road with little chance of finding a ride that late at night—I didn't think you'd do that either—and finally the footpath over the mountain—and I was certain you wouldn't do that, especially at night. Actually, I thought you'd curl up under a tree somewhere and sleep till daylight. But we checked out all three, estimating times, et cetera. Routine again. It took a while, even though we have contacts all over the island, but at Kamares we found a taxi driver who remembered someone who fit your description and looked pretty ragged that he had driven here to the Hotel Minos." He turned to Caroline. "I didn't know anything about you until then."

Caroline had sat down in Reilly's chair and had been turning from Reilly to Ben as each one spoke, obviously trying to understand what had occurred between them before she had entered the room, but her face had taken on a dull, heavy-lidded expression in the last few minutes, and she looked half asleep.

"So your . . . agency . . . isn't perfect," Ben said.

"Far from it, Professor. We don't even know what happened at Papandakis' two nights ago—what his reaction to the package was, for example, or anything else."

"He was angry . . . pissed . . . to put it . . . plainly. . . . Wouldn't . . . you be?" Ben was struggling more and more with his speech, and his breathing was becoming heavier each moment.

"I guess I would," said Reilly.

"Said he was . . . going to get . . . daughter back . . . any way . . . he could."

"Good. Anything else?"

"He thought I was . . . messenger boy . . . all right. . . . And when I sat . . . like a moron . . . thought I was . . . teasing. That's when he . . . got angry."

"Sorry about that. But you must have realized that you were in no danger."

"Why?" Ben's tongue occupied his entire mouth now, like a fat snake filling a cavern in another country, a snake he had heard rumors about but never seen.

"Because as far as Papandakis was concerned, you were his only link with the people who were going to help him get his daughter back."

"You mean . . . Concerned Father?"

"Right."

"I didn't know."

"I thought you'd figure that out, if nothing else, and sit tight. Papandakis wasn't going to let anything happen to you."

Ben didn't say anything. Even through the widening fog inside his head, he could see the logic of what Reilly had said.

"What did he say when he opened the package and read the letter?" asked Reilly. His words were still clear, but his voice was becoming smaller and smaller, as if he were speaking to Ben from the other end of a fading long-distance telephone line.

"Told you . . . was angry . . . determined . . . to get her back." Ben was trying to talk forcefully, but his mouth was beyond the horizon now, where he couldn't control it.

"No, I mean, did he bargain?"

"Bargain?"

"Tell you what he needed?"

"Said something. . . . Hundred thousand dollars."

Reilly whistled. The sound hissed through the telephone wire, sliding over mountains and plains.

"A hundred thousand!" Reilly repeated and whistled again.

The room was only a faraway dimness now, a shower of gray sequins occasionally lit by red or gold grains. Only Reilly's face was visible, and it was grainy, too, made of a skyful of dead lights.

"What happened at the house, sir?"

Ben didn't answer. His heaviness had been replaced by a rolling torpor, and he was trying to keep himself from sailing away, a huge balloon filled with breath.

"Professor? What happened at Papandakis' place? The men watching the house said all hell broke loose around eleven thirty."

"Watching the house?"

"Of course. We leave as little as possible to chance. We knew you were in no danger, but we wanted to know about all of Papandakis' movements."

"No . . . danger? At table . . . stabbed me . . . tried to. . . . " Ben was no longer part of his body.

"Who did?"

"He . . . five there . . . a prisoner . . . until I . . . told them." Lips were slapping against each other somewhere, waves on a shore.

"Who was a prisoner?" The voice on the telephone was speaking from the mouth of a tunnel.

"Me . . . but I . . . didn't know . . . escaped."

"So that was it. Well, now you know, so there'll be no danger."

"What?" Calling.

"You're going back, Professor."

"Jesus!" *Had Reilly really said that?*

"You've got to. We can't switch now. They'll let you go when you deliver the message."

"Shit!" *How can he do this to me?*

"I told you how important this is."

"Don't care! . . . Not going!"

"I know how you felt about Vietnam and our foreign policy in general, sir, but this is beyond politics."

"Shove it!" said Ben.

"As you've probably figured out by now, you're not drunk. I drugged both of you." Reilly's voice was farther back in the tunnel.

"Damn! . . . Stupid!" said Ben. When the words opened into meaning, he felt like crying, like curling up and crying himself to sleep, but he didn't know where his body was.

"You've got no choice, and I've got no choice. Can you hear me? Professor? I'm sorry this has happened. I mean it, but the operation is too important."

"I'll tell . . . tell him . . . blow your . . . agency. . . ."

"No one would believe you. Reilly is not the name on my passport anyway, and I didn't mention the intelligence agency I'm connected with, remember? Besides, Papandakis is going to keep on with it, no matter what you tell him. It's the only way he can get his daughter back."

"You bas—" said Ben. Then a question emerged from the darkness, one that he had meant to ask Reilly a long time before. "Real . . . son-in-law," he said. He was drifting off now, but he was fighting his way back for this last time.

"No, I'm not," said Reilly. "It was a ploy to make the story about the package plausible." His voice was beyond the tunnel, but there was only darkness beyond the tunnel.

"No . . . " called Ben. "*Real* . . . son-in-law."

"Real son-in-law? I told you, it was a ploy," said Reilly's small voice.

"No . . . son-in-law . . . *there* . . . at Papan—"

"What are you talking about?"

Ben felt two hands grab his shirt front and shake him. But that was impossible; he was a disembodied head drifting through thickened air.

"Professor? Professor? Answer me. What son-in-law?"

"The . . . one . . . already . . . there."

"But we didn't have a—what do you mean? Professor Ames? Professor?"

Ben was a head suspended in a heavy darkness, held up by two areas of pressure in front of him, areas miles below, that forced the back of his collar to act like a sling on the nape of his neck and hold his head up. Reilly's face loomed before him, a sun surrounded by darkness, a frowning sun that was continually disintegrating in several directions into red and gold blotches. *Reilly didn't know everything*, thought Ben, and he felt his whole head smile. The smile lifted him out of Reilly's grasp. It was a moon rising over mountains, one huge smile rising over the other side of the planet, right in Reilly's face. *No, sir, Reilly didn't know everything*.

"Professor? Professor? What son-in-law?"

It was the smile that answered him, Ben was sure of that. It was the smile that, as everything collapsed around it, said "Fuck . . . you!"

Chapter Thirteen

He woke slowly. He was lying on his side, and his eyelids refused to come unglued. When he could open them and focus his eyes, he saw that Yorgo was sitting beside the bed, the sleepy, whalelike smile still on his face, the tips of his teeth showing between his lips. The black bandanna was still tied around his head, its black fringe hanging halfway down his forehead, ending in minute, fuzzy cloth balls that looked like charred acacia blossoms.

Ben tried to raise himself up, but his skull seemed to be filled with sand and his body felt like a beached carcass. He fell back onto the pillows, realizing with a groan that he was back in the bedroom at Papandakis' house.

"Awake, yes?" said the Cretan, his smile broadening to reveal the enormous teeth. Not waiting for an answer, he hopped up and bounded from the room shouting "Keria Papandaki! Keria Papandaki!"

There was a trampling of booted feet on the stairs and in the hall, and then Papandakis entered with a savage-faced Pandelis and Uncle Kosta behind him, and the three younger men following them. *Jesus!*

All six had seemed to tumble through the doorway as if it were too small for them. They had ducked down as they entered the room, and once inside had shaken themselves erect like steaming horses tossing their manes in the early morning sunlight. Ben liked the image, the sense of animal energy it suggested. And he enjoyed the Cretans' entrance in the same way he would have enjoyed the horses—aesthetically, from a distance, although he knew the danger these men presented was as close as his bedside.

He lay there, groggy, still not fully aware of the situation or even that there *was* a situation. His throat seemed to be lined with chalk, and the sunlight that poured through the balcony windows was cutting like broken glass into his eyes.

The six men were now gathered on one side of the bed, solemn as a group of monks in a medieval painting, but Uncle Kosta and Pandelis were shifting impatiently from one foot to the other, twisting their eyes and heads this way and that, and clearing their throats, while Yorgo, Pavlo, and Manoli, all in the black bandanna headdresses, were straining to see past them to the bed.

"So you are awake now," said Papadakis. He was standing in front of the others, his voice unusually soft as he bent toward Ben.

"Yes," rasped Ben.

"*Yorgo, fere Nero, s'parakalo!*" said Papandakis over his shoulder, and the smiling young Cretan left the bedroom. Papandakis called after him, "*Kai café—gliko!*"

Papandakis turned back to Ben. "Yorgo will bring some water and coffee. Then we will talk. This whole matter is very strange. Why should you want to jump from the balcony like that?" He shook his head, and Ben realized that Papandakis had addressed the last remarks to himself more than to him.

"It makes little sense," Papandakis continued. "Then the phone call in the middle of the night informing us that we could find you in a deserted shepherd's hut outside of Gergeri, and when we arrive there we find you asleep on the straw with a young lady at your side, both of you obviously drugged. You see? It makes little sense."

Papandakis straightened up, turned, and walked to the glass door that led to the balcony, the four Cretans moving aside almost formally to let him pass. The old man stood there, his back to Ben, staring through the gauze-covered glass until the water and coffee arrived. Pandelis and the others continued to watch Ben, although if he had to describe their expressions in a word, he would have said, surprisingly, *concerned* and added that they looked more curious than hostile.

Slowly Ben's head began to clear. The gentleness of Papandakis' comments and his obvious confusion, as well as the almost purposeful way in which Pandelis had avoided approaching the bed—as though he were not sure that Ben wasn't in some way contaminated— had relieved Ben's initial feelings of trepidation on seeing them again.

Ben drank the water, sipped the small cup of strong black coffee, asked for another glass of water, and then felt ready for the interrogation he knew was about to begin, except that now he had to go to the bathroom.

Papandakis had returned to the bed and was looking down at him. "So. We are ready now."

Ben nodded, his bladder about to explode.

"Good. Is there anything else we can get you?"

"The girl—what about her?"

"She is here, still sleeping. The women are looking

after her. But she is fine, you are not to worry. Now we will talk."

"Wait," said Ben, and scrambling from the bed, he stumbled from the room in his shorts, aware that his sudden movement had startled them all and that they were staring after him as he lumbered down the hall to the bathroom.

He washed and returned to the bedroom much refreshed, although his face and head still felt swollen and his muscles were still sore from his climb over the mountains.

"Okay," he said, sitting on the bed, and first Pandelis and then the others, none of whom had moved or changed expressions since he had bolted from the room, burst out laughing. Papandakis smiled thinly.

"Hookay! Hookay!" roared Pandelis through his guffaws, repeating the phrase again and again until his eyes were groggy with tears and he was coughing and sputtering.

Ben shook his head. He could see what a comical figure he must have looked like charging from the room in his shorts. Christ, he felt like an inept nephew.

The laughter subsided with snorts and throat clearings, and when it was quiet Papandakis began to speak.

"Where does one start?" he said. "Truly we are more confused than before. You jump off a balcony and run—why?"

"Well, if you remember, you had threatened to turn me over to laughing boy over there, who had already tried to kill me, if I didn't answer your questions," said Ben, trying to regain some of his dignity.

"But certainly, then you would have answered the questions."

"The only thing wrong with that logic is that it assumed I knew the answers. I didn't. I wasn't the courier."

"But you brought the package."

"And I got hold of it in exactly the way I told you. I was duped by the man who gave it to me. He told me he was your son-in-law. The people he represented wanted to keep themselves out of the picture."

"The other concerned father."

"Yes. Well, it's not as cut and dry as all that, but let's leave it there for the time being."

"Why did you not tell us this before?"

"I didn't know it. I only found out last night."

"From whom, may I ask?"

"The man who drugged me."

"The man who drugged you? Can you understand how confusing this whole thing sounds to us?"

"Yes," said Ben. He paused. "The man who drugged me was the same one who had been my student and who, posing as your son-in-law, gave me the package in the museum. Last night he found me—"

"He found you? Where?"

"Ayia Galini."

"All the way down there. How could he know you would be there? Did you have a prearranged meeting place?"

"No. As I told you, I had nothing to do with this whole thing. I didn't even want to come back here. That's why he drugged me."

Ben saw the confusion in the old man's face, and he knew that Papandakis would never understand his story if he told it in bits and pieces. He also knew that he owed Reilly nothing, neither secrecy nor loyalty. Reilly had involved him in this twice against his will and had made a fool of him both times. A wave of anger surged through him.

"Look," he said, "the only way you're going to understand what this is all about is if I tell you everything he told me." And with that he told the entire story Reilly had told him the previous night, emphasizing Reilly's activities as an intelligence agent and the importance he attached to the American agent who was arrested with Papandakis' daughter in Turkey and the document he was carrying. He finished fifteen minutes later.

". . . and he said that even if I told you all this, you'd go through with it, because of your daughter."

"And he was correct," said Papandakis, who had drawn a chair up to the bed and was sitting there now with the others standing in a semicircle behind him. His elbows were propped on the armrests and he was kneading his temples with the fingertips of both hands. "So that is your story," he said finally, dropping his hands and looking up at Ben. "So," he repeated wearily. He looked very tired. Pandelis, who had been looking quickly from his brother to Ben for the last several minutes of the story, now leaned toward Papandakis and whispered a vigorous message to him in Greek, and Ben realized that he didn't know if Pandelis spoke or understood English. He had only heard him speak Greek to his brother.

Papandakis nodded to Pandelis and waved him away. "Tell me, Professor, do you accept this story as true?" he asked.

"Yes," Ben said immediately, although he suddenly wasn't sure. He had accepted Reilly's story completely, but now that it had been questioned, he saw there was no reason why he should have. "At least I think I do," he added.

Papandakis nodded. "I mean, Professor, do you believe the story about this memo?"

Ben was silent, and Papandakis continued. "Does it not sound highly improbable to you?"

Ben nodded.

Papandakis nodded in return. "Yes. To me also. But so improbable that it may just be true. I have heard stranger. You see, Professor, we have so many things to consider. Everything has changed since your departure. The offer of money is still acceptable to my Turkish associates, but they have added other conditions. They called yesterday and told me that it will be necessary for me to enter their country with a small group of men. They said my request is too great, especially with the way things are in Turkey at this time. All they can do is distract the guards, unlock the jail, and escort us back and forth. But we must make the release of the Americans look like a true jailbreak."

He paused. Ben said nothing.

"I can see you do not understand the significance of this, Professor. Let me explain. At one time I was operating mainly with a friend of mine, a Turk of Cretan heritage named Nazmi Kursad. Our families had been friends for years before the Kursads were moved to Turkey. With Nazmi's death seven years ago the separation between our family and the Kursads became complete. I am now dealing with people in Turkey, some in high positions, whose allegiances are governed by self-interest. I do not trust them, although they have done nothing to deserve my suspicions. Recently the Turkish government has been investigating corruption among its high officials, and with the Cyprus trouble renewing the traditional hatred between our countries, these investigations have evolved into a zealous reform movement. My associates may now view their dealings with me, should these be discovered, as an embarrassment. Do you understand?"

"Not really," said Ben.

"Professor, my dealings with these people have always been done on the water, in boats. Both sides are protected by the water, since there are no borders to cross at sea, really. We come fully armed and exchange what we have to exchange and go our separate ways. I have never set foot on Turkish soil. Now, suddenly, I am asked to enter Turkey. Do you not agree that my presence there would provide nervous bureaucrats with the perfect opportunity to rid themselves of their embarrassment?"

"I see what you mean."

"Do you know what it means for a man like me—a Greek as well as a dealer in contraband—to be caught in Turkey?"

"I think so."

"*Think*? You need a history lesson, Professor, if you only *think* you know. The Turks occupied Greece for almost four hundred years, beginning even before the fall of Constantinople. The hatreds one would expect between conqueror and conquered were increased a hundredfold by Ottoman cruelty and the religious differences between Moslem Turk and Christian Greek. By the time of our War of Independence in 1821 these hatreds had become so fanatical, so deep-seated, as to seem almost like racial inheritance on both sides. You are aware, no doubt, that two million Greeks lived in Turkey before the Greek invasion of 1922. That event provoked such murderous Turkish reprisals against these people that an international commission arranged for Turkey and Greece to exchange minority populations the following year. It was that exchange that sent the Kursads to Turkey. Since then the hatred between the two peoples has smoldered on the island of Cyprus, always waiting to erupt into full-scale war. Now do you see what it means for me to enter Turkey?"

Ben nodded.

"And while listening to your story a moment ago I was forced to wonder if in reality this concerned father of yours might not have a Turkish name."

Ben shook his head. "I've told you exactly what Reilly told me."

"And I believe you, Professor Ames, I sincerely do, although it is possible that you and the lady could have had a confederate phone us, and then you could have drugged yourselves with the sleeping potion. But why, I ask myself? Why such an elaborate masquerade? Your escape could have been undertaken so that you could make contact with your friends, but then I realize that you could have accomplished that with a phone call from my study, or they could have called up at an appointed time with instructions. And what can the woman have to do with this, if it was not, as you told us, merely that she knew the outline of the events that brought you here and therefore was sent along with you so there would be no possibility of our plans being disclosed before the document has been recovered? No, Professor, I believe you, but I am not at all sure I believe your Mr. Reilly's story." He paused, then continued. "However, an entire episode that was left out of your tale did make me sure of one thing—my daughter is well rid of Henry Reese."

Ben looked up. "Those are pretty harsh words, sir, for someone so recently dead."

"Really? What kind of man is it, Professor Ames, who leaves his wife in prison in a hostile foreign country, comes to visit a father-in-law he has never met, and not only says nothing about his wife being in any danger, but fabricates another story to hide the true one? That was one of the things Pandelis was just telling me. The idea struck us both separately as being one of the more curious side-issues in this affair."

"Maybe he was frightened," said Ben. "I mean, he didn't know you and—"

"Come, come, Professor! Your classroom Socratic stance, although classically Greek, is at times exasperating. Consider this—if you were Henry Reese, would you have acted in such a manner?"

Ben shook his head.

"Exactly. He was a dog and is better dead. His fall at Samaria has saved me the trouble. Come, Professor, do not look so shocked. I am not a harsh man. My daughter will never know—his death spares me not only the pleasant duty of ending his life, but the unhappy one of telling her what kind of man she married. Nevertheless, do you see what I mean about the curious ramifications of your friend Reilly's story?"

"Yes, I do," said Ben, his head reeling. "I don't know what to believe, but *I* don't have to believe anything. You do. I just wonder what you're going to do about all this."

Papandakis shrugged. "I am going to do what the letter instructed me to do."

"Sit tight and wait for the courier," said Ben, looking down at the rumpled bed.

"The *second* letter, Professor."

Ben looked up again.

"The one that was pinned to your shirt when we found you in the hut," continued Papandakis, watching Ben's eyes and smiling at the surprise he saw in them. "You see what I mean about this entire affair being very strange?"

"Dare I ask if the letter contained any information I haven't given you?"

"No, only that the money would be here today and that I should consider making the exchange within the next day or two, because the prisoners might be transferred to the military jail in Izmir."

"Yes," said Ben, "and there are only five—no, that was last night—there are only four days left to get the memo."

Papandakis waved away Ben's remark. "The instructions in the letter conform with my plans, so I will accede to them. We go tonight."

"Tonight?" said Ben, startled.

"Yes. Yesterday my Turkish associates informed me that they had received word that the prisoners are to be transferred the day after tomorrow. Therefore, it would be safer to release them tonight, and then and there we made arrangements to do so. Presumably Reilly knew nothing about my associates' request that I enter Turkey, nor that the prisoners were being transferred, when he wrote the letter. Therefore, I find it a curious coincidence that his letter mentions an earlier release date and a possible transfer."

"I see. Was there anything else in the letter?"

"Only that he thought it would be advisable for me to have the woman call her friend in order to reassure her of her safety, and that I should refrain from extracting information from you in a brutal manner—he called it 'using unpleasant interrogation techniques'—since you knew no more now than you did on the evening of your first visit here."

"Then why did he send me back?" asked Ben. He was thinking out loud rather than asking a question, and he knew the answer even before Papandakis replied.

"For the same reason he sent the young lady, I would think. He knew that I would want no word of this undertaking to transpire before my daughter's release, any more than he did, and that I would insist that you both remain here as my guests until the operation was concluded. Your friend seems to have put us both in an awkward position, Professor. He is a clever young man."

"Not really," said Ben. "You and I weren't expecting anything. He told me that himself. I'd say he was just an expert at sticking people where they're most vulnerable. In America we call a person like that a bastard!"

Papandakis winced, a little taken back by the ferocity in Ben's voice, but Pandelis grinned broadly and muttered something to his brother. He understood English all right.

"Pandelis says that you were displaying the balls of a goat."

"Tell him he shouldn't underestimate his enemies," snapped Ben.

Papandakis' face remained impassive, but Pandelis' grin grew wider. "My ears can hear your words,

Teacher. And my mouth can speak my own," Pandelis said. "No insult was given you. I was to be understood to say you were showing yourself a man in my eyes. But tell me, I know these around me are curious, where you go the other night?"

Now it was Ben's turn to grin. "I jumped into the back of a truck, the truck took me to Anoyia and from there I strolled over to Kamares."

"Kamares?" said Pandelis, his eyes bulging. "You go over Psiloritis? In dark?"

"Why not? Good moon, lovely night, perfect time for a stroll," said Ben, hoping he wasn't overdoing it but enjoying the stocky Cretan's surprise.

Pandelis clicked his tongue against the roof of his mouth and exclaimed, "As I said, 'balls of a goat'! And I am thinking you are one to watch with much closeness."

He nodded at Ben, squinting his eyes, and turned and translated Ben's words to the other Cretans. They clicked their tongues and whistled and stared at Ben as Pandelis spoke. Somehow a bond had been formed between Pandelis and Ben that Ben didn't have too much difficulty understanding, and Pandelis was relating Ben's escape to the others so vigorously and at such length that he seemed to be extolling the deeds of a heroic bandit.

Even Papandakis seemed amused. He smiled and took the opportunity provided by his brother's prolonged narrative to enter the conversation once again. "It would seem that you have won Pandelis' admiration. I hope you will not be foolish enough to be taken in by it. He admires you as he would a worthy adversary, not a friend. He does not trust you. Henry's death and Stella's arrest are too much of a coincidence, and this foray into Turkey is filled with too many hazards and too many chances of betrayal. I must agree with him."

"I thought you said you believed me?"

"I do. I really do, Professor. But there is a possibility that you and your friend Reilly have been hired by my Turkish associates to lure me into Turkey, and I must take every precaution. Too much is at stake."

"So? I'm here. I'm not going anywhere. And don't worry—I'm not going to try to escape again."

"Yes. And to insure that you do not, I have assigned Pandelis to you until this is over."

"Oh, great! Just what I wanted!" said Ben, shaking his head and looking at the thick-set man rhapsodizing over his walk through the mountains. Then he stopped and turned back to Papandakis. "Wait a minute. Isn't he going to Turkey with you?"

"Yes, he is, Professor. And so are you."

"What?"

"If what you tell me is true, then the only danger to you in Turkey will be our danger also. If you are lying, we will slit your throat like a diseased dog's before the Turks get us. And should your life mean nothing to you, I am leaving Uncle Kosta here with the woman. If it turns out you have been lying to us, he is instructed to cut her throat should we not return."

Chapter Fourteen

From the moment Papandakis had tumbled open the package on the table three nights before, Ben had sensed an inevitable linking of events over which he had no control and which eventually would threaten his life. He had lectured on this phenomenon many times, but it had never been more than an interesting topic for discussion until now. And now there was Caroline. Now she had been dragged into this seemingly inescapable progression as into the hurtling course of a river.

Papandakis turned toward the door.

"Wait a minute!" said Ben, still sitting on the bed.

Papandakis halted in mid-step and looked back at him. The other Cretans had turned away with him and they also looked back. Their silhouettes were edged with the white sunlight that flooded through the windows on either side of the balcony door.

"I've had just about enough of this."

"I think you have little choice in the matter, Professor."

"Guess again. I've cooperated with you, now I expect you to do the same. There are so many things that could upset your little Turkish adventure that I just plain refuse to go, and I won't be held responsible for anything that goes wrong."

He waited for Papandakis to respond, but the old man said nothing. He stood there, without turning all the way around to face him, looking at Ben with tired eyes.

"Listen, man, you're going into a hostile country," Ben continued. "And you said yourself that your own contacts may want to get rid of you. And that has nothing, absolutely nothing to do with me or Caroline!"

"I also said that you and this friend of yours—Reilly—might be acting in conjunction with my associates in order to lure me into Turkey, Professor," said Papandakis wearily.

"I don't buy it. That still doesn't give you any reason to hold Caroline responsible. You're holding her like a sacrificial animal."

"True. Let us say that if we are deceived, she will be our sacrifice to the god of vengeance."

"That's not very funny. In fact, it's damned barbaric, Papandakis, and you know it."

"I know nothing of the sort, Professor. It is a matter of definition. To you my decision is barbaric; to me it is merely Cretan."

"You have saying," interjected Pandelis, looking at Ben and touching his stubby right forefinger to his right eye, "'one eye for one eye.'"

Ben ignored him. "Look, I'm telling you the truth," he said to Papandakis. "But there are so many things that could go wrong and make it look as if I've been lying. Your contacts may not have planned this, but they may find it a perfect opportunity to get rid of you. And, Christ, you're actually invading the damn place, a whole country, and against odds like that you're willing to say I was lying, and kill me for it, along with a totally innocent woman? *Me*, I can understand—if I accept this crazy reasoning of yours—but her?"

"Professor, you have just described the position I find myself in. It is, I grant you, a most uncomfortable one, and one I do not particularly enjoy. You and this Reilly, and possibly my Turkish associates, have put me there. Everything I have, everyone I know and love, including my daughter, have been put in jeopardy. I think it is only fair that you share this ordeal and whatever conclusion evolves from it."

"But—"

"And now, Professor, if I can do nothing more to make you comfortable, I must leave you and make final preparations for tonight." Again Papandakis turned to go.

"Wait!" called Ben. He realized the hopelessness of his position, but still wanted to salvage something. Again Papandakis looked back. "Let me see her—the woman, Caroline."

Papandakis hesitated, then turned to Pandelis. "Take him to her," he said. "Leave them if he wants, but be sure the balcony doors are locked, and wait outside."

Pandelis nodded, and without looking at Ben again, Papandakis and the others left the room.

Ben showered and put on a pair of tan slacks and a yellow Banlon T-shirt. Pandelis casually watched these operations with a thin smile, but Ben couldn't determine whether the smile was good-humored or sardonic and found it more than a little unnerving when he remembered that this leering pumpkin with the upswept mustaches had tried to kill him a few nights before.

As Ben was scrubbing the dust from his shoes with a small brush he took from his valise Pandelis said, "Hey, you, Teacher. Say some words so I know you are here." He laughed, but Ben hadn't replied and there was no further talk between them.

They walked down the hall, knocked on a white door, and walked in.

Caroline was sitting up in bed. One of the old crones in black who had served supper two nights ago was sitting in a chair beside her, and there was a tray of sliced bread, honey, and Greek coffee on the bed, untouched.

Caroline was still dressed in the green blouse she had worn the night before. Her hair was tousled and her face haggard, and when she saw Ben, her eyes had widened and her lips began to move, but Ben shook his head and she remained silent.

Pandelis said a few words in Greek to the old woman, and she left the room. Next he checked the balcony doors, holding up a key for Ben to see before he dropped it into his sash with an exaggerated gesture. And then, still smiling, he left the room, saying at the door, "I am outside, Teacher."

When the door closed, Ben went over and sat down on the bed. He didn't know what to say. He took one of Caroline's hands and covered it with both his own. She seemed calm, but every so often she trembled.

"Where are we?" she whispered. "I was so frightened when I woke up!"

"We're at Papandakis'," Ben said in a soft voice. "Reilly drugged us and called Papandakis and told him where we were, and I guess he came and got us."

Caroline pushed herself upright and looked at him. "But why—"

"It's all my fault. Reilly asked if I'd told anyone about the package, and I said yes. I don't know—I was half drunk and probably drugged already, but it was stupid of me, stupid! I actually believed he was through with me and would let us go."

Caroline was staring at the blankets. She began to speak. "When I woke up, I didn't know where I was, and the old woman couldn't speak English and kept rattling on in Greek. And then those men came in and just looked at me for a while and left. I thought—"

"Hey, you're okay now. They won't hurt you."

"I thought—"

"It's nothing like that, nothing. It's okay," said Ben and put his arms around her and held her, rocking her back and forth. He decided not to tell her about Papandakis' threat.

"But I don't understand," she said several moments later, raising her head. "Why would Reilly drug us and send us here?"

"It's a long story," Ben said, sighing, and proceeded to tell her everything that had happened from the time he had gone up to Reilly's hotel room the night before to the moment he had walked into her bedroom that morning, carefully neglecting to mention that he would be included in the expedition to Söke and the threat to her life should the expedition end unsuccessfully.

By the time he finished she was looking at him with troubled eyes. "This whole thing sounds like a bad movie. Do you believe what Reilly said about the memo?"

Ben looked at the rumpled bedclothes. "I don't

know. I didn't at first, but I don't know. If it's true, it could be a weapon that would make the hydrogen bomb and the laser beam look like toys. I keep flashing on Knossos and the Minoans and how it was weather that destroyed them—a tidal wave. That whole civilization gone like that," he said, snapping his fingers. "And then there's the Vlatchkov story. All that talk about Transcendentalism. I don't know. Sounds crazy, but it could be."

"But what if this is a set-up and Reilly *is* in on it?"

Ben nodded. "That's a definite possibility."

"If it is, what will happen to Papandakis?"

"The Turks and Greeks hate each other worse than the Protestants and Catholics hate each other in Northern Ireland."

"And what will happen to us?"

"We'll be all right," he said, but he had paused a moment too long before answering.

She drew away and stared at him. "I know what you're doing, Ben, and it's not fair. I want to know everything."

"It will be okay," he said, "you'll see."

"Why can't you be honest with me? I can take it."

He reached over and touched her arm with his fingertips, but didn't reply.

"Christ, sometimes I hate being a woman!" she said, wrenching her arm away. Then her head drooped and she began to cry.

Ben let her cry, knowing he should have told her. What gave him the right to assume the role of her protector? He looked at her, watched her sobs die away, and knew he had lost the moment. *Lost*. He could hear Julia snickering. He was a sorry specimen, all right.

Caroline dried her eyes.

"It seems that you've also got to call Gail and let her know you're okay," he finally said, but Caroline didn't answer, and he waited for several moments before he began speaking again. "Look, you're letting your imag—"

But she shook her head violently, put one arm up as if to ward him off, and said, "Don't say anything! Just don't say anything for a few minutes!"

He moved away from her and looked toward the balcony window.

Finally her body relaxed. "I'm sorry," she said, brushing the hair out of her eyes. "It's just that—"

"You don't have to explain. I understand."

"What are we going to do?" she asked.

"I don't know. Why don't you eat some of that bread and drink some coffee."

But she shook her head and pushed the tray away.

He smiled at her before he could catch himself.

"What do you think is going to happen?" she asked, ignoring the smile.

"I don't know." He shook his head. While he was staring out the balcony windows he had been trying to figure out if Reilly was lying and how he was going to get Caroline and himself out of Papandakis' house, but he had not arrived at a solution to either problem. Reilly would have to make an incriminating move for Ben to tell that he was lying, and that wasn't likely. And the situation at the house had changed drastically since three nights ago. Now he was being watched, and he wasn't sure that he would be a match for Pandelis if he should attempt to overpower him. He also knew that Caroline's presence would make any escape plan he devised doubly difficult to carry out.

"I'm sorry I got you into this," he said. "I should never have come to Ayia Galini."

She smiled at that, and swam toward him under the covers. She put her hands on either side of his head, stared into his eyes, kissed him softly on the lips, then put her arms around him and cradled him. "Together, okay?" she said. "Let's make a pact—you and I. We'll get out of this. You'll see. And I'm glad you came to Ayia Galini, do you hear? I'm glad, Benjamin Ames, professor of history at Claremont College."

Professor of history. Claremont College. My God, was that who he was? He hadn't felt like that person once in the past three days. Benjamin Ames was a label in a suit he had hung away in a closet and forgotten.

The door opened. Ben turned. It was Pandelis. The old woman was behind him, and she slipped past him into the room. Pandelis looked at Ben and Caroline. He wasn't smiling.

"Phone call, Teacher. Downstairs," he said.

"What?" said Ben.

"Phone call. Now. We go, both together."

"But—" said Ben, but he was already pulling away from Caroline's embrace.

Pandelis stood in the doorway, square-faced and expressionless. Ben walked toward him.

"Ben?" Caroline called.

He turned. Her eyes were wide again. The old woman was sitting in the chair beside the bed once more.

"I'll be back," he said. And he and Pandelis left the room.

Chapter Fifteen

Several more men joined them in the hallway. The whole house seemed to have been alerted. There were doors closing and hurried footfalls, and by the time Ben and Pandelis reached the study downstairs, they were being followed by five men. The study was a shadowy room anchored by massive furniture and lined with bookshelves on three sides and twin glass doors that opened onto the veranda on the fourth.

Papandakis and Uncle Kosta were waiting for them. The old man nodded toward a heavy mahogany desk in the center of the room, where a phone squatted with its receiver off the hook. Ben went to it. The others, led by Papandakis, crowded around him as he lifted the receiver.

"Hello," he said.

"Good morning, sir. Did you get a good rest?"

"Well, well, Reilly. Listen, you bastard—"

"Now, now—"

"What do you think this is, some kind of game? Where the hell are you?"

"Settle down, Professor. I was beginning to get the impression last night that you were rather enjoying this."

"Do you have any idea what's going on here? It's

bad enough you got *me* involved in all this, but why Caroline?"

"Professor, I may make light of the situation, but I'm serious when I tell you that I didn't think things would get this complicated. I just couldn't chance your telling the authorities about this until it was over. Anyway, Papandakis will only hold you until his daughter and the others are brought out, then he'll let you go. And I've been assured that he's known all over Crete for his hospitality. So don't worry and just be patient."

"Listen to me, Reilly, and listen good—he thinks I'm in this with you."

"And he'd be a fool if he didn't. I'm reassured."

"Damn it, you shithead, be serious!"

"I am, Professor. Look, you've got nothing to worry about. When the Turks have brought the others out—"

"Brought out! Will you listen to me! No one's being brought out. Papandakis' contacts want him to go in and get them and make it look like a break."

There was silence on the other end of the line. Ben continued. "He thinks they may be using this fiasco to get rid of him, and—"

"How does he usually work?"

"On a boat. In international waters. He's never gone in before. Never. N-E-V-E-R! Are you getting the picture?"

Silence again.

"Add this to it. He thinks you and I are setting him up."

The silence continued.

"You want me to go on, wise guy?"

"Go on."

"He's taking me in with him. And if anything goes

wrong, he's going to slit my throat. But since you tell me not to worry, I won't."

Reilly didn't reply.

"Still there?"

"What else?"

"It's not only me, it's Caroline. He's going to leave someone with her, and if we don't get back, she gets it, too. I won't worry about that, either. . . . Well, say something!"

"I told you how important this is—"

"What are you going to do, man, walk away from this and award posthumous medals when it's over? Are you going to rationalize it out of your conscience by saying it was *oh, so important*? For all I know, you *are* working for the Turks."

"Calm down for a second, will you? Think. Why would his contacts want to get rid of him?"

"I thought you knew that. You're supposed to know everything. There's a shake-up there. The government's looking for officials who've got their hands in the till, his contacts among them, and he's the reason their hands are dirty. So if they get rid of him—"

"Shit!"

"That's a truly intelligent statement, Reilly. Go to the head of the class. Now what the hell are you going to do about this?"

"Don't worry. We'll come up with something."

"That's reassuring. Really. Listen, man, Caroline and I are caught in the middle, thanks to you, and we can't get out without your help."

"Where are you landing?"

"Hold on." Ben turned to Papandakis. "Where are we landing?"

"Bodrum," said Papandakis. "In a boat. It is all arranged. Let me speak to him, please."

"I'll take care of it," said Ben holding the phone away from the old man's outstretched hand. He spoke into the mouthpiece again. "Bodrum. It's all arranged."

"How many? And is he coming out that way?"

"How many and are you coming out the same way?" Ben asked Papandakis.

"Seven and yes," Papandakis said.

"Seven and yes," Ben repeated into the phone.

"Okay. Tell him I'll try to get him some Turkish clothes. Is he going into Söke by truck?"

"By truck to Söke?" Ben asked, flushing at the amusement on Papandakis' face.

The old man nodded.

"Yes," Ben said into the phone, realizing how absurd these antics made him look.

"Okay. Now listen to me, Professor. I'm going to alert all our people to get down there. The place will be crawling with them all the way to Söke and back. If the Turks start anything, they'll get more than they bargained for."

"What are you going to do, Reilly, start a war?" asked Ben, but he had to admit that Reilly's words had reassured him.

"I told you how important this is. I'm not lying, Professor. We've got to bring that man out. In fact, it seems obvious now that we've got to make sure that everyone gets out."

"That's fine, Reilly. And how do you propose to make sure of that?"

"Do you want me to break you out of that house

right now? They'd slice you like a grapefruit, probably both of you, before we hit the front door."

Ben was silent.

"I've read your file, Professor. I know you can handle yourself in any kind of trouble when it comes up. You were trained for it."

"That was years ago, Reilly, and it was strictly military."

"All right. You've told me the situation. I'm aware of it. Give me time to do something. Now let's get on with this, so we can wrap the whole thing up. Okay?"

"No. There's no time. The prisoners are being transferred day after tomorrow. We go in tonight."

Silence.

"Damn it, wise guy, say something!"

"I'm thinking, I'm thinking."

"That's not good enough."

"Then you give *me* an answer."

Ben clenched his teeth.

"Okay," said Reilly after a pause. "Let's get on with what we do have answers for. You have a pencil?"

Ben looked at the desk. There were several pens and a pad of paper on it.

"Ready?" asked Reilly.

"For what?"

"Take this down."

"Screw you, Reilly!"

"You're acting like a child, Professor. Now let's get on with this."

"I don't have to *get on* with anything."

"Have it your way. Put Papandakis on."

Ben handed the phone to Papandakis and stepped aside. He felt foolish and, yes, he *had* acted like a child. But he had to show Reilly that he wouldn't fall in with his plan. He wanted Reilly to see that he wouldn't do whatever Reilly or his agency ordered him to do. No one was going to orchestrate his life—or his death.

"Yes, I am Stavros Papandakis," Papandakis said into the phone. He stood stiffly and solemnly. He listened for a few moments, staring at the olive grove outside the window. Then he reached for a pen and turned the pad toward him, writing as he listened and interjecting comments as he wrote. "From Siteia, about three P.M. . . . Yes, I understand. . . . We will need additional materiel . . . tommyguns with at least one hundred clips of ammunition and one hundred grenades. The last is most important. . . . about two P.M. . . . Yes. . . . A truck with a green canvas cover. . . . I understand. . . . Northeast, one street back. . . . I understand. . . . Over left front tire. . . . Yes. . . . five A.M. tomorrow. We should have plenty of time. . . . I understand, yes. . . ." Finally he put the pen down on the pad and said, "Now, Mr. Reilly, I hope you understand *our* position. Both your friends are our hostages. Should anything happen to us, they will be eliminated. From your letter I know you are familiar with my dossier and are aware that this is no empty threat. For my part I am to bring out all the Americans and I will endeavor to do this. Where do you propose we make the exchange? . . . I would prefer Spinalonga. . . . On the northeast side of the Gulf of Mirabello. An island. You'll find an old Venetian fort there. Some of my men will wait there with the girl for our arrival. . . . Say three P.M. tomorrow?. . . . Until then, Mr. Reilly. . . . Yes. . . . Good-bye."

Papandakis turned to Ben, holding the receiver out to him. "He wants to speak with you, Professor."

Ben took the phone. "Yes?" he said.

"Listen, Professor, I may have got you into this, but we're going to have to get you out of it together. So cut the self-pity. We're not going to get anywhere until you start using that celebrated mind of yours for more than chewing me out."

"Are you lecturing me, Reilly? When I see you, I'm going to kick—"

"Look, I don't want to argue. Let's call a truce and figure out how we can make this thing go as smooth as butter."

Ben clenched his teeth and remained silent.

"That's better. I'll be in touch as soon as I can figure something out. But the road to Söke will be paved with our men. That I guarantee. You can tell Papandakis that, too—I take it you told him everything else I told you, anyway."

"That's right."

"I figured as much. You don't let me down too often, Professor. Christ, what an asshole operation!"

"I owe you nothing, Reilly, understand?"

"Yeah. Yeah. I figured you'd say that. By the way, what were you blabbering about just before you passed out?"

"What do you mean?"

"You were saying something about me being the real son-in-law."

"So?"

"So I told you I wasn't. I was only using that as a pretext—"

"I wasn't talking about you. I was talking about the real one."

"What real one?"

"The one who died here the week before I arrived."

There was a pause, then Reilly said, "Tell me more, Professor."

"He was Papandakis' daughter's husband. Named Reese—Henry Reese. American. They had gone to India from San Francisco and were returning through Turkey to visit her father because Reese had never met him. But you must know all this."

"Keep talking, Professor."

"There's nothing to talk about. He arrived without her—said she was staying with a sick friend in Athens. And he was killed the day after he got here."

"How?"

"Accident. A fall while he was out hiking."

"And?"

"That's it. Except this morning when I told Papandakis everything, he cursed Reese up, down, and sideways."

"Why's that?"

"Because Reese had lied to him about Stella's whereabouts and hadn't come to him with the real story."

"That's crazy as hell, Professor. Why wouldn't a guy report his wife missing to the American Consulate? And—hmmm . . ."

"What?"

"And how did the guy get out of the Turkish drug bust to begin with? Supposedly the Turks hit them when they were all asleep and arrested everyone. Listen, Professor, ask the old man what happened to the body and the kid's papers."

Ben turned and repeated the question. Papandakis answered him with an uncomprehending frown. "He says the body was taken to the Heraklion morgue, and the police took Reese's passport and belongings," Ben said into the phone.

"That's standard. I think I'll look into this—check the body and the belongings and any info we may have on Mr. Henry Reese."

"Why?"

"Because it's too much of a coincidence, besides being weird. I impersonated his son-in-law to fool you, not Papandakis. We knew his daughter was married to an American, but that was it. And there was no Henry Reese on the list we got of the people in jail at Söke. I pulled the whole son-in-law business out of thin air."

Ben said nothing. There was a pause and then Reilly continued. "It's probably nothing. The guy was either too scared to tell the old man what really happened, or he *was* an asshole, like Papandakis says. But we'll check it out anyway. It's routine procedure. . . . You feeling better now, tiger?"

"Don't patronize me, Reilly. There's no way I'm going to let you off the hook. If I ever get out of this, your ass is mine."

"That's my boy. I'll be in touch with you soon."

"Yeah, I'll *bet* you will."

"I promise. And, Professor?"

"Yes?"

"Watch out for a skinny Russian with a pink birthmark on his cheek, reading Emerson."

"Very funny, Reilly."

"That's it, tiger, stay angry—you'll live longer."

Reilly hung up without waiting for Ben's reply.

Ben put the receiver back on the hook and turned

to the others, deep in thought. He looked up when he felt the silence in the room. Everyone was looking at Papandakis, and Papandakis was looking at him.

"We leave in one hour," the old man said.

Chapter Sixteen

The car, a dusty gray Volvo sedan, wound around the curves above a steep gorge while the blue waters of the Mediterranean sparkled several miles away to the left. A hot wind bundled through the windows and all of them were gritty with sweat. Ben sat in back with Pandelis, and Yorgo sat in front with the driver, a tall, stringy man with graying hair and a long nose who kept squinting through the sun-splashed windshield and muttering.

Papandakis' Citroën swept along in front of them. The two cars had passed Heraklion half an hour before, and when Ben asked Pandelis their destination, he had pointed through the windshield and said curtly "Siteia." Aside from stray comments, that had been the extent of the conversation for the past hour. At times Ben thought that Pandelis was dozing, but when he turned to look he saw that his square-faced companion was staring ahead unblinkingly, his chin and jaw thrust forward and his upswept mustache looking as if it had been pasted on his upper lip.

Ben welcomed the silence. He had his own concerns to think about. The farewell with Caroline had been too hurried—he had left too much unsaid. When he told her he was going with Papandakis, she remained calm and assured him that she would be fine, he shouldn't worry, and he should only be concerned about himself. As if to show proof of this, she had marched into the study, asked Papandakis to place a phone call to the Hotel Minos, and, with Ben and Papandakis both listening, told Gail that she and Ben had gone off on their own for a few days. After she hung up the phone, she turned toward both of them and smiled brightly. She was a fine woman. Christ, he felt guilty about involving her in this craziness and then not leveling with her about the threat Papandakis had made.

He looked out the side window at the narrow winding road and the bush-clustered walls of the canyon below, and acknowledged that he was frightened. It was one thing to defend an air base against known enemies and another to invade a country with a handful of men who weren't sure of their allies and who were holding you as a hostage at forfeit of your life if anything went wrong.

The fact that Reilly hadn't called back before they left didn't help matters. Ben wasn't really surprised, but he had to admit that he was disappointed. He still couldn't make out if Reilly was in the employ of the Turks and had lied to him in Ayia Galini. But he kept thinking that if the Turks *were* plotting to get Papandakis, they didn't need to use Reilly's circuitous methods—they had the old man's daughter. On the other hand, if Reilly's story was true, there were only four days left to get hold of the memo, four days before a series of events began that in the end could sweep all life from the planet in forest fires of atomic holocaust and leave the continents charred, wind-scraped wastelands.

Four days. And now he was driving along the side of a canyon toward that final day. In fact he had been approaching it inevitably, when he was flying east from California to Athens, driving west on the bus from Herkalion toward Papandakis' house, stumbling south over the mountains toward Ayia Galini, or wandering nowhere in particular through the ruins at Knossos in his nightmare. Those ruins, he suddenly realized, could be the model of what the entire civilized world might look like shortly. Now, winding through the canyon in the dead afternoon heat, he saw the events of the last few days as part of a gigantic labyrinth in which he had been wandering, unable to find his way. His entire life, in fact, now seemed to be a series of interlocking events, connected but meaningless, that had been leading him to the snuffling form that waited somewhere in the shadows ahead. He could smell the heavy animal odor, hear the bushes thrashing, see the furious, bloodshot eyes. "Jesus!" he muttered.

"What, Teacher?" said Pandelis hoarsely, clearing his throat.

"Nothing," said Ben. "Just thinking."

Pandelis nodded, settled his chin on his chest, and resumed staring through the windshield.

When Ben had discovered that he was not going to ride in the Citroën with Papandakis, he felt slighted. He thought that Papandakis had no use for him any longer and was telling him this by assigning him to ride in the Volvo with Pandelis. But as the preparations for the trip continued it became obvious that Pandelis was just as much a leader of the group as Papandakis. Each had his job: Pandelis with the organization and direction of the men, and Papandakis with planning and liaison. In addition to this Ben had noticed that the men regarded each brother differently. He had seen it in their eyes and in the way they stood when the brothers approached them. They had laughed and swaggered while they were working with Pandelis, following his gruff orders with good-humored complaints as they loaded the cars. But whenever Papandakis, abstracted and aloof, had either walked by or offhandedly addressed them, they had become hesitant and uneasy and had begun nodding their heads and bowing. Even to Ben, who hardly knew the brothers and tended to discount his initial impressions of people, the two old men seemed as different as earth and sky. Pandelis was the vigorous, cursing peasant, and Papandakis the austere, lonely aristocrat forced by the gods to live without solace in this blasted landscape.

So by the time he had climbed into the back of the Volvo, Ben wasn't feeling slighted at all. Besides, Pandelis had been assigned to watch him, and that was as likely a reason as any for Ben to be riding in the same car with him.

Pandelis nudged Ben's arm. "Hey, Teacher," he said, pointing through the window at Ben's side. "Neapolis. Here with English I make big boom of German petrol dump."

They were entering a provincial town baking in the early afternoon heat. It was one o'clock, the beginning of the afternoon nap, and the streets were empty. Men were sitting under awnings in outdoor cafés, sipping drinks at small tables, talking, reading newspapers, or sleeping in their chairs, but other than that there was only the white sunlight glaring off buildings and pavement, except in the tree-shaded park in the center of town.

Ben had not responded to Pandelis' words. He was, in fact, confused by them, and the stocky man, seeing this, elaborated on his statement energetically, as if vigor could make up for lack of vocabulary. "Big resistance on *Kriti. Germanee* come from sky in parachute: bang, bang. I fight in Heraklion, then up on Psiloritis with English. Four, five year. All of us in cave."

Ben nodded. "I'd heard you and your brother were in the Resistance in World War Two."

"*Nai,*" said Pandelis, dipping his head in a curt nod as he continued his story. "I go as runner here to explode the petrol. Big boom. Fire for days. At night sky is orange here all the way to Psiloritis. I see it, and my brother, his eyes, too, waiting for me there."

"You were in the Resistance during the whole war?"

"All years. Stavros, me, old Uncle Kosta. First we take *Australyas* and English over mountains to Moni Preveli, monastery on south coast. They all escape. Then up in mountains, on Psiloritis with Petrakogeorgis. Next start own band on north side below Michael Xylouris' down through Garazon all the way to sea. Very bad. Very dangerous."

Pandelis was totally absorbed in his words. Ben could detect the same intonations he had heard that morning when Pandelis related the story of his hike over Mount Ida to the others, but now there was no humorous edge to his words. Now he was completely serious, as though recalling an experience he was pledged to discuss with the utmost gravity.

"In mountains three years when English steal General Kriepe. You call this—ah—keednap. Stavros help with this, planning how they go over mountain to sea, and I take them partway to boat, changing direction four times when *Germanee* on all paths. Is very bad next. *Germanee* come into village and kill all men, burn houses. At Anoyia worse. Most men there, they know and hide, but *Germanee* come and shoot two hundred—old womans and children. The ones sick, who cannot move from bed, they burn in house, and all animals in stable. For two week they boom houses one by one. I see Anoyia just stones at my feet. Three churches left only, and the town in pieces around them, and the death smell in my nostrils deeper than in my whole life it has ever been. That was town you climb through at night, Anoyia, and I tell you this now so you know these things. The paths your feet went with, others travel, great men and brave, many I love as comrades and bury with these hands." He lifted his hands and stared at them while he was saying this, much as a surgeon raises his scrubbed hands before beginning an operation. There were tears in his eyes.

Ben looked away. *Kali Eleftheria*—isn't that what the guidebook had said? *Good Freedom*. The Cretans knew the meaning of this more than most. After the fall of the Minoans the island was invaded by Mycenaeans, Dorians, and Ionian pirates. Next the Romans and the Byzantines. Followed by the Venetians for four hundred years. And then the Turks for the last two hundred, with a short respite before the arrival of the Germans.

Pandelis sniffed, wiped his nose with the back of his hand, and swept his mustaches to their full extent with thumb and forefinger. Then he said in a low voice, "When very bad things happen like in Anoyia,

we have words we speak, what English call 'saying.'
All *Kritis* know it—"

"*Kali Eleftheria*," Ben muttered.

Pandelis stopped in mid-sentence and looked at Ben for several moments, then nodded. "*Kali Eleftheria*, yes. You know this. I think you know many things maybe. You know how it means in English?"

"Good freedom," said Ben.

"Good freedom. Yes. Good freedom. In Anoyia, the womans, they say it. I hear them say it standing with rock pieces all around. In caves we say it. At night, walking, we say it, and when we meet friends."

Ben nodded.

"You know these things. Is good, Teacher. Is good," said Pandelis, nodding and smiling. He took a pack of Greek cigarettes from his shirt pocket and offered one. They smoked in silence.

The car, now beyond Neapolis, passed a row of low turretlike whitewashed buildings. Pandelis pointed to them with his cigarette. "Windmill," he said. "For making the water spread through the groves."

Ben was relieved. Pandelis' words were saying one thing, but his tone of voice was saying another. It said, *You are all right, Teacher. I have misjudged you.* And as Ben embarked on this tricky little outing it was downright comforting to know that the man who had tried to kill him two nights ago was making overtures of friendship. *Kali Eleftheria.* It had been as simple as that.

Pandelis was looking at him. "Tell me, Teacher. How this thing with Stella is your thing?" he said, as if the question were being asked for the first time. And Ben realized that in a way it was the first time, for now he was asking a companion instead of a stranger.

"Just as I told you," Ben replied, then added, "You love Stella very much, don't you?"

Pandelis hesitated for a moment. "The *Germanee*, they shoot my wife and two daughter. They burn house." He paused, his eyebrows narrowing, and looked through the windshield for a few moments. Then he shrugged. "After war I come live with Stavros and watch Stella grow. Is like my own daughter, Stella. But is Stavros I think of now. Since Eleni she die, only Stella is in his head."

"Eleni?"

"Stavros' wife."

"Oh."

"They love for forty years, then pneumonia. A great sadness in him now. I see it from when we play as boys, but is bigger now, and only Stella is to stop it. He was to be great man. Was Venizelos said this. Venizelos! Father, Stavros, me, with books everywhere on all sides in room where today you stand, and Venizelos say to Stavros, 'One day this *Kriti* you lead!' I hear it with these ears and feel big inside with happiness. Then to England Stavros go to learn."

"How come *you* were never sent to England?"

Pandelis grinned. "Pandelis? England? Father, he try. Is a true thing that Uncle Kosta try. But mountains only is good for me. Friends is. *Raki* is. This English sleep in my head and is not waking on my tongue even now. One great man, Stavros, I say, is enough for this family. Two is asking of God too much."

"And Stavros? Did he become a great man?"

Pandelis stared straight ahead. "He is good when he come from England and afterwards before war, but when *Germanee* burn villages and shoot children, I see in him this sadness beginning. And when Communist fight and Nationalist fight, and Kefalogiannis and Petrakogeorgis fight, he is saying nothing."

"Kefalo what?"

"Kefalogiannis. Petrakogeorgis. Is families. Is those of one name that fight those of other name."

"You mean 'feuds'?"

"Is those of one name fighting those of other name, yes?"

"Yes."

He nodded. "Then Stavros is always staying near house. Communists come. He say, 'No.' Nationalists come, he say, 'No.' Kefalogiannis and Petrakogeorgis come. He say, 'No.' Is staying at house, and Eleni, Stella, Dimitrios, and Nicholas, they grow around him, and the olives grow and the fruit, and the mills and everything owned by us grow."

"Who are Dimitrios and Nicholas?"

"Stavros' sons. Lawyers. In Athens now."

"I don't understand. What exactly happened?"

"Yes. Is best I speak of day in olives. Both Stavros and me walking there. 'Pandeli,' he say, 'this *Kriti* is never change. Turks and Germans, they kill us like dogs. Us, we of one name kill those of other name because they steal sheep or curse our cousins. Is stupid,' he say, and I see tears in his eyes and shaking in his chest. 'I do nothing,' he say. 'Death come for others if I do.' Then he stay here and is not going to Athens when asked."

"Who asked him?"

"Government. Mainland government. He is big man there. But he stay here and work, and is as you see him now."

Pandelis fell silent and once more stared grimly at the road ahead.

Papandakis, the melancholy aristocrat, thought Ben. *Prospero on his island. Childe Harold brooding among the ruins. A fitting Byronic legacy.* And Ben remembered the melancholy spirit which brought Byron at last to Greece. He had come to Greece to die, the world too much with him, too much a disappointment—a world he could no longer deal with. But if Papandakis had become a misanthropic recluse, why had he become a smuggler? He asked Pandelis.

Pandelis smiled. "Is in 1923. Kursad family, these friends we have, are being sent to Turkey, and leave with us much chairs and desks and jewels. Later we are bringing these things to them from boat to boat, and no one is knowing. Then come here Turkey Greeks who leave these same things there, and we get Kursads to bring them here as was done before, boat to boat. Then Turkey Greek is telling this to friends in Athens, who is telling others, and they are coming to us. One is museum man. He ask us get holy things, Greek things, and Islam things for museum. All this was done by us and Kursads. But soon others, Turkey peoples, they find out, they say, 'We do this thing, too, or we tell police what is being done.' Then us and Turkey people is trading these things from boat to boat. War come, this stop. After war, it begins bigger—Greek museum, *Amerikanee*, and peoples, other peoples, with much money."

"I see."

"Is no bad thing. In Turkey these things all fall down and Turkey government leave them down and do nothing. We give money to Turkey people and to our own—fishing people and farming people. Many are poor people with nothing left from war."

Ben nodded. "It sounds like a profitable business."

"Listen to me, Teacher." Pandelis spoke almost angrily, emphasizing his words by jabbing his right forefinger into the palm of his left hand. "After war my brother say, 'Pandeli, we do not need these monies. To those who work with us in war and lose everything, we give it.'"

He sat back and nodded his head triumphantly.

Papandakis the philanthropist, thought Ben. The picture of the old man that emerged from Pandelis' words was of a provincial landowner disappointed by the world who had retreated to his estate and concerned himself with the welfare of his family and neighbors; a person much like a benevolent English country squire in a Fielding novel, who has decided to make what little he controls of the world a better place for those under his jurisdiction. *A shortsighted view of things*, thought Ben, *one in which all sorts of national and international corruptions are allowed to exist which may eventually intrude on the squire's little realm and destroy it.*

Immediately, Ben saw himself in Reilly's hotel room the night before, refusing to help his former student. At least Papandakis had done something. Where was the sense of social responsibility Ben always lectured about to his classes, for God's sake! If Reilly's story were true, millions, possibly billions, of people would be affected by the outcome of this boat ride. The whole thing was ironic, in a way. He had daydreamed many times in the past few years about joining the handful of historians who were eyewitnesses to events of great moment, historians such as Thucydides, Guicciardini, Marx, De Tocqueville, and Finlay. But now, when the opportunity might really have arisen, he only felt concern for his own safety and Caroline's. Inadvertently, he remembered Vlatchkov, and saw him shaking his fist at Reilly as he bawled out that Transcendentalism was a fraud. The drunken Russian. What did he have to do with all this?

Pandelis nudged him and pointed toward the front window. The car had wound around several hairpin turns and was now descending toward a large white town clustered on the edge of a wide blue gulf. "Ayios Nicholas," Pandelis said. "Siteia, one hour." Then he leaned close to Ben. "We have talked good words, Teacher. I do not want things should be bad in Turkey. Stavros tell me, 'You are one will cut his throat if things bad in Turkey.' I do it, Teacher. Is family. Is honor. But I tell you this—I do not want things should be bad in Turkey."

In the distance, beyond the gulf's farther shore, barren pink mountains trembled in the heat.

Chapter Seventeen

Siteia lay on the western shore of a small bay, the last harbor of any size in eastern Crete.

They drove straight toward the port, where a fleet of fishing boats was moored, the masts nodding and dipping in the afternoon sunlight. The Citroën turned into a narrow shaded street a block before the harbor and stopped some distance in front of a battered truck with a dull-green canvas roof. The Volvo followed and drew up behind the black car.

Papandakis stepped out of the Citroën, and with Manoli, the young Cretan with the bulging left eye, ostentatiously guarding his back, he walked briskly to the truck, inserted a hand under the left front fender, straightened up, unlocked the door on the driver's side, and hopped in. He emerged a moment later, holding a wrapped package the size of a shoebox, and quickly stepped to the rear of the truck. His movements were so light and graceful that, seeing him from a distance, one would have thought him a much younger man.

Meanwhile Pandelis had jumped from the Volvo and with his right hand hooked inside his sash was slowly strolling down the street of squat, crumbling houses, looking in all directions, every once in a while turning around and walking backwards for a few steps, so that he seemed to be spinning down the sidewalk in slow motion like a teetering barrel.

Leaving the long-nosed driver with Ben, Yorgo was performing a similar routine on the opposite side of the street, his lazy, whale's smile looking more dangerous than ever.

Everyone had moved so suddenly and with such precision that Ben knew they were following a set procedure each had performed many times before. Ben realized that he had underestimated Papandakis and his men. It was obvious that they were a professional unit and had been doing things like this for years—in the case of Papandakis and Pandelis, come to think of it, since they were teenagers, maybe fifty years ago.

Papandakis had reemerged from the rear of the truck, still carrying the shoebox. He nodded to Manoli and returned to the Citroën. Manoli strode over to the back of the truck and a moment later trudged back to the Citroën carrying a three-foot-square wooden crate on his shoulder, which he loaded into the trunk. Then he and Pavlo—the sad-faced, dreamy-eyed one who had so lackadaisically guarded the back yard the night Ben had escaped—swaggered back to the truck together.

Meanwhile, Pandelis and Yorgo, their reconnaissance completed, had gone to the rear of the truck and were now bending over a coffin-sized wooden crate with rope handles at both ends. All four men made two trips, hauling four casket-sized crates over to the Volvo and the Citroën. Then, flushed and breathing heavily, they got back in their cars and drove to the docks.

The whole episode had taken two and a half minutes. It was now two-thirty. They were ahead of schedule.

The period the Greeks allot for an afternoon nap was not yet over, and the tree-fringed harbor, with its castle and its outdoor cafés and shops broiling in the sun, was almost deserted.

The Cretans unloaded the crates and the other supplies they had packed at the house onto a forty-foot white fishing boat that was banded below the gunwales with broad swathes of maroon and yellow enamel. Ben, feeling like a prisoner for the first time, was brought on board after the unpacking was finished.

Papandakis and Pandelis had disappeared immediately into the wheelhouse with the captain, a tall, elderly man with a bristly face. They emerged on deck several minutes later; Pandelis stopped beside Ben while Papandakis and the captain strode onto the dock, continuing to talk solemnly, and walked over to the cars. Papandakis said something to both drivers and then, to Ben's surprise, the cars drove off.

Papandakis returned to the captain and together they strolled down the dock and boarded another white fishing boat, this one painted with lines of blue and green. Both men vanished into the wheelhouse.

Pandelis tapped Ben on the shoulder. "Is lucky, Teacher. Good day. No *meltemia* wind. Pandelis like ocean, but stomach, it does not."

Pandelis' words seemed friendly enough, but he was standing so close to Ben, practically hovering over him, that Ben was positive Papandakis had told his brother to guard him closely. Now Pandelis and Ben stood together on the deck of the fishing boat, sweating in the sultry air, staring down the dock, everything around them silent except for the bantering of the young Cretans behind them and the slow slapping of the sea against the hull.

Papandakis and the captain reappeared on the deck of the other boat with two men. One was dressed like the captain. He stayed behind and waved, calling "*Adio!*" and then as the three walked back up the dock, "*Kalo taxidhi! Kali tihi!*" The other man was tall and bony and was dressed in white slacks and a short-sleeved white shirt with a collar. His silver hair, slicked back against his skull, seemed almost luminous against his deeply tanned face. As he came closer his long nose and chin made Ben think of the coyote in the Road-runner cartoons he used to watch with his kids on Saturday morning TV.

"Is Jeem! Is Jeem!" shouted Pandelis, and when Ben turned toward him, he saw that Pandelis was grinning and that his face had once again lit up like a jack-o'-lantern beneath his mustache. "Jeem!" Pandelis called, and the next moment the two men were standing on the gangplank hugging and kissing each other on both cheeks, slapping one another's faces and shouting insults.

Papandakis was standing stony-faced behind them, and during a lull in the greetings he said, "And this man is Professor Ames, Jim. Professor, may I present an old friend and associate, Jim Cooper."

Ben nodded and held out his hand. Cooper grabbed it and seemed to be lunging forward, as if he were pulling himself onto the boat by holding on to Ben's hand. But there was no strain on Ben's arm, and he realized that Cooper's lunging was an illusion projected by the man's lean, stoop-shouldered frame.

They shook hands, Cooper still smiling from his meeting with Pandelis, and Ben noticed a pouched puffiness on either side of the man's upper lips, as if two enormous eyeteeth were housed beneath them, and he also saw that Cooper's metallic gray eyes weren't smiling at all.

"Pleased to meet you, sport," Cooper said.

"English?" asked Ben, nodding.

"Aussie, sport, Aussie." He was still smiling, but his eyes were staring expressionlessly into Ben's. Fleshy knobs at the end of his nose and chin blunted the sharpness of his features, but he sure as hell had a lean and hungry look.

By now the three young Cretans were casting off the lines, and the boat's motor started with a roar. In a few minutes they were clear of the harbor.

Most of the boat was open deck, and to get out of the sun, they had crowded into the wheelhouse, which was outfitted with battered, shoe-brown benches along the sides and a long wooden table bolted to the floor in the center. The tabletop was made of bleached gray planks that had once been the same brown as the benches but now had only a few scaling brown slivers adhering to their surfaces. The engine throbbed below the floor, shaking the entire boat, and the captain, his back to his passengers, was shifting the wheel from side to side and staring out the front window.

Ben counted eight people in the wheelhouse, not including himself. Besides the captain and his mate, there was Papandakis, Pandelis, Cooper, Yorgo, Manoli and Pavlo.

"Time to break open the CARE parcels," said

Cooper, after they had all smoked a cigarette in silence and looked out at the glaring, sun-white deck where the crates were stacked.

The sky was light blue above them and the sea was dark, almost indigo, below. The hull cut through the blue water and the water opened on either side of it with the sound and look of crumpled cellophane. Ben could hear the sound above the engines as he and the others went out on deck as two good-sized islets trailed away to port.

Yorgo and Manoli took crowbars and opened the small square crate with a groaning shriek of nails. There were clothes inside—rumpled, shapeless, gray and black suit jackets and trousers, short-billed gray cloth caps, and scuffed shoes.

"What's this? What's this? A bloody costume party?" said Cooper. He was smiling and the Cretans were smiling with him. He lifted a huge charcoal-colored jacket from the crate and held it in front of his long, emaciated chest, then tried it on. It was as big as an overcoat on him. "Won't pass for a blasted Turk in this," he said as the others laughed, Pandelis loudest of all.

"I think your Mr. Reilly is underestimating us, Professor," said Papandakis with an ironic smile. "We have already provided ourselves with the appropriate clothing."

Ben nodded, realizing that he had forgotten to give Reilly's message about the clothes to Papandakis, and more impressed with the old man's organization with each new disclosure. Since they had arrived in Siteia Papandakis had become a different person—singleminded, efficient, and as limber as an athlete. It hadn't even occurred to Ben that they would need to disguise themselves as Turks. The whole episode was beginning to seem like a Hollywood commando raid.

Yorgo and Manoli, now wearing their black bandannas rolled into headbands, were busily wedging open one of the long crates. It contained a large number of grenades set like ribbed khaki eggs in a nest of sawdust.

Yorgo, the toothy smile still on his face, removed a grenade, blew the dust off it, and suddenly shouting *"Pavlo!"* tossed it into the air. Pavlo, his usually perplexed expression breaking into a grin, caught the grenade and threw it to Manoli. A brisk game of catch ensued, the three young men giggling and every so often wrenching back their heads and guffawing at a near miss, Manoli's froglike eye seeming to gaze everywhere around the deck except at the approaching grenade.

"A stomatate! Me bezes mufta, Vlakes!" yelled Pandelis before the game was half a minute old, and the Cretans, still chortling, immediately stopped and began to search for other grenades in the crate. They blew off the sawdust and packed them in the gray wool knapsacks that Cooper had brought from the wheelhouse.

A bare, rugged gray promontory had just slid away behind them to starboard. "There it goes now," said Cooper, dropping several more knapsacks near the crate and staring back at the promontory. "Akro Sidheros, old Cape of Iron. That's the last we'll see of Crete for a bit."

The others were staring at it, too. All of them were silent. The young Cretans had even stopped smiling. Then Pandelis slapped his hands together, exclaimed something in Greek which made the Cretans snort with laughter, and they all set to work as vigorously as before in the searing sunlight.

Ben felt out of place. He wanted to join the others in their preparations, in their camaraderie, but that was clearly not his role. So he strolled around the deck, watched the others go about their tasks, and attempted to hide his awkwardness with a nod and a butterfly smile when anyone happened to look at him.

Pandelis opened another crate. He grunted and, with everyone watching, reached in and lifted out a machine-gun. He shook it free of sawdust and turned it from end to end and looked it up and down, as if he were either inspecting it or wondering exactly what to do with it.

"Grease gun," said Ben.

Pandelis looked at him.

"Grease gun," Ben repeated. "Loads with a clip. Very accurate at short range."

Pandelis continued to stare at him.

"We used it in the Air Force," Ben continued.

"Grease gun?" grinned Cooper. "Looks more like a bloody bicycle-pump to me, with a nozzle stuck out of one end and a bent wire clothes-hanger hooked on the other."

Ben smiled at the description. Many times he had looked ironically at the hollow cylinder with the short barrel on one end and the skeletal steel stock on the other. Cooper's description was tellingly accurate, but Ben wasn't going to let the Australian get away with his raillery.

Rolling with the boat, he made his way over to Pandelis and took the weapon from him, turning it upside down.

"Clip goes in here, in front of the trigger housing,"

he said. "Fifteen bullets, if I remember right. Squeeze off a burst or one at a time."

Everyone was watching Ben and he felt good to be able to join the group, even if in so marginal a way.

"The clips are probably in the other crate," he said, looking down at the even rows of grease guns, their trigger guards facing up, that glinted black and heavy from the sawdust in the crate at his feet.

Cooper and Pandelis opened another crate. This one contained the clips. The black rectangles, each already loaded with its complement of bullets, resembled elongated women's compacts, and like the other weapons had been packed in sawdust. Ben reached down and grabbed one, shook it clean, and jammed it into the belly of the grease gun with a click. The movement was as quick and efficient as he had hoped it would be, although he hadn't handled a weapon in more than twenty years.

Pandelis jumped back, his eyes wide. Cooper had gone into a crablike crouch next to him, and Ben, as surprised at their reactions as they seemed to be at his, could hear the intake of breath on all sides. The silence that followed it was relieved only by the pounding of the engine and the slapping of the water before it fell away on both sides of the boat.

Suddenly, as if watching it all from a great height, Ben could see himself standing on the deck with the grease gun, the six men paralyzed around him, and the blue day, polished with sunlight, surrounding them all. Did they really think he was going to use that gun on them, or yell to the captain to turn the boat around or else? The idea hadn't even occurred to him. He had taken the weapon from Pandelis simply because he wanted to take part, to be of some use. Even now, that was all he wanted.

He turned toward the stern of the boat and pulled the trigger, loosing a burst of bullets which kicked up the water like giant raindrop spouts in the wake behind them. Even over the engine noise the loud metallic rattle stopped his ears and deafened him momentarily. Next, he tried to squeeze off one, two, three blasts in some sort of pattern so the others would understand what he was doing. But his finger control was slightly heavy after all those years, and this maneuver was not as smooth as he had hoped.

He emptied the entire clip. The others stood as rigid and still as statues while Ben released the spent clip and dropped it on the deck with a clatter, grabbed another clip from the crate, and slapped it into the grease gun. He pointed the muzzle toward the water and handed the weapon to Pandelis. "Try it," he said.

Pandelis' eyes were still wide open. But when his fingers felt the warm metal of the gun, they clamped around it and his face broke into a grin.

Ben could hear the others exhale, and their bodies relaxed as if he had released them from a spell. He turned. Everyone was smiling, except Papandakis, whose face showed more curiosity than relief.

Pandelis loosed a stream of bullets into the boat's wake and snorted with satisfaction. "*Oopah!*" he shouted.

Cooper was standing behind him, his silver head almost topheavy on the long stem of his suntanned body. He was nodding and grinning. Ben could see his teeth and, as he had suspected, they *were* long and fanglike under the pouched upper lip. "You gave us a start there, sport. That you did," he said. "I just about shat myself."

Behind him the three young Cretans were convulsed with throaty laughter, yelling comments at Pandelis, who grunted and growled over his shoulder at them in mock anger. In a few seconds he had emptied the clip and stood swaying with the pitch of the boat, fondling the grease gun and looking at it with affectionate astonishment as he snapped the bolt back and forth.

"How about the rest of you?" asked Ben. He bent over the crate and handed out the weapons to the others. With much shoving and pushing they lined up at the starboard rail. He gave them each a clip, demonstrated how to insert it, and while they were familiarizing themselves with that maneuver he picked up the empty crate and heaved it over the side. It whirled away astern, spinning heavily, then slowed, bobbing in the wake like a tired swimmer with one shoulder lifted out of the water.

"Fire!" called Ben, and the whole episode reached a thunderous crescendo in the explosion of sound that followed. Seven machine guns roaring concussively, and twenty yards behind the boat, slipping astern, the crate began to shake and jig and split and shatter into a shower of splinters and wood chips and water spouts, leaving an undulant trail of scattered wood bits on the dark water.

Everyone on deck was elated. They laughed and hooted, shouting war whoops. Pandelis clapped Ben on the shoulder, then threw his head back and half-growled, half-shouted a laugh from somewhere deep in his chest. The whole group was so exhilarated by the power they had released that Ben expected them to break into a dance at any moment. He knew what they were feeling. He was feeling it himself.

Only Papandakis, who had responded stiffly throughout the proceedings, horseplay, was not smiling. He was looking down at his grease gun as if it were a wayward child. His silent, distant manner soon caught the others' attention. Their laughter began to falter, and soon they broke up into groups of two and three, and silently finished unloading the crates, each man with his grease gun at his side.

Chapter Eighteen

Ben couldn't believe how quickly the mood on board had changed. He stared at Papandakis, more bewildered by his abstracted manner and expression than surprised by it. He turned. Cooper was looking at him, and with a nod he pointed to the other side of the boat. Ben walked over, and he and Cooper leaned on the rail looking out at the sun-glazed water.

"The old man's got a hell of a lot on his mind, he has," said Cooper absently, still looking at the water. "You know, sport, Stella's all he's got, now Eleni's gone."

"I know," said Ben. "Pandelis told me."

Cooper turned to him, smiling. "Been talking to him, have you? Mad as a bull, but a good old sod, that one. Saved my bones in '41, you know. You can trust whatever he says."

"That's what I'm afraid of," Ben exclaimed, remembering Pandelis' friendly but grim promise as they sat in the back of the Volvo.

"How's that? Oh, right. The old man told me. If you're clean, though, it's no worries."

"It's a little more complicated than that. A lot of things can happen that could make me look guilty as hell. And Papandakis won't listen."

"He's always been a queer one, he has. When Pandelis brought me in and introduced him as his brother, I nearly crapped myself. He was a bit merrier then, but even just standing about he seemed a general or a duke lording it over the mountainside. You know, always on parade. It's not like he's a dandy or anything —he's never at ease, is all. And when I got to know him, I see he's got worries bigger than mine or his brother's —or even yours. That's the only way a body can describe it, I think. He's seeing grander things than you or me in the simplest happenings. Like the shooting just before. He saw more than wood skipping about out there, and all the others saw it, too, through him. The war, dead relatives, tonight's danger. See? That's why those blokes love him, and why I do. Don't worry, he didn't cop your show."

"What show?"

"The bloody bit with the tommies," grinned Cooper. "That play won them, I'd say. Could have turned the blasted thing on all of us. It was a stupid thing to let you do, take that gun and load it and all. But you waltzed us out of it with that show, handing Pandy the tommy and lining us up like you did. Saved the others' faces, so to speak—and these *Kritis* won't forget that soon, if I know them."

Cooper was looking at the sea again, leaning on the rail.

Ben shook his head and smiled. For all his raucous humor, the Australian was no fool. He had seen Ben's intentions clearer than Ben had. Ben looked at Cooper. "Where you from in Australia?" he asked.

"Perth," said Cooper, turning his face toward him. "Know it?"

Ben shook his head.

"On the west coast. But I've lived in Melbourne and Sydney at different times, working one job or another."

"What do you do?"

Cooper turned completely toward him, grinning. "Favors for friends, sport. Favors for friends." And the way he said it let Ben know he should change the subject.

"What are you doing in Crete?" Ben asked, realizing as he said it that this, too, might be the wrong question, yet not really caring if it was.

But Cooper answered without hesitation. "Live here. Have since '56. Couldn't make a go of it down under anymore. Tried, you know. Drove a truck from Melbourne to Sydney, then worked outback at various jobs, from drover to housepainter. Wife, two kids—I still send them a little something monthly—but it wouldn't wash. When I got back there in '45, these bones were too full. *Kriti* sunlight had got into my blood, I guess, or the killing had. I'd seen too much of both." He paused, took a pack of cigarettes from his shirt pocket, offered one to Ben, then lit them. "Old man tells me you're a history professor. That true?"

Ben nodded.

"Know anything about the war—the last one?"

"A fair amount, but not what happened here."

"It was a bloody mess. The Jerries in battle were one thing, but what they did in the villages, to the people—there's no way a body could stomach it. That's what did it for me, sport, I'm sure of it."

"Pandelis told me about Anoyia on the way to Siteia."

"That was one place ripped me for sure, it did. And before that the nine days when Jerry invaded in '41. Wasn't expecting that. No one was. Not that way—come at us with bloody parachutes and drove us south into the mountains. I was with the Australian Nineteenth Brigade, Two-Seven Battalion. Good bunch of blokes, hellraisers all—could drink or laugh any man under the table. Even in the end they was laughing, faces all grimed, marching on the road from Vrises over the mountains. Marching? More like wandering, it was, staggering, some of the blokes crawling.

"There were thousands of us chaps—all in the same condition, mind you. Sun like a furnace, no water, and the Stukas swooping out of the glare with guns blazing. All day you'd hear, 'Take cover! Take cover!' coming down the line. It was like some bloody game, except everyone's throat was sandpaper and everyone's eyes was hollow, and after the Stukas chattered by, a lot would be dead. Wreckage was all over the road, with blackened bodies half out of the vehicles, heads down and arms falling past the heads. And everyone passing by, not looking, just clinking and clanging over the bends, the ravines all dusty bushes now and getting steeper.

"Stuka got a mate in the leg. Name of Dyson. Couldn't walk. Dragged him with me while he worked the tourniquet, and we went on like that into the evening, winding up, headed over the mountains for Sphakia, where a mess of Royal Navy boats was to take us all off to Egypt.

"The mountain peaks was quartz-white in the moonlight, and then, cutting through the sweat and machine-oil and the stink of Dyson's rotting leg, there was wild thyme from somewhere, and lavender. Back in Melbourne afterward, I'd be sitting home or steering the truck, and that smell would rise up from nowhere and I'd hold my breath and start shaking. . . ."

He paused and tossed the cigarette into the passing water. "Sky was orange behind us. Someone said Jerry had burned Vrises. Think Dyson slept a bit. Don't know. By midnight the moon was down and you could hardly see the stars. We all lurched about like dying men. No order. Exhausted. Some fell on the road and slept. Dyson and me kept on till we came to a pass the bloody engineers had blown, the bastards. Brought rock down on the only road, with most of us on the wrong side. Had to leave Dyson. Lots of other wounded left, too. And never saw the poor bloke again.

"Scrambled on rock face next, me and hundreds more. On hands and knees mostly, ripping my palms, so's I could regain the road on the other side. Two hours it took me. Afterwards I kept climbing on the road, staggering about, the peaks always ahead, darker than the sky and seeming to pack closer together, and it getting colder all the while.

"Then, just before dawn, I came round a bend and the peaks moved back. Below was a valley—trees and fields and running streams, birds already singing, and a breeze smelling of sage and rosemary blowing right up at me. Most beautiful place I'd ever seen. Didn't know it then, was Askifou plain, and when I go up there even now, I remember that night, and, you know, sport, it's still the most beautiful place. I ran down into it, drank from a stream, collapsed under an olive tree, and slept.

"It was all downhill from there. Got to the coast by noon. Kept out of the bloody heat a mile out of Sphakia in Komitadhes Ravine. There were thousands of us in it, and more coming in all the time. Even renamed it Rhododendron Valley. All shaded rock walls, it was, where only a finger of sun could reach.

"Stayed there three days. No food now. Supplies not coming in. At evening ships came in to Sphakia and took us off by the thousands. But after the fourth night we heard there'd be no more. Still thousands of us there. Just left, we was, the Admiralty blokes afraid they'd lose their blasted ships. Can't blame them, though. But that left us to pack it in or go farther east. Rumor started there'd be ships at a place called Roumeli. I set out along the coast with one or two others. We were few and far between, we was. Most stayed at Komitadhes and packed it in. Not me. If I got that far, I figured, I'd bloody well go on.

"All the way people in the villages helped us, the most miserable sods I'd ever seen, yet they all would part with bread, cheese, anything, with a smile and a 'bless you.' So when no boats came to Roumeli, I decided I'd stay. Just wandered in rags through the hills for a few weeks till Pandelis found me and brought me in."

"So you were in the Resistance, too."

"The duration, sport, the duration. Mostly it was mapping and spotting troop concentrations and materiel. You didn't want to attack Jerry, because he'd take reprisals on the villages. Ten lives for every German. See? Villagers would feed us and we'd move about at night and enlist this *Kriti* or that.

"Lived all the time high up in caves and dressed as Cretan as you please—all rags, black kerchiefs on our heads, and strips of old tires on our boot soles. Four years of rain, snow, bone chill, sun, lice, and filth.

Sounds bloody awful. But it was the best time I ever had. Think it was for them, too," he said, jerking his thumb over his shoulder at Pandelis and Papandakis. "The comradeship, the bloody adventure of it. You know—the corking good health a body feels living in the mountains and doing a job he thinks is doing some good in the world. We were all young then, we were, and we knew who the enemy was. All of our lives depended on the others. Even slept with arms around each another for warmth, all of us close as brothers.

"Well, after I was demobbed, there was no way I was going back to truck driving and later just sitting in front of the telly. I tried, sport, I really did. Ten years. Got into some nefarious things to keep the blood up, but in the end came back here. Been doing one job or another since, a lot for the old man, but bringing out other things from Turkey myself and trading on my own all over the Mediterranean—drugs, money, Islamic antiques, what have you. Sometimes a courier, sometimes a middleman. Jack of all trades, so to speak."

He fell silent, looking out at the early evening sea. Cooper's story had made Ben uneasy, although he couldn't figure out why. He stared at the water for a few moments, but his uneasiness persisted, and now the silence was making him nervous as well. "Pandelis thinks that the war ruined his brother," he said, continuing to stare at the water.

"The war and the civil stuff after that, yes," the Australian said, still gazing beyond the boat. "He was different there. Saw it for what it was, clearer than any of us. Even then. The senseless murders, the butchery. It was an endless round to him that he'd seen going on through all history. Him and me have talked about it. Old man feels he's in a cage. Understand that? He's trapped here. Knowing what's going to happen and can't do a blasted thing about it. Cursed, you might say. So each moment the old boy feels helpless, imprisoned in his life. . . . We all do."

They stood silently, looking at the water.

"And now you come along, sport, and tell him the only thing he's got left is rotting in a Turkish jail."

Ben remembered the way Papandakis had looked down at the grease gun after the barrage had shattered the crate.

Cooper looked at his watch, then pointed astern to port. "That tiny egg-shaped rock we passed twenty minutes ago was Avga. Egg Rock to you." He straightened, turned, and pointed to starboard, past where Papandakis was standing. "Stakida. Beyond that, Karpathos, under those blasted clouds." He was pointing to an islet silhouetted against a steep mountainous island that hovered like a tan phantom ship on the southeastern horizon. Then he tapped his watch. "Six P.M., sport. Right on time. Hear those engines below? That's a smuggler's special. We'll do the hundred twenty miles in ten hours total."

"I'm impressed. You seem to know these waters like your back yard."

Cooper smiled. "A body has to in my business." He tapped his watch again, shoved himself away from the rail, and started toward the wheelhouse. Then he turned back. "The old man told me that story of yours, about the memo and all. That true?"

"That's what the man told me."

"Any chances it's real?"

Ben shrugged. "Only time will tell."

"If it is, it makes what I've just told you small crackers, right?"

Ben didn't answer, hearing the change in Cooper's voice.

"Well, it don't, sport. It don't at all."

"Never said it did, friend," replied Ben, "never said it did. But if Reilly's story is true—"

Cooper nodded. "Right! And you, sport, you on the square?"

Ben didn't answer again.

"Only time will tell there, too, right?" He flashed a smile and strode over to the wheelhouse, disappearing into its shadows.

The others had finished loading the weapons into the knapsacks and were crouched in the wheelhouse, watching the evening sun turn the water into a burning honey. Only Papandakis was still on deck. He was looking toward Karpathos rocking in the distance, standing in the same spot he had been before Cooper had motioned Ben to the other side of the boat. He seemed a lonelier figure than ever, with his back straight and unbending and the sun-glazed water beyond him already inky black on the underside of the swells.

Ben turned away and stared at the black tracks the sun was making in the water on his side of the boat. Although Cooper was gone, Ben's uneasiness had persisted, but now he knew what was disturbing him. As he had listened to Cooper's story he had the crazy idea that not only was his trek over the mountains similar to Cooper's, but that his life in some strange way paralleled the Australian's. He now realized that Cooper was what he could have become after Korea, if he hadn't developed his interest in history. This thought was kept in bounds by the obvious differences between them—any way he looked at it, he was no Cooper. But how was he different? And in reality were the differences—and this was what kept nagging at him—only superficial?

He turned away from the rail. Papandakis was still standing on the opposite side of the boat with his back to him, facing away from the last of the day's sun.

For a man who was reluctant to disturb the movement of things for fear he would cause unintentional harm to others, Papandakis' life had taken an ironic turn—first the war and now the smuggling operation. It sounded harmless enough from the way Pandelis talked about it, but the smuggling had finally brought the old man to embark on this raid to rescue his daughter, which might in the process destroy both her and the others who were closest to him. What had the old man been thinking about, standing out here for so long? His daughter? His wife? The insanity of this whole venture?

Ben thought of Papandakis alone, except for Stella—Pandelis alone, his wife and daughters shot by the Germans, Cooper alone, his wife and children far away in another life on a dusty continent. He realized that he was alone in the same way, and he was reminded of something else, something he had not come to terms with and had avoided thinking about for months—his daughters. Not only were they far away, but every time he had seen them on the court-appointed weekends, they seemed to be more estranged from him, living lives which had less and less to do with his—lives that he now suddenly envisioned coming to an end under toppling buildings. California and the children seemed hopelessly lost to him. Everything seemed lost. And even as Julia's face appeared in his mind at the repetition of the word, he felt a sense of helplessness expanding inside him that he couldn't control.

"Hey, sport! Grub!" called Cooper.

Ben turned toward the Australian's voice and started across the deck, wondering how Cooper's children reacted to him when he saw them, and if they, too, lived in a city where buildings would come crashing down on them in the near future.

It was stuffy inside the wheelhouse. The three young men had laid out a meal on the gray table, and they were still tossing plates and glasses to each other from three cartons Ben had seen them load into the cars at Papandakis' house. Pandelis and Cooper were already eating, and within a few minutes the younger men joined them, all except dreamy-eyed Pavlo, who smiled bashfully at Ben, handed him a plate, and motioned for him to help himself.

Ben was touched. He took the plate and smiled back. Pavlo stood in front of him, nodding and gesturing toward the food, so shy, so boyishly awkward that Ben was struck by how young he was, much younger than Ben had first thought—no more than twenty, maybe twenty-one. Ben was reminded of his daughters once again. His jaw tightened.

Pavlo nodded once more, then filled a plate for himself and joined his friends. All three joked and roughhoused, taking care not to disturb Cooper and Pandelis, who were speaking together in low tones.

Ben stood with the empty plate in his hand, lost in his thoughts. The distance to the other side of the cabin where the five men sat seemed immense, impassable.

By the time Papandakis entered the wheelhouse several minutes later, Ben felt hopelessly isolated, totally alone.

Chapter Nineteen

Everyone was friendly with Ben during supper, and this had somewhat revived his spirits. There was, in fact, much merriment during the meal, led by the three young Cretans. They continued to tease Pandelis by singing songs that mockingly echoed his name, while Yorgo, with a great flare for mimicry, imitated Pandelis' swagger and appeared to act out some of the more celebrated episodes of his past history. Pandelis responded with mock anger—snorting through his huge mustache or growling beneath it, while fixing each of his tormentors with a fierce, glittering eye. It was obvious that the young men regarded him with affectionate respect and that he thought of them with the same indulgence that allows a lion to tolerate the irreverent playfulness of his cubs.

After Ben had taken some food, Pandelis had made room for him on the bench between Cooper and himself and had continued to spear morsels of cheese or chicken with the long Cretan dagger he kept in his sash. At times Ben could hear the blade cracking an olive pit as Pandelis thrust the knife into the olive bowl. Pandelis ate heartily, his eyes flashing, not somber or brooding as he had been the night of Ben's first supper with him. In fact all of them were extremely animated, as though the prospect of this new adventure had filled them with raucous enthusiasm and large appetites. Even Papandakis was cordial during the meal, and nodded and smiled benevolently at the goings-on around him.

The food had already been reduced to a pile of bones and pits when Papandakis said a few words in Greek to the company. Immediately the laughter ceased and everyone began clearing the table. The remains of the supper went the way of the crates—over the side.

Then Papandakis spread a chart of the Turkish coastline on the table, and with everyone gathered around him in the deepening shadows he outlined his plan. He spoke in Greek, and Cooper translated for Ben.

"The old boy says we'll skirt the east coast of Kos, change vessels, and enter Turkey dead on at Bodrum. That will be about one A.M."

"Why change boats?"

"To a Turkish one, sport. The Turkish coastguard don't look kindly on strange boats flying Greek flags. Trigger-happy as well, they are. The old man's had one of his Turks provide the other boat."

Cooper was silent for a few minutes, listening to Papandakis. The others greeted Papandakis' next words with tongue-clicks, elbowing, and grinning nods, and Cooper was smiling, too, as he turned back to Ben. "Says this same bloke got him the Turkish boat expects a payment of fifty thousand dollars at Bodrum and a courteous good-day. I know him—fat pig name of Yussuf—wouldn't trust him around his own mother's knickers. Wanted payment through a courier, but the old man insisted he'd only pay such a sum to the man himself. And here's why"—Cooper paused and grinned—"we're going to snatch him, says the old man. Clean as that, and hold him hostage till we finish. If anything goes wrong, we'll cut the bugger's throat—but you know about that side of the old boy's planning, don't you, sport?"

Cooper listened to Papandakis again, then turned back to Ben. "We'll take a truck to Söke. It's about a hundred fifty meters north of Bodrum, say ninety miles. Over those roads, about three and a half to four hours, I'd say. Be there between four thirty and five A.M. A long way, but it's quicker than by boat and a perfect diversion. Another bloke will be waiting in Söke with his hand out. This one takes care of the jail. Big police official, he is. I know the bastard well. He wanted a courier to pick up his fifty thousand, too. We'll snatch him along with Yussuf, get the lot from jail, and dash for the coast."

"But you just said it was more than three hours from Söke to Bodrum," said Ben. "And it'll be light by then. They'll have us cold, if they want us."

Papandakis had finished speaking and raised himself from the map. The other men had been grinning, and at his last words they clapped each other on the back and began shouting, *"Bravo!" "Efia!" "Bravo!"*

Cooper was smiling too. His eyes sparkled and he couldn't suppress a grin. "We ain't going back to Bodrum, sport. We're going out another way that the Turks don't know about. Part of the diversion. He's made arrangements with another party, a cousin who lives in Chios—a good sort, though he's never cracked a smile in his life—with the fastest smuggler's special in the Aegean."

"But he told Reilly he was going out through Bodrum," said Ben, confused.

"Did he now?" said Cooper, nodding his head and laughing with the others. "Well, what do you know? You know, sport, we're liable to make it out of this bloody party yet." He laughed loudly now at Ben's confusion. "Oh, by the by, you're going in with Pandelis and him and young Yorgo there," he added, pointing to Yorgo, who was laughing and roughhousing with Manoli.

"Going where?" asked Ben.

"The jail, sport, the jail. Wants you in the thick of it should everything not be on the up and up."

"You're kidding," said Ben, aware of a slight tremor in his stomach, although he wasn't really surprised by Papandakis' decision and knew that he would do the same thing if he were in his position.

"Don't worry, sport. You'll be fine."

"Yeah . . ." began Ben, his voice trailing off in a series of nods. Pandelis would be right alongside him. He remembered the dagger cracking the olive pits. "Where are *you* going to be?" he asked Cooper.

"I'll be with Yussuf and the others, holding the truck in front, with a shiv at the driver's throat."

Ben didn't say anything. He had just realized that although everyone was laughing and clapping each other on the back, this raid wasn't the game he had been thinking of when he'd fired the grease gun into the boat's wake that afternoon. He began to experience the same knotting in his bowels he used to get in Korea, just before he went out on a reconnaissance mission with his squad. He tried to swagger it off. "Someone could get killed," he quipped.

Cooper snickered, turned, called to the others for

quiet, and translated Ben's words to them. Immediately all of them, except Papandakis, who looked on impassively, began laughing uproariously, rolling over each other and holding their sides until the tears spilled down their cheeks. "Holy Jesus!" muttered Ben.

The sun sank behind them, glazing the swells on the black water with red and yellow streaks. Then it was dark, and several hours later a lopsided moon rose low in the east, the direction they were heading, and laid a shimmering silver track on the water that seemed to be pulling them forward.

The darkness and the night chill subdued the men's good humor. They sat in the shadowy wheelhouse, their faces lit only by the green lights from the instrument panel, whispering to each other or silently intent on their individual thoughts. The engine pounded below. Just after the moon rose, Cooper pointed to a light at starboard and said, "Gaidharos. We're off the north end of Tilos, sport." Then he checked his watch and lapsed into silence.

The moon polished the sea, and the boat seemed to be moving across a huge hammered-silver dish.

At eleven Ben saw white lights blinking on a large shadow that rode heavily in the water before the boat. "What's that?" he asked Cooper.

"Nisiros. East side," Cooper replied and checked his watch again. "Be in Kos by twelve or twelve thirty."

Papandakis left the wheelhouse a few minutes later and walked over to the same spot at the rail where he had stood that afternoon.

Ben followed him.

The night was still clear, but the moon, still low,

although now off to starboard, had lit up the sky with a soft, smoky luster which almost seemed like an overcast, and the sea shifted and rolled about the boat, heavy, flat, and luminous.

Papandakis was looking at the moon.

"Excuse me, sir," said Ben.

Papandakis turned. "Yes, Professor?"

"I'd like to talk to you, if I could."

Papandakis nodded, eyes and lips in shadow, moonlight spilling through his hair.

"Cooper told me that you weren't coming back through Bodrum. Well, sir, you told me to tell Reilly that Bodrum would be our exit route."

"Yes. That is exactly the reason why we are going in another direction, Professor."

"Are you aware that Reilly intends to line the road with his agents so nothing can go wrong?"

"Professor, my single concern is the success of this operation. To me that means the safety of all those involved in it. You stated this morning that you were not sure of Mr. Reilly's motives, and obviously I am less sure than you are."

Ben couldn't argue with that. He stood there, groping for the words, trying to find a phrase that would allow him to withdraw gracefully. The conversation had been briefer than he had expected. He wanted to say more to the old man. *Why?* To reassure him of his good faith? To commune with his Byronic melancholy? *Ben, you're being a sentimental ass. Just shut up and tramp back into the wheelhouse.*

But it was Papandakis who spoke first, spoke in a soft, almost wistful voice, looking out over the water at the moon once more, his back to Ben and his hands clasped behind him. "Your display with the machine guns this afternoon was impressive, Professor. Accept my apologies in advance, if you are the innocent party you profess to be. Unfortunately, I will have to continue with my precautions. After we disembark from the boat, therefore, consider yourself my hostage and please act accordingly."

"I understand," said Ben. "I understand, but I don't like it. You're putting me in a precarious position. I could be caught between both sides with no way to protect myself if trouble broke out."

"I am glad we understand each other, Professor."

"All I understand is the reason you're making this trip."

"Do you?"

"Yes. I talked with Pandelis and Cooper today, sir, and they told me—"

"Oh. Now I am the one who understands. The two blind men have told the deaf man what they saw."

The insult stung, but Ben didn't reply. They stood silently for a few moments. Then Papandakis turned toward him, his face once more in shadow, and said, "Forgive my sarcasm, Professor. I have actually been looking forward to talking with you. If one chooses to live on a remote island, one has little opportunity to speak with educated men, and history is a subject that has been continually in my thoughts for some years now. Some nations choose God, and it is true that we are a godly nation, but all Greeks of any education know that they must find the reason for their existence in the study of history, since our country is filled with history's ruins."

Ben said nothing.

"What did my brother and my friend Cooper tell you about me?"

"They told me about your wife and your love for your daughter—"

"And that I am a man who is continually depressed— am I correct?—and morbidly preoccupied with what you would call nihilism. . . . My brother is a man who is both spontaneous and good. I feel great love for him, truly. He is an innocent soul—put food in front of him, he eats it; put a gun in his hand, he shoots it. No qualms. No questioning. I do not say this condescendingly, mind you. Before God, I wish I were like him! Cooper is more subtle, as changeable as a chameleon, and in the end more dangerous—to himself as well as to others. I love them both. In a manner of speaking, they are all that I am not."

"And your daughter?"

"She is all that I am, as well as all that I am not." He paused, then continued. "She is all I could have been and nothing I could have been. And now she is everything that remains with me in this life and all that will remain of me after I leave it."

Papandakis' elaborate statement had caught Ben off guard. There was nothing in their previous conversations that had prepared Ben for it. He peered at the old man's shadowy face. "Your brother said that you could have been a great politician," he said.

"That is most probable. But there is in power an element I find repellent." He laughed. "And yet it is power that is always given me."

"Like this operation, you mean?"

"That is what I mean, yes. And the war also. And after the war if I had wanted it. If I had, I would have destroyed thousands."

Ben began to speak again but stopped, feeling he had already overstepped his bounds.

"Come, Professor, there is no need to stand on ceremony. What is on your mind?" said Papandakis.

"I was just thinking that there was another side you hadn't considered, sir. You could have helped thousands as well as destroyed them."

"How?"

"By taking responsibility for them—by simply accepting the power you find so repellent."

"Through action, you mean?"

"Well, yes."

"Like yourself. You leaped from the balcony of my house and walked over a mountain at night—all to shape your own fate. And in that you have achieved your destiny. There is no need to snicker; I am not being humorous in saying these words. All Americans I have known, no matter how intellectual, in the end find solutions to all their perplexities in action. Action is what is responsible for all the most enduring aspects of your culture—the cowboy shoot-out, I believe you call it; the crimes in your cities; and your imperialistic foreign policy. But where has your great leap got *you*, Professor? You are again under my control, more involved in this situation than before you attempted to escape from it, and you have involved another person, Miss Hooper, who, like yourself, may pay for your action with her life. The entire situation is one in which Sophocles would have found much amusement, do you not agree?"

"So we should do nothing?"

"Or as little as possible. As you surmised, I was thinking today of the ironies which have forced me to act and involve those I love in dangerous circumstances. But I have also been thinking about how little difference it makes what we do. Events and situations force us to act, and the man who seeks inaction will always find the opposite."

Ben was silent.

"But there has been some good come of this," said Papandakis, leaning his back against the rail. "I was observing you this afternoon as you worked the machine-gun, Professor. You are not the same man who stepped into my car three days ago. I could see it in the manner in which you grabbed the weapon from Pandelis and organized us into a firing squad. The men saw it, too. They have accepted you. It will disturb them greatly if they discover that you are playing a double game—more than it would have before. I should not want to be in that position if I were you."

Ben remained quiet.

"Do you know why they have accepted you, Professor?"

Ben shook his head.

"They have seen how excited you were when you pulled the trigger, how much you enjoyed it. They could identify with that. It demonstrated that you were one of them. Beneath the veneer of the civilized, educated man you were full of animal bloodlust."

"I don't accept that appraisal. But that animal bloodlust is what you hate so much, isn't it?"

"Yes, in a way it is. Did Pandelis tell you that?"

"Yes."

"And that is your appraisal of my condition?"

Ben nodded.

Papandakis sighed. "There are things Pandelis will never understand," he said in a guttural half-whisper. Then he paused, clearing his throat. "Maybe the time has come to clear up this misconception, since it is probable that in a few hours we will all be dead." He paused again, drawing a quick breath, and continued in a low rush of words. "Now I will tell you something. If you cannot understand it, I do not know who will. . . .

"During the war I learned that one of my cousins was giving information to the Germans. I had ordered that all traitors were to be executed. I could have assigned the task to Pandelis, but my brother would have only understood that he was being asked to kill a relative, and one of whom we were both fond. I chose to do it myself, and on the pretext of taking a stroll with him led my cousin into a ravine. I drew my pistol and pointed it at him. He knew immediately that he had been found out and stoically accepted his fate, asking only that I hear his reasons. I listened.

"He said the Germans had discovered that he was a runner for us, and they had threatened the lives of his wife and three children if he did not supply them with information on our movements and the whereabouts of the British officers who were coordinating the work of the various resistance bands. After much deliberation he had decided that his wife and children were more important and had told the Germans what they desired to know.

"His explanation finished, my cousin stepped back and prepared to die with that defiant bravery, that lack of concern in the face of death which has become accepted as a Cretan birthright down through our history. But I could not pull the trigger. I do not know how long we stood there without moving, but I could not fire at him. And this is the point—it was not my feelings for him that prevented me from shooting him, nor my sympathy with his situation, nor his bravery in meeting death, nor even the compassion one human being feels for another at such moments. It was simply the pleasure I was experiencing at literally holding his life in my hand.

"This must have become apparent to him, however slowly. I may even have been smiling. If so, it was a smile that would only be seen on the face of a halfwit, I am sure of that, or a drunken man overcome with lust. And, yes, Professor, it was lust I was feeling. I was aroused . . . and I was waiting.

"Soon his eyes began to shift back and forth and his lips were trembling. His whole body began to shake. I was consumed with pleasure from head to foot. At that point he fell to his knees in front of me and with hands clasped together imploringly looked up. It was then I shot him.

"From my finger on the trigger I felt the power jump out in a blazing line that hurtled from the barrel into his forehead. The impact shocked me with delight. I could see the bullet enter the forehead, Professor, the actual hole, the red, and the bone chips and sticky gray matter I knew was brain flying from it.

"The concussion had rocked him backwards at first, but then he fell forward and lay curled up at my feet like a sleeping child. I was elated, soaked in sweat, and totally exhausted.

"Later I was horrified, and hated myself for what I had done. Then I began to have dreams of those last moments, and the dreams have returned many times. They confirm what I have known from the moment I pulled the trigger: I must not allow myself ever again to be in a position of power."

He fell silent, the silhouette of a man, head and shoulders haloed in the moonlight.

Ben felt nauseous. Unformed thoughts whirled

through his head. Once more he had been surprised by Papandakis, and he was beginning to get the impression that he was out of his depth in this entire misadventure, in the same way, he now realized, that Reilly had been out of his when Vlatchkov had harangued him at the embassy reception.

When the old man spoke again, his voice had taken on that weary tone Ben had become familiar with but had not really understood until now. "I was thinking about my cousin when you came up to me just now. I had much affection for him, yet I felt nothing, neither love nor hate, when I shot him, only my own arousal. I was thinking of him and of Stella, and of the possibility that your Mr. Reilly's memo actually exists. If it does, it means what I have told you, even my concern for Stella, is of no consequence. Or is it, Professor?"

Ben didn't answer. He was thinking of Vlatchkov and the mysterious message, 'Transcendentalism defective'. The message seemed to take on a new but unexplained significance in the light of what Papandakis had just told him.

They stood in silence for several minutes. The boat was sliding by a long dark shadow to port. Soon a shadowy headland appeared to starboard, and above it a bright white light flashed a double signal every five seconds.

"Look, Professor," said Papandakis in a tired and, Ben thought, excessively quiet voice, pointing toward the lights. "Turkey."

Chapter Twenty

They changed boats a mile northeast of the island of Kos, taking with them only the grease guns, the knapsacks filled with grenades and ammunition, and Papandakis' shoebox, which Cooper grinningly told Ben contained $100,000.

The Turkish boat was no different from the one they had just left, except that the odor of rotting fish was stronger and its engine seemed to be composed of loose parts—it clinked and jiggled with each revolution, like a pile of nuts and bolts revolving into a washing machine.

Cooper spoke to the captain in Turkish and the captain shrugged and pointed to several cartons filled with rumpled, sweat-reeking clothing. Then they all changed clothes, stuffing their own clothes into the bottom of their knapsacks, Yorgo and Manoli cursing at the filthiness of the disguises. Cooper instructed Yorgo to pack Ben's clothes with his own. Ben was at first nauseated by the stench of the Turkish clothes, which reminded him of the worst odors of Athens and Heraklion, but hardly noticed it a few minutes after he had put them on.

After they had changed, they went out on deck and silently watched the Turkish coast slide toward them.

The moon was behind the boat now and outlined the shapes on land with pallid light, except where curved inlets and small bays between overhanging cliffs were obscured by blocks of darkness and bordered by jagged edges or upswept, bladelike walls. Soon the mainland was stretching away endlessly on all sides; they were virtually enclosed by it.

Ben's heart had been fluttering for the past half hour, and now he acknowledged that he was terrified. He was also aware of the somber quiet that had settled over his companions in the last few minutes, and that didn't help matters.

"Twelve forty-five, sport," said Cooper. "Be there in twenty minutes. You ready?"

Ben's throat was so dry, he couldn't answer. He merely nodded.

Cooper patted his arm and moved on to the others, his hunched shadow giving Ben the impression of a sergeant hurrying down the length of a trench to give his troops final instructions before an assault. The image seemed all too apt, and Ben looked up at the approaching coast again.

The hills were low and chalky in the moonlight, and he could see the white towers of ruined windmills, much like those Pandelis had pointed out to him on the way to Siteia, dotting the headland to starboard. Directly in front of him on a low peninsula between two bays he could just pick out the gap-toothed battlements of a massive castle, indistinct against the distant hills like the subject of a poorly lit, grainy black-and-white photograph. Beyond the castle and sprawling all the way up to the semi-circle of hills that curved around the twin bays was a town of small two-story white houses interspersed with many clumps of trees and several slender minarets. The town shone in a hushed, moonlit silence that made Ben think he could see the whitewash flaking from its walls.

Papandakis was beside him, pointing to the town. "*Bodrum,* Professor. Your Halicarnassus before the Turks renamed it."

Halicarnassus. So that's where they were landing. He should be coming here as a pilgrim, not a raider. Here in 484 B.C., Herodotus, the Father of History, was born, and a hundred years later, on top of one of those cliffs the boat had just passed, Queen Artemisia had built a tomb for her husband, Mausolus, a tomb so grand it was included among the Seven Wonders of the World. In time the tomb had been destroyed, leaving only a scattering of hewn marble blocks and its name to recall the memory of the dead king. It was called the Mausoleum. This castle, then, must be the Castle of St. Peter, built by the crusading Knights of Rhodes who ruled the coast until 1523 and fitted into its walls the last of the Mausoleum's marble slabs.

Ben leaned forward as the boat passed the castle and rounded the breakwater of a small harbor, aware that he had forgotten his terror in the single excitement he never failed to experience. He called it "the historical moment," and in this case it had come upon him in that instant when he looked at the quiet town and realized that he was witnessing the combined achievement of almost three thousand years of human existence in its moon-chalked buildings.

They docked with a bump and went ashore in inconspicuous groups—first Papandakis and Manoli; then, two minutes later, Cooper and Pavlo; and, three minutes after that, Pandelis, Ben, and Yorgo. Each of them was dressed in baggy, nondescript Turkish clothing, a gray cloth short-billed cap on his head and a grease gun looped over his shoulder, out of sight beneath a bulky knapsack. Ben, who had been given neither gun nor knapsack, felt more like a prisoner every minute.

Ben's group made their way from the cement pier to a small square fringed with palm trees. The square was fronted on three sides by open-air cafés, all closed at this hour.

They walked quickly up a narrow side street, hearing their footsteps detonate the silence, turned left at a corner and found the others waiting near a canvas-covered truck. Cooper, with Papandakis at his side, was speaking in whispers to two men near the truck's cab. One of the men was slight and bareheaded, with a pencil-thin mustache. He was wearing a pinstriped suit over a white shirt and neatly knotted dark tie. The other was a heavy-set, ordinary-looking man dressed in slacks and a checkered sport shirt. Manoli and Pavlo were standing behind them.

The man in the pinstripe was shaking his head vigorously and hissing words at Cooper in an agitated whisper. Suddenly each of the young Cretans lunged forward and grabbed the man in front of him around the neck, wrenching his head back with one hand and holding a dagger against his throat with the other. The movement had caught Ben off guard, and suddenly a thick sweat seemed to spring from every pore on his body.

Pinstripe stopped talking, and now Cooper was talking to him emphatically. Then Cooper turned and sauntered back to Pandelis, Yorgo, and Ben.

"All right, into the back, you three, and keep it hushed. The rest will be along shortly. Have to do some phoning first," he whispered, then grinned. "Would you believe that sod Sali? Didn't want to join us. Not a friendly sort, these Turks. Not friendly at all."

They scrambled into the rear of the truck. Ben was relieved to be off the street and enclosed by a darkness that smelled of gasoline, rope, and rotten vegetables.

Five minutes passed. Ten. Ben looked at his watch. It was one twenty. They were cutting it close if they expected to reach Söke by five. Then he heard footsteps, and Papandakis, Pinstripe, and Manoli, now holding the Turk in a hammerlock, appeared and scrambled into the rear of the truck. Immediately, the engine turned over and the truck lurched forward.

Ben was unable to see the others in the dark. He knew that Cooper and Pavlo were missing, but he assumed that the other Turk was driving with Pavlo sitting next to him, his dagger jabbing the Turk's ribs, while Cooper sat on the other side of Pavlo, giving the driver directions.

They bumped and bounced through the sleeping town, turning from one narrow street into another. The rear of the truck was open, and the white houses, a milky blue in the moonlight, fell away in the distance.

Soon they were climbing through pine-covered hills, and the town receded behind them down the slopes. Beyond the town the sea was a flat sheet of lead, and Kos, with the moon behind it, a solid shadow in the distance.

No one had spoken. It was chilly now, and the men began to mumble and scramble about, trying to get comfortable. Guns clanked, knapsacks clattered. Ben had not moved since he had crawled into the truck, remembering a similar truck ride he had taken four nights before and a similar scene he had observed through a canvas frame much like this one. He looked at Papandakis' hunched form in the darkness and remembered that the old man had said almost exactly what Cooper had said about the memo. "If it does exist, it means that what I have told you, even my concern for Stella, is of no consequence. Or does it, Professor?" Cooper had said almost the same thing, but perhaps the old man been baiting him, just as Julia used to? He knew damn well it was of consequence. Every man's life *was,* if only to himself, no matter what changes history held in store for him and his children. Artemisia's love for Mausolus was important because it made a difference to Mausolus, no matter what happened to their kingdom or to the Mausoleum—no matter if the Mausoleum had never been built. But what really bothered Ben about Papandakis' question was something he had not acknowledged at the time, and that was the old man's willingness to believe Reilly's story. If Papandakis could accept the reality of the memo, the story might really be true.

He peered through the darkness at Papandakis. The old man was squatting several feet away, his face half in shadow, and seemed to be staring at the floor.

They were winding up around innumerable curves. Pine trees surrounded them on all sides, and the road hadn't seemed straight for more than a few yards at a time when Pinstripe began to talk to Papandakis in a high sharp voice, although Manoli was still holding him in a hammerlock.

"Why do you do this, sir? Have I cheat you before? Is not good."

The man waited. Papandakis didn't reply.

"I would be pleased for you to answer me, sir. This is not right. Five years now I do for you good things—*evet*, yes?"

Papandakis remained silent.

"*Evet*—yes?" repeated the little man, pausing for a reply, then shrilling, "*Ingilizce Konusuyor?*"

Manoli snorted. There was a thump. The little man yelped and was quiet.

"Things are now changed, Sali," said Papandakis in his tired voice. "Never before have you people asked me to enter Turkey. Why do you ask now? And when I arrive, Yussuf does not come to the meeting place, but sends you instead."

Ben was instantly alert at this. Papandakis and the others were behaving as if nothing had happened, but something had obviously gone wrong.

"Too dangerous to do this thing you want. Much difficulty. Sayun Orhan Çalika can help no longer, sir. He is in deep suspicion at Istanbul, and the others are too frightened to do as was planned."

"Then why did they agree to the plan in the beginning?"

"The plan is a thing that can be done, sir. But the meeting is a thing too dangerous. In the plan they are as wind—no one is able to see them, yet all can feel their power. In a meeting they are in a light for all to see."

"If this undertaking is dangerous for Yussuf and the others, I am sure, Sali, that you realize it is twice as dangerous for us. That is why I wanted Yussuf to meet us. And that is why I had you call him from Bodrum and tell him to be in Söke when we arrived there, and to make sure Hassan was there, too. He could be there thirty minutes to an hour before we arrived, if I am not mistaken."

"Yes, the road from Izmir is good and the distance less. But, sir, why have I been so treated by you—this knife, this man who is bending my arm so?"

"We are insuring our safety, Sali. Did you hear what I said to Yussuf on the phone?"

"No, sir, I think not."

"I told him I was taking you hostage. I know how much he appreciates you, Sali. That should induce him to be more cooperative. But in such troubled times you may not be as valuable as I thought. Therefore, I have also informed him that I would only deliver the money to him personally. And should I encounter any difficulty on the way, I would destroy the money."

The truck was descending through steep curves in the pine-clad hills. Ben had listened to the conversation with increasing concern. Something sure as hell had gone wrong. "Excuse me," he said. "Is everything all right?"

"There has been a change in our agenda, Professor, but there is nothing to worry about. The person who was to meet us at Bodrum, a very important person, sent Sali here instead. I phoned this person and told him to meet us in Söke if he wanted the money and expected to see his friend Sali alive again."

"But—"

"Everything is *fine*, Professor," said Papandakis, with an emphasis that told Ben not to question him or to show any concern in front of Sali.

"And the money for Hassan, sir?" said Sali. "What if he is not in Söke to receive it? What is to become of me then?"

"If I estimate Hassan's appetite for money correctly, he will be there, even if he is laying a trap for us. As prefect of police for the entire district, he will be there to direct the operation and win glory for himself—and also, I think, to make sure that the money does not escape him. Such a twofold success would be much to his liking. Besides, I am positive Yussuf was in touch with him moments after we rang off."

"Sir, I am hearing much suspicion from your words. Why would we want to do you harm? For five years we have done together good things, with *para* for everyone."

"Forgive me if I have given offense for no reason, Sali. Once this is over and we have reached our boat in safety, you will be released."

This seemed to satisfy the Turk, since he asked no more questions and fell silent.

But Ben could feel the tension inside the truck; it was building with every mile. Pandelis, sitting beside him, was breathing heavily and his body seemed ready to spring at the dark huddled shape out of which Sali's voice had spoken.

The truck had left the hills and was sweeping down a level road that curved through cultivated plains separated by wooden knolls. The sea glinted off to the right as Ben looked back along the road, and they had traveled through this bumpy but level landscape for half an hour before they passed a huge medieval fortress and several minutes later entered a town with a distinctly Islamic atmosphere—domes and minarets rose above the darkened houses. A river zigzagged through the town under several bridges. "Milas," whispered Sali, although no one had asked him. "It is from here little more than sixty kilometers to Söke. We will arrive in one hour and a half."

They left Milas behind, passing—was Ben dreaming?—the moonlit columns of an intact Roman temple rising out of a dark grove of trees. They went through several small towns separated by cultivated fields at the foot of the forested slopes. The sea, always on their right, was joined half an hour beyond Milas by a huge tree-lined lake on their left that appeared to be several miles long. In half an hour the lake had disappeared and once more the truck was sweeping through fields, forests, and hills, the sea still on their right but farther away now.

Ben's watch said four forty-five, and the sky was paling with pre-dawn light when they bounced into a large town with several small parks and neatly-spaced trees growing along all the streets. Everyone sat tense and quiet, until Sali's voice broke the silence once again, saying softly, "It is Söke we are now entering."

Chapter Twenty-one

The truck stopped on an unlit side street full of small shops and lined with trees. The men climbed down from the back as quietly as possible, although the clanging and clattering of their gear seemed to reverberate through the silent town.

They had parked behind a black Mercedes sedan, which shone even in the lifting darkness. Beside it stood a fat man of medium height wearing a panama hat and a baggy white suit. Next to him was a tall, haughty-looking, bareheaded man, also dressed in a loose-fitting suit, although his was black, and under it he wore a white shirt open at the collar.

Papandakis walked toward the two men. Manoli pushed Sali forward, followed by Ben with Pandelis and Yorgo on either side of him.

Pandelis was inspecting the street as he walked, moving his head almost imperceptibly from side to side. He seemed to be walking on tiptoe, and this gave him the appearance of a stout old matador warily approaching a bull.

Cooper and the other two had already gotten down from the cab of the truck, and now Cooper and Papandakis came up to the two men standing by the Mercedes and began to speak to them in whispers.

Ben and the others were standing only a few feet away, but he couldn't distinguish a single word, or even what language they were speaking.

The conversation quickly became heated, and the Turks began to wave their hands and hiss out their words. The fat man had dragged out a huge handkerchief and was clutching it like a tattered battle flag, when he wasn't mopping his cheeks and forehead with it or shaking it, crumpled up big as a softball in his fist, at Cooper and Papandakis.

The other man was speaking in a frenzied whisper and slapping the back of his right hand into the palm of his left with each word. Both men were middle-aged, and although the fat man's features were indistinct, his companion's slicked-back, thinning hair, and his long, thick nose, neatly trimmed mustache, and flashing white teeth gave him a pantherlike, almost predatory appearance.

Papandakis and Cooper seemed to be totally at ease. They stood calmly as the Turks rasped and bleated at them, and their inaudible replies seemed to send the other two into such paroxysms of snarling and hissing that anyone passing might have thought the four of them were watching a cat fight. Standing on either side of Ben, Pandelis and Yorgo continued to scan the street, apparently paying no attention to the conversation.

Finally the tall Turk threw up his hands with a sneer and said very distinctly, *"Tamam yaparim!"* Then he climbed into the back of the Mercedes, followed by the fat man and Papandakis.

Cooper turned to Ben and the others and beckoned to Pavlo, who had been standing behind the truck driver during the conversation. Then he waved to

Manoli and pointed to the Mercedes. The two young Cretans, pushing Sali in front of them, strode over to the Mercedes, shoved the Turk into the driver's seat, and got in on the other side.

Meanwhile Cooper had come up to Ben's group, taken the truck driver by the arm, and guided him towards the cab.

"Here we go, mates," he said as he closed the door on the driver and started around to the other side of the truck. "Into the back with you lot," he said. "And hop it!"

Pandelis grunted.

"Come on, Pandy. Just a few more streets."

"What went on up there?" asked Ben.

"Another change of plan, sport. This time ours. Papandakis let 'em know that Hassan was coming in with us—like we was holding a gun to his head and forcing him to release the lot. Hassan's the tall one, a top bloke in the police, which is really like militia over here. He'll get us in. Didn't like Pappy's plan a bit, though. But Pappy knows just where he's ticklish."

"Where's that?"

"In his money belt, sport, his money belt."

"And the other one?"

"Fat one's called Yussuf, important political bloke . . . Now in with you lot and let's get on with it."

They scrambled into the back again, Pandelis and Yorgo following Ben. Cooper remained in front with the heavyset Turk in the checkered shirt, who was still driving.

Yorgo knocked on the small window in the back of the cab, and the truck pulled out with a lurch.

* * *

The town had been laid out with wide boulevards lined with trees, and yet it didn't give Ben the impression of an elegant suburb as much as it did of a provincial market town.

The streets were empty as they drove by a park and a mosque, through a large square, and squealed to a stop a block later on a narrow side street. It was five after five on Ben's watch.

"We go!" growled Pandelis. He swung the knapsack from his back so it hung around his neck like a bulky, outsized bib and then unslung the grease gun from his shoulder. Next he slapped in a clip and jumped down from the truck. Yorgo and Ben were close behind him. Ben hadn't had time to think; Yorgo had grabbed his shoulder and shoved him after Pandelis so roughly that Ben had almost fallen out of the truck. But he had regained his balance and now, tense and alarmed, sprinted after Pandelis in the direction of the Mercedes, aware of Yorgo, his grease gun, and his toothy smile right behind him.

Papandakis and Manoli were nudging Hassan out of the Mercedes at gunpoint. They directed him toward a three-story building with five wide marble steps leading up to a narrow doorway with a marble column on either side and a marble plaque with a Turkish inscription over the entrance.

Pandelis, Ben, and Yorgo followed them, as Cooper and Pavlo started pushing Yussuf and Sali back toward the truck.

Hassan jogged up the steps, followed by Papandakis and the others. They shoved through the heavy wooden outer door, into a small foyer, then through a second door made of wood and glass, and burst into a large grapefruit-colored room lit by a dim yellow light with official-looking posters drooping from the high, grimy walls. The room was sweltering.

Two men in olive-green uniforms were playing cards at a table in the middle of the room, and even before they had time to look up, Papandakis and Manoli were shoving Hassan toward them, while Pandelis moved far to the left of the door and Yorgo to the right, both of them pointing their weapons toward the table.

Ben was left a few steps behind Papandakis and Manoli, and he was frightened. He felt totally exposed, with no way of protecting himself, and he had no idea what would happen next.

Hassan was very agitated. Papandakis had jabbed him twice in the kidneys with the barrel of his gun, and the second time Hassan had turned and glared at him. Now Hassan spoke to one of the policemen in a snarling voice. They still hadn't had time to get up from their chairs, and were still holding their cards like ladies' fans in front of them. They stared at Hassan, goggle-eyed at first, mouths open. Then, as he continued to rant at them, one of them rose slowly and tiptoed like a tightrope walker over to a long, high desk that ran the length of one wall, took down a large ring of keys from the wall, carefully made his way over to a door at the back of the room, unlocked it, turned back toward Hassan, and waited.

"Pandeli, parte ta diavateria!" said Papandakis over his shoulder, then he pushed Hassan forward with the barrel of his gun and both of them strode toward the door. Manoli remained at the table and looked back at Ben, his round left eye staring past Ben's right shoulder.

"Teacher!" rasped Pandelis, and when Ben turned

he saw that Pandelis, a furious expression on his face, was nodding for him to follow the others inside. He obeyed, and Manoli fell in behind him.

They walked down a peeling, dimly lit corridor until the policeman lumbered over to a door on the left, unlocked it, flicked a switch on the wall, and all five, still in single file, went through the doorway. They found themselves in a narrow aisle between two blocks of cells. Honey-colored light, that seemed as thick and sickly-sweet as the air, filled the cellblock.

Three of the cells were occupied. Two of the occupants, half-wrapped in gray blankets, were already sitting up, and in the third, on the other side of the corridor, another person was struggling to extricate himself from the bedclothes.

The first prisoners were young men. Both seemed to be tall and bony, and both had beards and curly hair. One of them was wearing a gray sweat shirt and was yawning. He stared at the intruders, his arms hugging his waist. The second prisoner was carefully scratching his scalp and pressing his skull with his fingertips, as if he were testing the ripeness of a melon. He wore a grimy, faded white T-shirt with a picture of a waterfall and the slogan *OLYMPIA BEER—It's the Water!*

"Hey, what's happening, man?" he asked sleepily.

By this time the third prisoner had thrown his blanket off and was striding toward his cell door. He was a good-looking, solidly built young man in his mid-twenties, dressed in a faded blue T-shirt and dungarees. The wild expression on his face was intensified by a disorderly tangle of black hair and an equally unruly beard. He was completely awake, possibly because of his struggle with the bedclothes, and even before he grabbed the cell bars he was scowling. "What the hell's going on now?" he demanded.

"Quiet, please," said Papandakis. "We have come to take you out."

The wild-faced boy was staring at Papandakis' grease gun, as if he were seeing it for the first time. He said nothing in reply.

"Tell him to hurry," Papandakis said to Hassan, jabbing him in the kidneys with the gun again. Hassan lurched forward with a yelp, turned and glared at Papandakis, and then shouted to the policeman, who began unlocking the cells.

"Hey, man, what you guys doing?" the boy in the Olympia T-shirt asked Manoli.

Ben looked back. He knew Manoli didn't understand English, and Manoli, as if he hadn't heard anything, kept his gun trained on Ben and the policeman and didn't reply.

"Hey, *you*—what's going on?" the boy in the T-shirt asked again.

"It's okay," said Ben. "We're going to bring you out."

"What?" He looked at Ben's rumpled Turkish clothes and then at Manoli.

"I said, we're going to get you out of here."

"American?" asked the boy in the gray sweat shirt as he hooked a pair of wire-rimmed glasses around his ears.

Ben nodded. He could sense their relief. He felt relieved himself, although he wasn't sure whether it was because he had found three fellow Americans or because the first stage of the raid had been accomplished without incident.

"Shit, Jeff, we're being rescued," said the boy in the

sweat shirt, his glasses flashing as he raised his head.

"Yeah, the cavalry has *arrived*!" The boy called Jeff smiled at him.

Ben didn't smile back. He was irritated by the boy's flippant remark. Didn't the idiot realize what was happening? "Come on," he said in a gruff voice, "and don't forget your shoes."

The three young men were out of their cells by now. The wild-faced boy was standing next to Papandakis, who looked at him and asked, "What has happened to the others?"

"Nextdoor," he replied.

Papandakis and Manoli prodded Hassan, Ben, and the policeman back into the corridor, and the three young men followed behind them.

In the corridor Jeff and his friend in the sweat shirt hopped up and down, trying to get their shoes on while standing up. But the wild-faced boy stood stolidly on his bare feet, carrying a shoe in either hand as if it were a brick. He was scowling again.

"You wait here," said Papandakis to the three young men as the policeman unlocked the other door, flipped a switch, and led the way into a second, identical cellblock.

Only two of these cells were occupied, and as they entered both occupants were already stirring in their narrow beds. A frizzy reddish-blond head emerged from one of the blankets, then a round freckled face with wide cheeks and a pug nose. The girl's face was swollen with sleep, and her eyes stared at them uncomprehendingly. The girl in the next cell had scrambled from the bedclothes and was sitting up now, looking out at them with startled black eyes. Ben remembered the eyes and the shoulder-length black hair from the photograph Papandakis had shown him in his dining room four nights ago.

"Stella," Papandakis called quietly. He pronounced her name so casually that Ben could almost imagine that he had been sitting with her in his study all evening and was about to ask her to bring him a glass of water. But Ben had heard the uncharacteristically low voice in which he spoke her name, barely more than a whisper, as if it had been uttered from deep in his throat, and he had detected the almost indistinguishable quaver that trembled around the edges of the word.

The girl's eyes opened wide. "Papa?" she asked. "Papa? Oh, papa!" She threw the blanket aside and ran to the cell door, grasping the bars and shaking her head from side to side several times. Then she rested her head against one arm; she was sobbing quietly. She hung from her straining fingers until they lost their grip on the bars and she slid to the floor. No one moved.

"Unlock it, please! Unlock it!" croaked Papandakis.

"*Ac! Ac!*" Hassan shouted at the policeman in a trembling voice.

The policeman began to rummage through the ring of keys, selected one, and poked it several times at the metal plate of the lock before he found the keyhole. He opened the blond girl's cell and then Stella's.

The blond girl, her face still puffy with sleep, stepped tentatively out of her cell. Ben told her to join the others in the corridor, and she started to wander toward the door.

"Your shoes!" Ben called after her, and the girl ambled back to her cell, retrieved her shoes, and started toward the door again.

Stella had gotten up by now and dried her eyes.

Ben was surprised at how slight she was, almost petite. She was wearing a pair of jeans and a collarless maroon-and-white madras shirt with long sleeves.

When the policeman unlocked her cell, she stepped toward her father. But he drew back and shook his head. She looked at the gun in his hands, nodded, and walked past Ben down the corridor, shoes in hand.

At that moment the door flew open and the wild-faced boy in the blue T-shirt burst into the room.

"Henry!" shouted Stella, and pushed past the blond girl and ran into the boy's arms, pressing her head against his chest and hugging him while he kissed her hair and held her tight.

The name had exploded like a shot in the room, and Ben immediately turned toward the door.

It was then that all hell broke loose.

Chapter Twenty-two

Ben heard a grunt behind him, and he turned around in time to see Papandakis sprawling on the floor of the cellblock. Hassan was standing over him, swinging the butt of Papadakis' grease gun upward, trying to brace the stock against his shoulder and get his finger on the trigger.

Immediately Ben understood what had happened. Papandakis must have looked toward the door as he had, and Hassan, who was probably waiting for such an opportunity, had jumped the old man, grabbed the gun from his hands, and shoved him backward.

Hassan looked almost ecstatic. His eyes flashed like black pearls, his lips were stretched back in a gloating grin, and his teeth sparkled. He was still having difficulty getting the gun into position, but finally he braced the stock against his shoulder and pointed the barrel down at Papandakis, who had started to rise to his feet.

"*Yat! Yat!*" Hassan shouted, and waved the gun at the old man's chest before leveling it at his head once more.

It may have been his eyes—most probably it was— or it may have been the way Hassan was holding the gun; but Ben realized that moment that the Turk was about to pull the trigger, and the next thing he knew, he was lunging at Hassan. He pushed his weight against the Turk and braced his feet. Then he grabbed the barrel with his left hand and swung it upward, wrenching the steel stock downward, toward his body with his right hand. Hassan's fingers dragged against the trigger and the gun went off; the heat of the barrel seared Ben's palm.

The sound seemed to detonate the room. And even as he tugged at the gun in Hassan's hand, sensing that the Turk had been thrown off balance, Ben had the momentary thought that the explosion had shaken the entire building and would reverberate outward forever.

A moment later Ben had jerked the gun from Hassan's hands and automatically smashed the stock against his chin. It caught the Turk on the left side of his jaw, and Ben could feel the bone cracking, just before Hassan hurtled backward, crashed against the wall behind him, and crumpled to the floor like a pile of empty clothes.

Ben stood staring at the wall for a moment, his ears still full of the sound of the shots and his hands holding the gun across his body, aware now of the scorching pain in his left hand. All sound and motion seemed to have been drained from the room. A plume of oily smoke floated upward before his eyes, followed by a bitter smell that reminded him of overheated car engines.

Then the girl screamed and everything began to move again, and when Ben turned around, his left hand throbbing, he saw that the scream was coming from the blond-haired girl who was standing near the door and staring past him at Hassan's body with huge eyes. The shrill sound quivered in his head like a vibrating needle.

Henry and Stella were also staring past Ben, but then as the scream subsided to a snuffling whimper, the young man turned and grabbed the blond girl by the arm. Stella turned anxiously toward her father, but Henry took hold of her arm as well and dragged them both from the cellblock.

Papandakis had already risen and retrieved the grease gun from Ben, who was shaking his burnt hand. The old man stood for a moment looking down at Hassan, his face turned away. Then he moved quickly toward Ben and the policeman, pressing Ben's arm and fixing him with a solemn stare. "Leave him," he said, glancing over his shoulder, and then looked at Manoli. "*Fuge, Manoli! Fuge!*" he said, and Manoli moved toward the door.

The policeman was the only one who hadn't moved. He had fleshy, almost pouchy cheeks, a long, fat nose, and a thick body, and he had been staring at Hassan with the same incredulous expression he had worn all along. Papandakis grabbed him by the shoulder and propelled him toward the door. The policeman stumbled backward, almost lost his balance, then turned and let his momentum carry him unsteadily through the doorway.

The five Americans were waiting in the corridor, huddled together, their faces like masks. The blond girl was shaking.

Papandakis pushed the policeman in front of them, and continued prodding him in the back with the barrel of his gun, so that the Turk staggered through the corridor with the Americans scrambling to keep up with him, Ben and Manoli bringing up the rear and herding everyone forward. Ben's hand was beginning to cool off.

They burst into the large front room, and Yorgo's and Pandelis' expressions showed that they had heard the gunshots and the screams.

The other policeman was standing against the wall opposite the long desk, with his back to them and his hands resting on top of his head.

Before anyone could say a word, the street door swung open and Pavlo dashed into the station, his grease gun nosing forward and his eyes glazed with apprehension. Apparently Cooper and the others had heard the shooting, too.

"Pavlo, ugaltous exo!" commanded Papandakis, and Pavlo stopped in mid-stride, turned, raised a hand, and signaled the Americans to follow him.

They ran toward the entrance in a shambling line, with Manoli behind them. Pandelis and Yorgo stayed behind, looking expectantly toward Papandakis at the back of the room.

Ben had stopped near the table in the center of the room. The cards were still on it, one set lying in a neat fan shape, the other in a snaking, sectioned line like a string of derailed toy boxcars.

No one said anything for several moments. Ben stopped flexing his left hand and looked over at Pandelis and Yorgo. He didn't like what he saw on their faces.

The silence continued. The only sounds were the rumbling footfalls of the group that Pavlo was leading out the door.

Ben turned to Papandakis, the pulse jumping in his throat. The old man was watching the receding backs of the Americans, seemingly oblivious to the expression on Pandelis' face. Ben was about to speak when a chattering fusillade of gunfire exploded in the street, followed by several short screams.

Pandelis didn't move. He hadn't seemed to hear the gunfire, but his face had become thickened and menacing, like a square stone effigy of a wrathful god. "Good-bye, Teacher!" Pandelis said, and pointed his grease gun at Ben.

Ben's heart clenched into a knot. "Wait!" he wanted to shout, but his voice wouldn't come. He was unable to move, even to shift his eyes from that vengeful demiurge's face that a moment before had been Pandelis'. With unexpected clarity it occurred to him that this was where the gods had been leading him, where all the events in his life had been arranged to convey him—here, to his death in a stuffy Turkish jail. He stared at Pandelis, knowing there was no hope.

"Oshee, Pandeli! Me tokanes afto!" yelled Papandakis.

Pandelis was still pointing the gun at Ben; his statue's face was impassive, but he shifted his eyes toward his brother, who was pushing the fat-nosed policeman toward his comrade standing against the wall.

"The professor . . ." said Papandakis over his shoulder, "he saved my life."

The stony edges of Pandelis' face receded into flesh once more. A smile slid from his lips, and he dipped his head at Ben. The vengeful demiurge had become a man again. Ben nodded in reply, an enormous wave of relief expanding through his constricted muscles.

If Pandelis thought that Ben's nod was curt, he was right. Ben wasn't exactly angry at Pandelis, but the dumb bastard had almost shot him, for Christ's sake, and only Papandakis' intervention had stopped him—

only the old man's words had given Ben his reprieve. And then Ben knew whose eyes Pandelis' had reminded him of a few moments before. They were Hassan's eyes after he had grabbed the gun and aimed it at Papandakis, and, yes, they were the eyes of the Minotaur in his nightmare.

More gunfire exploded outside, followed by the sound of shattering glass. Ben, Pandelis, and Yorgo turned toward the small windows high above the desk. One of the windows was broken, and the jagged ends of glass glinted like icicles. A moment later Papandakis shouted at them, and they turned as he began shoving both policemen toward the front door. Except for a mild stinging sensation, Ben's hand was all right now.

Several bursts of machine-gun fire rattled the windows again as Papandakis flung the two policemen through the inner doorway. He waved for Ben, Pandelis, and Yorgo to follow him, and waited for them behind the front door. Then, pushing the two policemen in front of them, the four burst out of the heavy wooden entrance.

The outside air hit them like a splash of icy surf. The light in the sky had widened into a cobalt blue clarity, but the other side of the street was still smothered in darkness.

They ran toward the stairs, but even before they reached the top step, more gunshots snapped out, spattering flashes of light from the darkness across the street.

One of the policemen screamed, grabbed his knee, and fell forward, tumbling to the bottom of the stairs. There was another body there, a man in a rumpled gray jacket. It was Pavlo. The other policeman had pitched forward headfirst and lay sprawled down the length of the steps.

Pandelis and Yorgo opened fire, spraying the buildings opposite them, then dashed down the steps and veered off to the right, toward the Mercedes and the truck. They ran past Pavlo's body without looking down, flanking Papandakis on either side and leaving Ben to bring up the rear. He sprinted behind Papandakis, who reached down and picked up Pavlo's grease gun as he ran past.

Ahead of them the boy in the sweat shirt was half bucking, half hopping toward the truck, dragging his left leg and holding his left arm with his right hand, like a man shouldering his way through a windstorm. Everyone else had disappeared.

The Mercedes was empty. All four doors were open. Several yards behind it, the truck was parked where they had left it.

More shots chattered from the other side of the street. Chunks of plaster crashed to the pavement from above Ben's head, and plaster dust showered his hair.

Suddenly Pandelis spun around in a half-circle, grabbed his left arm and crashed to the sidewalk. Blood was rolling over his fingers.

The others ran on, but Ben, still bringing up the rear, reached down and hooked his elbow under Pandelis' right arm as he passed, and tried to pull him to his feet. Pandelis was as heavy as a sack of concrete.

"Go, Teacher. You go," Pandelis gasped from the pavement.

"Bullshit!" said Ben. He hauled him up and started to run toward the back of the truck, pulling Pandelis after him.

At that moment, a car hurtled into the street and swept past them, and the next instant a deafening volley of gunfire raked the buildings across the street. This was followed by several screams and a confused series of shouts in Turkish as the car accelerated and squealed out of sight around a corner.

A second later a second car sped into the street and swerved to a halt in the middle of the road, next to the truck. The driver jumped out. He was a small, thin man with a skinny black mustache, who wore a short-sleeved sport shirt. As he ran toward Ben and Pandelis, his head was turned toward the cab of the truck, and he was shouting in several languages, the last of which was English. "To turn! To turn! Around, please! Around!"

As the man ran up to help Ben, who was staggering under Pandelis' weight, the truck was already lurching forward. By the time it had swung around in the opposite direction, Ben and the stranger were carrying Pandelis under each arm and had almost caught up with the truck.

Yorgo was leaning toward them from the rear of the truck, and on all sides other hands were grabbing them and hauling them into a soft, shadowy clutter of bodies and bony lengths of arms and legs.

Ben fell into the truck, surrounded by the odors of sweat, garlic, rotten vegetables and the unmistakable bitter scent of fear.

The truck lumbered back through the town the way it had come. No one appeared behind them until a block past the mosque, when the same car that had fired on the Turks sprang out of a side street and followed several car-lengths behind them. It was a boatlike black 1956 Buick. The stranger waved at it and everyone else stared, but no one attempted to do anything about it. Whoever was in the Buick was obviously an ally who was protecting their retreat. Besides, everyone was busy catching his breath and organizing his thoughts, and a harsh chorus of inhaling and exhaling was interrupted only by somebody whimpering—Ben thought this sounded like the blond girl—and somebody else moaning—Ben thought this must be the boy in the sweat shirt.

Pandelis, tense and silent beside him, was sitting straight-backed and rigid by the tailgate, and when Ben's eyes got used to the dark, he could see that he was staring at the car that was following them.

"You all right?" Ben asked him after he had caught his breath.

Pandelis nodded. "I no forget this, Teacher," he said, then noticed the stranger. Pandelis stared at the little man for several moments as the truck bounced and shook through the outskirts of the quiet town. "Who you?" he finally asked.

The little man smiled. He had taken a pack of cigarettes from his shirt pocket and was offering one to Yorgo as he replied, "Kemal. Meester Reilly, he send me."

Chapter Twenty-three

It was five thirty-five by Ben's watch as the truck rumbled over a bridge over a dry riverbed, the Buick still right behind them. They were beyond the outskirts of Söke now and winding up through a low range of hills whose broad slopes were covered with clumps of bushes and dotted with yellow and white flowers.

"Mr. Reilly, he send me," the little man had just said.

"Reilly?" Ben muttered. He had almost forgotten the name during the events of the last half hour. "Reilly," he kept repeating to himself. *The place will be crawling with our people.* Good old Reilly.

"It would seem we owe you and Mr. Reilly our apologies, Professor Ames." It was Papandakis speaking. He was bent over Pandelis' wounded arm, probing it with his fingertips and every so often speaking to his brother in Greek, perhaps apprising him of the progress of his examination.

Pandelis was glaring at the other car now, but his face was distorted with pain rather than anger. "Pavlo, Pavlo," he kept muttering and shaking his head.

Papandakis leaned close to him and whispered several sentences in which the word 'Pavlo' was repeated twice. Pandelis nodded and looked down, then unexpectedly wrenched his head up, and with eyes swimming and lips trembling, he shouted, "*Na prosefhitoume ya Pavlo!*" to which Yorgo added in a low voice, "*O Pavlos, to Pallikari, mas afisay! O Theos mazito!*"

Stella had been sitting at her uncle's side, holding his hand, and now she hovered over his good shoulder and kissed him on the cheek. Pandelis merely grunted and swung up the back of his hand, his expression still grim.

In the depths of the truck the Americans were taking care of each other, aided by Yorgo, while Manoli kept his terrible eye and his grease gun trained on Sali and Yussuf, who sat with their hands on their heads.

"I would like to extend my appreciation," Papandakis was saying to Ben, "for what you have done for my brother and myself at the jail!"

Hassan crumpled against the wall like a pile of old clothes. *Appreciation? I may have killed the poor bastard!*

Ben's thoughts must have been apparent from his expression, for Papandakis added, "He was still breathing when I looked at him, Ben—may I call you that? You must understand that there was nothing else that could be done. I am sure he meant to kill me. I could see it in his eyes. And it was a thing he had to do sooner or later."

The last statement struck Ben as curious. "I don't understand," he said. "Why would he have to kill you?"

"Because he had prepared a trap for us, as I suspected he would."

"How can you be so sure? Everything was going so smoothly."

"The ones outside, that is why."

Ben stared at the old man.

"The gunfire from across the street, Professor. Surely it would take them longer than two or three minutes after hearing gunshots to get into such an excellent position for an ambush."

"He is right, sir." It was the stranger again. Ben turned to him. He was squatting on Ben's left, smiling beneath his thin mustache—which looked a lot like Sali's—a lighted cigarette in his hand. He hunched his shoulders and dipped his head, as if to excuse himself for entering the conversation uninvited. "We saw them deploying to one hour previous of your arrival, directed by the tall man you took into the jail with you. That one I recognized to be Hassan Mutgil, director of internal security for these provinces."

Ben nodded and sighed. "Then why did he let us get near the jail in the first place?" he asked.

"He most probably wanted to catch the Americans attempting to escape so he could kill us all together," said Papandakis. "That would prove the Americans' guilt to the world, would it not? I am sure Hassan realized that his country had no case against them, and thus he would avoid the international embarrassment of another fraudulent drug trial and possibly achieve further prestige for himself."

Ben nodded again. He was exhausted, and the thought of such deviousness was beyond him at the present time. His left hand was fine now, the prickly sensation in his palm so slight he could ignore it.

"Please, sir," said the stranger, with enough urgency in his voice to make Ben look up once more. "We are not traveling for the correct roadway to Bodrum."

"What?"

"We are not directed to the Bodrum roadway, sir."

Ben looked at Papandakis. The old man was smiling and nodding. "He is right, Ben. As you know, we are going to the coast—to Kusadasi, to be precise. It is only twenty-five kilometers away."

"But, sir, if it is permitted for me to say, whatever we can provide for you in the manner of protection we were told to place on the roadway for Bodrum and into the town."

"Yes. I was attempting a stratagem. Bodrum was the gambit. At the time I suspected both Mr. Reilly and the professor. To inform Mr. Reilly of our real escape route would have been foolish, to say the least, and as a point of entry Bodrum was perfect."

"I cannot understand this, sir."

"It is not important. We are on our way to Kusadasi, and that is the way we will leave."

"To Samos, sir?"

"Yes."

"Then our difficulties are not yet beginning. The police in Söke will phone Kusadasi, and the police there will be waiting for us."

Papandakis nodded again. "I considered that. Is there another road that runs north beyond Kusadasi? We would be able to turn south then and enter the town from an unexpected direction."

"Now that we have chosen onto this road west from Söke, sir, there is none other until we come over the hills to the coast south of Kusadasi. And any other road of which I speak runs south away from the town."

Papandakis reached into his knapsack and took out a map, which he spread on the floorboards in front of him. Pandelis looked at it, as did Kemal and Ben.

"If I may be permitted, sir," said Kemal. "Relatives of mine live near here. We would be able to stay with them for one day."

"That is not possible," said Papandakis, shaking his head. "The police will be more numerous if they are given more time, and I have a boat waiting in Kusadasi which has been instructed to sail without us if we are not there by seven A.M."

The black Buick suddenly began honking wildly. Everyone in the back of the truck looked up. Arms were waving from the windows of the big car and fingers were jabbing backward. Ben and the others glanced in the direction the hands were pointing. Down the hillside, past the Buick, weaving up the switchbacks toward them, were three military-looking trucks. At the base of the hills, the town of Söke, identifiable by its neat, tree-lined streets, appeared at the edge of a long valley bordered by mountains and bisected by a wide river that was now a winking copper track winding out of a distant haze in the day's first moments of sunlight.

"It would seem our Turkish friends have decided our route for us," said Papandakis. He continued to stare at the convoy. In the shabby, ill-fitting clothes and small-billed cap, the barrel of the grease gun nudging his shoulder, he looked the perfect picture of a resistance fighter, or a bandit. "There is little to do now but head for Kusadasi—am I not correct? If they stop us, we will bargain with them for the life of the eminent Deputy Minister of Commerce, Mr. Yussuf Asmali." He nodded to Yussuf and Sali, who sat with their hands on their heads in the depths of the truck and said nothing.

Ben gave the two men a peripheral glance. He was

more intent on Papandakis, who had delivered his last sentences in a tone that was too oily and with an expression that was downright smug. *He's enjoying this. Christ!*

Papandakis was now whispering to Pandelis, whose shoulder was being wrapped by Stella, and whose expression was still grim. As his brother continued Pandelis began to nod; when he had finished, Pandelis turned to the front of the truck and began shouting orders to Yorgo, who was tending the boy in the sweat shirt.

Everyone watched as Yorgo rose, stepped over to the back of the cab, drew his dagger from his belt, and using its handle, tapped on the small rear window of the cab.

Cooper's face appeared in the window. Yorgo motioned to him and he nodded. Then Yorgo took off his rumpled jacket, held it up against the window, and looked back toward the others. They could hear metal beating on glass and then a crunch. Yorgo turned back to the cab, and now using his jacket as a funnel, sifted the shattered glass onto the floorboards near his feet.

"Good morning, you sorry-looking crew," said Cooper through the jagged opening. "Just putting in a more direct communications system here. What's up?"

Yorgo spoke to him in rapid Greek, motioning to the road behind them, and Cooper smiled. "Right," he said. "Got it, Pappy." Papandakis replied with a nod; his lips were still twisted in a smirk. Cooper passed six grenades, one at a time, through the broken window to Yorgo, who dropped them into his knapsack, turned, collected Manoli's knapsack and dumped it, along with his own, on top of the map that was lying in front of Papandakis and Pandelis. They had already piled their knapsacks on the same spot. Yorgo sat down with the two older men, and the three of them began removing the grenades from the knapsacks and stacking them in a single pile on the floorboards in front of them. Every so often Pandelis or Yorgo would lift a grenade and hold it up to the light as if it were a jewel. At these moments they turned to each other, nodded gravely, and then fell back to work.

Ben couldn't understand what was going on. He and the other Americans were watching uneasily as the three Cretans went about their curious preparations, and when Ben looked at Kemal, he found the little man staring at him with an expression of bewilderment and apprehension.

Papandakis caught his eye. "Do not worry about the Turkish convoy, Ben."

"But I *do* worry about the Turkish convoy. What are we going to do about it?"

Papandakis nodded. "We are taking care of that at this very moment."

"What do you mean by that?" asked Ben.

"You are not to worry, Ben. Be patient, my friend," Papandakis said and turned back to work.

Finally, the three Cretans repacked the knapsacks, putting twenty-four grenades in one (after removing the grease-gun clips and redistributing them among the other packs) and fifteen in each of the others.

Yorgo handed Manoli his knapsack and slung his own over his shoulder. Papandakis did the same, after stuffing his brother's Cretan clothes into the bottom with his own. The knapsack containing the twenty-four grenades remained on the floorboards in front of Pandelis.

Papandakis and Pandelis, still sitting by the tailgate, were loading fresh clips into their grease guns when Henry spoke. "Is there anything I can do to help, sir?" he asked Papandakis. His scowl had been replaced by an amiable smile, and now the whipped black wavelets of hair around his face merely looked unkempt.

Papandakis looked up and studied the young American for a moment over his shoulder, as if he had been reminded of something. Then he swiveled his entire body around and focused his complete attention on him. "Yes, you can help me. You can tell me who you are, young man. Do you understand that I was almost killed because my daughter called out to you? Who are you, sir?"

"He's Henry, father. Henry—my husband," said Stella, making her way unsteadily to the boy's side.

Papandakis said nothing. He merely nodded once and smiled enigmatically. "Henry Reese?" he finally asked.

"Yes, sir," said the boy.

"What?" gasped Pandelis, hunching up his unwounded shoulder and opening his eyes wide. "Is not possible."

"I think it is possible, dear brother," said Papandakis, and he nodded at Ben.

Ben didn't say anything, but he had to agree with the old man. Things were beginning to become clear.

Papandakis had turned to the boy again. "Tell me, Henry, who are the others?"

The boy looked over his shoulder. "The blond girl's Stephanie Hodges; her husband's the guy in the sweat shirt and glasses, named Doug; the other guy's

Jeff Stone, a friend of theirs. We met them in Kayseri. Why?"

"Is anyone missing from your group?" asked Papandakis.

The scowl returned to Henry's face. His jaw tightened. "You're damned right there is. That bastard Robinson."

"Stephen Robinson?" asked Papandakis.

"That's right. How did you know?"

"Never mind for now. Just answer, please. Had this Stephen Robinson been with you since India?"

"No. Stell and I met him the day after we arrived in Turkey. In Erzerum. He struck up a conversation and—"

"He introduced himself?"

"Yeah. He struck up a conversation with us at the bazaar. Saw us bargaining for a jet ring with a gold setting, came over and got it for us at a quarter of the price. Spoke excellent Turkish. Then he invited us for a drink, and when he found out we were into archaeology, he offered to show us a few out of the way places. Said he had a car and asked if we'd join him all the way to Izmir. He was happy as hell when we said yes. So were we—we hadn't met an American who knew his way around since—"

"And then?"

"And the next day we ran into the other three at Kayseri, and he asked them to come along. We visited a couple of sites, and everyone agreed to go wherever Robinson wanted—he really knew his stuff and he was great company."

While Reese was speaking Papandakis studied the map. He was tapping the fingers of his right hand rapidly against his temple, and every so often he nodded. Then he looked up at Ben. "Do you understand, Professor?"

Ben was only half paying attention to the conversation. He was constantly glancing beyond the Buick to the Turkish convoy, which remained far below on the winding road. Henry was watching it, too, but Papandakis and the other Cretans seemed unconcerned.

"Do you understand, Professor?" Papandakis repeated.

Ben nodded.

"I thought you would. Reilly said the memo was brought from Soviet Georgia. If so, then it could easily have come over the border at Batumi, right here." Papandakis pointed to a spot on the map in front of him. "A crossing that would be both casual and inconspicuous. Yes? Robinson picks it up there or just over the border at Artvin, over here, and then must go south to begin his westward journey on a major roadway, which he finds, look, here at Erzerum, where he surrounds himself with other Americans either to avoid suspicion or to confuse anyone who might be following him." He was tracing the movement on the map with his finger as he spoke. Now he said, as much to himself as to Ben, "He picked up the others at Kayseri, still moving west, but look, he is avoiding the major route through Ankara. He must think someone is following him, but that he has lost them. . . . Hmmm." He paused, then turned to Henry. "Where did you go after Kayseri, Henry?"

"Through Konya," Henry replied, looking back at the Turkish trucks.

"And from there to"—Papandakis paused to follow the route on the map—"Afyon?"

"No. He insisted we go south, the road that parallels

the Afyon highway, to Denizli, so we could see the ruins of Kyorara and Hierapolis."

"Yes, yes," nodded Papandakis, still staring at the map.

Ben noticed that Sali and Yussuf, their hands still on their heads, were watching the Turkish convoy and nodding, and the other Americans were glancing at it as frequently and uneasily as he had been.

"So Robinson takes still another circuitous route," Papandakis said to himself, although Henry answered him.

"That's what we thought, since we wanted to go to Sardis, which would have been on the way to Izmir on the Afyon highway. But he said we'd double back to Sardis from Izmir and that the driving was easier on the Denizli road. And, well, he seemed to know what he was doing, so—"

"So you allowed him to continue his itinerary. Yes, I know."

"Say, who is this guy anyway? Do you know him?"

"No, Henry. No, we do not. As for who he is, I think I can definitely tell you that if you will answer one more question. What happened at Söke?"

"Excuse me, sir. I don't mind answering your questions, but those trucks are really putting me uptight—"

"Do not trouble yourself about it, Henry."

"But—"

"You are not to worry, Henry."

Henry looked at Ben and shrugged. Papandakis returned to his question. "Again, Henry, what happened in Söke?"

"Damned if I know. Robinson said we'd go to Izmir the next day, but for that night he knew of a good hotel at Söke, a town a little off our route but worth the extra twenty miles or so. He was right again. It was a clean, pleasant town with a good *gazino*—I mean restaurant—for a change. And that night the cops busted in while we were asleep and busted us for drug smuggling. There you have it, except for the cops calling me by his name all the time and getting rough when I told them my name was Reese."

"I am sorry, but would you explain that last statement?" asked Papandakis.

"You mean about the cops calling me Robinson?"

"Yes, that, please."

"Confused hell out of me until they showed me my passport. It turned out to be Robinson's, but somehow my picture had been pasted in it. Sloppy as hell, too, even the Turks admitted that, but they thought I'd stolen it from someone else, put my own picture in it, and was using it as a false ID to fool the Turkish narcs."

"Did they find any drugs?"

"That's the craziest part of it. There was a packet of the stuff in every one of our knapsacks."

"And no Stephen Robinson," concluded Papandakis.

"And no Stephen Robinson! I think the bastard was using us to transport the stuff for him and then took off when the going got hot."

Papandakis fell silent. Ben looked at him, then back at the road. Although the Buick was hugging the truck's tail now, the Turkish convoy was still far behind. But what would happen when the convoy crested the hill and started to accelerate, or when they reached a level stretch of road, if there was one, between here and Kusadasi? And what sort of instructions had they radioed ahead to Kusadasi? Would Papandakis find half the Turkish army waiting for him there?

Papandakis was looking at Henry, still ignoring the danger that seemed to be closing in from all sides. "Your supposition about Robinson is not correct, Henry. But do not feel uneasy—we have more information than you do. Robinson is not the man you think he is. Do you not agree, Ben?"

"Yes, it seems that way," Ben replied offhandedly. He turned his complete attention to Papandakis now, beginning to realize the full implications of the old man's last words. "It looks like we've come over here on what we in America call a wild goose chase."

Pandelis bellowed and brought his fist down on the bed of the truck like a sledgehammer. The whole floor shook. "What goose chase? Pavlo dead, and what you talk about? Is crazy thing, making no sense!"

Ben turned to Pandelis, whose face was fiery with frustrated rage, and smiled affectionately at him. "This Stephen Robinson, it seems, is the agent we came to rescue, along with the others. But he had already traded passports and identities with Henry here, the real Henry Reese, and come to Crete." He turned to Henry and Stella. "I take it you three got pretty chummy, and you told him who you were and that you, Stella, were going to Crete to introduce your new husband to your father."

"Yes." Stella was frowning.

"And he asked your father's name and address."

"Yes, he did. He said he knew a Papandakis on Crete and wondered if my father was the same man."

Ben turned to Papandakis. "Seems he had it pretty well planned. But what I don't understand is why they got busted, where the drugs came from, and why Robinson continued the masquerade on Crete."

Papandakis shrugged. "About the drugs I am as confused as you. As for continuing the masquerade, I would think that either he could not make contact with Mr. Reilly or he knew that he had been sighted."

"This Robinson, where he now?" asked Pandelis.

"Lying in the morgue at Heraklion, I'd guess," Ben replied. "Wouldn't you agree, sir?"

"Yes, it is probably so." Papandakis smiled. "I think your Mr. Reilly will be most surprised when he sees the Stephen Robinson we have rescued."

Ben remembered Reilly frantically questioning him about "the other son-in-law" as he slid into unconsciousness two nights before in Ayia Galini, Reilly's continued probings the next morning on the phone, and his intention to see the body in the Heraklion morgue that afternoon. Ben smiled. "I think he already knows."

"How so, Professor?"

"He told me he was going to visit the morgue right after I spoke to him."

"I see. Then that leaves only one mystery—the most disturbing one of all."

"What's that, sir?"

"We must now assume that Mr. Reilly was telling the truth and that the memo is real. Would you not say so?"

Ben nodded, suddenly realizing what Papandakis was going to say.

"And we have three days before the directive goes into effect. Am I right?"

Ben nodded again.

"But where *is* the memo, my friend? And how does Mr. Reilly propose to find it now?"

Ben nodded once more, then said, "That's not our only problem. I'm afraid we've also cleared up a mystery whose solution is not a pleasant one."

"Oh?"

"We now know that Vlatchkov is real, too, and that Reilly was right when he suspected him of being the one who radioed the 'Transcendental' message."

"You are speaking about Mr. Reilly's Russian?"

"Yes. Obviously he's on Crete looking for the memo. And he's had more than a week's start on us."

Chapter Twenty-four

The truck had reached the top of the hill and was descending the other side through a series of switchbacks. As it hurtled around the curves everyone could see Kusadasi lying several miles to the north, far below them past scrubby slopes and cultivated fields. It was a prosperous-looking resort town set at the foot of low hills on the shores of a long gulf. The sun was just rising over the near side of the hills, and the sea was still a heavy pewter in the early light, marked by glossy black hollows and inky tracks and the dim hulk of a large island emerging from the shadows of the southwestern horizon. Papandakis pointed to the island and identified it as their destination, the Greek island of Samos, estimating that it was thirty miles from Kusadasi.

After the revelations about Robinson's real identity, the authenticity of the memo, and Vlatchkov's probable presence on Crete, Papandakis had begun to brood once again and the atmosphere in the back of the truck had become tense and silent.

Henry and the other Americans had gathered at the tailgate and were straining to catch a glimpse of the convoy every time the truck swung around a curve. This had developed into a peculiarly engrossing game, and the Americans reminded Ben of hens who know that a fox has snuck into the barnyard and is sliding around the outbuildings where they can't see him. Whenever one of the Americans caught sight of the convoy, he would call out, "There!" and point, and the others, in a dither of alarm, would look in the direction his finger was pointing and either gasp or groan if they saw the trucks. Even Pandelis and Manoli were beginning to show some interest.

Ben was scanning the road with the rest of them, but his thoughts were on the memo and the first of what might well be a chain reaction of cataclysmic events that would be set off in three days if the memo was not found. He was contemplating these possibilities with increasing alarm, when Kemal, who had been sitting in gloomy silence staring at the floorboards since Ben had finished speaking to Papandakis, suddenly spoke in a sharp, high voice that made everyone turn toward him. "If I may be permitted," he began, glancing toward Papandakis.

Papandakis looked up.

"This man you speak of—Robinson—you say he come to your house on Crete?"

Papandakis nodded.

"And that he is dead."

"That's right," interrupted Ben. "You sound as if you know him."

"He does," said Papandakis. "Of course. It is so obvious now. Think, Professor. Reilly arranged to protect us in Söke. Through whom? Kemal. Why? Because Kemal is employed by Reilly. Robinson disappears from Söke. He is employed by Reilly, too. Who helps him disappear? A Reilly employee in the area. And who is that person and at the same time the link between the two cases? Kemal. Am I correct, sir?"

Kemal nodded.

"What else do you know about this, Kemal?" asked Ben.

"Mr. Robinson, sir, he call me the day previous to Americans' arrival in Söke and say it never before so important for him to proceed from country."

"Because of the memo? Did he mention the memo or any kind of paper?" asked Ben.

"No, sir. He only say it is never before so important. He sound much excitement in his words."

"Then?"

"Then, sir, he tell me what is to be done by me."

"At Söke?"

"Yes, sir."

"What?"

Kemal looked away.

"Damn it, Kemal, what the hell went on in Söke?"

"Sir, if it is permitted—"

"Listen to me, Kemal. We've only got a few minutes to get this straightened out. Robinson's most likely dead and a document which may mean the outbreak of World War Three has disappeared. Now what the hell were you supposed to do in Söke?"

Kemal stared at the floorboards again, then looked up, shuttling his glance between Ben and Papandakis. "Mr. Robinson, he say that he is followed. To stop this, he tell me to bring to Söke next night two hundred grams of opium divided into five small packages. Then I am to give money to man at hotel desk to get passport of Henry Reese for one hour only, after Americans register.

"When next night Americans all sleeping in hotel, Robinson and me, we meet. He change picture on passport. Then, sir, he go to hotel with opium. I go to man at desk and return Robinson passport with Reese picture.

"We meet one hour forward, sir, Robinson and me. I have arranged new car for him and fishing boat at Kusadasi. This boat is for to take him to Crete. No other contacts he will use, he say. Then he will go to Athens from Crete—'backwards,' he say. As for me, I am to tell no one where he is gone, not even Mr. Reilly, in case Russians now monitoring our messages. Then he tell me call police and say opium in packs of these others where he put them. That is last I see him."

Ben shook his head. "And he gave you nothing—no letters, no papers?"

"No, sir. No thing."

"Just framed these people and took off?"

"Yes, sir."

"Damned! Why the hell would he do a thing like that?"

"To lose the people following him for one invaluable day and perhaps two, Professor," said Papandakis. "It was all, as you say, a smokescreen. Stephen Robinson would be arrested, safe in jail—and the memo would be useless, as far as his pursuers knew."

"Yeah," said Ben, "and as far as John Reilly knew, also."

"A devious man, this Robinson," said Papandakis. "Rather brilliant as well as unscrupulous."

"You sound as if you admire him, for God's sake!"

Papandakis smiled and said something in Greek to

Pandelis, who grunted, his expression still grim. Ben looked at Pandelis inquiringly.

"Stavros say this Robinson part Cretan," said Pandelis.

Ben looked at Papandakis. "Your daughter could have been killed because of that bastard," he said.

Papandakis smiled and shook his head. "Professor, you still fail to appreciate the exquisitely monstrous. My daughter did not die, and although it is quite probable that we may all be dead in the next few minutes, we will die knowing several things we did not know before. And what more can we ask than that a few mysteries of this strange world we inhabit together be answered for us? In this instance what they have revealed is an unfinished masterpiece of deceit by a master deceiver. This man came into my home, tricked me and my brother, and died after accomplishing his plan—or at least most of it. His legacy was your arrival and all that has followed. We can at least give him our homage, can we not? As we would give homage to a unfinished work of an El Greco or a Rembrandt? Yes?"

Pandelis was nodding in agreement.

Ben shook his head. "I'm never going to understand you people. Never, I swear." But despite himself, he was smiling.

"Aha, the smile," said Papandakis. "I think you will understand, Ben. I think perhaps you already do." Then, as he glanced out the back of the truck and saw the Turkish convoy sweeping down the switchbacks above them, he continued. "But now to the problem before us." He turned to Kemal. "Tell me, what is the road like from the bottom of this hill into Kusadasi?"

"Is good one, sir. Flat. A little from coast in beginning, then along it."

"How many lanes?"

"Four, sir."

"And the coastal plain?"

"Please, sir?"

"What is it like along the water—cliffs, sand?"

"*Plaj*—beach, sir, entirely the whole way forward to Kusadasi."

"Would they set up a roadblock outside the town?"

"Is most likely possible."

Papandakis looked at his watch. "It is now five fifty-five. Is there much traffic on the road at this hour?"

"No, sir. A farmer, a camel or two only."

"Will there be many people in the streets of Kusadasi?"

"Only fishermen at this hour, sir. And they at harbor, in cafés."

Papandakis thought for a moment, then spoke several sentences in Greek to Pandelis, who began shouting to Yorgo and Manoli. While the shouting was going on Papandakis made his way to the cab window and spoke to Cooper for a moment, pointing to the rear of the truck, before returning to where Kemal and Ben were now standing near the still seated Pandelis. Pandelis lifted the knapsack containing the twenty-four grenades up to his brother.

"Everyone, please, your attention," said Papandakis, gripping the bulky knapsack in one hand. "This is what we are planning to do. When we reach the flat road, the truck will stop and you, Kemal, will give this sack to your friends in the Buick. It contains twenty-four hand grenades. Do your friends know how to use them?"

"Yes, sir."

"Good. They will slow down until they are four to six seconds ahead of the convoy. Then they will throw the grenades from either side of the car onto the roadway, two at a time, until five have been thrown from each side. They will then pause to observe the results before resuming the maneuver. Do you understand that?"

Kemal nodded.

"Good. After that, if God is willing, we will all continue on toward Kusadasi's harbor, where a white fishing boat with a plain green ensign under the Turkish flag will be docked. We must get to that boat by seven . . . If we should run into a roadblock before we get there, the truck will slow down and Yorgo and I will jump from either side and attack the roadblock with grenades, ideally before the police realize what is happening. Meanwhile, everyone will run for the beach and approach the harbor from that direction. Remember, you must reach the boat with the green ensign by seven or it sails without you. Is that clear to everyone?"

"Wait a minute," said Ben, suddenly remembering something.

"Yes, Professor?" asked Papandakis.

"The money. What happened to the money in the shoebox?"

Papandakis smiled, patted the knapsack slung over his shoulder, reached into it, and brought out a stack of ten or fifteen bills shaped into a brick. "Unfortunately, I didn't have time to pay Hassan—or Yussuf for that matter," he said, turning to Yussuf and Sali. There was a smirk on the old man's lips.

Papandakis returned the money to his knapsack and handed the other one, Pandelis', with the twenty-four grenades to Kemal.

The truck was approaching the bottom of the slope, and as they swung around the last switchback they could see where the highway leveled out and hugged the coast for several miles north along white beaches. Beyond a low hill, and out of sight, lay Kusadasi.

"No!" shrieked a terrified voice. It was the blond girl. "Grenades? Are you insane? I won't do it! Doug, tell them. I won't do it!"

"She's right," said the boy in the sweat shirt. His glasses made him look studious and pained. "You can't go around killing people this way. We'll have no part of it."

Papandakis looked at them with tired eyes and shrugged. "If you want to remain in the truck, do so. You are not forced to come."

"Wait, papa." It was Stella. She turned to the blond girl. "Stephanie, remember what it was like in the prison? Those men? They even refused to inform the embassy of our arrest. That's not unusual in drug cases here. Even when they do, the result of the trial is always the same: they make an example of convicted drug-smugglers and sentence them to life, and keep them in jail no matter how much the consulate complains. Believe me, your only chance is to do what my father suggests."

The blond girl was quiet, looking down at her hands. The boy in the sweat shirt was looking at her, as if waiting for a signal.

Then Ben heard himself speaking, as if he were listening to his voice on a tape recorder. "The kids are right, Papandakis. You'll start a goddamn war if you do this."

"You are forgetting your position, Ben. You came into this country illegally, and at the very least broke the jaw of a prefect of police. If they catch you—well, I would not like to be in your position. And what about the memo? What are your obligations there? There are only three days left, and your Mr. Reilly will need all the help he can muster."

Now it was Ben's turn to remain silent. He had voiced his protest because he thought that he should, that it was expected of him—an obligation to a vision of the world that he, as teacher, had been pledged to maintain. But he knew his protest was a sentimental gesture even as he heard himself voice it. The convictions he had espoused so completely five days ago seemed like empty phrases now. The world was not a friendly place, never had been, and probably never would be.

Henry stepped forward. "Is there anything I can do to help?"

"Do you know how to use these guns?" Papandakis asked.

Henry nodded.

"And grenades?"

"I was in 'Nam for two years," Henry said.

Papandakis turned to Ben. "Shall I give him Pavlo's gun, Professor? I was keeping it for you."

Ben shook his head. "No. I'm in."

Papandakis nodded, picked up Pavlo's gun and handed it to Ben. Then he took his brother's gun and gave it to Henry.

"Mr. Papandakis, sir?" It was Sali, his hands on his

head, still sitting beside the fat man. "Please, what is to become of *us*?"

Papandakis turned to face him. "You and Yussuf will come with us as hostages. You will run with the others, should it come to that. Manoli there has been instructed to guard you. If either one of you attempts to escape, his orders are to shoot you both immediately."

"But, sir, this thing you cannot accomplish."

"Hope we do, Turkish," said Pandelis in a flat voice, "or you are dead before the sun come up again." Then he said something in Greek to Manoli, which caused him to snap the safety catch on his grease gun. Sali fell silent.

Pandelis was looking at Sali almost hungrily, his bandaged shoulder giving him the air of a barbarian warrior. Yussuf began to blubber. His hands were still on top of his hat, crushing it down almost over his eyes. Fat tears were rolling down his cheeks and he was sniffling.

"Quiet, fat one," said Pandelis.

"*Mon coeur, mon coeur,*" mumbled Yussuf. "*Nos amis pour années.*"

"In English, fat one," said Pandelis.

"We have been friends for years. Partners. Why now do you do this? Why?"

"Listen, Yussuf," said Papandakis. "Hassan did not betray us alone. You had to know about it also. That is why you sent Sali to Bodrum instead of coming yourself as we had planned. Am I correct?"

Yussuf didn't reply.

The truck was out of the hills now, sweeping north on a level highway. There was no traffic in either direction except for the Buick behind them. The convoy had not come into view yet. There were just the slopes to their left and the coast with its slim strip of white beach snaking away behind them on their right.

"Now, Kemal!" said Papandakis, and Kemal began to beckon to the Buick as Papandakis looked toward the cab and called to Cooper to tell the driver to pull off the road and stop.

The truck rolled to a halt by the side of the road, the Buick pulling up behind it. Kemal jumped over the tailgate, the knapsack slung over his arm, and dashed to the car, stuffing the knapsack through the window and speaking excitedly as he pointed up and down the road and waved his arms. Then he sprinted back to the truck, Ben and Henry hauled him in, and the truck lumbered off once more, but at a slower pace, the Buick falling farther and farther behind it.

Soon the convoy appeared behind the Buick, the lead truck larger on the horizon with each second. The Buick maintained its speed, everyone in the back of the truck watching it silently. The only sound was the whine of the engine and the jolting rattle of wooden slats when the truck hit a rough spot in the road.

The Turkish convoy was several hundred yards behind the Buick when hands emerged from the rear windows on either side of the car and flung something backward before being pulled inside again. This gesture was repeated five times in the next six seconds.

Even before the arms were pulled back into the car for the fifth time and the Buick accelerated, the first of the explosions flashed on the road behind it. Two. Four. Then the lead Turkish truck seemed to rear up like a horse on top of a rolling orange cloud. A moment later, as the sound of the explosions reached them, the truck seemed to vault into the air, and at the peak of its ascent it began to come apart, fragments flying from it in all directions, and a fireball emerging in its center. An enormous explosion shook the air a second after that, and the truck was momentarily blotted from view by the brilliant splash. Then the vehicle reappeared, landing heavily on its wheels, a burning hulk swerving off the road, wrapped in flames. The truck behind it was burning, too. It seemed to have collided with the truck ahead, and was skidding off the road farther into the underbrush. The third truck was still intact, though, and swerved into the brush on the opposite side of the road to avoid the debris before turning to the road once more.

Everyone in the truck was stunned.

"My God!" muttered Ben. He hadn't seen anything like it since Korea.

The blond girl began to whimper.

"Holy shit!" said Henry. "One of the grenades must have got the gas tank."

Ben turned to Papandakis. The old man was staring, mesmerized, at the wreckage on the roadway behind them. His features were swollen and his eyes inflamed, and he looked like the statue of the demiurge that Pandelis had become when he was about to take Ben's life. Ben felt sick and turned back toward the road.

The hands flew out of the Buick again, and several seconds later two more flashes roiled out of a thin oily smoke, detonating harmlessly on the road in front of the last Turkish truck, which emerged from the smoke, still gaining on the black car.

The men in the Buick must have realized that the

truck was gaining on them, for hands began to fly in and out of the windows—once, twice, three times, four. It looked as if the men in the Buick were feverishly trying to paddle their car out of danger.

"They're throwing them all!" shouted Henry, and even before the words were out of his mouth the explosions began, like a synchronized mortar attack, and the Turkish truck disappeared in intermittent orange flashes and heavy smoke.

When the smoke cleared, the truck was dwindling behind them, in flames, men jumping from it on both sides.

"*A' Pedia, tous fagame!*" shouted Pandelis, and Yorgo began whistling through his teeth and dancing in a tight circle, his head down, hopping from one foot to the other like a grasshopper.

"That for Pavlo, Turkish bastards!" shouted Pandelis, and he waved his good arm happily at the Buick, apparently forgetting that its occupants were as Turkish as the soldiers in the convoy.

The black car was hugging the tail of the truck once again, and its occupants could be seen grinning and roughhousing with each other, as elated as the Cretans in the truck.

Sali and Yussuf were sitting with pinched faces. The Americans had remained silent, too, clearly stunned by the violence and bewildered by the celebration going on around them.

Ben was unable to suppress a grin, and when Yorgo grabbed him around the waist, he jumped up and down with him and crowed just as loudly. Kemal was jumping up and down with Henry. Then all four of them were jumping together, and Stella was jumping and howling with them. Ben was dizzy and could hear himself laughing, but he could see the other Americans behind him even as he reeled, stomping and yodeling, around the floorboards. He didn't want to look at them.

Cooper's voice cut through the festivities. "Muzzle it, you blokes! We've got a welcoming committee," he said, and pointed ahead of him when everyone was quiet.

Through the small window they could see past the windshield. A low hillside lay before them. At the foot, several hundred yards away on the road ahead, three Jeeps were blocking the highway in both directions. A military truck was pulled up on the coast side of the road next to them, and about twenty helmeted men in beige uniforms, all carrying rifles or machine-guns, were milling around the vehicles.

Chapter Twenty-five

The truck slowed down several moments later, as if they were stopping for an inspection.

Waiting for Cooper's signal, Papandakis and Yorgo squatted on either side of the tailgate, grenades with pins already pulled in either hand, grease guns slung over their shoulders, and knapsacks hanging over their chests.

It was completely quiet in the back of the truck now. Everyone was crouched down, ready to move.

Along with Pavlo's grease gun, Papandakis had given Ben two grenades and assigned him to guard the rear. Now, the grenades bulging in his front pants pocket, Ben waited behind the others, gripping the gun across his chest in the ready position and watching Henry on the other side of the truck.

Ben was surprised at how easily his body had accepted the situation. It was reacting just as it had each day in Korea. All fear, all emotions, in fact, had been compressed into a tiny area that flickered every so often somewhere deep in his bowels.

He was positive the police at the roadblock had heard the explosions, and yet, since Cooper was not shouting an alarm, they must have been showing no signs of extraordinary vigilance or hostility. The explosions had probably happened too fast, were only distant sounds to them, noises to question and maybe to puzzle over. Possibly this truck or the black car behind it had seen what had happened and could tell them.

"Now!" barked Cooper, and Papandakis and Yorgo sprang from the truck and immediately disappeared from sight.

The Buick stopped behind the truck and five men bounded from it, leaving the doors open. They rushed to the coast side of the road, in front of the truck, where they fell to the ground and began firing at the roadblock.

There were shouts and confused yelling and commands in Turkish coming from somewhere in front of the truck as Ben and the others jumped from the back and ran behind the prone men firing at the roadblock. Kemal dropped to the ground beside them as Ben ran past.

The grenades went off a moment later—four closely-spaced explosions that staggered Ben, almost throwing him to the ground for a moment. When he turned, he saw that two of the three Jeeps were on fire and twisted at odd angles to each other, and that an orange balloon of flame was billowing from the canvas roof of the truck behind them. Bits of wreckage were still tumbling through the air and bouncing on the road, and several Turkish soldiers were running for cover in the brush on both sides of the highway, while others were scattered over the roadway itself— some dead or wounded, but some already firing at Ben and the others. Ben could hear the staccato snapping sounds of automatic weapons.

He would have raked the area with a quick volley,

except that Cooper was in his line of fire, running toward him, and behind Cooper, running low to the ground, were Papandakis and Yorgo. The heavyset driver was lying on the road behind them, midway between the truck and the flaming roadblock, identifiable only by his checkered shirt.

The five men from the Buick had scrambled up and were sprinting behind Papandakis and Yorgo.

"Get a move on, sport," said Cooper as he ran past.

Ben turned and dashed after him, the grenades joggling in his pockets, two dead weights, their ridged surfaces bumping against his thighs. He heard Papandakis and Yorgo wheezing behind him as bullets whined past his head.

The sandy shore was only fifty yards away now. It ran north and south in an uneven line of white sand and surf-ruffled sea. To the north it curved white and clean for another hundred yards to a cement causeway that led out to a tiny forested islet topped by a castle.

Papandakis and Yorgo were running alongside him now. Kemal caught up with them and pointed to the island. "*Kus Adasi*, Bird Island," he panted. "Harbor two hundred meters forward of that, sir."

The gunfire behind them continued. This alarmed Ben, for they had reached the sand and the going was slower. They seemed to be running in place, getting nowhere, and Ben's ankles were aching. He heard a grunt behind him and turned. One of Kemal's Turks had dropped his gun and was swerving off to his left, toward the surf, clutching the right side of his ribcage and doubling up. Then he fell to his knees, gasping for breath, and just before he pitched forward, he looked up at his comrades, an expression of bewilder-

ment on his face. One of the other Turks rushed to
help him and waved the others on.

By now the sun had turned the pewter sea into a
cauldron of bronze.

They ran on, spurts of sand flicking around them.
Up ahead of them Pandelis, his left arm bound in a
makeshift sling, was humping down the sand behind
the three Americans, and exhorting them to hurry
with growls and hoarse oaths. The boy in the sweat
shirt limped along as best he could, his left arm also
in a sling, but the blond girl kept veering off and
throwing her arms down at her sides. Whenever she
slackened her pace, Pandelis would shout louder and
smack her across the rump with the flat blade of his
Cretan dagger, which he was holding in his right hand
like a goad. She, in turn, would immediately yelp,
bring her hands back to protect her rear, and scamper
on, shrieking angrily.

Stella and Henry were running on their right flank,
away from the sea, and Henry kept looking over his
shoulder and scowling, holding the grease gun by the
trigger guard, pointed toward the sand.

Manoli was trotting behind Yussuf and Sali on the
other flank, and every time Yussuf slowed down,
Manoli would jab his gun barrel into the fat man's
kidneys. Yussuf's back would arch up at each thrust
and he would drag one leg in a stricken limp for several steps, then run a few yards at full speed before
once more lapsing into a girlish waddle.

Behind the others, Cooper, Papandakis, Yorgo,
Kemal, and Ben ran in a protective line. Ben looked
over his shoulder. The three Turks were racing over
the sand behind him, the fourth was sprinting to catch
up with them, and the fifth lay immobile, forty yards

down the beach. Beyond the beach six or seven Turkish soldiers were running toward them through the brush.

They slogged through the sand, reaching the causeway in less than a minute. Everyone was out of breath. The first line waited gasping for the last, no one speaking. When the four Turks caught up to them, Pandelis and his group climbed up on the causeway and started to jog toward the mainland, their backs to the island castle. The other groups followed in order. The handful of Turkish soldiers were still several hundred yards behind them.

The causeway led them to a cement esplanade after less than a hundred yards. The esplanade ran north and south. On the left, to the north, it curved along the waterfront, running parallel to a two-lane paved road and, beyond that, to a large hill, disappearing around the hill within another hundred yards. This was the same hill Ben had seen through the windshield of the truck, and as he and the others charged down the causeway they seemed to be running toward it. Its green slopes loomed ahead of them from the opposite side of the road, scuffed with patches of lion-colored dirt, gray outcrops, and a dozen or so white houses on its lower levels. On the right, in the distance, an oily black cloud billowed from the roadblock, but that was all Ben could see of it. There seemed to be no traffic in either direction.

They reached the esplanade and then the bend in the road and kept running, everyone gasping and panting but refusing to stop.

The other side of the hill opened onto an amphitheater of hills facing the sea. A jumble of whitewashed houses with red-tile roofs were clustered together on the slopes and around the shore, thickest in the center where a town square fronted a small harbor, complete with fishing boats and several yachts rolling at anchor. People were sitting in outdoor cafés in the square and strolling back and forth on the docks.

The esplanade continued to wind along the waterfront, parallel to the road and leading directly to the harbor.

They ran on. The harbor was no more than three hundred yards away, and Ben was infused with new energy at the sight of the boats.

Maybe that was why he didn't hear the Jeep until it roared around the bend behind him. Before he could swivel around, he heard the cackling of machine gun fire. He turned in time to see three of Kemal's Turks falling toward him, eyes bulging. Soldiers standing in the Jeep shot spurts of flame in his direction, and pulverized cement was kicking up around his shoes. Six soldiers were standing on the Jeep's running boards, all so far off-balance they couldn't even point their weapons, and Ben supposed that they must have been the squad of soldiers who had chased them across the beach.

"Ben! Yorgo! Grenades!" yelled Papandakis, just as several of the soldiers jumped from the running boards. The momentum of the Jeep thrust them forward before they could steady themselves. Then someone behind Ben opened fire, and two of the soldiers grabbed their chests and fell.

The Jeep slowed down. Ben threw down his grease gun and kept running, his body half turned to the road. He plunged his right hand into his pocket, he grabbed a grenade, pulled the pin, and heaved it toward the Jeep as it bore down on him. The grenade fell into the back of the Jeep, bouncing off the shoulder of a soldier with a boyish profile and shiny-black curly hair who was standing up and firing back at the fallen Turks from the Buick. The grenade dropped at the soldier's feet, behind the front seat. Ben saw all this even as he turned and searched for cover.

Papandakis was sprawled on the pavement, his hands over his head, and Ben dived to the sidewalk. But even before his body hit the pavement, the first explosion tore through the early morning. There seemed to be a cushion between the sidewalk and his stomach that lifted him up and whirled him over. He landed on his back with a grunt and lay there helpless, the breath knocked out of him, as another explosion, and then another, went off and turned the morning upside down.

He could see the blue sky clearly above him, hear the screams and shoe-scrapings on the concrete, but he seemed paralyzed, stranded in the confines of his body, the breath lost somewhere in his upper chest and clawing for a way out. He was terrified.

Cooper's face appeared above him. It was frowning with concern. "Hit, sport? Where?"

Then, as Cooper helped him up, his breath found passage and rushed out of him. He was standing up now, still breathing hard, still shaky.

"All right?" asked Cooper, who had retrieved Pavlo's gun and now handed it to him. "Then let's hop it!"

The smell of burning gasoline and machine oil and the bitter odor of cordite hung around them, and the screaming continued. But the machine-gun fire had stopped. Ben saw why.

The Jeep had crashed into a lamp post on the opposite side of the road. It was on fire, and men were trying to raise their arms and heads from inside it. Five bodies lay on the road. Two of them were floundering on the asphalt as if it were slippery, and every time they tried to rise they fell back into a prone position.

On the sidewalk across from the burning wreck, the American in the grimy white T-shirt was lying face down, his right arm flung over his head and the palm of his left hand turned upward along his side. A puddle of blood was spreading from beneath his face; he wasn't moving. Directly in front of him Henry was being helped up by Stella. He was clutching his left arm and blood was spurting between his fingers. A few yards beyond them Pandelis and the boy in the sweatshirt were dragging the blond girl after them. She was screaming and looking back at the boy in the white T-shirt. In the lead now, Yussuf and Sali stumbled ahead of Manoli, staggering through the sunlight toward the harbor. Everyone, in fact, was starting to move again. Papandakis passed Ben, pulling at his coat sleeve as he went by. Then Yorgo, dragging his right leg, limped by; his right hand clutched his thigh. He was gritting his teeth, his black eyes flashing. Ben started toward him and from the corner of his eye saw the four Turks from the Buick still on the ground. Three were not moving. One was on his knees, bent over two of the others, and Kemal was cradling the head of the third.

"Kemal!" yelled Ben.

Kemal looked up. "You go!" he shouted back, looked down at the man in his arms for a moment, then up at Ben again and called in a softer voice, "This one my brother."

The words made the situation seem brutal and

meaningless to Ben, and he suddenly felt empty, helpless. He fought against it, turned and tried to put an arm around Yorgo in order to support him, but Yorgo pushed him away.

"No! You go! *Torah!*"

"Shut up!" snapped Ben. Shoving the Cretan's hand aside, he looped an arm around Yorgo's waist.

Yorgo pulled away for a moment, then leaned heavily on Ben's shoulder, and they hobbled quickly after the others.

The remaining twelve kept running, their shoes thumping on the pavement. The ones in front slowed so the others could catch up. Then they all ran on in a tight group. *Wrong*, thought Ben, realizing that they presented an easy target bunched up that way, but at the same time understanding the protective impulse that had caused them to pack together.

They were nearing the center of town now, and people were standing motionless at café tables and on the docks, staring at them.

They jogged on, feet tramping, past small shops and houses and narrow side streets, staring grim-faced at the harbor, nobody breaking stride, even when two Jeeps appeared from a wide thoroughfare, sped through the square, and jerked to a halt in front of the palm-fringed entrance to the wharf. Eight helmeted men in dark-green fatigues, each armed with a machine gun, jumped out and hastily formed a line that blocked their way.

"Yussuf!" called Papandakis. "Now you. Tell them who you are. Tell them you are a hostage—and that we will shoot you if they refuse to let us pass!"

Immediately the fat man began shouting in Turkish at the line of men fifty yards ahead. If the Turks opened fire now, they could probably wipe out all of them. Ben knew that, but he also knew that their luck might hold. *Luck?* Yes, luck—that and the element of surprise had been on their side, as well as the boldness of their attack and the unexpected use of grenades. All had been rabbits pulled out of Papandakis' hat, and the last rabbit was about to be produced—Yussuf, a high official of some sort.

"Keep running! Keep running!" Papandakis called out while Yussuf was gibbering at the phalanx of uniformed men ahead of them. The group slogged on in perfect step, as if they were one body with many legs.

Thirty yards.

Twenty.

Fifteen.

The line of Turkish soldiers began to shift nervously. Several were glancing sideways at a slim man with a neatly clipped mustache and sunglasses who was standing next to one of the Jeeps. He wore a tan uniform with two gold stars glinting on the shoulders of his jacket, and a black-billed cap with a yellow star-and-crescent insignia above the visor. He had started forward before Yussuf had begun to shout, his right leg bent and lifted and his right arm raised in the middle of a command, and he had remained in that position ever since the fat man had begun proclaiming his identity.

Yussuf was screaming now, almost bleating. It seemed like the eleven people behind him were pushing him forward. They were packed into a solid mass, all sensing, it seemed from the louder tramping of their boot soles, that the uniformed men were wavering and that their commander was confused.

Then the officer in the dark glasses yelped a command, the line of uniformed men parted, and the tightly grouped survivors of the raid went past them. Ben, his arm still around Yorgo, sensed they were one creature, one grinding mechanism, as they continued their tight, pistonlike progress on the cement dock, where astonished fishermen leaped out of their way or stared at them from the decks of their boats.

Ben's back was a shimmer of nerve ends. At any moment he expected to feel bullets thud into it. He strained to hear what was happening behind him, but could distinguish only the tramping of boot soles as the group stamped along the dock.

Masts swayed overhead. Nets sprawled from rigging. Turkish flags drooped from their halyards.

"*Natous! Natous!*" barked Pandelis, and still they kept running.

Then Ben heard an idling engine sputtering above the noise of their boot soles. The sound grew louder, and suddenly the group was splintering, falling away in front of him, and everyone was jumping onto a large white boat and turning around, reaching to help Yorgo and him aboard.

The engine roared, and within seconds they were speeding out of the harbor, past the breakwater, and swinging back past the island castle and the causeway and the huge hill on the mainland.

The island Papandakis had identified as Samos swayed in the distance ahead of them, a ghostly presence in the early morning sunlight.

Ben looked back at the harbor and the town. Several policemen had charged onto the pier, and now, small figures without faces or names, they stood at the end of the dock and helplessly watched the fleeing boat.

Had it really been that easy?

Then Ben saw the thin smoke rising from the wreckage on the esplanade, and a few moments later the billowing black clouds where the roadblock had been, and farther down the highway the shimmering smudged air above the demolished convoy—and he remembered the destruction and the dead men he was leaving behind. Suddenly he was exhausted, too tired to think.

"Hour an a half, sport, and we're home free," said Cooper.

Ben nodded, unable to reply. Hassan was crumpling against the cellblock wall, and the soldier with the curly black hair stood in the Jeep firing the machine gun as the grenade bounced off his shoulder.

Ben exhaled and looked down at the grease gun in his lap, and as he stared at it he realized that he was still clutching it in both hands in the ready position.

Bird Island was fifteen minutes behind them, and they were headed southwest through an immense morning of sunlight and blue water, the green Turkish coast off to port and the island of Samos far ahead to starboard.

Aside from Yorgo and Henry and the dead they had left behind, no one else had been wounded in Kusadasi. The blond girl had merely become hysterical at the sight of the dead boy in the white T-shirt, and now, although still sniffling, she was quiet.

They had patched Henry's arm well enough to stop the bleeding, wrapped Yorgo's leg with the rest of Pandelis' shirt, and then had hungrily devoured the bread, cheese, and wine that had been waiting for them. They were sitting in the stern of the boat, staring dazedly into the sun-speckled water, when the captain called from the wheelhouse.

He was a lanky, dour-looking man with white hair, who had been introduced by Papandakis as a relative from the island of Chios. Pandelis had elaborated on this introduction by describing to Ben the man's activities in the Chian resistance during World War II. This information was sketchy, however, since Pandelis seemed more interested in extolling the wonders of the boat's powerful engine, and from his words Ben gathered that the captain was not only a relative but an important element in Papandakis' smuggling operation.

"*A' Prosohe!*" the captain called.

They all looked forward. Sweeping toward them from around a headland on their left was a sleek, fast-moving cutter.

"Turkey coastguard," whispered Pandelis.

Several minutes later they were all waiting, weapons in hand, when the gray coastguard cutter came alongside.

The cutter had been talking to them for the last several hundred yards, blaring instructions in Greek, French, and English over a breeze-slurred amplification system.

A small naval gun, mounted in front of the cutter's bridge, was being aimed at the Chian's deck by three Turkish sailors, and ten more sailors stood along the prow of the cutter, automatic weapons at the ready.

Papandakis stood at the starboard rail, facing the cutter. He was flanked by Yorgo and Manoli, who were standing behind Yussuf and Sali, holding daggers to their throats. Pandelis and the Americans stood in a group behind Papandakis, Henry in their midst, his left arm in a sling and his right hand at his side, clamped, Ben knew, around a grenade with a pin already pulled, as Papandakis had instructed. Cooper and Ben were standing on benches below the port gunwales, on either side of the Americans, their grease guns aimed at the sailors on the cutter. The dour Chian captain was in the wheelhouse, his back to the entire scene, standing at the wheel.

The engines of both vessels were idling. There was a slight chop to the sea now, and water slapped against the hull of the boat, rocking it from side to side.

An officer in a starched white uniform strode past the sailors in the prow of the cutter and addressed them through a white megaphone. "You will be pleased to put down your arms," he said. "We shall board in one minute." He repeated the instructions in Greek and French.

Papandakis turned to Yussuf and whispered something, and the fat man began shouting at the officer in Turkish.

The officer appeared to listen attentively, then he turned and went back toward the bridge of the cutter.

Nobody moved. Several minutes went by. The boat continued to rock, and the sunlight was a hot plaster on Ben's back. Sweat rolled down his face and trickled from his armpits and down his sides.

Finally the officer reappeared. He stood in the prow of the cutter again and spoke through the megaphone. "Great crimes have been done. Many Turkish citizens killed by you. My government cannot accept your request. We hope you are aware that should any harm be visited upon Mr. Asmali, the situation will be certain to go more adversely for you. Be pleased to put down your arms immediately!"

Yussuf began to shout, but Papandakis interrupted him. "We will comply with your request," he called out. "You may come aboard to discuss Mr. Asmali's release, but for reasons I am sure you will understand, we will stay with our weapons until we have reached an agreement."

No one on the boat moved.

The officer hesitated, then ordered several sailors to throw a metal gangplank across the gunwales of both boats. When this was accomplished two armed sailors came aboard the fishing boat and positioned themselves beside Yussuf and Sali on the crowded deck, and the officer began to cross over himself. When he was nearly across, Papandakis, in a firm voice, said *"Torah."* The officer leaned forward as if he had been spoken to, and Papandakis grabbed his arm with one hand and pulled him aboard. At the same time, a knife flashed overhead in the old man's other hand and swept down to skewer the officer in the center of his white uniform.

Meanwhile, at Papandakis' command, Yorgo and Manoli slid the blades of their daggers across Yussuf's and Sali's throats, as if drawing bows across the strings of two cellos, and almost simultaneously shoved the two Turks, their necks spouting blood, against the two armed sailors. Yorgo and Manoli leaped at the sailors, daggers glinting in the sunlight.

At the same instant Ben and Cooper opened fire, Henry's arm arced forward as the other Americans sprawled for cover on the deck, and the Chian captain gunned the engine full throttle, whisking the boat over the water with a jolt that sent Ben and Cooper toppling onto the deck.

The entire action had taken less than three seconds.

Ben, sprawled on the deck with the others, could still see the Turkish sailors falling on the deck of the cutter. He and Cooper had agreed to shoot inward, toward the center of the line of sailors, in order to provide two crossing lines of fire.

Papandakis had hastily devised the plan when the Chian had spotted the cutter, and it seemed to have worked perfectly. Ben didn't think that the Turks had gotten off a single shot. But even as he was thinking this he heard the clatter of machine gun fire and wood chips were spraying around him. Somewhere glass shattered and the blond girl screamed again, but not in the same way as she had before. The cutter's deck gun fired with a sound like a slamming door, but the shot must have been off to the side—it would have had to be, the boat was moving too fast and the cannon had been trained on it when it was stationary and at point-blank range. Papandakis had thought of that, too.

Ben lay with his hands over his head, waiting for the explosion of the grenade; but whether because of the noise of the engine or the increasing distance between the two boats, he never heard it. The next thing he knew, Cooper was bending over him, smiling and helping him up.

He and Cooper looked back toward the cutter. A puffy gray plume of smoke was rolling from the prow.

Manoli was whooping and vaulting high into the air, slapping the heels and toes of his boots with open hands, while Yorgo watched, leaning heavily on his good leg, a pained expression on his face. Both were patched all over with blood. Papandakis, on one knee, was rising slowly, looking down at the Turkish officer.

The officer and the two sailors were dead, but Yussuf and Sali were still alive, spurting blood and jerking in convulsions at the feet of the two Cretans.

Henry, Stella, and Doug were bending over the blond girl, who was blubbering and rolling from side to side on her stomach, a pink froth gathering on her lips. Beyond them in the wheelhouse Pandelis knelt below the shattered windshield, where the Chian captain lay motionless. "Jeem!" Pandelis called to Cooper. "The steering!" And Cooper hurried into the wheelhouse and took the wheel, steering a course for Samos.

"Steph! Steph!" called the boy in the sweat shirt, kneeling next to the blond girl. She lay still now. "Steph?" His voice trailed off.

Henry touched his shoulder. "She's gone, Doug." Henry tried to lift the boy off her body, but he shook off Henry's hand with a jerk of his shoulder.

Yussuf and Sali were still flipping like landed fish, but their convulsions were weaker. Manoli was slipping on the blood-slick deck as he went from one to the other and peered curiously at them. Blood was everywhere—splashed on the white walls to the gunwales and rolling in puddles on the planks of the deck.

"For Pavlo!" hissed Manoli.

"For betrayal!" muttered Papandakis.

"You could have told them," said Ben, realizing that this was the end Papandakis had planned for the two Turks all along. He was staring at the blood, but he was too dazed and exhausted to feel any more than a slight nausea at the sight of so much of it.

"What good would it have done, Ben?" asked Papandakis. He was staring at the blood also, unable to take his eyes from it, his features thickened once more. A slow smile curled his lips. "Besides, if they had known, they might not have helped us at the wharf or just now with the cutter."

Ben looked at him. "You really are a heartless bastard," he said in a tired voice.

"No," said Papandakis, still gazing at the blood as if hypnotized by it. "It had to be done. These men were without honor." Then he turned and stared at Ben with his expressionless black eyes. "Do you understand that, Professor?"

Ben nodded, too exhausted to be drawn into a discussion.

"I thought you would. Whatever other reasons were involved, that was the central one. Please remember this."

Ben turned away. He wasn't sure of anything anymore.

"And now," continued Papandakis in his tired voice, "we have only one concern left."

Ben looked up.

"The memo, Professor," the old man said. "We have only three days to find it."

Chapter Twenty-six

They arrived on Samos by seven thirty, mooring several miles west of the town of Pithagorion in a small cove on the south coast, where they were met by six middle-aged men in four cars.

They had tossed the bodies of the five Turks overboard half an hour before their arrival, and now Papandakis instructed several of the greeting party to wash down the boat and sail it, with the blond girl's body, to the hospital at the island's port city of Samos, where they were also to take the captain, who had been shot in the back but was not mortally wounded. Pandelis handed the Americans their passports, explaining that he had retrieved them from the main desk in the front room of the Söke jail. The boy in the sweat shirt refused to leave his wife's body, and when Pandelis, mumbling condolences, gave him his dead companion's passports as well as his own, he did not acknowledge his expressions of sympathy. He accepted the passports in silence, and did not say a word throughout the preparations that followed, nor did he say good-bye to any of the others before they drove off.

Ben and the others—Papandakis, Pandelis, Cooper, Stella, Henry, Yorgo, and Manoli—were driven to a house owned by one of the men who had met them at the cove. There they ate, bathed, had their wounds looked after by a doctor, and changed into their own clothes, which had lain all night at the bottom of their knapsacks. Then they distributed the weapons and ammunition among the men who had greeted them, and after much hugging and vows of affection on all sides, they were driven by their hosts to the Samos airport to fly back to Crete.

"Why didn't we fly here to begin with, and go from here to Kusadasi and then over the hill to Söke? It would have been ten times shorter," Ben said to Papandakis while they were waiting to board the plane.

Papandakis had made several phone calls and spoken privately with at least fifteen visitors to the house near Pithagorion; now he looked wizened and tired. But he smiled, put an affectionate arm around Ben's shoulder, and replied, "My dear Ben, we were much more inconspicuous by sea. Besides, we *had* to go to Bodrum. I knew Hassan and Yussuf would betray us, and since they expected us to return through Bodrum, it seemed likely that they had laid a trap for us there, or along the way, in the final contingency that their ambush in Söke should fail. I would not doubt that an ambush party is waiting for us in Bodrum at this moment. You see, they knew that the boat which took us to Kos could never reach Kusadasi by the time we broke the jail at Söke and could get there ourselves. Therefore, they discounted Kusadasi as a possible point of departure. That is why the resistance we met there was so haphazard. They were unaware that the day before I had arranged by phone with Alexi, my cousin from Chios, to meet us there."

* * *

The hour-long flight to Crete was not a happy one. All the Cretans were somber and held whispered conversations in which Ben heard the word *Pavlo* muttered many times. Ben had hardly known Pavlo, and he sensed that it was not his place to join in the conversations, but he felt a sadness that had nothing to do with the standard response a person experiences on learning of the death of one so young. There had been something different about Pavlo. He and the other two young Cretans were not an inseparable trio in Ben's mind, performing a ballet of exuberant horseplay. Pavlo's dreamy eyes, his incompetence on guard duty in Papandakis' garden three nights before, and the way he had offered Ben the plate on the boat before taking food for himself, suggested a gentleness, a certain kind of serenity, which seemed to imply that if Pavlo had had his choice, he would have done something else with his life, something as unpretentious as tending sheep or watching the stars wheel around the heavens night after night, or working in the olive groves and singing to the birds. And that sense of the boy, no matter how sentimental it was, made Pavlo's fate that much more pitiable to Ben. *And what about Hassan's fate? And the young soldier with the curly black hair?* Yes, theirs, too. In Julia's terms Ben had regained something this morning that he had lost over the past twenty years. Now he wondered at what cost he had regained it.

The Cretans continued their whispered conversations. Left to his thoughts, Ben had time to consider the escape from Turkey in retrospect, and now he added a third reason for their success. Not only had they done the unexpected and been armed with grenades, but they had struck with such murderous disre-

gard for life that it was enough to set all but the most
hardened opposition at a disadvantage. Yet he acknowledged
that if he had to do it again, he would
carry out every act as he had before, and such was his
respect for Papandakis now that he knew he would
follow any orders the old man gave him, no matter
how callous or sadistic.

Inevitably, these reflections brought Ben back to
the most important question of all, the one that kept
intruding on his other thoughts, and that was the
whereabouts of the memo. There were still three days
left before the directive went into effect, but now
that Robinson was dead, how were they going to find
it? And Vlatchkov—where was he on the island, what
was he doing this very moment, and more important—
what had he been doing for the past nine or ten days?

They arrived in Crete at one P.M.

Nikos and Uncle Kosta met them at the Heraklion
airport with the Citroën and the Volvo. Uncle Kosta
informed them that there was no need to go to Spinalonga,
since Reilly had phoned to cancel the meeting
an hour after Papandakis had called from Samos to arrange
for the cars. "The American, he is at the house
now," said Uncle Kosta with tears in his eyes. When
the old man had gone ahead for the car, Pandelis took
Ben's arm and nodded at the old man's back. "Pavlo,"
he said, "is Kosta's grandson."

Ben almost didn't recognize the young man who
greeted them when they arrived in the graveled yard
behind Papandakis' house. He walked toward them
against a backdrop of olive trees, as if the searing
white sunlight had somehow detached his bleached

figure from the dark green foliage. He wore a neatly-pressed blue-and-white hopsack suit, a pale blue shirt, and an indigo-and-white-striped tie, and his blond hair was combed back in orderly waves. It was the eyes that gave him away, the bright blue china-doll eyes that shifted quickly from Ben's face to Papandakis'—the eyes and the man in the white suit who was leaning against the fender of a gray BMW sedan several yards to his left.

"Hello, Reilly," said Ben with an involuntary smirk. They both seemed vastly different since their last meeting, and Ben liked his own difference better.

Ben introduced Reilly to the group. Reilly nodded impatiently to each one, and so Ben extended the length of the introductions, enjoying his former student's discomfort.

Caroline entered the yard in the midst of the introductions but remained on the edge of the group until Ben saw her and nodded. Then she came up to him, and he took her hand, pressed it, and looked into her eyes for a moment. She stood next to him for the rest of the introductions, her hand in his.

Papandakis suggested that the conversation be continued in the shade, and with the old man and Reilly leading the way, Ben, his arm around Caroline, and the rest of the group, whose gloom seemed to have deepened as they neared home, filed into the house, trudging to the study without a word, Reilly striding ahead of them, tense and silent, and Uncle Kosta quietly bringing up the rear.

When everyone was comfortably seated in the study, Papandakis instructed Manoli to have the old women bring cold wine and *mezedakia*. Papandakis was seated behind the desk. Ben, Pandelis, and

Cooper sat in upholstered straight-back chairs in front of the desk to his right and Reilly sat in a brown leather easy chair to his left, his hands tightly clasped together. Behind Reilly, Caroline, Stella, and Henry shared the sofa in front of the glass doors with Yorgo, whose bandaged leg was propped on a chair, while Nikos and the man in the white suit stood on either side of the door to the hall. Uncle Kosta had disappeared.

"Let's get on with it," said Reilly.

"What's your hurry?" drawled Ben, settling back in his chair.

Reilly glared at him, his jaws clenched.

Ben smirked. "We've got some interesting news for you, Reilly. So relax."

"I already *know*, *sir*. I went to the morgue. He was due to be shipped back to the States tomorrow."

"Stephen Robinson?" asked Papandakis.

"Yes. Anyway, that's the name he went by. Our man in Turkey, poor bastard. Lucky we got to the morgue in time."

Ben knew it was petty, but he continued to taunt Reilly, remembering how the agent had twice made a fool of him and relishing his frustration. "Tell me, Reilly, how come you didn't know about Robinson before? I thought you people knew everything. Even when I told you about Reese visiting Papandakis, you seemed shocked."

Reilly clenched his jaws again and looked down at his hands. He took a deep breath and looked up. His blue eyes were icy, and he spoke in a toneless voice, though at times he almost spat the words at Ben. "Yes, we're thorough, Professor. But time was against us. We knew Stella was married, but not that her husband was with her, because our check was run on her, not him. Understand? And remember Reese's name was not on the list of Americans in the jail—for good reason, of course. Robinson was using his passport. Normally the embassy sends my office a copy of the death certificate of every American national, but Reese's supposed death occurred at the time I was checking out the names on the list and trying to devise a way to get the guy I thought was Robinson out of jail, and I had turned over all routine matters, such as the deathwatch, to another operative." He paused and looked at Ben with his icy eyes. "Satisfied?"

Ben smirked.

"Okay, you've had your fun, Professor. Now bug off. We don't have time for this. We've got more important things to take care of!"

"'Bug off'? Reilly, your eloquence cuts me to the cuticles."

Papandakis interrupted them. "Mr. Reilly, I am confused about two matters," he said. "With such an important document, why didn't Mr. Robinson go to one of your air bases in Turkey to insure the memo's safety? And why did he continue his masquerade when he reached Crete?"

Reilly turned to Papandakis, and Ben could see that he was trying to compose himself. When he spoke, his voice was calm, but Ben could detect a shakiness around the edges of the words. "Each of our armed forces, as well as several civilian departments, has its own intelligence service, sir. Each agency is separate and autonomous. Unless it is engaged in a joint operation, whatever information each one discovers, no matter how important, it works itself and keeps to itself until the operation is completed and the results processed. This is mainly for reasons of security, and I think you'll find this is standard policy with intelligence agencies around the world. . . . That's one reason Robinson didn't go to any of our military installations in Turkey. Another was that he was ordered not to under any circumstances. There are special problems on our Turkish bases—the security on them is zero. The Turks themselves launched their 1974 invasion of Cyprus from two of them by taking them over without a shot, and we've suspected that at least ten workers on every base are in the employ of intelligence agencies representing no less than six countries."

"Christ, Reilly," said Ben, "are you trying to tell us that you deferred to precedent and procedure in something as crucial as this? What do you people think you're playing at?"

"Get off my case, Professor, I'm warning you—" Reilly shot forward in his chair and aimed a finger at Ben. "You people did enough damage in Turkey!"

"Yeah, well, we had a little difficulty over there, trying to find someone who didn't exist," replied Ben, suddenly flushing with anger. "It seems some imbecile sent us on a wild goose chase. And in case you haven't heard, several people got killed over there."

"I'm damned well aware of *that*!" said Reilly. Suddenly he smacked the heels of his hands against the armrests, sprang up from the easy chair, and began stalking back and forth across the room. "Just what the hell did you people think you were playing at?"

"Shouldn't send men to do boys' work!" Ben snapped.

Reilly lurched toward him, his finger a dart. "Listen, you—"

"Please, please, Mr. Reilly," interrupted Papandakis.

"Try to remain calm. You have been on edge ever since we arrived. And you, Ben, come now."

Reilly went back to the easy chair and sat down, gripping the armrests tightly.

"Tell me, please, Mr. Reilly," Papandakis continued, "I would be most interested to learn how you know about our action in Turkey. Was it in the news?"

"Yes, it was in the news. The Turks think the Greeks have staged an unwarranted and unprovoked commando raid against them for the sole purpose of taking Turkish lives. The Greek government denies all knowledge of it—the usual shit—but over there that's enough to start a war. Luckily it will blow over when it comes out that the Turks were holding five Americans incommunicado. The Turks will be on the defensive after that. But, my God, when Kemal told me the details—"

"Kemal? So that young man is all right. Good. He and his friends were invaluable to us," said Papandakis.

"How's his brother?" asked Ben.

"Kemal was pretty broken up about that. The kid's dead. Kemal and the other guy got away, though."

The silence in the room seemed to deepen. It was a silence that excluded Reilly and he knew it. He looked around the room and seemed to recognize, as if for the first time, the unity of the people around him and the bond which in one day had united them to two men whom he had worked with perhaps for years but may never have known.

Then the old women brought in trays filled with *mezethes* and jiggling glasses of raki and cold lemonade. Reilly galloped his fingertips on the arm of his chair as the women went from one person to the next, and he waved them away when they stopped in front of him. Finally, the women left the room, and after several more silent minutes, during which everyone but Reilly ate and drank, he leaned forward, cleared his throat, and began speaking again. "Here's some news I *can* give you. Robinson didn't die from any fall. His neck was broken by a neat hand-chop. You'd never notice it if you didn't know what to look for."

Papandakis looked up. "Then we must assume—"

"—that he was followed. Right. And knew it. And that was the reason for the masquerade you asked about before. I can only guess, but it seems as if he came here posing as Reese to see if he was sanitized— I mean, to see if he had lost the opposition—because he didn't want to lead anyone back to our area HQ. Remember, he had more than two weeks before the memo became operative, so time wasn't as much of a factor then." Reilly jumped up again and started his pacing. "That leaves only one problem."

"The memo," said Papandakis.

"Yeah. It has to be on the island," said Reilly, "somewhere safe, where Robinson could have gotten his hands on it quickly and given it to us. Someplace as small as a hatband or a wallet." Reilly paused, looked around the room again. His blue eyes were shining. He knew he had everyone's attention now.

"The post," said Cooper. "Could he have posted it to you?"

"No, it would have arrived by now. And he wouldn't have taken the chance, anyway."

"A bank vault, Mr. Reilly?" asked Papandakis, leaning forward.

"We thought of that. Checked all the banks on the north coast here. No American—no foreigner, in fact—

signed for a bank vault during the two days Robinson was on the island. And we checked out the five Cretans who did. No, it has to be somewhere here, in this house."

"Why do you say that?"

"We checked Robinson's body and his effects. Nothing. By the way, is this everything he had with him?" Reilly withdrew a folded sheet of paper from his inside breast pocket and spread it out on Papandakis' desk.

Papandakis bent forward, looked at the paper closely, and raised his head with a shrug. "My brother would know," he said. "He was the one who took care of Robinson while he was with us and assembled his belongings for the police afterward."

Pandelis rose heavily and trudged over to the desk, his bandaged left arm in a sling. Ben and Cooper got up and followed him. Reilly didn't try to stop them, and they both read the list over Pandelis' shoulder.

PASSPORT INFORMATION
DECEASED EFFECTS SHEET

NAME	ID TAG NUMBER
HENRY LAWRENCE REESE	(1312)
BIRTHDATE	BIRTHPLACE
December 5, 1946	California, U.S.A.
HEIGHT	HAIR EYES
6 feet 2 inches	Black Brown

WIFE	PASSPORT NO.	ISSUE DATE
STELLA IRENE REESE	E1895781	May 26, 1976

MINORS	EXPIRATION DATE
xxx	May 25, 1981

EFFECTS

QUANTITY	ITEM	ID TAG NO.
1	Jacket, windbreaker (blue)	1312A
1	Jacket, sport (brown)	1312B
2	Shirts, sport (blue, yellow)	1312C
3	T-shirts (white, yellow, blue)	1312D,E,F
1	Trousers, denim (blue)	1312H
2	Trousers, sport (blue, brown)	1312I,J
1 pr.	Boots, knee high	1312K
3	Undershorts (white)	1312L,M,N
3 pr.	Socks, cotton (black)	1312O,P,Q
2	Handkerchiefs (white)	1312R,S
2	Ties (blue-and-brown-striped)	1312T,U
1	Wallet (black)	1312V
1	Ring, finger (gold, ruby inset)	1312W
1	Keyring (7 keys)	1312X
1	Money (2,000 Turkish lira)	1312Y
1	Money (600 Greek drachma)	1312Z
1	Shaving kit (toothbrush, toothpaste, floss, comb, brush, Noxzema)	1312A1
1	Book (*Antiquities of Eastern Turkey*)	1312A2

Something seemed wrong, out of place on the list, but Ben couldn't decide what.

"Are those the things you gave the police?" Reilly asked Pandelis.

"Is, yes."

"Did you leave anything out?"

Pandelis jerked his head up, his face furious.

"No, no!" said Reilly. "I mean something you forgot or maybe didn't find till afterwards—say, something you remembered later and never got around to bringing to the police."

Pandelis shook his head.

Reilly looked at Papandakis. "What room did Robinson stay in?"

"Stella's, of course. Why?"

"May I have your permission to search it? He may have put the memo in the mattress or behind a picture—or even under a floorboard."

Papandakis nodded, sat back, and waved his hand, a play of amusement on his lips.

Reilly turned to the man in the white suit and instructed him to search Stella's room.

"Manoli," said Papandakis, and Manoli showed the man in the white suit out of the room and went out after him.

Reilly turned back to Papandakis. "It's not just time we're fighting now, sir. There's a new wrinkle—we weren't the first ones to view the body. The day after it arrived at the morgue, two American consular officials came to examine it. Signed in as Hodges and Turner. There's a Hodges and Turner at the consulate, all right, but they never went to see that body. Policy says the security officer or one of his staff is supposed to do that, if anyone does. Hodges is an administrative clerk and Turner's the public information assistant."

Ben looked at Reilly, knowing what he was going to say next.

Reilly stared back at him and nodded. "Yes, it's Vlatchkov. Attendant at the morgue confirmed that one of the two was tall, blond, and had a bright pink birthmark on his right cheek. I've no doubt now that his radio message was nothing more than a challenge to me. He's fighting some kind of private war that I wasn't even aware of, and can only assume is somehow connected with the incident at the embassy party."

Papandakis nodded, no longer smiling, and said quietly, "So at least two of their agents are on the island, yes?"

"Yes."

The old woman who had been sitting with Caroline on the morning of her arrival at the house crept into the room, spoke to Papandakis, and left.

"Aliki says lunch is ready to be served," announced Papandakis to the group. Then he extended his hand toward the door. "Please," he said to everyone. "We can continue this talk afterward."

Everyone rose. Cooper, Stella, and Henry had started toward the door, followed by Caroline and Ben, as Papandakis turned to Reilly once again. "I almost forgot, Mr. Reilly," he said. "We have brought you a gift from Turkey." Then he beckoned to Pandelis who stepped forward with one of the knapsacks.

Papandakis handed the knapsack to Reilly. Everyone had stopped and was looking back at Reilly and Papandakis.

Reilly reached into the knapsack and withdrew his hand with a quick snort of laughter. He was holding a wad of dog-eared American dollars. "This much at least is yours, you know. You earned it," he said, holding out the bills to Papandakis.

A thin smile curled Papandakis' lips. "I do not accept money for rescuing my daughter, Mr. Reilly," he said.

Chapter Twenty-seven

They ate lunch in silence while the man in the white suit continued to search Stella's room; Reilly had gone up to help him.

A somber atmosphere hung over the dining room. The quiet, dignified presence of Uncle Kosta seemed to direct everyone's thoughts toward Pavlo, and this invested the meal with a churchlike solemnity.

All the men were exhausted, yet they remained tense and on their guard knowing that at least two men no one had seen, two Russian agents who had already killed someone they had known, might be watching them at that moment, and had been observing them most probably for the past thirteen days.

All of these things combined to make Yorgo and Manoli uncomfortable to the point of restlessness. They kept glancing out the glass doors, twisting their heads from one side to another, and tapping their silverware on the tablecloth. This kind of fidgeting was not permitted, however, and was immediately silenced by a rumbling glower from Pandelis or a muttered phrase from Cooper, at which the two young men froze and glanced at Uncle Kosta. But each time the old man seemed not to have noticed.

Papandakis had once again lapsed into an abstracted silence, and unconsciously patted Stella's hand whenever she touched the sleeve of his jacket. Like the others, Ben was exhausted but still tense, and his tension was heightened not only by his apprehensions about the Russian agents but by the recurring thought that they no longer had three days to locate the memo; now they had to find it before the Russians did. At first Ben had gone along with the Cretans' insistence on having lunch, realizing, as the Cretans did, that it would take Reilly and the man in the white suit time to search Stella's room, a process all of them would merely confuse if they tried to help. But now he found that he was identifying with Reilly's impatience more with every minute. He hardly touched his food and spent most of the meal pressing Caroline's hand and nodding at her when she turned toward him.

Reilly returned to the dining room just as coffee was being served, the man in the white suit behind him. "Nothing," he said. He looked at Pandelis. "Did Robinson spend a lot of time in any one room? The study? Here? Or walking near any particular trees?"

Pandelis thought for a moment, then shook his head.

"Anything he sent out to be cleaned or repaired?"

Pandelis shook his head again.

"That last day, the day of the hike, did you stop anywhere on the way to the gorge—like for a drink or a bite to eat?"

Once more Pandelis shook his head. "Eat here. Only stop pick up cousin Grigori for guide."

"Anything he might have put somewhere for safekeeping, or stowed at Grigori's before you went on the hike?"

"No," Pandelis said, paused, then shrugged and remained silent.

"What was that shrug for?" asked Reilly.

"Shoes," said Pandelis.

"What shoes?"

"He have no shoes for walking in mountains."

"So?"

"Grigori, he lend Ro-bean-son boots. Is very funny; boots so small Ro-bean-son walk like woman. All laugh. Then Ro-bean-son say, 'We come back, yes? I leave other shoe, but we come back?'"

Reilly was biting his lips as Pandelis spoke. Everyone at the table was watching him. "I don't know," he said, but his eyes were shining. "That could be it, but I don't know."

Pandelis resumed speaking. "This Ro-bean-son is all day asking about shoes, 'We go back?' 'Not forget them?' 'Is safe there, yes?' Then he die, and I no remember till now—"

Of course, thought Ben. *That's what was strange about the list—there were no shoes, only heavy boots.*

Reilly snapped his fingers before Ben had finished the thought.

"Yes, yes! That's it all right! It's got to be!" He glanced at his watch, then looked over at Pandelis. "It's five now. How long will it take us to get to your cousin's?"

Pandelis shrugged. "Two hour."

"Okay, we can make it by seven and get back to Heraklion by ten or eleven. That's still three days before the deadline." He turned to the man in the white suit. "Andoni, call HQ and tell them what's happening. The old man here will tell you where we're going. Oh, yes—" He turned to Papandakis. "Can you phone this Grigori and tell him to sit tight with those shoes till we get there?"

"Impossible, Mr. Reilly," said Papandakis. "Grigori lives in a high mountain village on the Askifou plain. It is very primitive there. He is a poor man and has no phone. But tell me, Mr. Reilly, if I may ask, how do you know you will not collide with the Russians before you get there? They may be outside at this very minute."

"I hope to hell they are," said Reilly.

"And Mr. Reilly—" said Papandakis.

"Yes?"

"Do you really think we should talk this freely in the house? There may be listening devices in all the rooms. In fact it seems from my vantage point that you have been altogether too open with information since this project began, that you have taken people into your confidence you had no way of knowing you could trust."

Reilly took a deep breath, tried to relax, and smiled at Papandakis. "We checked the house for bugs before you got back, sir. Routine. As for my being free with information—yes, this is a sloppy operation, the worst I've ever been on as far as security is concerned. But we had no choice. We've been running scared ever since our units in Russia began collapsing. And we had to get that piece of paper, you know that . . . I didn't want to tell the professor—I knew what his political ideas were—and I knew he might blab the minute you put pressure on him. But we had no choice. We had to keep the agency out of it, if we could, use him as a middleman, and get you to rescue your daughter and, we thought, our man with the memo. Now the memo is within our grasp, and sloppy or not, we're going to get it. If Vlatchkov and his buddy are around—and I'll bet they are!—then it may come down to a very hard-nosed confrontation." He paused. "In that case, sir, Andoni and I aren't enough. I want the odds to be overwhelmingly in our favor." He stopped again. "Look, I know you've got what you want out of this, but it would be helping a greater cause than your family if you and some of your men would come along with us."

Papandakis nodded. "Pandelis, Cooper, Kosta, Manoli—do we go?"

They all murmured, "Yes," except Uncle Kosta, who nodded gravely.

"Thanks," muttered Reilly.

"It was not as difficult a decision as all that, Mr. Reilly," smiled Papandakis. "One of us had to introduce you to Grigori, anyway. Besides, it is not every day my friends and I have a chance to both rescue my daughter and save the world."

"You're forgetting someone, aren't you?" asked Ben, attempting to hide the slight he felt at not hearing his name called.

"No, Ben," said Papandakis with an impish smile as he sat back in his chair. "I was waiting for you to offer."

They were ready to leave in twenty minutes. It took them fifteen minutes to choose from the assortment of both modern and antiquated World War II weapons in Papandakis' arsenal, and another five to decide on cars and seating arrangements. At first Reilly muttered to himself, then attempted to hurry the proceedings along by swearing at everyone, but he finally gave this up and stood by the cars, with his arms folded, staring at the Cretans, whose somber mood had turned sullen.

Papandakis had not included Yorgo in his original selection because of his bad leg, but Yorgo had insisted on coming and was limping about the yard with a grim expression, and Pandelis, unshaven and weary, glared at Reilly and muttered under his breath as he loaded the cars. Then Yorgo and Manoli quarreled over who was going to use an antique Mauser with a shiny black barrel. But when Manoli, his disfigured eye glaring, found that Yorgo wasn't hobbling toward him after he had snatched the weapon from Yorgo's hands and danced away with it, holding it with both hands above his head as he twirled in circles, he dropped his arms, trudged back to his friend, and handed him the weapon without a word, and they continued their preparations in silence.

Finally, Papandakis instructed the group to get into the cars, and Ben, who had been standing next to Caroline watching the preparations, took her hand and walked with her toward the Citroën. Although both of them turned to each other several times as if to say something, neither one spoke, and they settled for a brief kiss by the car door. Then Ben climbed into the Citroën with Pandelis, Cooper, Yorgo, and Nikos, and the car drove off, following Papandakis, Uncle Kosta, Henry, and Manoli, who were riding with Reilly and Andoni in the American's gray BMW.

They drove west along the coast in the late afternoon sunlight that was laying out cities of long shadows in the rock crevices and making the distant mountains on their left into hazy sand castles. The blue water on their right was streaked with copper when, an hour later, they lost sight of it for several minutes as they drove through the crumbling Venetian streets of Rethymnon and by a large park which was as unkempt as a jungle behind its fence. They rejoined the sea on the other side of town, and when Ben happened to look back he saw a huge castle, with the dome of a mosque rising from inside it, sitting on a promontory overlooking the water.

The sullen mood had persisted in the car, and everyone was silent. Cooper, sitting on Ben's right, had tensed, and Ben knew why half an hour later when the Australian muttered "Vrises" as they came into a small town. This was the town in which Cooper had begun the ordeal that had haunted him for the past thirty-five years. Now the village he had fought in and had later seen burning from high in the mountains was a peaceful town where men sat in small outdoor cafés under the wide canopies of plane trees, talking, reading newspapers, sipping raki or white wine, and watching the evening approach and the traffic pass by.

The BMW turned left in the center of town, and the Citroën followed. Within minutes they began climbing. Soon, on the slopes below, miles of olive groves seemed to be sliding toward the sea. Branches and gnarled, arthritic trunks slumped into shadow, and individual trees merged in vast banks of darkness, but Ben could still detect white chapels among the groves and small clusters of white villages, like so many sets of dice or knucklebones scattered about the landscape by half-mad gods.

They passed the village of Alikampos. By this time the broad curves had become a series of tight switchbacks that were now so familiar to Ben that he couldn't tell the difference between this road and any

of the others he had traveled during the past four
days. He no longer knew whether he was winding up
to Anoyia, clinging to the sides of the gorge on the
way to Siteia, snaking over the mountains between
Bodrum and Milas, or climbing the hill that separated
Söke from Kusadasi.

All the landscapes had also become one. The miles
of olive groves or pine trees inset with small villages
of whitewashed houses topped by red tile roofs seemed
to be repeated endlessly in his mind. The columns of
Minoan ruins, Doric temples, and domed Orthodox
churches were jumbled together with Crusader castles,
Ottoman mosques, and concrete-and-glass high-rise office buildings. Had he seen that Turkish neighborhood
in Heraklion or Athens? Athens or New York? Was
Kusadasi actually Ayia Galini, or were they both
Bodrum?

At the same time he had an unrelenting sense of
different epochs occurring simultaneously in the same
place. His climb to Anoyia, that moon-weird town
erected on the bones of World War II reprisals, had
become Cooper's climb through wreckage and gunfire
thirty-five years before on the road they were traveling at this moment, for past and present seemed to
have merged. That was the tension he had begun to
feel in Cooper. Now he saw Cooper's trek, which had
ended at dawn with rolling streams and birdsong, as
his own trek past Zeus' cave on Psiloritis, a journey
made by countless others throughout a history as continuous and shadowy as the evening that was now descending on him.

He turned toward Cooper. The angular face was
staring straight ahead, the jaws still clenched. Cooper
was leaning forward, looking into the past, reliving an

endless march to the sea, a march to which he had sacrificed family and country in order to wander aimlessly over the terrain of his youth.

Ben thought of Cooper, Pandelis, Papandakis, and old Uncle Kosta together in World War II, and although he knew he could never step inside their feelings no matter how many different epochs overlapped in his historian's imagination, he no longer felt like an outsider, for he knew he was wandering in the same landscape as they did, and that landscape was history, which had trapped them all in its labyrinth. For History was the Labyrinth, or rather the past was. (Yes, he could say that now without any self-consciousness.) And this Labyrinth was only partially formed. It took shape around them with each of their steps. And though it seemed more metaphorical than actual, it had its Minotaur who waited in the shadows, Ben was sure of that, and the Minotaur's name, Ben now knew, was the Future.

And as Ben thought this the memo became everything to him. He had to have it. Everything in his life, and everyone else's seemed to depend on it. He saw himself sprinting down an endless street with buildings collapsing behind him and others swaying overhead. The memo was the thread, the way out, and it was the only thing that could stave off the mindless, shadowy figure that was grunting hungrily somewhere in the darkened rocks ahead, waiting for all of them—the human body of the Minotaur, who no longer had the head of a bull but was wearing a papier-mâché bull's mask, and the papier-mâché was made from a document printed all over with Russian typescript. Ben could see fragments of the Cyrillic text where the mask curved into the snuffling muzzle and around the frothy nostrils and under the blood-slick lips.

"Askifou, sport," said Cooper in a strained whisper, and Ben woke with a start.

Chapter Twenty-eight

It was twilight by the time they drove onto the high plain. The plain, enclosed on all sides by flinty ravines and mountain peaks, was dotted with small groves and sectioned into rectangles by cultivated fields and slow streams.

The two cars drove off the main road at the end of a village, which was located in the center of the plain, and halted a little later on a dirt track in front of a square one-story house made of whitewashed rocks.

Reilly charged ahead of the others and knocked on the door. It was opened quickly by a tall, lean man with huge, finlike mustaches and gray hair, who must have heard the cars drive up and stationed himself on the other side of the door. He stared solemnly at Reilly, swaying slightly. But when Papandakis and Pandelis came up behind the American, the man's face brightened. And after effusively hugging them, kissing them on the cheeks, and shouting at no one in particular, he herded everyone inside and ordered an old woman with frightened eyes to bring raki and *mezedakia*.

Meanwhile he had crowded everyone into a small, low-ceilinged room that was hot and stuffy, commanded them to sit in awkward straight-backed

wooden chairs that he brought from another room,
and, to increase the light thrown out by the room's
one overhead bare yellow bulb, lit five oil lamps
which spread the heavy stewlike odor of lamb fat and
the mildewed attic mustiness of old clothes to every
corner.

Ben, already damp and wilting in the room's heat,
could hardly keep from gagging, and several others
were coughing when the gray-haired man finally
seated himself on a stool as abruptly and vigorously as
he had opened the door, seated his visitors, and lit the
lamps. Now he slapped his thighs with his open hands
and smiled. Ben and the others smiled back. He nodded,
drew a deep breath, and smiled again. They did
the same, all except Reilly, who sat opposite Ben with
clenched jaws and stared at the old man. Not a word
had been spoken since the greetings at the door. Both
guests and host seemed to be waiting for the other to
begin, and now they sat smiling and nodding at one
another as if miming the Greek equivalent of "after
you, Gaston."

Finally the woman brought in two bottles of raki
and glasses on a tray, and with an enthusiastic
grin and an exclamation of "Aah!" the gray-haired
man dived for the glasses, poured the drinks, and
began to speak rapidly in Greek to Papandakis as
he handed the drinks around.

Papandakis replied, then turned to Ben and Reilly.
"My cousin Grigori expresses great happiness that his
relatives and their friends have come to visit him. I
told him that we were happy to see him and that our
visits with each other do not occur often enough.
Then I told him that you were Americans and requested
he speak English so you could talk with him

directly and understand what he was saying in reply."

Grigori followed this speech with evenly-spaced, enthusiastic nods and a continuous smile. And when Papandakis had finished, the man raised his left hand from his thigh, thrust it toward the Americans with his thumb and forefinger less than half an inch apart, and said, "Speak this much English."

Reilly, who had been clenching his teeth and shifting in his chair since he first entered the room, leaned toward him. "We've come about the American who was here with Pandelis ten days ago."

Grigori's head drooped dramatically. He looked at the floor with a forlorn expression, tucked his head into the hollow of his left shoulder, and sighed. "Poor American!" he said and shook his head.

"Yes. Well, what we want to know," said Reilly, "is what happened to the shoes he left here."

Grigori's head snapped up. Ben could detect a troubled, slightly frightened look on the man's face that seemed different from all the elaborate expressions he had exhibited since he had met them at the door. "Americans come," he said.

There was a quick intake of breath on all sides following this announcement. Ben gasped, too. Everyone sat bolt upright, not moving. Grigori was looking from Reilly to the others, his smile dwindling and his eyes becoming more and more frightened.

"What Americans?" asked Reilly in a flat, tight voice.

"Americans from Cowan-sue-lit. Two mens."

"What did they want?" Reilly snapped, his face shiny with sweat.

Grigori continued to glance from one face to another. "The shoes," he shrugged.

"And—? And—?"

"I give them."

All of them sagged in their chairs, loudly releasing their breaths and looking down.

"I go to hurry Anna with *café* for guest," continued Grigori, "and when I come back they are going. They hand me shoes. 'He will not need,' they say. 'You take.'"

"You mean they gave them back to you?" said Reilly, almost lunging out of his chair.

"Yes, yes. Gave them back," said Grigori, leaning away from Reilly's tensed body and loud voice.

"Well, where the hell are they!"

There was a crash of pans in the kitchen and Grigori, who seemed happy for any pretext to get away, hopped up and ran to the other room before anyone could stop him.

"Hey!" Reilly called after him, jumping to his feet. But seeing it was too late, he took a deep breath and turned to Papandakis and the others. "Bastards realized at the morgue that the boots were out of place. Killed him in Samaria, so they must have followed him and your brother up here that day and they must have known this was the only place he could have changed shoes."

"Yes, Mr. Reilly." Papandakis nodded. "But there is another possibility that I hope you are not ignoring. Certainly the Russians examined the shoes while Grigori was in the kitchen, but they seem to have found nothing in them."

"They found wrong! Do you hear?" Reilly stabbed his forefinger down at Papandakis. "We know what they don't. Robinson was pretty damn concerned about those shoes! The memo's got to be there. The

Russkies just didn't look hard enough. Why should they? They were probably playing a hunch, not sure, and they let it go after a casual once-over."

Grigori had returned, slightly stooped, bowing and nodding and assuring them that everything was all right—his wife had been unnerved by the yelling from the front room, that was all.

"Yes, Mr. Reilly," said Papandakis. "You are frightening poor Grigori and his wife out of their sanity. Grigori is not your enemy. In fact you are his guest. Please take control of yourself."

Reilly nodded tightly several times, took a deep breath again and turned back to Grigori, who had resumed his seat on the stool and clasped his hands together on his lap. "Sorry, fella. No offense," Reilly said, then paused, took another deep breath, and continued. "The shoes—you said the Americans gave you back the shoes, right?"

Grigori nodded, looking at Reilly closely, it seemed to Ben, as if staring at the American's face would allow him to understand the man's words better and the meaning behind them which was agitating him so much.

"Okay," continued Reilly, pronouncing each word slowly and clearly. "Now will you please bring us the shoes."

Grigori shrugged again, separated his clasped hands and placed them, palms upward, on his thighs. "Not here," he said.

Reilly whirled around and slammed his right fist into his left hand. "Damn!" he hissed.

Pandelis leaned over and whispered to Papandakis. Cooper caught Ben's eye, raised his eyebrows, glanced toward Reilly, and pressed his lips together. Ben murmured, "Yeah," in reply and nodded.

Reilly, who seemed to have counted to ten, had turned back to Grigori, and with the same slow, clear pronunciation he had used before, but with his voice higher in his throat now, said, "Where *are* the shoes, Grigori?"

"Americans give to me. Good shoes, but too big—plenty too big for Grigori. A poor boy, a shepherd, Demos—I give shoes to him."

"You gave the shoes to a shepherd named Demos," said Reilly in the same methodical voice.

"Yes, a boy. Good boy, but poor, very poor."

"Where can this Demos be found?"

"He is with sheep over hill. There," said Grigori, and he pointed through the wall to his right.

"How far?" asked Reilly.

"Two kilometer, maybe. No more above that."

Reilly whirled around toward the others; they had already begun to rise, Ben among them.

Grigori looked from one to the other. They were waiting in a crouch—almost, it seemed, ready to spring. But Grigori had an idea, Ben could see it in his eyes and in the smile that was widening on his lips. "Come," he said, slapping his thighs and rising. "I will take you."

And all of them rushed out of the house.

Night had fallen and the first stars were out. A cool breeze slipped down the mountainside and brushed past them as they climbed the rocky path behind the village. Shadows filled crevices and widened rocks, and Ben could hear his companions' shoes clattering on pebbles and stones, and their weapons, which they had hurriedly retrieved from the cars as they left Grigori's house, occasionally clanging on the ground.

Grigori was springing up the path, holding their only source of light, an oil lantern that danced ahead of the others and swung spidery shadows in all directions.

Reilly, who had once more pushed ahead of his companions, was following close behind him and cursing between clenched teeth whenever he stumbled or slipped in the growing darkness.

All of them except Grigori were out of breath before they reached the top of the hill. He waited for them and pointed to another hill about five hundred yards higher which was set farther back than the one they had just climbed and thus had not been visible from the base of the track behind the village. "Strouga there," he said.

All of them looked in the direction he was pointing and could make out a steep hillock topped by a low, dark building.

They continued to climb.

There were no trees. They were beyond the treeline, had been for fifteen minutes before they entered the plain. The slopes around them were all edges, rock, and talus, except for occasional bushes clinging to the slopes. The landscape jutted out at them, sharp and barren, softened only by shadows and the widening darkness.

They reached the top of the hillock, their shoes full of flinty pebbles which made Ben and Cooper hobble and probably accounted for Yorgo's having fallen far behind. But none of them stopped to empty their shoes.

Ben, his heartbeat thudding in his ears, took several

swallows of air and looked back. He seemed to be on top of the world. The plain was a sea of darkness far below.

He turned toward the others once more and slogged ahead.

Led by Grigori and Reilly, the group tramped straight toward the long low building. It was merely four walls of stacked stones patched together with dried mud and roofed by braided bushes covered with lumps of dirt. The building was no more than six feet high and they had to stoop to enter the low doorway.

There was only one room inside. A fire of dried dung and brush crackled in a fireplace against the farther wall, flickering indecipherable shadows on the other walls and making the windowless hut stifling and hot.

Dripping cheese baskets hung from the ceiling, and except for some stone shelves and piled rocks, obviously for sitting, and a shallow stack of bushes gathered near the left-hand wall, most probably for a bed, the hut was bare.

Smoke stung Ben's eyes, and the odor of excrement and the sharp smell of sour milk pervaded everything.

A young boy of twelve or so stood with his back to the fire. It was too dark inside to see his face, but the awkwardness of his posture told Ben plainly enough how frightened the boy must be to have his quiet evening suddenly invaded by twelve panting men.

Grigori pointed at the boy and turned to Reilly. "Demos," he said.

Ben looked at the boy's feet, sensing the others were doing the same. The boy was dressed in indistinguishable shirt and trousers, but there, below his cuffs, glinting in the firelight, were a pair of still-shiny brown loafers that seemed totally out of place in this small mountain hut so high above the civilized world.

"American's shoes!" gasped Grigori, and he began hopping from one foot to the other, completely involved in his guests' excitement and feeling triumphant at finding them what they had wanted, as if he had somehow redeemed himself in their opinion.

Reilly rushed toward the boy, Andoni at his side. "Tell the kid to give us the shoes," he said to Andoni.

"*Thoste mas ta papoutsia, parakalo!*" snapped the man in the white suit.

The boy didn't move. He seemed to shrink back toward the fire.

"*Ta papoutsia! Ta papoutsia!*" shouted Andoni, as he and Reilly lunged forward, grabbed the boy's ankles, and wrestled the shoes from his feet.

Whimpering, the boy sprang past them, bounded through the bodies of the men surging forward around him, and disappeared out the door. They let him go without a word. Everyone was converging on the shoes, as if mesmerized by the two empty pieces of footgear glinting in the firelight.

"Watch the door! Someone watch the door!" shouted Reilly.

"Manoli! Yorgo!" ordered Papandakis hoarsely over his shoulder.

Everyone gathered around Reilly and Andoni, who had already started tearing the shoes apart. They tossed the cushioned insoles in front of the fire and began dismembering the shoes in unison.

First the heels with pen knives. They held each one

up, looked inside, prodded and sliced the rubber with
the knife blades.

Nothing.

They tossed the heels aside.

Next, they began cutting the soles away from the
sides of the shoes. It was laborious work; the pen
knives were too dull.

Pandelis grunted. "Wait!" he said, went over to
Yorgo, now stationed at the door, and then handed
the two agents the young Cretan's dagger and his
own.

The cutting went more smoothly now. They stripped
the soles carefully, layer by layer.

Again, nothing.

They stripped the padding from the broad tongues,
and ripped off the ribbed ornamental leather band
stitched across the shoes in front of the tongues.

"Nothing!" gasped Reilly.

Ben's body was slick with sweat. His face was pouring. Everyone else's face was shiny in the firelight.

Reilly looked toward the cushioned insoles lying
next to him in front of the fire. He lifted one and
flapped it from side to side. It wagged back and forth.
He turned it over. "Thick," he said and bent closer.
"Two tops. Stuck together." He was already stripping
the two halves apart.

There was nothing inside. He tossed the scraps over
his shoulder.

Everyone looked at the other insole. Reilly lifted it,
flapped it. It didn't wag, seemed to be stiffer.

Everyone leaned closer.

Ben was holding his breath.

"Two tops again," said Reilly, and he began stripping the insole down the middle.

The two halves came apart easily. One side flopped limply. Reilly tossed it aside. The other side remained stiff, and when Reilly held it up to the firelight they could see where the foam rubber had been hollowed out and there, clearly, was a folded sheet of paper that had neatly replaced the foam wadding.

Reilly removed the paper, unfolded it, held it up to the firelight, and began to read it. Suddenly his arms dropped to his sides and the paper, still grasped in his hand, rustled in the shadows where no one could see. Reilly remained kneeling, his head bowed, not moving.

Ben reached forward and took the paper from his hand, tilted it to the firelight and began to read the neat, tiny lines of writing to himself.

"Read it to all of us, please, Ben" said Papandakis in a quiet voice, and Ben proceeded to read aloud the contents of the message.

> My dear Emerson,
>
> I wonder if you can appreciate the satisfaction with which I write this. I think not. For three years the insect bite you gave my career at the embassy party has infected my every hour. Now all has been rectified. Suffice it to say, I have the memo. Of course, it was not genuine to begin with, merely the final phase of an operation begun two years ago to expose your deep-penetration agents within the Kremlin and the KGB. By including a strike date in the memo, we hoped you would dispense with normal security procedures. You did.
>
> Seismic regulation does not exist. It never has.

Do you understand what has happened, my Transcendental friend? No? Briefly, then, I will explain.

Radio-trackable chemicals were brushed on to the document so that it could be traced from operative to operative. Headquarters estimated that all important exposures would be made within an 800-kilometer radius of Moscow, at which point the operation was to be terminated. But I recognized in the operation a way of regaining the promotion you had cost me, and furthermore I could implement my plan without my commander's knowledge. I would simply let the memo continue on its way, eliminating or at least identifying your agents wherever it went. Convincing my KGB colleagues in the alerted areas to do the same was also simple. I merely pointed out the rewards that would accrue to all of us.

My station's role in Headquarters' plan was precautionary: if the memo reached Georgia, we were to intercept it before it crossed the border. I reasoned that even if the memo did not come into my area, Headquarters would commend the initiative displayed by my expanded plan.

Everything proceeded well until Moscow terminated the operation and demanded the memo. Somehow they had failed to learn about your negotiations with the Chinese, and now the memo was a liability.

Within two days Andropov had made my colleagues tell all, and sent Colonel Zimansky for the document, holding me responsible for it. But by then I had undertaken my variation of the plan and had dispatched three men to track the memo, ordering radio silence as an added precaution. I sent others after them, but the original group was in deep cover by then. When the original group finally surfaced, Robinson was dead and the memo gone. It seems that metals in the mountains around the Askifou plain had weakened the limited signal range of the chemicals on the memo, and my men, with Robinson under visual surveillance anyway, had switched off their receiver, only to find that the signal had vanished when they switched it on again near Samaria. At that point they panicked and unfortunately eliminated Robinson.

Within twelve hours I was on Crete, retracing Robinson's movements. I think you can imagine the rest.

So there you have it.

Knowing you Americans are fond of souvenirs, I had thought to leave you the memo, but that, of course, is not possible. I will leave this letter instead. One way or another I know that eventually it will reach you, my dear Emerson. The radio message will insure that. The radio message is the final stroke, the one which will involve you directly in this, my first triumph, and I will send it after I have recovered the memo and planted this missive in its place.

Until we cross sabers again,

> I remain,
> *The Defective Transcendentalist*

Everyone remained silent. There were only the sounds of the fire crackling and the cheese baskets dripping. Ben put the paper back into Reilly's hand.

Then Cooper snickered and got up. "Well, what do you know?" he said and ambled to the door. He whispered for Yorgo and Manoli to follow him into the night.

Papandakis rose, too, shaking his head. With a mournful smile, he stood looking at Ben.

Pandelis was staring up at his brother, his shoulders hunched. "What this mean?" he asked him, sliding his hands back and forth in a threshing motion.

"Nothing, dear brother, nothing," Papandakis replied. He reached down to Pandelis and helped him up. "It is only a Russian joke," he continued. "They must have found the memo while Grigori was in the kitchen and replaced it with their letter before he returned."

"But—"

Papandakis put his arm around Pandelis, hugged him, and led him to the door, followed by a bewildered Grigori and a silent Uncle Kosta.

"But—" Pandelis protested again.

"It is nothing, brother," said Papandakis. "Nothing we did not already know."

Then they were gone.

Ben, Henry, and Andoni were watching Reilly. The blond American hadn't moved; he was still on his knees, staring at nothing, the paper trembling in his hand. Finally, he staggered to his feet. "Jesus!" he said, swaying and shaking his head slowly from side to side. Then, still staring ahead vacantly, he stumbled from the hut with Andoni and Henry behind him.

Ben was totally disoriented. His whole body seemed to be a splintering shower of nerve ends. He had watched the others from what had seemed like a great distance. Now he took a deep breath, looked at the shadowy shepherd's hut with the meaningless firelight images capering on the walls, and turned toward the door.

Outside, it was chilly and completely dark. The last of the mountain peaks were silhouetted against the lower part of the sky, and the stars were bits of sapphire above him. He was, in fact, surrounded by sky. It was a vast jeweled crown above his head, a crown that belonged to him and to the men descending the hill and to the people in the village below them and to everyone clinging to the sides of this spinning planet. But it was a crown that was too large.

He looked down. The others were already climbing down the path. He saw their outlines but could identify only Reilly lurching down the steep gradient, his arms dangling.

He could hear tiny voices floating in the still air. They were calling and laughing from the village, and he could sense more than see the plain and far beyond it the slopes of olive groves and the lighted villages sprinkled here and there among them, like so many star clusters, glittering all the way to the sea. And he imagined other light clusters scattered throughout the darkness beyond the sea, and an infinite number of other voices floating up to the stars—endless light clusters erected on crumbling stone walls, endless voices, and the darkness sprawling and swaying between them.

How could everything be so petty, brutal, and meaningless, yet at the same time so full of grandeur and wild beauty?

He stared at the sky for several more moments, unable to reach any conclusions, then began to descend

the path, realizing almost immediately that that was a
kind of conclusion. He was descending to the voices,
to the crumbling stone walls that housed them, to the
community that existed inside those walls. And maybe
that was the only history lesson in the end—to put one
foot in front of the other, as he was doing now, no
matter what lay ahead.

He had taken several steps down the path when he
heard noises. They were coming from his left, from
behind a cairn of some sort—wet, snuffling noises,
half gasps, half grunts. He froze. But even as he
turned toward the sounds, the image of the bull's
head with its bloodshot eyes was fading from his
mind, and in its place rose a much different shape,
one that made him recognize what the noises were,
what they had to be. And that awareness sent an overwhelming
sense of shame surging through him, even
before he took the first step toward the pile of rocks
where he knew the shepherd boy lay huddled and
whimpering.

Epilogue

Only seven major American newspapers ran a short UPI report of an alleged Greek raid on the east coast of Turkey. Heavy gunfire had been reported in the Turkish resort town of Kusadasi, and several people had been killed. Details were still sketchy and no names were given, although the Turkish government, outraged at this wanton aggression on the part of the Greek government, was preparing a detailed statement of charges, and had closed ferry service between Kusadasi and the Greek island of Samos as a preliminary step to the possible severance of diplomatic relations. The Greek government categorically denied the charges, claiming that the Turkish Foreign Office was attempting to provoke an incident. The Athens News *carried a somewhat different story, reporting that the incident actually grew out of a jailbreak by three Americans who had been detained illegally by the Turkish police. The article took great pains to point out that this information had not been verified, but added that two of the three Americans had been killed and that their names were being withheld pending notification of next of kin.*

In a separate incident only The New York Times *and the* San Francisco Chronicle *carried* brief items about a mistake in the identification of an American killed in a hiking accident on the Greek island of Crete. The Matthew Reeses of 2153 Pacific Heights, San Francisco, both smiling broadly, told local television reporters that they were "elated" that their son Henry was alive. They also stated that they were not holding the State Department responsible for the mistake in identity. The Athens News ran a more elaborate story of the incident, revealing that the real victim was an American importer of Middle Eastern artworks named Stephen Robinson.

Two weeks after the raid, Time magazine, in its "World" news section, reported a story that had originally appeared in Pravda concerning the arrest of ten KGB junior officers on charges of "gross insubordination and flagrant dereliction of duty." "Not since the nadir of the Stalinist purges," stated Time, "could Kremlin watchers recall a similar mass roundup of secret police personnel, and consequently it was still too early to evaluate the significance of this latest purge." Chief among the accused was a KGB captain named Yevgeny Andreievich Vlatchkov, who had been arrested the week before on charges of sabotage and anti-Soviet agitation. Vlatchkov, who was awaiting trial in Lubyanka Prison on Moscow's Dzerzhinsky Square, had allegedly been working for the CIA and at one point, under the guise of running an operation on his own, had actually left the Soviet Union illegally to receive orders from his CIA case officer on the island of Crete. "CIA officials," the Time article concluded, "were unavailable for comment."

Benjamin Ames, Professor of history at Claremont College, Claremont, California, saw none of these articles. At the time they appeared he was visiting the

Minoan sites on the island of Crete, accompanied by several older members of a local family named Papandakis and two women identified from their passports as Caroline Hooper and Gail Hutchinson.

Afterword

The weather manipulation experiments by the U.S. and the U.S.S.R. alluded to in this book are not fictional. For those readers wishing to know more about the subject, I have appended the following information.

Nikola Tesla was born in Croatia, Yugoslavia, then part of the Austro-Hungarian Empire, in 1856. After emigrating to the United States in 1884, he worked for a time with Edison. He was the inventor of arc-light systems, the Tesla induction motor of alternating-current transmission, the Tesla automobile coil, generators of high-frequency currents and a system of wireless communication. It is because of his findings that the U.S. uses alternating electric current instead of the direct-current method discovered by Edison. In addition, Tesla designed the huge power system at Niagara Falls and once lit 200 electric lamps from a distance of 25 miles without the use of wires, envisioning the use of this technique for weather modification. This information and more can be found in the standard edition of the *Encyclopedia Brittanica*. His statements as to how the earth could be used as a conductor for "terrestial stationary waves" can be found in the Macro edition of the *Encyclopedia Brittanica* as well as in

Lighting in his Hand: The Life Story of Nikola Tesla by Inez Hunt and Wanetta W. Draper (Denver, 1964).

How Tesla's discoveries could be implemented in the upper atmosphere were examined by Paul Scott in the Manchester (New Hampshire) *Union Leader*, February 28, 1977.

The approach by the Soviets to Tesla's old assistant, Arthur H. Matthews, was recorded by Stephen M. Aug in the *Los Angeles Herald-Examiner*, February 1, 1977, a little less than three weeks before Patrick Young, writing in the *National Observer* for February 19, 1977 (pp. 1, 21), reported that high-frequency radio transmissions emanating from Russia had disrupted radio communications in several nearby countries, and that the Soviets had admitted "testing something."

On the other side of the coin, Lowell Ponte's article, "Weather Warfare," in the Oakland *Tribune*, January 24, 1974, discussed the complaints in the U.N. of U.S. weather experiments in the Caribbean.

The Tangshan earthquakes were covered in detail by *The New York Times* (July 29, 1976, p. 1, col. 8; July 30, Sect. 1, p. 1, col. 1). Final revelations of the quakes' destructiveness were reported in the same newspaper by Peter Griffith (Reuters) on June 1, 1977, p. 1; June 2, p. 1; June 5, Sect. 4, p. 18. *The New York Times* also reported the Italian earthquakes (May 8, 1976, p. 1).

Regarding the U.S.S.R.'s possible role in the Tangshan quakes and their mastery of seismic regulation in general, Captain Yevgeny Andreievich Vlatchkov says all that needs to be said on p. 339 of this book.

Dell Bestsellers

- ☐ TO LOVE AGAIN by Danielle Steel $2.50 (18631-5)
- ☐ SECOND GENERATION by Howard Fast $2.75 (17892-4)
- ☐ EVERGREEN by Belva Plain $2.75 (13294-0)
- ☐ AMERICAN CAESAR by William Manchester ... $3.50 (10413-0)
- ☐ THERE SHOULD HAVE BEEN CASTLES
  by Herman Raucher $2.75 (18500-9)
- ☐ THE FAR ARENA by Richard Ben Sapir $2.75 (12671-1)
- ☐ THE SAVIOR by Marvin Werlin and Mark Werlin . $2.75 (17748-0)
- ☐ SUMMER'S END by Danielle Steel $2.50 (18418-5)
- ☐ SHARKY'S MACHINE by William Diehl $2.50 (18292-1)
- ☐ DOWNRIVER by Peter Collier $2.75 (11830-1)
- ☐ CRY FOR THE STRANGERS by John Saul $2.50 (11869-7)
- ☐ BITTER EDEN by Sharon Salvato $2.75 (10771-7)
- ☐ WILD TIMES by Brian Garfield $2.50 (19457-1)
- ☐ 1407 BROADWAY by Joel Gross $2.50 (12819-6)
- ☐ A SPARROW FALLS by Wilbur Smith $2.75 (17707-3)
- ☐ FOR LOVE AND HONOR by Antonia Van-Loon .. $2.50 (12574-X)
- ☐ COLD IS THE SEA by Edward L. Beach $2.50 (11045-9)
- ☐ TROCADERO by Leslie Waller $2.50 (18613-7)
- ☐ THE BURNING LAND by Emma Drummond $2.50 (10274-X)
- ☐ HOUSE OF GOD by Samuel Shem, M.D. $2.50 (13371-8)
- ☐ SMALL TOWN by Sloan Wilson $2.50 (17474-0)

At your local bookstore or use this handy coupon for ordering:

Dell DELL BOOKS
P.O. BOX 1000, PINEBROOK, N.J. 07058

Please send me the books I have checked above. I am enclosing $_____
(please add 75¢ per copy to cover postage and handling). Send check or money order—no cash or C.O.D.'s. Please allow up to 8 weeks for shipment.

Mr/Mrs/Miss _____

Address _____

City _____ State/Zip _____

THE SUPERCHILLER THAT GOES BEYOND THE SHOCKING, SHEER TERROR OF *THE BOYS FROM BRAZIL*

THE AXMANN AGENDA

MIKE PETTIT

1944: Lebensborn—a sinister scheme and a dread arm of the SS that stormed across Europe killing, raping, destroying and stealing the children.
NOW: Victory—a small, mysteriously wealthy organization of simple, hard-working Americans—is linked to a sudden rush of deaths.

Behind the grass-roots patriotism of Victory does the evil of Lebensborn live on? Is there a link between Victory and the Odessa fortune—the largest and most lethal economic weapon the world has ever known? *The Axmann Agenda*—it may be unstoppable!

A Dell Book $2.50 (10152-2)

At your local bookstore or use this handy coupon for ordering:

Dell **DELL BOOKS** THE AXMANN AGENDA $2.50 (10152-2)
P.O. BOX 1000, PINEBROOK, N.J. 07058

Please send me the above title. I am enclosing $_____
(please add 75¢ per copy to cover postage and handling). Send check or money order—no cash or C.O.D.'s. Please allow up to 8 weeks for shipment.

Mr/Mrs/Miss_____

Address_____

City_____ State/Zip_____

BY REASON OF INSANITY

Shane Stevens

author of *Rat Pack* and *Go Down Dead*

"Sensational."—*New York Post*

Thomas Bishop—born of a mindless rape—escapes from an institution for the criminally insane to deluge a nation in blood and horror. Not even Bishop himself knows where—and in what chilling horror—it will end.

"This is Shane Stevens' masterpiece. The most suspenseful novel in years."—Curt Gentry, co-author of *Helter Skelter*

"A masterful suspense thriller steeped in blood, guts and sex."—*The Cincinnati Enquirer*

A Dell Book $2.75   (11028-9)

At your local bookstore or use this handy coupon for ordering:

Dell	**DELL BOOKS** BY REASON OF INSANITY $2.75 (11028-9)
	P.O. BOX 1000, PINEBROOK, N.J. 07058

Please send me the above title. I am enclosing $_____
(please add 75¢ per copy to cover postage and handling). Send check or money order—no cash or C.O.D.'s. Please allow up to 8 weeks for shipment.

Mr/Mrs/Miss _____

Address _____

City _____ State/Zip _____